For Tanera
Thank you for your never-ending support, for always believing
in me and my books, and for working your socks off every
single day!

1

BYRON ACADEMY COLLEGE, BASINGSTOKE, HAMPSHIRE, UK

'Not gonna lie, this place sucks and Kirsty is a total bitch.'

Eve Collins desperately wanted to nod in agreement to Josh's statement but that wasn't the done thing when you were in a student support role. Yet Josh always made excellent points when asked to underpin his angst and Eve always listened.

'Expand please, Josh.'

Josh did his usual dramatic shrug and the back of the flimsy plastic chair he was sitting in warped as if it was made of bubble-gum. Eve asked constantly for more comfortable seating but apparently another vending machine full of sugary overpriced snacks was preferable over her 'harmony hub' meant to soothe. College courses were harder than ever before, the pressure to achieve even greater and the number of stressed-out, brain-fried pupils lining up for a session with her could be likened to an airport security queue.

'This is student support,' Josh began. 'You're supposed to support *me*, but lately I feel this is just a place for me to vent my rage, so I get it off my chest and don't get so worked up that I go and... I don't know... spray obscenities or hairy penises on the walls.'

Josh paused to inhale, and Eve contemplated why his anger might lead him to graffiti a hairy penis. Freud would be her go-to for that...

'No matter what I say, here or on Tik Tok to a sad soundtrack, nothing changes. I end up in here with you trying not to think about how my addiction to Polos is getting really out of control!'

As Josh said these final words, he popped another hard white mint into his mouth and sucked.

'Kirsty tells me you haven't been completing your assignments,' Eve said.

As she dropped this onto Josh, she watched his expression to see how he might react. There was no accelerated sweet movement from cheek to cheek, no quirk of his eyebrows. She pulled at the hair scrunchie on her wrist and then carried on:

'So, are you just trying to be bad-ass by challenging Kirsty to take things further with a warning on your file... or is there anything going on at home that might be making things difficult?' She had gone from good cop to bad cop in one swift and fluid motion. This usually sorted those taking the piss from those who really needed help.

'Expand,' Josh quipped, the word drenched in sarcasm.

'Is everything OK with your parents? Any worries about money? Your sister, is she still into the occult?'

'What?' Josh exclaimed. 'My sister isn't into the occult! She's into animals. Practically a zoologist!'

'I know,' Eve answered. 'I was just checking you were listening.'

'And *you're* not listening to *me*! My only problem is Kirsty thinks I can do all this work as well as have time for my shifts at Noo Fork in Chan's and, you know, also have a few moments on my weekends to explore my more creative side.'

She didn't miss a beat. 'You mean play *Animal Crossing*.'

'Are you judging me, Eve?' Josh snapped. 'You're not supposed to judge me. It says so in the college handbook.'

'I'm not judging you, Josh. But I find the best form of defence with tutors is attacking the assignments. Then they don't tend to come at you with: "Josh, can you stop discussing *The Great British Sewing Bee* when you should be unravelling the mindset of Lord Sugar".'

Josh let out a gasp then, fingers going to the student lanyard around his neck and gripping hard. 'I feel seen! Do you have cameras in the classrooms? Because, if you do, that's a breach of my civil liberties.'

There weren't cameras, Eve simply knew her students well. That was at the absolute heart of what she did here. Her qualifications in psychology and philosophy meant she could be working at a clinic earning substantial sums out of stressed out divorcees still quibbling over that wine cooler they received as a wedding gift from goodness knows who or business owners on the verge of a breakdown. But Eve had long ago decided that the people she really wanted to help were people struggling the same way she had when she was a student at this very college. She might be giving Josh a little tough love here, but she was also going to be his shoulder to cry on if it was required.

'Josh,' she said, more softly. 'You know you can tell me anything and it will go no further unless I'm concerned about your safety.'

'I'm concerned you know I watch *Sewing Bee*.'

'Listen, I can fend Kirsty off but only if I know what I'm dealing with... what I'm *really* dealing with.'

Josh sighed, folding his arms across his chest and adopting a brooding look. And then it hit Eve. Not what was there, but what *wasn't*.

'Josh, you haven't mentioned Kit-Kat for a while. Is he doing OK? Still cleaning himself more than people on a body wash ad?'

Kit-Kat was Josh's calico cat who had turned eighteen in January. Josh had dressed him up in a pet tuxedo on the special day and posted a pic to his socials stating, '18 today. Lick... I mean like.'

And that was when Josh's expression changed. His solid-set obstinate jawline folded like a concertina and his lips began to quiver. Eve was already, instinctively, reaching for the tissue box.

'I can't... even pass by the canteen and see those two-finger chocolate bars without shedding a tear. It was... last month. He had a bowl of his favourite food – the one for gravy lovers – and then he just sauntered out into the garden, lay under his favourite bush to sleep and never woke up.' Josh sniffed. 'He was already stiff when I found him, with an expression I've never seen him wear before. He looked like... Alan Carr. It was... chilling.'

Eve passed him a tissue and Josh took it, wiping at his eyes.

'Josh,' she began, softly. 'Losing a pet is a valid excuse to give yourself a time out.'

'Seriously, have you seen the other students on my course? I'm already the gay geek. I don't want to be the gay geek who weeps over the loss of his old pussy. I mean, can you imagine?'

Eve gritted her teeth. She knew the group of students Josh was referring to. They embraced difference as well as Will Smith had reacted to Chris Rock's Jada joke at the Oscars. She'd spoken to the principal before about stamping out this kind of slow drip-feed social bullying, but complete eradication didn't seem easy to achieve.

'Josh, I will get you some extra time on any outstanding assignments. I will speak to *all* your tutors and I'll speak to Mr Gilligan about sorting out Brent and his crew.'

'How... how did you know?' Josh asked, still sniffing. 'About Kit-Kat?'

Eve passed him the whole tissue box. 'You always talked about him a lot. You haven't mentioned him in our last couple of sessions. When we're upset about something, we do one of two things. We either talk too much or not enough.'

And that last sentiment had always been the crux of what ran through Eve's family. There was her mother, Glenda, who always talked too much to gloss over whatever was really going on. And then there was her brother, Ben, who shut down completely the minute he was challenged about anything. Her dad, Dave, he hadn't run deep at all. What you saw was what you got and he'd pretty much operated on one level. Eve had always been a bit envious of that non-emotional freedom, that ability to almost switch off your brain for a bit and take life as it came without question.

'Thanks, Eve,' Josh said with complete sincerity, dabbing at his eyes with another tissue.

'You're welcome,' she answered.

2

THE HUNTER'S MOON, BROOKLY HEATH, HAMPSHIRE

'There we go. Two Old Viceroys,' Eve said, setting the pint glasses on the bar.

'Ta, Eve. What d'you think of the Old Viceroy then?' Ted, one of the regulars, asked her as he put the slight foam head to his lips and sipped. 'I'd say it's not as aromatic as Foundland Kipper, but it does have heavy tobacco notes that suits me just perfect.'

'Suits me perfect too,' Stanley added, lifting his bald head from the newspaper. 'Like smoking inside again.'

Eve shook her head and recommended polishing the glasses now her only two customers were served. Being a bar person was her other job. Not that she really needed a second, but this one was personal. She had worked evenings here at The Hunter's Moon for the past six years and it was a job she had literally begged for. This used to be her dad's local pub, where he had brought her as soon as she was old enough to get up on the bar stools. Long afternoons spent watching the locals win and lose on the spin of three matching fruits, listening to an eclectic mix of Queen-meets-Pink Floyd on the jukebox, the television blasting out the horse racing and Ben dropping pork scratchings on the sticky carpet and picking them up and eating them. And every Friday and Saturday evening the fish lady had arrived with pots of prawn cocktail or cockles and crab sticks to feed hungry patrons bored of Scampi Fries and pickled eggs.

Not much had changed in The Hunter's Moon since those days. The wallpaper was still pheasants and deer but the feathers and antlers had faded with age; the banquette seating had been recovered but looked no cleaner; and the straws were made of paper not plastic now. Some might say it was well overdue a complete refit and ready to be taken over by Wetherspoons but, for Eve, this was *her* 'harmony hub'. This was where she wanted to be, where her dad had spent so many hours of his life teaching her how to cheat at dominos and where to stand for her height on the darts oche. Back then, to Eve, Dave Collins had seemed invincible. Her tall, broad, dark-bearded dad who could carry her on his shoulders for miles and knew all the words to America's 'A Horse with No Name'. Pancreatic cancer had felled him in the end, slowly to begin with – pain he shrugged off as 'my joints from all those years of climbing scaffold' and then with the inability to walk very far: 'it's my age' until all too soon he was chairbound before making that last trip to the local hospice. Eight days he was there, going from reading the newspaper and discussing the football results to a glazed look and unintelligible conversation and then slow, rattly breaths until the next breath simply didn't come. A teenaged Ben had cried exactly like he had when he was a toddler, rubbing a snotty nose with The Hunter's Moon beer mats, while Glenda had stood at the foot of the bed and simply observed, eyes watching the rise and fall of her husband's chest until it rose and fell no longer.

Although only nineteen at the time, Eve had been the one to manage everything that came next – the funeral director, the vicar, the stonemason – but after that, she'd distanced herself completely from her mother, moving into her best friend, Gabby's parents' house. Because how could you grieve alongside someone who had spent their husband's last months of life sleeping with another man? Perhaps Eve's one regret back then was not taking a fifteen-year-old Ben with her.

'Eve, you all right, love?'

It was Ted asking the question and she suddenly realised that she had been hugging the catering-sized pickled onion jar to her chest and rubbing the cloth over the lid like it was a prized ornament. That's what thinking about Glenda did. It distracted her and brought back all those intoxicating feelings of anger. Feelings she probably should have had counselling for. Because if there was one thing a counsellor couldn't do so well was counsel themselves.

'I'm fine, Ted, thank you.' She put down her cloth and leaned against the wood of the bar that had been peeling its varnish for as long as she could remember. 'So, what are your plans for the summer, you two? Any adventures I should know about?'

'Adventures?' Stanley asked, chuckling into the newspaper. 'These days my adventures consist of worrying late frosts are going to sabotage my tomato plants and hoping that the good ice cream van is going to be at the vehicle show this year.'

'I'm going to Cornwall,' Ted announced. 'Staying with me daughter and the grandchildren.'

'That sounds nice, Ted.' She paused. 'I'm actually going away too. To Greece. One of the islands. Corfu.'

She was going to be spending the summer with Gabby, finally visiting the gorgeous Greek island her best friend had made her home on. It had been two years since Gabby left. It had started with her answering an ad to be a nanny for a wealthy family, staying for a few months at a luxury villa and then, when the family had returned home, it had turned into something much more permanent. Gabby had fallen in love with the island and its animal population and was now running a sanctuary that looked after old, injured or abandoned animals, as well as supplementing her income with bar and restaurant work. But it wasn't the photos of the sheep wobbling on three legs or the turtle housed in an old bath that excited Eve about the trip, it was the cloudless blue skies, the sunshine illuminating beautiful vistas of sea and swimming pools and the idea of being somewhere her roots weren't entangled. Even though she loved the familiarity of the pub, she knew getting away from the village was long overdue.

'You're visiting Gabriella,' Ted stated, the penny finally dropping. 'I saw her mum and dad in the big Lidl t'other day. They still had their tan from when they visited in April. Hotter than Dubai they said.'

'Hotter than Penzance, that's certain,' Stanley answered.

Suddenly the doors of the pub swung open rather viciously and all three of them turned to look at what had caused it. Eve stood up a little straighter. She took in the England football shirt, the skinny jeans and Adidas trainers as the owner of those and a head of sandy-coloured hair nosedived onto the carpet.

'Think someone's had three too many,' Ted remarked.

Eve was already on her way out from behind the bar as the figure on the floor gave a groan and tried to buck himself as if he was a dolphin needing to propel himself forward. Dropping to her knees, she rolled the man over and looked into those familiar blue eyes – the same eyes he had shared with their father.

'Eeeeeeeve!' Ben greeted her, a stupid grin on his face. 'I'll have a pint of San Mig.'

'You'll have coffee,' she said firmly. 'Get up.' She tugged at his arm.

'I'm tired,' Ben slurred, cheek still attached to the carpet, body like a dead weight. 'I'm just going to go to sleep.'

'Oh no you don't,' Eve said, wrenching his arm with a strength she usually reserved for hauling barrels down in the cellar.

She dragged Ben to the edge of the banquette seating where he slumped down like a straw-filled scarecrow. She strode across the carpet, picked up the jug of water and lemon slices next to the ice bucket and, when she was one stride away from Ben again, launched it at him.

'What... what's going on? Is it raining?'

Ben's eyes were wide open now but he looked as if he had no idea where he was. Water was trickling down his forehead and there was a lemon slice stuck in his hair. Suddenly Eve had a flashback. Ben aged six or seven, a Fab lolly stuck to the side of his face, chubby fingers coated in sand from the castle he'd just demolished. In many ways he was more vulnerable now than he had been then.

'You need to go home,' she told him. 'I'll call a taxi.'

'Taxi won't take him in that state,' Ted said.

'I'll drive him then,' Eve said, still trying to coax Ben up from the carpet.

'I'm staying... at Mum's,' Ben slurred.

'What?' She was gritting her teeth before she even realised. 'Why are you staying there?' She didn't want to deliver Ben to Glenda's like this. She didn't actually want to deliver Ben to Glenda's *at all*. Perhaps she could stay in the car, make sure the front door opened and that Ben fell inside and then bomb out of there as fast as the speed humps would allow.

'Got kicked out of my flat, didn't I?'

'What?' This had to be a joke. Because Ben had only been there three months and it was the best place he'd ever been able to afford. He'd Instagrammed photos of it. The grey herringbone curtains, white walls, the bamboo lanterns around the fireplace Eve had bought him. It was somewhere fresh and clean that spoke of new beginnings. That was all Ben needed. Somewhere to call his own, somewhere to enjoy taking responsibility for himself, somewhere to maybe bring a girlfriend back to...

He had a hand on a stool now, attempting to pull himself up from the floor. 'Couldn't afford it.'

What?

'D'you want me to take him?' Stanley asked, leaning closer to her. 'I've only had a few glugs of the one.'

Ben was up now, flailing his arms and spiralling about in the style of interpretative dance no one wanted to be witness to. And then it turned almost balletic, Ben spinning like an awkward sugar-plum fairy until he barrelled into one of the small round tables, scattering beer mats first, then a stool, then his foot caught on the edge of the old Wurlitzer jukebox...

Eve grabbed Ben's arm and pinched. Hard. 'Outside. Now.' She eyeballed her customers. 'I'll be ten minutes. Ted, you remember how to work the taps? Stanley, don't take the piss with the pickled eggs.'

'You go,' Ted reassured her as she pushed Ben towards the door. 'We'll be fine.'

Eve took a deep breath as, before they had even crossed the threshold and arrived out on the street, she heard the lid of the jar being opened.

'Ow!' Ben moaned, stumbling forward, still not in control of his faculties. 'You're hurting me.'

'Not as much as your head is going to be hurting you in the morning. Get in the car.'

3

HERON'S WALK, BROOKLY HEATH, HAMPSHIRE

Eve pulled up outside the two-bedroomed ground floor maisonette their mother had lived in since she'd decided the family home at the other side of town was 'too much for her'. At the time, Glenda had said 'too much for her' like the rooms could speak and the anaglypta wallpaper had memories seeping out of it rather than age-old bubbles of badly spread paste. However, Eve suspected 'too much for her' was actually 'heavy council tax' and 'needing closer proximity to the places singles went to mingle'. Not that Eve was still raging. Not that Eve still relived that last day in the hospice and the nuances of all their mother's expressions as their dad passed away. Not that Eve was still social-media stalking Gene Reynolds.

Gene Reynolds. Single. Interests: Italia 90, classic cars, *Airwolf*. Studied at: University of Life. Her fingers had once hovered over her laptop keyboard on a Messenger tab with Gene's profile photo at the top – Gene dressed in very small swimming trunks holding a very large fish. But what did you say to someone who had been sleeping with your mother whilst your father battled cancer? 'Hello' didn't seem appropriate. And 'fuck you, knobhead' was counterproductive if Eve hoped for any response. Not that she had actually thought that far ahead. Anger did that to you. It messed with your usually balanced internal wiring, setting light to circuit boards.

'See,' Ben said, grinning. 'Told you I wouldn't throw up.'

Eve turned away from the apartment and brought her attention back to Ben. He had delivered the line about not being sick as if he should be presented with a local personality of the year prize. And now he was fumbling as if his fingers were all useless thumbs, trying to find the door handle.

'Ben,' Eve said, channelling the kind of calmness she demonstrated when the college dog peed on the floor and she knew she would have to be the one to clear it up. 'What happened with your flat?'

'Told you. Couldn't afford it.'

'But... you *didn't* tell me, Ben,' Eve continued. She could feel her emotions swinging from concerned to cross and back again. She needed to keep that in check or she'd be in danger of getting nothing from her brother but clamming up. But perhaps, as Ben was living here in this widow's-new-beginning pad, Glenda was now sat on the Throne of Confidants, rocking new Bonmarche robes to impress whatever man she currently had her eye on.

'Have you locked me in?' Ben said aggressively.

'Ben, you're pulling at the glove box now.'

'Let me out!'

'Ben,' she said. 'You know there's nothing you can't tell me, right?'

They weren't the kind of siblings to fight. They had always been close despite the five-year age gap. She loved Ben fiercely, would do anything to protect him. He had had difficult times and had always come to her before, so why did she feel he was hiding something now?

'People say that,' Ben replied with a sniff. 'But they don't ever *really* mean it.' He looked at her then, with their father's eyes, beautiful yet piercing and oh-so-serious.

'What do you mean?' she asked, her heart rate increasing. '*Is* there something you're not telling me?' More than not having told her he was no longer at his show-home of an apartment. The place she imagined him watching Aston Villa, feet up on the coffee table, awful too-salty popcorn in a casserole dish on his lap. Happy. *Safe*.

Ben opened his mouth as if he was going to respond or perhaps go back on his promise not to puke, when there was a rapping on the car window. And behind Ben's head, outside against the darkening sky, was Glenda. Eve felt herself freeze from the tips of her trainers, right up through her body. She felt suddenly cornered in the Dacia Sandero...

And then Ben pressed the button to lower the window.

'Hello, Mum!' he said, sounding drunk again as he reached out and lightly punched her shoulder as though she was one of his mates.

'Where've you been?' Glenda demanded. 'You told me you'd be back for dinner. I microwaved a cottage pie.'

Eve didn't want to be here. She didn't want to be involved in this domesticity that she'd cut out of her life. She'd be there for Ben. Always. But this woman? She barely recognised her as the mother who'd once made a whole float's worth of costumes for the Girl Guides at the Brookly Heath carnival. That had all been nothing but a charade, a part she had been playing as if she were in witness protection and had to adopt an entirely different and managed persona...

'Did *you* get him like *this*?'

The 's' had been elongated at the end and although the

sentence had been phrased like a question, Eve felt the accusation with no doubt whatsoever.

'Evelyn, I asked you a question.'

Using her full name, the name Eve never *ever* used, well, Glenda knew exactly how to push her buttons. No one called her Evelyn, not even her doctor.

Eve addressed her brother. 'Ben, take two paracetamol before you go to bed and a big glass of water. I'll phone you in the morning and see how you are.'

Ben had at last found the door handle. He opened it and swung his legs out of the footwell and onto solid ground. A surreptitious glance sideways showed Eve that Glenda was now making her way round the car, like a bull on a charge, and then her face appeared at Eve's window and her knuckles began rapping on the glass again.

'Evelyn, open this window!'

Eve remained still, drawing a long, slow breath. She was not going to be brought into this. On the day of her dad's funeral she had put her emotions on display on the street outside their family home. She was not going to put them on display again here in this unfamiliar cul-de-sac. She could picture Glenda playing the victim at her very next coffee and cake morning. *My daughter has always been a bit of an oddball. My Dave used to say she had a unique spirit. Well, it might well be unique but, where I'm concerned, it's always felt more like ectoplasm than spirit...*

Eve was broken out of her train of thought when she caught sight of her mother's face right up close to the glass.

'If you don't open this window I'll... I'll...'

This was going to be interesting.

'Lick it!' Glenda blasted. She opened her mouth and stuck out her tongue and that was enough for Eve.

She yanked at the door handle and as the door opened, Glenda reeled back, falling against her green wheelie bin.

'What sane person threatens to lick someone's car window?' Eve yelled, the calmness she prided herself on evaporating as she got out of the car.

'What sane person won't speak to their mother when they're being asked a question?' Glenda countered, brushing herself down as if she had actually landed inside the bin.

'I have nothing to say to you,' Eve said, gritting her teeth.

'No, because you know you can't take the moral high ground in this situation. You've gone out and got your brother drunk and it's going to be me who has to pick up the pieces.'

'I said... I'm not going to be sick,' Ben called from the other side of the car.

'*I* didn't get him drunk,' Eve told her. 'I've been working. He came into the pub already like this. But while we're on the subject of picking up the pieces, why is Ben living here with you? What happened with his flat?'

In Eve's mind, this had nothing to do with Ben's financial situation and more to do with Glenda's need for control. Perhaps single, divorced or widowed men over sixty were in short supply and she craved the company. A promise of pay-per-view sports when he wanted it and a few months rent-free and Ben wouldn't have taken much more persuading. Despite the restraint on his independence. Meals cooked for him – albeit microwaved ones apparently – washing and ironing done, all of it was a lure to a lad who had always felt the pressure of being the only man left in the house.

Eve watched her little brother now, wondering if she should go over and intervene, try to prevent him from falling off the few inches of kerb and potentially turning his ankle.

She looked back at Glenda.

'Is he gambling again?' she asked firmly and in a low voice. Eve squared her shoulders, rooted her feet to the floor, held herself firm. She did not want to give away the fact that she was terrified of the answer.

'No!' Glenda responded quickly. 'Of course he isn't! That stupidity is all over now.'

'How do you know?'

'Because I have people looking out for him,' she continued. 'Vera at Ladbrokes. Warren at Bet Fred. Someone with a lip ring at William Hill.'

Did she? Because when Ben's gambling had first got out of hand, Glenda had wanted to put it down to 'boys being boys', like losing every penny you had and putting bets before having enough money for food was some kind of stag night game.

'Charlie would know if there was something going on,' Eve said. 'I'll give him a call.'

Eve turned back to her car and Ben started to hop towards them from across the road looking like a pissed-up children's entertainer.

Charlie was Ben's best friend. They had met at work and had been hanging off scaffolding with each other ever since they'd both joined the building firm. Charlie was probably the only one of Ben's friends who had a few more interests than Formula One, football and fight nights. Eve had always thought he was a sensible, stable companion for Ben and that took the weight off a bit.

'No!' Glenda said.

And here it was. This was the moment Eve *might* get some insight into this situation. She turned around and faced Glenda again.

'Why can't I speak to Charlie?' Eve asked.

'Because... he's on holiday.'

All the tell-tale signs of a lie were written on Glenda's expression. The game was up and even Glenda knew it.

'OK... Ben is... in between jobs at the moment,' Glenda said, lips tight as if this unsavoury information might blemish her Lipcote.

'He's what?'

'Don't shout,' Glenda hissed. 'You know how Ben gets.'

'He's lost his job!' Eve stated bluntly. 'And *that's* why he can't afford the flat any more. What happened?'

'I don't know,' Glenda admitted. 'He won't tell me and believe me, I've tried.'

Eve's gaze went to her brother, who was currently swinging himself around a lamppost singing an out-of-tune rendition of The Wanted's 'Glad You Came'. She knew all too well how Ben could clam up faster than an unnerved oyster. Well, Eve wasn't about to let Ben give up on himself. He needed to find purpose. He needed to deal with his left-over grief.

'Well, *I* haven't tried,' Eve said, her words fuelled with determination.

She marched over to her brother and got him in an arm-lock, forcibly shifting him towards the front door of the maisonette.

'What are you doing? Get off!' Ben moaned, wriggling like a worm on a fishing line.

'Ben, I want you to get inside, have water and paracetamol and, in the morning, when you're feeling slightly more normal, I want you to start thinking about packing a bag.'

He started singing again. 'You trying to make me go to rehab?' He sniffed. 'My answer is the same as Amy Winehouse.'

As Ben fell onto the carpet, Eve turned back to Glenda. 'Can you make sure he has everything he might need for some time away?'

'Time away where?' Glenda asked.

'I'm taking him to Corfu.'

4

VERONA, ITALY

It was a scorching summer day outside, but here in Gianni Riccardo's father's suite, every scrap of what lay beyond the walls of the stone villa had been blanketed out. From the thick tapestry curtains to the blackout blinds stretched over every inch of the glass, this room had been turned from master bedroom to almost mausoleum since Riccardo Riccardo had been confined to his bed two months ago.

Gianni was still screwing up his eyes now, trying to get his pupils to adjust to the difference here compared to the bright office overlooking the gardens. He stood at the foot of the huge, four-poster bed, his father's form prostrate, Riccardo's head propped atop three thick duck-feather pillows. Despite his father's size and stature, for the first time in Gianni's life, Riccardo looked weak. His skin was mottled – a muddied hue between purple and grey – the tanned olive tone fading, Riccardo's strength diminishing as the cirrhosis took hold.

'How long now? Do you think?'

It was his mother, Valentina, whispering into the ear of the nurse. They were standing a little closer to the bed. Had his father heard? Didn't they always say hearing was the last sense to leave? How must it feel to hear that everyone was waiting for the sad inevitability?

'I do not think very long,' the nurse replied gravely.

Gianni stepped closer, moving around to the side of the bed where his mother wasn't standing and pressing icons on the screen of her phone. Was this really going to be the end for the king of coffee? They had known it was coming for almost a year now but it was still so hard to comprehend. At the beginning there had been time for laughter, champagne and trips around the Med; the diagnosis hadn't seemed real. But then, instead of plunging himself into everything like a confident cafetiere, Riccardo had retreated. Gianni's father had holed himself up in this cavernous bedroom with its velvet and gold thread and its floor-to-ceiling arched windows with unrivalled views of the lawns, ordering the windows to be covered and hunkering down under the covers, feasting some days, fasting others, existing not living.

His mother sighed. 'You have been saying this for days now. And each time we have to put aside our work and mount the many stairs to enter into this dreary cave dwelling Riccardo has made for himself only to watch his chest rise and fall like it has been doing since the first time his body came out from between his mamma's legs.'

'Mamma,' Gianni protested. He didn't like the way his mother was dealing with this. She had kept well away from this wing of the house for the last few weeks, making excuses about the business or one of her friends, or sometimes not bothering to make excuses at all. He knew how she felt about illness, how she was all about the organisation, no pill or potion unexplored in an attempt to control if not cure, but when it came down to the handholding and showing empathy, she had always been severely lacking.

'We have an important meeting, Gianni. In,' she looked at her watch, 'just over twenty minutes. If this is going to happen then it needs to happen now... or after five o'clock.'

'Mamma,' Gianni said. 'Come sit with me and Papa.' He pulled up an ancient wooden chair and sat down right next to his father, reaching for one of his hands. The skin looked paper thin, like tissue or the fragile petals of a poppy.

'This was not the way things were supposed to be,' his mother said, finally showing some emotion as she looked at her ailing husband.

'I know,' Gianni replied with a sober nod. He toyed with the gold sovereign rings on his father's hand. This jewellery, this villa, the luxury that surrounded them, it was everything Riccardo had worked for and the man barely had time to enjoy it. His father had always been the hands-on CEO even though he hadn't needed to be. He loved the buzz of business, the meeting and greeting, the deals done in person. Never mind email signatures on dotted lines. Riccardo's handshake had always been his word and the importance of honour was something he'd passed down to Gianni. You didn't do deals under the table, you did them face to face and with integrity. But as much as his father had lived business, got drunk on it, family had always come first.

'It is so selfish of him,' his mother continued, shaking her head. 'He promised me this illness would not get in the way and look at him. Luxuriating in death like it is something to be savoured.'

'Mamma!' Gianni exclaimed.

'Don't look at me like that, Gianni. Riccardo knows how I am with sickness.'

The 's' word had barely passed her lips when she rolled her eyes and retched a little. Gianni shook his head then. Surely, now, for as long as it took, she could be here for her husband. Be here for *Gianni*. They might have known this was coming, but what did that knowledge really give you? A brief warning that your world was going to come crumbling down whenever Fate or God or whoever decided it was so.

'Mamma,' Gianni whispered softly. 'It is Papa lying here. Not the illness. Think only of him.'

It was then his mother began to cry. Silently to begin with, the first trails of tears slowly snaking down her cheeks, until her shoulders started to shake and then noise followed. Gianni left his chair and made his way around the bed to comfort his mother. He leaned in to embrace her, but she was up and off the seat before he could make any contact.

'Don't do that, Gianni,' she said, brushing her hands through the air as if she might be dispatching a fly or three and not his attempt at consolation. 'Riccardos are strong. They do not crumble. They do not show weakness. That was always your father's way.'

'No, Mamma,' Gianni responded a little roughly. 'That is always *your* way.'

His father had always hugged everybody in greeting or vigorously pumped their hand until their whole body shook, his loud laugh vibrating off the walls of the boardroom or the boat or the bar until his infectious personality was pulling at your purse strings and you were more than happy about it. He hadn't just loved business and family. He had loved life.

'Gi... anni.'

It was his father. Gianni edged forward, taking his other hand this time. 'I'm here.'

His father hadn't spoken at all in three days, a sign that his body was beginning to shut down, the nurse said. The room had been darkness, a silence heavier than the curtains and a stale odour mixed with the scent of an extravagant display of lilies his mother had ordered to counteract the other smell.

'You... are my boy,' Riccardo whispered. His eyes were half-open now and he was slowly turning his head on the pillows, the effort visible in his expression.

'Yes, Papa,' Gianni said, swallowing a lump in his throat.

'You... have always been... my boy. In my... head. And... in my heart.'

'Papa,' Gianni said. 'Please rest now. There is nothing here for you to worry for any longer. I will look after Mamma and I will take care of the business. Build Riccardocino even bigger. Make it stronger than your signature espresso, remember?'

His father was shaking his head. Gianni felt his grip tighten on his hand a little. And were there tears in his eyes?

'He is tired,' his mother said, suddenly back at Gianni's shoulder. 'And the morphine. The nurse says that and his illness will make him say things that make no sense.' She turned to the nurse who looked to be sorting through bottles of medication on the dresser. 'You said this, didn't you? Tell my son.'

'Valentina,' Riccardo croaked. 'Do... not... be afraid.'

'See!' she said, so loudly it echoed off the walls. 'See, he speaks no sense.'

Except Gianni's interest was now piqued. The behaviour his mother was exhibiting was the kind she put on when she was attempting to cover something up, like when they had difficulties getting supplies to customers. Honesty was always his and his father's go-to principle but, with his mother, it was more a case of 'what people didn't know couldn't hurt them'...

'Papa,' Gianni tried again. 'Whatever is on your mind, now is the time to say it. I am listening.' He squeezed his father's hand again. This time Riccardo found the strength to weakly pull Gianni nearer.

'Blood... it is just blood,' he carried on, his voice a mere rasp. 'But... it cannot... be ignored... and it should not... be ignored.'

Were these words of wisdom? Some spiritual message Gianni could cling to as time went on? Or were these the ravings of a man under the influence of medication about to part with the world?

'I... have loved you... with the strength of... a thousand coffees. But now... it is the turn... of someone else. To be there for you... when I cannot.'

Now Gianni really didn't understand. And his father's voice was becoming fainter with every passing second.

'Papa,' Gianni said, tears filling his eyes.

'Find him, Gianni,' Riccardo pleaded as he struggled for breath. 'Find the father... who gave you that jawline I do not possess. The father who... passed to you a gentle side that you must not... shut down.'

Tiny fragments of what his father was saying began to join together and form larger pieces which Gianni's mind was trying to decipher as if they were code.

Blood. Someone else's turn. The father who gave him his jawline.

'What is he saying? I cannot hear,' his mother said.

She was next to him and Gianni watched his father's eyes roll back, his fingers falling from Gianni's grip to the covers where they began to scratch at the high-thread-count sheet. And then... nothing. No movement. No sound. No life.

For a second, Gianni didn't know what to do. He was torn between taking his father's hand again, shaking it, demanding something, a last breath, more words and backing away, running from the room and out of this wing of the house. It was over. And it felt sudden, as if death had come by accident.

'What happens now? Do I call the funeral director? Will you stay and wait for him? If I drive very fast I can still make my meeting.'

Gianni turned from his father and looked at his mother. Her

eyes were dry now and she was asking these questions of the nurse who was hastening towards his father. His father's *body*.

A stethoscope was placed on his chest, the nurse leaning in. Then she stepped away and gave Gianni a grave look.

'We have to wait for the doctor,' she told him. 'Although your father has passed, the doctor will be the one to fill in the documentation.'

Gianni looked at his mother again, who was taking her phone from her bag, preparing to make a call. Suddenly he did not feel gentle or kind, he felt angry and out of a loop he didn't even know existed.

'Do not make that call,' Gianni said. It had sounded forceful in the air, the first words in a while that were louder than a whisper.

He watched as the nurse scurried away, leaving the room as if she anticipated the dramatic unfolding of this situation.

His mother heaved a sigh. 'Unfortunately, there is nothing more we can do for your father now.'

'Is there not?' Gianni asked, taking steps towards her. 'Because my *father* just told me that I get some of my appearance from someone else.'

He watched the colour drain from his mother's face, a tell-tale tightening at her temples. There *was* something in this. It *hadn't* been the morphine talking. But he needed to know the extent of it and he needed to know now. He held his breath for a second before he found the courage to continue.

'Tell me. Is it true? Is Riccardo not my father?'

'Gianni,' she said, her lips trembling. 'This is not—'

'Answer the question, Mamma,' he ordered.

He watched his mother get caught between a nod and a shake of her head. Tears were there now, slowly trickling down her face. More tears now than for the death of her husband only a few moments ago.

'I'm sorry, Gianni,' she sobbed. 'It... it is true.'

Gianni hadn't realised exactly how much he was tensing until the release rushed up through him. He bolted for the door of the suite and only just made it outside before he vomited over the balustrade.

5

A WEEK LATER, CORFU, GREECE

'...And that is how Antigone at the pharmacy is with her brothers. Families. They are always about the drama, yes?'

'Yes,' Eve replied quickly, snapping her closing eyes open and forcing herself to pay attention to their driver who had been only too happy to chat *all the way* from the airport. Gabby's text that she had organised a lift had come in at the same time Ben almost had a coming together with an enthusiastic traveller desperate to elbow-barge his way to the front of the luggage carousel. They wouldn't have had any baggage to collect if Glenda hadn't filled Ben's cabin bag with 200 ml bottles of sun cream, after sun and an Avon product that allegedly repelled mosquitos like Britain repelled a heatwave. But with Ben being fair-skinned and not knowing whether a Factor 30 in Greece meant the same protection it did in the UK, Eve had stumped up for the extortionate hold case fee. With Gabby's message also stating 'a kitten emergency', they had left Corfu Airport to find their driver, this very tall, wiry man with a bushy cloud of thick grey hair.

Eve's eyelids had been drooping from the moment the door of the Fiat Doblò had been slammed. It was hot in this van. The windows were open but all that seemed to be doing was blowing in warmer air mixed with the husks of dried roadside grasses and the occasional wayward wasp. And their driver wasn't hanging about. He was careening around these winding roads as though he was on course for a chicane certificate.

'You have family drama?' the driver asked, his light eyes appearing in the rear-view mirror.

'Always, dude,' Ben said. 'That's why we're here.'

The driver laughed loudly – something he'd been doing often since he'd thrown their cases in the back – and stepped on the accelerator a little more. 'Well, let me tell you about Antigone's husband, Vasilis. He has had three heart attacks yet still he smokes cigars and eats like a colossus.'

As their driver launched into another animated talk about the members of a local pharmacist's family, Eve focused her attention on her brother. Ben had his arms folded across his chest, sunglasses on and his head turned to the boiling breeze blowing in the window. He had barely said anything since she'd picked him up in the early hours of the morning. There had been no usual pre-flight pint of Stella, the picture posted to Facebook early doors with laddie comments like 'on it, bruv' and the sunglasses smiley face emoji. Thinking back, he had said hardly anything about this trip since she'd first told him he was coming. He hadn't even agreed, just kind of submitted.

The three-hour flight had passed by in a blur of meal deals and perfume offers and it seemed being in Greece was not helping with the conversation. Perhaps Eve needed to start slowly, the way she had drawn the demise of Kit-Kat out of Josh. She opened her mouth to speak—

'Goats!'

It was a shriek from their driver who pressed his foot on the brake even harder than he had been touching the gas pedal. Eve's seatbelt dug into her neck as she was thrown forward, auburn fringe grazing the seat in front, and the van skidded to a stop, only just short of a herd of mainly brown hairy four-legged animals meandering in the middle of the road.

'Are they not cute?' the driver said, the engine idling almost as much as the goats. 'Look at their beards and the way they look so unhappy with us.'

Eve could have been an unhappy goat right now. Apart from the beard – she hoped. Whiplash hadn't been on her arrival agenda. And as much as she knew Gabby was busy, she'd built up their reunion at the airport to be akin to a soldier coming back from a war zone cuddling the child he had never met. It had been too long since she had seen her best friend. There was no one else in the UK she gelled with quite like Gabby. The friendships she had with the college staff were all somehow at a superficial level. Eve would pass the time of day, ask them about their weekends, share the odd wine and cheese night – and sometimes they really were *really* odd – but that was it. She actually had deeper conversations with Ted and Stanley at the pub.

But Gabby had always just got her. She could tell her anything without a speck of judgement. Like the time she admitted she had a real fear of the pommel horse at school and had nightmares that it would come to life just as her feet landed on its leathery skin. Gabby had confessed she hated it too – perhaps not to the same degree as needing deep breathing exercises to be in the same room – and they had drawn crazy caricature pictures of it and burnt them in Gabby's parents' fire pit.

'What kind are they?'

Hearing Ben's voice shocked Eve almost as much as the jarring braking had. She slid into a more comfortable position, watching her brother remove his sunglasses and lean out of the open window.

'They are Greek,' the driver replied.

Eve fanned a hand in front of her face, waving her fringe up off her forehead. It was very hot now they had stopped moving and there was no wind rush. And it seemed the goats weren't moving anywhere in a hurry either.

'There is not always goat herd here in Corfu,' their driver announced. 'Goats, they have free spirits.'

'Lucky goats,' Ben muttered, loud enough for her to hear.

The driver continued. 'They will roam if they can and they will not stay where they are not happy.'

Well, currently Eve wasn't happy in this sweatbox of a vehicle with her pissed off brother. She sat forward again.

'Shall we... I don't know... stop looking at the goats maybe and... go around them?'

'We will wait,' the driver said. 'They will not be long to cross the road, have grass and take a moment.' He turned the engine off.

Was he now... rolling a cigarette? This was not on! Eve put a hand on the door handle and pulled. There had to be something somebody could do. She put a sweaty trainer-clad foot onto the dusty not-quite-tarmac ground and inched her body out of the van. Not a hint of a breeze. But the view really was something.

Walking away from the van, Eve found a little space to breathe and look around her. Greenery was rolling down from their position as if someone had unfurled a sumptuous carpet. Dips and curves, cubes of pastel buildings almost hidden were dotted amongst the trees, all framed under a clear forget-me-not blue sky. It was as if time was standing still. A bit like the goats were doing. Eve's eyes went to the animals then, which were bleating loudly, teeth tearing at the scrub, coats long and shaggy.

'It looks nothing like Bournemouth, does it?'

Eve hadn't heard Ben's approach, but he was standing next to her now, facing the breath-taking scenery. She smiled. 'No.'

Bournemouth had been their dad's holiday destination of choice when they were little. *Why go abroad for sand and sea when you have one of England's best right down the road?* The beach *was* wide and golden and when they were kids burrowing into the sand making castles, burying their dad right up to his neck, all they had wanted was that, coins for the arcade and chips that wasps were ready to go to war for.

'He'd have liked this view though,' Ben continued. 'Dad.'

'He'd have loved the heat too,' Eve said, a trickle of perspiration running down from her forehead.

'God, yeah,' Ben said with a laugh. 'His pasty British skin burning up under anything above eighteen degrees. Zero sunscreen because he thought that was for wimps. I'm surprised it wasn't skin cancer that got him.'

Ben's reverie was as sad as it was heart-warming, but what really touched Eve was that this was the first time her brother had spoken about their father since he'd died. Eve hadn't wanted the memories to die along with him and during those heavenly birthdays, Christmas, etc. she often brought up some of his funny sayings or talked about the times he'd made special. But Ben never engaged, always changing the subject. It was almost as if he wanted to sweep everything under the rug, pretend what had gone before had never happened. And none of her usual counsellor techniques worked on someone so utterly closed off. But maybe now there was an opportunity...

'Ben—'

'So, what's this place we're going to like? Because the Gabby I remember never liked breaking a nail. I can't see her mucking out goats and stuff.'

He had shut her down before she'd even had a chance to begin. But he *had* spoken about their dad; that was a leap in itself. Softly, softly...

'I know,' Eve answered. 'But before we all discovered Rimmel she was in charge of the animal hut at school. She was the only pupil to ever teach a squirrel a trick. Sammy tapped "Happy Birthday" on a Yamaha organ in assembly. And she's been a nanny,' Eve reminded.

'Come on, Eve. She was a nanny for rich people. Do their kids even take a crap?'

He did have a point. The stories from Gabby's days in the villas had been more about making fruit smoothies, even for the under twos, than it had been changing nappies. And that was why Eve *needed* this catch-up with her best friend. To reconnect and to remind herself that there was stuff going on outside her village.

'The goats have moved!' their driver called. 'I will just finish my cigarette and we can drive again.'

Ben shook his head, a grin on his face. 'D'you reckon he arranged those goats just so he could have a smoke?'

Before Eve could make a response, their driver spoke again. 'I expect you think I make goats come here so I can smoke, yes?' He laughed.

6

VERONA, ITALY

'You look a little pale, *amore mio*.'

'But you still look very attractive.'

'Giuseppe says now you are worth more than all the Sheiks.'

Gianni was being fanned on one side and patted on the arm the other. His cousins, Luna and Bella, were paying more attention to him than they were to the ongoing wake for his father. He zoned out from their chatter and watched his mother working the room – their family dining room was trussed up like a grand banqueting hall, decorated as if a royal family were expected. *The king of coffee*. Their patriarch had been interned in the family crypt with his parents and his younger brother, an uncle who had died before Gianni was born. Another family member he didn't know and another family member he was not related to by blood.

His mother laughed hysterically – *inappropriately* – about something one of their 'influential' friends had said to her. Her head was thrown back like a horse unhappy about something its jockey was doing, except this was not displeasure from his mother but a show of ostentatiousness. She might be dressed like a grieving widow but there was an undercurrent of management about this whole thing and it had been that way since the first meeting with the undertaker when the man had been offered langoustines with his coffee...

'Will you buy a boat?' Luna continued.

'Or another house? Or... two houses?' Bella added.

'Perhaps Gianni will wait before making decisions. Until he has a wife to help make them,' Luna suggested, leaning into him.

Gianni got to his feet then, the room suddenly feeling as suffocating as if he were encased in a stone shrine himself. 'Excuse me.'

He heard Luna and Bella bleating after him and he kept on striding, relishing the idea of being outside, the heat on his skin as blistering as it felt restorative. A little light was creeping in through the open door. He could divert to the terrace, leave the mourners to their so-called grief and expensive catered buffet. But, alternatively, his mother was only a few steps away. And she had made this last week exceedingly difficult for him. If it wasn't bad enough that he'd lost the man who had brought him up, it felt as if he had lost him twice. Once just before he took his final breath with his bedside revelation and then again straight after. And as the funeral was arranged, Gianni found himself going over and over details from his life, looking for any signs he had missed. When Riccardo had been unwilling to take him fishing or to the coffee factory, was it really work getting in the way or a weak connection? How had his parents managed to keep this a secret for so long? Wasn't it practically the law in these matters to tell the child when they were old enough to understand? Well, Gianni had been old enough for many years now and this new knowledge was punching him hard.

He watched his mother put a hand on the arm of their operations manager, Paolo, and squeeze the sleeve of his Gucci suit. Did Paolo know? How many others here knew? Had Gianni been the *last* to find out?

'Mamma, I need to speak with you.'

His mother turned her head a little, made eye contact and then at once diverted her attention back to Paolo.

'Excuse me for a moment, Paolo,' she said, giving another squeeze and the smile that persuaded many a café chain to stock only their brand of coffee. But the smile dropped away as soon as she looked at Gianni.

'What is it? Can you not see I am busy? Paolo and I are trying to do business.'

'At my father's funeral?' The word 'father' now felt wrong on his lips. He corrected himself. 'At Riccardo's funeral.'

His mother pursed her lips and made sure her voice was low as she gave her reply. 'He is still your father, Gianni.'

'But it was his last wish for me to know that I was not his son.'

It hurt. No matter the good intentions Riccardo might have had, everything that had gone before now felt flimsy, a mirage.

'Riccardo was not in his right mind,' Valentina said, one eye on the hordes of people feasting on the buffet banquet, proof that she was not 100 per cent invested in this conversation.

'No more excuses, Mamma. Tell me who my real father is,' he said bluntly.

'This is not the time or the place. Now I am going to—'

'No,' he said, putting a hand on her arm. 'This *is* the time and the place. My father here is gone and now he has been interred. He wanted me to know and you are the only person who can tell me. I want his name. I want his address. I want to know if he knows about me.'

'Keep your voice down,' his mother said, giving a side-eye to the group of guests nearest to them.

'I will *not* keep my voice down.'

'Gianni, think about this. We are a family, an established family in the community of Verona. One day there will be a statue dedicated to us, perhaps next to Dante in the Piazza dei Signori. We need to protect our reputation.'

'Our *reputation*?'

Now Gianni's temper was frothing like hot milk before it spurts into a cappuccino. Was his mother really putting their standing in the city above his feelings?

'Tell me his name,' Gianni said firmly.

'I wish you would see that he is not important.'

'I wish you would give me a straight answer.'

His mother sighed. He was going to get this out of her here and now.

'If you do not tell me my father's name right this second, I will announce to the entire room that I am not Riccardo Riccardo's son. How will that be for your social standing?'

He watched his mother whiten, her pallor changing to something close to the lilies that, lately, were in every corner of this place. He was not going to back down like he sometimes did during business negotiations, giving her the respect he knew she thought her age and maternal status granted her. This time it was different.

'His name... It is... Pan,' she said, her voice trembling as the words left her lips.

Pan? What kind of name was Pan? For a second Gianni had no words. Was this a joke?

'Do not look at me like that. I cannot bear it. I cannot bear *this!*' His mother gesticulated to the room and Gianni didn't know whether she meant the house, the funeral, the guests, the situation or all of those. One thing was certain: his mother's control was slipping. Her guarded nature was beginning to look as if it was about to unravel like a skein of thread.

'I made... questionable choices when I was younger, Gianni.

Sometimes I wish I could go back and make different decisions, but here we are.'

The string quartet they had booked began to strike up a rousing rendition of 'Amor, Amor, Amor'.

Questionable choices. Did she mean *mistakes?* And he was one of them? He held his nerve and bit his tongue, standing tall the way his father had taught him from the youngest of ages. *Real power comes from within, Gianni. But never underestimate the strength of stature. No one ever has respect for the tiny mouse unless he stands up straight on his two back legs.*

'I learned too late that naivety does not just belong to silly girls who have no brain cells. It can infect those who, in usual circumstances, should know better.'

Tears were running down his mother's face now and guests were starting to direct their attention to them both. Her fingers went to her neat stack of hair and she began to unpick the strands at the sides. She looked as vulnerable now as he had ever seen her. The only other time she had behaved like this was when someone spoke about his long-since-passed-away *nonna.* Sometimes if a family member mentioned his grandmother she would break down and shut herself away for the rest of the evening, only to reappear later as if nothing had happened. But whether she was finding this difficult or not, Gianni still wanted the truth. *Needed* the truth.

'Where is this Pan, Mamma? Or, at least, tell me: where in Italy did you last see him?'

Valentina shook her head, hands scratching at her hair again.

'Mamma, is he from Verona? Or somewhere else in this region?'

Then he remembered; his mother had spent time in Sicily. Was that where she had met this man?

'It was not Italy,' she said, shaking her head as more tears started to fall. 'It was Greece.'

'Greece?' Gianni exclaimed.

'The island of Corfu,' his mother continued. She looked directly at him then, her weeping eyes full of pain and sorrow. 'Gianni, your father, he is Greek.'

7

SAFE ANIMALS SANCTUARY, EPISKEPSI, CORFU

'Look at you!'

Gabby squeezed Eve tight and it felt as if she might be a tube of toothpaste that needed brute force to remove the last remnants. When had her friend got so strong? And so tanned? Every inch of Gabby exposed from the cut-off denim shorts and vest was a warm bronze. Well, time had passed by, there were bound to be changes in her friend, but thankfully one thing that was exactly the same was her hair. It wasn't just the visual effect of the huge extravaganza of dark curls that was familiar, it was the smell. Gabby's hair had always *always* smelled of coconut and as Eve inhaled now it reminded her of all the hugs they'd had as children, through tears and laughter, sleepovers and fun fairs, those pickled eggs and bottles of Coke at the pub...

'Are you smelling my hair?' she asked, laughing as she finally let go. The hair sniffing had never been a secret between them.

Eve smiled. 'Maybe.'

'Well, it probably smells of horse poo and cat sick right now. It's been a bit of day for it.' Gabby made her trademark excited noise –

a kind of squeal – and grabbed Eve again. 'It's so good to have you here. Come on, let me show you around the sanctuary.' Gabby pulled her towards a group of outbuildings, the ground a mix of concrete and dust, but olive trees were all around, providing shade from what was an intense heat.

Eve looked back to the Fiat Doblò where Ben was leaning against the bonnet, eyes on his phone. He hadn't moved when their driver had pulled the vehicle to a halt and announced their arrival at Safe Animals. And when she had asked him if he was getting out, he'd ignored her completely, eyes hidden behind those large sunglasses. At least he was out of the vehicle now, if not bounding over to greet their host.

'Sorry,' Gabby said, linking arms with her and slowing their pace a little. 'I'm rushing you and in Corfu one thing our guests don't do is rush. Especially when they've have had a three-hour flight, a hideous queue at passport control and I suspect an even worse experience with the drive here.' Gabby grinned. 'Did he have to stop for "goats"?'

Gabby had said 'goats' as if the word was slang for a Class A drug.

'Well, there were actual goats,' Eve answered. 'I saw them myself. And even Ben seemed to pay a bit of interest in them.' More interest than he was currently paying to her and Gabby.

'Is Ben OK?' Gabby asked as they headed towards something that looked like a stable block. It had a tiled roof but not all of the tiles were present and correct.

Eve sighed. 'I really don't know. But thank you for letting me bring him with me. I just think he needs to get out of Brookly Heath for a bit.'

'As do you,' Gabby said with a nod. 'And you need to rethink your job at the pub. Or one day you're going to wake up and you'll be literally part of the furniture... or the crusty pheasant wallpaper. Please tell me that's not still there.'

Eve smiled. 'Of course it's still there.'

'Of course it is,' Gabby repeated, shaking her head. 'Right, are you ready to meet some of the animals?'

'How many are there?'

'Gosh, I have no idea on the numbers,' Gabby said as she led them on, 'but all the animals have a file, except the ants in the ant farm. I mean, that would be craziness.'

She clapped her hands and within seconds a group of geese had come waddling at speed around the corner of one of the sheds. There was a mixture of white ones, grey ones and some that were speckled with both, orange feet flapping and beaks opening and closing as they honked a greeting.

'*Koritsia mou!*' Gabby greeted, spreading her arms wide as two of them flew up and at her, landing in her embrace as if they were returning to their mother. 'My girls!'

A white one looked at Eve, up and down and then down and up as if wondering whether she was a good egg or a bad one. Should she pet it on the head? Or just stand still?

'Oh, Eve, geese aren't like swans. They aren't going to break your arm with their wings if you get too close. They might make a lot of noise but it's all bluster.'

And Gabby was coddling them with so much affection. This was not the same person who had moaned over FaceTime about the irritating children she had to entertain for hours on end while their parents were getting pampered or pissed – or both. This was pioneering Gabby, teaching a squirrel to play music, elbow deep in rabbit feed in the school animal shed as they listened to Mumford and Sons.

'Are you OK?' Gabby asked, putting the geese back on their feet and perhaps even wondering whether she might have to do something similar with Eve. 'Is this a bit much straight away? Because we can just grab a Fanta Lemon and leave the look around until later.'

'No, it's fine. It's just, you look so at home here.'

Gabby reached out and put a hand on Eve's shoulder. 'I may never be Richard Attenborough but look at this place. And I mean *really* look at it. What's not to love?'

Eve's gaze was drawn to their surroundings. The outbuildings were in amongst the most tranquil of settings. Olive branches trailed over the brickwork, cicadas chirped a rhythmic tune, broken plastic buckets spilled with bright flowers and two cats were perched inside a wheelbarrow silently assessing the world. Nothing was symmetrical or ordered, it just simply *was*. Was it Eve's imagination or was the base of her neck a little less tense all of a sudden?

Gabby let out a satisfied sigh. 'It might take you a little while but by the time your return flight is ready to depart you'll feel lighter and a lot brighter... or maybe you won't go back to England at all.'

Something in Eve stalled and she suddenly had a vision of The Hunter's Moon with someone else standing behind the bar. Someone who had ordered in cashews and pistachios, someone set on changing the décor...

Gabby laughed then and thumped Eve's shoulder with the flat of her hand. 'Oh, Eve, I've missed you. It's like having a piece of Brookly Heath over here.'

Eve didn't know whether that was a compliment or not. She smoothed her hair behind her ears. 'It's David Attenborough by the way.'

'What?'

'The BBC version of Doctor Dolittle. It's David Attenborough, not Richard.'

Gabby grinned. 'See, you know almost as much about animals as I do.' She slipped an arm around Eve's shoulders and hugged her close. 'Come and meet Savage. You'll love Savage.'

'Please tell me Savage isn't a lion.'

'It's an animal sanctuary, Eve, not a safari!'

8

Eve was exhausted. She hadn't meant to keep zoning out when Gabby was telling her the names of all the animals – the tortoises were named after Teletubbies and Tinky Winky currently had an eye infection – but with the heat and the early morning start they'd had it was difficult fighting the draw to close her eyelids, especially now she'd lain down on the bed in the cosy, if not cool, upper level of Gabby's little stone house.

Eve let her eyes shut and tried to recall the details of the whistle-stop tour. This whole set-up had been established by a never-disclosed owner with mystery trustees to provide a place to care for Corfu's waifs and strays. Gabby earned a small salary as the manager and had also been given the stone house to live in but bills were her own responsibility. She then had a small team of volunteers. To supplement funds, the shelter held fundraising events – from quiz nights to sponsored runs. Gabby had shown Eve some of the photos – there was their driver from the Fiat Doblò dressed in shorts and a singlet, an orange bandana across his forehead, having completed a run to the top of Mount Pantokrator and another where pork *souvlakia* was being barbecued in the outside space at the sanctuary as a Greek band performed to scores of dancers.

The living quarters were rustic but beautiful: two stone houses next to each other with a front outside terrace. Each had a minute kitchen with barely room to move a frying pan, a downstairs sitting or eating area, a bathroom with only just enough room to draw the shower curtain, and one bedroom. However, Gabby's house was laid out slightly differently from its neighbour with a second bathroom and another bedroom upstairs where there were twin beds with enough room between them that Eve hoped she wasn't going to be disturbed by her brother's snoring. There was also a balcony up here with views through the olive groves. Gabby had explained that if she stood at the very edge of the balcony on tiptoes, she would be able to see the sea. Eve hadn't tried that yet.

And, as for Savage, he hadn't been a member of the cat family; he was a hoopoe bird. Perfectly able to fly off and live wherever he chose with his broken wing fixed over a year ago, but the bird seemed to have decided to stay at the shelter. Why he was called Savage, Eve had yet to find out. But that could come over dinner later. For now, she was going to just relax and take a power nap as the rusty pedestal fan did its best to move the warm air around...

'Eve, have you got any money?'

Her eyes snapped open at the sound of Ben's voice but her tired brain took a second to catch up. The question he'd asked was all too familiar and as she struggled into a sitting position, she was hit with a flashback of Ben asking for cash the last time she had ever given it to him. It hadn't ended so well.

'What kind of money?'

'Er, you know, euros, the kind they take here,' Ben answered.

'Didn't you say Glenda had given you some?'

'Yeah, like enough to send her a postcard if you can even send postcards around here. The driver dude is going to give me a lift down to the main town. Can't remember what it's called. Thought I'd get some bottled water and crisps and that. D'you want anything?'

'I could come too,' she said, swinging her legs off the bed. 'It might be nice to have a look around. See what else is here.'

'You look tired though. Why don't you get some rest.'

He definitely didn't want her coming with him. And that was raising all kinds of red flags. What was the best thing to do? If she went in too firmly now there might never be a way back in. But letting him have money and him heading off miles down the mountain to another town, that was a recipe for disaster, wasn't it?

'I'd better not sleep really,' she said, standing up. 'I'll not be able to get off tonight. Do you think the driver has room for me as well?'

'I... don't want you to come with me,' Ben said bluntly.

Now that was honesty at least. And how did she follow that up? Perhaps it was best to keep things simple.

'Why not?'

Eek. It had come out hard and confrontational despite her intention to be measured.

'Because I don't need a fucking babysitter.'

His reply was much harder than hers and the sentence reverberated around the almost-loft space like gunfire. Eve stood still, locking any sense of emotion in and trying to make Ben hold eye contact, wanting him to realise how rough his response had been. Perhaps she should let him go. Show him a little trust. She had two conflicting voices making suggestions including one that sounded very much like Glenda...

'OK,' she said quickly. 'You're right. Sorry.' She picked her handbag off the floor next to her cabin case which she hadn't even unzipped yet and took out her purse. 'Will ten euro be enough?'

Ben shrugged. 'Dunno how much crisps are around here.'

'Well,' she began. 'Get some really really luxury ones. Not cheese and onion.' She palmed him a twenty-euro note.

'That's not fair,' he protested. Cheese and onion had long been his favourite flavour but weirdly Eve was sure it made his snoring worse.

'Get me some ready salted if you must get C and O.'

'Right.'

He was stalling for some reason. He had pocketed the money but wasn't leaving. Eve waited.

'Listen, I know I was a bit of a shit before we left England...'

He stopped and left the sentence hanging. Eve let the silence trail.

'Anyway,' he said, then cleared his throat. 'I'll try not to be such a shit.' He paused, dropped his eyes and gave a smile. 'Can't promise not to snore though.'

'Well,' she said. 'If it gets too rough, I can bed down with the donkeys.'

'They make noise, you know.'

'Yes, but they won't moan about the Arsenal back four in their sleep.'

'You're out of touch. I moan far more about the forwards these days.'

'Right, well, noted.'

Now it felt a bit awkward. She smiled and hoped that would be enough.

'Right, I'm going. Crisps, water and maybe a bottle of wine? What's that type Gabby used to like?'

'Rosé,' Eve answered.

'Cool.' He headed for the door of their room. 'All right, see you later.'

'Bye,' Eve said.

She heard him thundering down the stairs then the mosquito-net swing door opened and clapped shut with a loud bang. On first appearances, Ben was unchanged from the little brother he'd been when he was twelve years old but Eve knew whatever was going on under the surface was far more complex than Arsenal's game strategy.

9

PETRA BEACH BAR, ALMYROS, CORFU

Half of Gianni was Greek. But which half of him was it? The top half? Or did you instead draw a line down the centre of your torso and sever your nationality that way? He hated this. He was *Italian*. He had always been Italian and had taken great pride in that. The whole foundation of Riccardocino was built on their Italian ancestry, lovers of coffee since time began. So now what?

Gianni took another slug of the dark alcoholic liquid and looked at his surroundings. He was at a beach bar, on a Greek island, having fled his father's wake and got a seat on the first flight. *Corfu*. Finally, the word had tumbled out of his mother's mouth as the tears fell from her eyes. Not a lot of what she'd said had made complete sense, but Gianni had clung to the snippets, made mental notes. This island was where Valentina had met 'Pan'. She had spent four weeks here before hopping to other Greek islands then a final two weeks on Corfu. On returning to Italy, she had found out she was pregnant. Apparently, Pan was the only one she had decided to take things further with.

Riccardo had been the unexpected shoulder to cry on when she had fainted on a train and he had literally picked her up off the floor. Gianni had heard that story before, minus the pregnancy aspect. It had been heartening to know that not everything he knew about his parents' relationship had been false.

Valentina and Pan had met somewhere near a place called Spartilas. His mother and the girlfriends she had been travelling with had stumbled upon the mountain café where Pan was working as a waiter. To Gianni, Spartilas hadn't sounded like a real village and he'd wondered whether his mother had remembered it correctly. But there it was on the map. It wasn't far from here – perhaps thirty minutes in a car, give or take the winding terrain it promised on paper. But he knew the likelihood of this man working at the same taverna some twenty-six years later was low.

Gianni pushed his designer sunglasses up his nose and looked again at the view outside the beachside eatery. It wasn't like Verona here. It was perhaps more like rural Italy, the places he would see as he travelled to Venice or Milan for meetings. This island was mountainous, yet green even in the heat of the summer. There was a laid-back vibe, from both the holidaymakers on the sand and shingle beach to the waiting staff, who were bringing out platters of grilled meats, vibrant salads and thick chunks of bread with accompanying dips. His stomach gave a groan then. Nothing had touched his lips since his cousin, Bella, had tried to make him eat some tortellini at the wake.

He didn't even have somewhere to stay yet. He had got a hire car at the airport and driven towards the nearest big town at this end of the island – Acharavi. Suddenly exhaustion rolled over him like one of the white-capped waves hitting the shoreline. He was tired for so many reasons: keeping the business going while his father was sick, trying to come up with a revolutionary idea to ensure Riccardocino had longevity in a time where drink connoisseurs were craving things new and inventive. And battling his mother over both of those things. But Gianni knew, like any good businessman should, that evolution was necessary, always. Those businesses that did not adapt to changing markets and trends were the ones that did not survive. And now there was this, him not being Riccardo Riccardo's son. He sighed. Whether Riccardo's blood flowed through his veins or not, Gianni was not about to give up on the one solid thing that he had helped shape just because his mother was too proud to admit the brand needed a refresh.

He put his hand in the air and beckoned a waitress.

'*Ne?*' the waitress asked, a tray in her hands.

He had no idea what that meant. Was it Greek?

'I would like another one of these,' he said in English, holding his near-empty glass aloft.

'I'm afraid you have the last of that bottle.'

'OK,' Gianni answered. 'Then perhaps you will open the next one?'

The waitress laughed then, her dark curly hair bouncing with the sound. 'Where are you from?'

'If I tell you, do I get to have more Averna?'

'No,' she answered. 'We really do not have any more of that. Sorry. Can I get you something else? Ouzo? *Tsipouro?* Limoncello?'

Limoncello. That reminded him of home. His mother had made some once with the lemons from their estate. Of course, such was her lack of skill in the kitchen it had been a complete disaster, but Gianni had never forgotten the sweet scent that had filled the kitchen and which had lasted for days afterwards as the sticky fluid clung to the worktop.

'I have never tasted ouzo,' Gianni said.

The waitress' eyes widened then. 'You've never tasted ouzo? I thought you were Greek.'

Gianni swallowed. He *was* Greek apparently. Half of him at least. But that thought wasn't sitting comfortably.

'What does it taste like?'

'It will get you pissed. Isn't that all you need to know if you are on holiday?'

Perhaps it was all he needed to know for now. He could leave the car here, the hotel he'd spied around the corner was only a short walk.

'I will have ouzo,' he agreed.

'OK, I will bring it over. Here we serve it just with ice, but would you like some water too?'

He shook his head. 'I am from Italy.'

And he had said it as if the statement somehow proved his worth in the world. He needed to work on that.

10

QUALITY GRILL, EPISKEPSI

'Sorry it's all been a bit mad,' Gabby said as she brought three Alfa beers over to the table and reached into her pocket for a bottle opener. She snapped the tops off like a pro.

Eve, Ben and Gabby were sitting in the outside area of a small grill room in what seemed to be the centre of this village. Episkepsi was only a short distance down a rather steep hill from Safe Animals. There were vines above them and, despite the humidity, there was a breeze making the leaves flutter a little, the occasional large grasshopper leaping from frond to floor with a light smack. Inside the eatery were a few tables, all occupied, the grilling station already sizzling with meats, and a large red fridge from which Gabby had helped herself to beers. Here you paid for everything at the end. *If Nikos lets me pay at all,* Gabby had said.

'Do you work here as well?' Ben asked, picking up the bottle and taking a slurp.

Gabby laughed and shook her head. 'This is probably one of the only places I don't work. But I love it here. And Nikos is a master at what he does. You are going to adore the food.' She looked at Ben. 'You think the kebab van back home is good? This knocks spots off anything you've ever tasted before. And his fried courgettes are to die for too. We'll have those to start with and tzatziki, and I would say Nikos's homemade wine, but I've got to drive later.'

This Greek life wasn't as slow-paced as Gabby had made out on their phone calls. Eve hadn't seen her friend sit still for one second.

'You going out?' Ben asked. 'Down to Acharavi?'

Ben had come back from his trip with monster-sized packets of ready salted crinkle-cut crisps plus some cheese and onion Lays. He had even offered to give her back the change. She hadn't accepted. There was very little he could bet on here for whatever coins he had left. But, more importantly, he had bought what he'd said he was going to – including a bottle of wine that was getting slightly colder in a fridge that was hot to the touch and made more noise than the archaic fan.

'Almyros, it's quite close to Acharavi,' Gabby answered. 'I work at a bar there in the afternoons and then some evenings I work at a hotel there. Sometimes I'm in the restaurant, other times I'm on the bar. Occasionally, I turn full-on chambermaid for late check outs.'

Gabby's working life was putting Eve's to shame. She was usually so exhausted from a day at college that pulling on her jeans for a shift at the pub afterwards almost felt as if it could be a Three Peaks Challenge.

She took a swig of the beer. It was very refreshing.

'Ever thought about having just the one job like most people?' Ben asked.

'*I* have two jobs,' Eve reminded him.

'Yeah, but you don't really need the job at the pub, do you?'

Her brother's comment jabbed at her and she took a firmer hold on her bottle. *You don't really need the job at the pub.* Maybe she didn't for monetary reasons but it was important to her. So she *did* need it. Did Ben think her working there was unnecessary? Stupid?

'What can I say,' Gabby said. 'Variety is the spice of life, right?' She whipped her curls back from her head, causing a grasshopper to leap from it and land on the edge of a plant pot. 'And I worry that one day the trustees are going to think that the sanctuary is just a money pit. Even people who want to do good aren't keen on forever if it just bleeds their bank account. I've done three extra fundraisers this year but we've had so many more vets' bills. I have to keep my other work in case I have to find somewhere else to live.'

'I hear you,' Ben said. 'I'd be happy for any work right now.'

'Hanging from scaffold lost its appeal?' Gabby asked.

'Something like that.'

Eve sat still and watched the interaction between her brother and her best friend. Was Ben going to open up to Gabby? She was caught between feeling pleased that he might want to talk to somebody and feeling aggrieved that it wasn't *her* he wanted to confide in. But that was stupid! What was the point of playing favourites? It was the end result that mattered.

'Well, what do you want to do next? Any plans?' Gabby asked.

Ben shook his head. 'Didn't plan to come to Corfu either but that's working out OK. It's sunny. It's got crisps and beer.'

Gabby laughed. 'That's what sold it to me too.'

'Really?' Ben answered. 'I thought it was the rich guys with the wives who didn't want to look after their kids.'

'That's what *got* me here,' Gabby replied. 'But the crisps and beer made me stay. And the horses. And Vincent Van Hoff.'

'You what?' Ben asked with a laugh.

'That's what we call the three-legged sheep. Because he's had his hoof off.'

'That's cracking,' Ben said, shaking his head.

Gabby whipped her hair back again, laughing and Eve suddenly felt prickles break out on her skin. What was that horrible, ugly crawling sensation settling on her like a tribe of mosquitos with evil intentions? If she didn't know herself better, she might have mistaken the feeling for... jealousy. Just that thought entering her head was enough to make her jerk in her seat and she jiggled the table leg with her knee, making the bottles of beer sway for a second. Then all eyes were on her.

'Sorry,' she said, quickly reaching for her bottle, then Ben's.

Gabby had reached out too, and their fingertips collided horribly, almost sending Ben's bottle right over. Eve laughed – overdramatically – and Ben grabbed his drink, shaking his head at both of them. The atmosphere was suddenly tighter than a *Love Island* bikini.

'I'm holding on to this. Neither of you can be trusted not to hit it with your elbow or flick it with your hair,' Ben said, taking a swig.

Gabby's hair was bouncier than ever. Bouncier and alive as if living in Greece had dipped her in an intense infusion of vitality. And Eve felt sour. And dry. Like out-of-date cereal that had lost its crispiness but was not yet bad enough to commit to the bin. She got to her feet. She needed some air. Whatever these feelings were had to be to do with the travelling and the humidity and her concerns about Ben. She adored Gabby and she had missed her so, so much. She had forgotten how great she was, how funny, how adorable, how together...

'I'm... just going to get some air,' Eve said, moving around the table.

'There's much more air here with the fan than there will be outside,' Gabby told her.

'I won't be long,' she said quickly, forcing a smile and waving a hand. She began to walk along the road, instantly getting hit with the heady scent of citrus and clematis.

She breathed deep and slow. Being here was a good thing. It was the break from routine she needed. It was spending time with her best friend. It was *Greece*. Yes, she may have shouldered the responsibility of Ben but, given his current no-work circumstances, if she had left him in England she would have been worrying about him anyway. Better to worry about him when he was in plain sight and she had some control...

'Eeeee!'

The word – if it was a word – was long and drawn out, a thick gravelly voice from the shadows. Eve stopped in her tracks and looked into the dark. There were figures under an awning outside a glass-fronted eatery that didn't look like it was open. Three people sat around a table in the dark.

'Eeeee!'

'Hello?' she offered. What was the Greek for 'hello'? Gabby had told her earlier. She had made her repeat it to the animals when she had taken the tour around the sanctuary. She was certain it had 'ass' in it. Then it came to her:

'*Yassas*,' she said tentatively.

'You are English,' a voice replied. 'That is the "e" you speak of, Aleka.'

'*Ochi! Ochi!* Eeeeee!'

Suddenly the table and its occupants were bathed in light as one of the outside lamps above the awning sprang into life. There were three people, two women and a man, all seeming as old, if not older, than Stanley and Ted back home.

'*Ela!* Come! Come sit with us.'

One woman got to her feet and beckoned her over.

Eve swallowed and looked back down towards Quality Grill

where she could just about see Gabby's hair and the outline of her brother.

'*Ela! Ela!*' the man said, standing up and pulling over an extra chair. 'Very good. Very good.'

'Come, please, my name is Vasiliki. This is Spiros. And this is Aleka. She cannot see you. She is blind. And she does not speak English. Neither does Spiros.'

Spiros laughed. 'Very good. Very good for you. Very good for me.'

Eve stepped towards the terrace and gave a nervous smile. 'I'm afraid I don't speak any Greek. I was just... having a look around the village.'

The woman called Aleka said something in a low tone, her opaque eyes seeming fixed on Eve. She was dressed all in black, in complete contrast to her white hair which was tied in long plaits. Eve had never been good with guessing people's ages, but Aleka had to be in her eighties at the very least.

'Aleka says that you mourn. You are the "e" she has been guided to tonight. But, Aleka's gift, it is erratic.' Vasiliki shrugged.

Spiros was pointing at the chair and there was nothing else Eve could do but sit down on it. The very next thing he did was pour her some clear liquid into a small glass and then add water from a tall bottle on the table. The scent of aniseed was thick in the air.

'Well, my name does begin with an "e",' Eve told the group. 'I'm Eve.'

There was a collective gasp. Vasiliki had gasped the loudest, putting the flats of both hands to her cheeks. Spiros drank the whole contents of his small glass. Only Aleka remained still, until her lips quivered slightly at the corners. And then her fingers moved to the wooden tray on the table nestled between the glasses, a tobacco pouch and an ashtray. In the tray were pieces of red wool, some longer than others, a mishmash of thread that Aleka was now combing through.

'Drink,' Spiros said, pushing forward the small glass he had filled for her. 'E.'

'You are here with Yabby,' Vasiliki stated, picking up the glass and pressing it into Eve's palm.

'I think you mean Gabby.'

'Like I say, Yabby.'

Eve took a sip of the drink and, as well as making her tongue catch fire, the scent nearly took the hairs from her nostrils. 'She's... my best friend.' She coughed. 'We used to live near each other in England.'

'Did Yabby try to fix everything in England?' Vasiliki asked. 'Is she someone to trust?'

'I... don't know what you mean. But I trust her very much.'

'She is good with the animals? When no one looks?'

'Yes?'

She had only seen Gabby in action once here, with a cat that had an unexpected infection – it seemed there was nothing that a tube full of Germolene couldn't mend until the vet got there.

Spiros nudged Eve's arm and directed her to look at the surprisingly nimble fingers of Aleka. The elderly lady was now positioning the wool strands on the tray to make shapes. Or were they words? From the bits of the Greek alphabet Eve had encountered already, some of the wool shapes could be those letters.

'Aleka is telling your riches,' Vasiliki informed her with a nod of satisfaction.

'I think you mean telling my fortune,' Eve said, the alcohol now bringing a warming sensation up through her torso.

'That is what I said,' Vasiliki answered. 'Look closely.'

Eve leaned forward, brushing shoulders with Spiros who had

done exactly the same thing, and tried to make out what this fortune was going to be.

Spiros said something in Greek and then knocked his elbow with Eve's again. 'Bicycle.'

Was it? Eve screwed up her eyes and looked closer.

A few more deft touches and then Aleka sat back in her chair, hands down in her lap, resting on the sagging fabric of her dress.

'It is not a bicycle,' Vasiliki said with certainty. Then she turned to the woman who had made the ensemble and spoke in her native tongue.

Aleka replied with one word. '*Kafes*.'

Eve looked blank.

'Aleka says "coffee",' Vasiliki interpreted. 'Does this mean anything to you?'

Coffee. Eve liked coffee but not so much it was running through her veins in unhealthy amounts. She shook her head. 'No.'

Vasiliki shrugged. 'It will come. That is certain.'

Spiros said something in Greek and then burst into laughter, slapping Eve's shoulder.

'What did he say?' Eve asked.

'Spiros said,' Vasiliki began. 'That it took four or five wool images until we understood the meaning of the aubergine for Kostas.'

'O-K.' Now Eve wasn't sure where this conversation was going.

'Crushed to death under a pile of them on the road to Sidari,' Vasiliki filled in.

'*Kafes*,' Aleka repeated, her head turning towards Eve again as if she could see her.

Eve smiled and picked up the little glass, downing the liquid in one.

Possibly death by Kenco. Great!

11

SAFE ANIMALS SANCTUARY, EPISKEPSI

It turned out that the heat stayed all night long here, only dropping a few degrees at approximately 5 a.m. Eve had opened the balcony door at half past four, unable to sleep again after the brief few hours she'd managed.

They'd had a belly bursting meal at Quality Grill: pitta bread and *tzatziki*, courgette fritters, *saganaki* (fried cheese), followed by lamb and chicken from the grill, chips and a huge salad filled with the ripest tomatoes, cucumber, deep purple olives and more cheese – feta this time. Gabby had left them at midnight to drive down to Almyros on her moped and the conversation had all but dried up despite Ben being fuelled by four or five large bottles of lager.

Eve rocked in the chair as a loud squawk broke the peace that not even the cicadas had chirped into yet. It was Savage. Well, it was a hoopoe bird, presumably the one that lived here. It had landed on the metal railings that bordered the balcony and was now strutting up and down, giving Eve the side-eye as if it was trying to tell her who was really in charge.

'Hello, Savage,' she ventured. 'Or should I say, *kalimera*.'

The bird stopped walking and carefully turned towards her on the rail. It ducked its head, Mohican-style plumage wavering in the slight breeze. Was he bowing to her? How cute!

'Aww, you're so sweet,' Eve said, slowly getting to her feet. Would he let her pet him? She reached out with a finger.

'Stop! Don't do it!'

It was Gabby's voice and Eve leapt back, her hand going to her heart as the shock of hearing another sound so loud and so close threw her for a second. Once she had regained some equilibrium, she saw Gabby was down below her, sitting astride her moped and looking up. Remarkably, Savage was still there on the rail, unperturbed by the shouting; in fact, he was starting to raise his wings up a little.

'Come down!' Gabby called. 'Before you lose a finger. Or worse.'

'What?' Eve exclaimed. 'What d'you mean?'

'Well, he isn't called Savage for no reason.'

The bird emitted a sound that Eve had never heard any creature make before and she backed away, almost falling into the little coffee table.

* * *

'Put this on,' Gabby said, passing over a helmet.

'Is the bird that bad I need head protection?'

'Well...'

'Gabby!'

'I'm kidding! Well, a bit.' She grinned. 'Put the helmet on and get on the back of my moped.'

'What? It's 5 a.m. or something. Where are we going?'

'Back to Almyros. I have to help set up at the hotel for breakfast and I'm late already. *And* we're short-staffed, so I'll need your help.

Also, I think I have visitors coming to the sanctuary later so every-thing needs to be perfect.'

There was a lot in that sentence but despite the described hectic nature of it, Gabby had delivered it with a smile. When was the last time Eve had spoken about her work with a smile? But then her friend's happy expression dropped faster than it had appeared.

'Come on,' Gabby urged. 'I'll let you drive on the way back up.'

'Gabby, I've not sat on a moped before. I can't drive one!'

'I thought that the first time I tried, but you get used to it. And it's *ride* not drive.'

The helmet fastened over her head, Eve put her leg over the body of the machine and held on tight to Gabby.

12

ALMYROS BEACH, ALMYROS

Gianni couldn't remember the last time he had felt this tired. The night before was a blur of ouzo, a rather unhelpful receptionist and then, finally, a room with a view. Then the calls had begun. Each time he got a call from his mother he let it go to voicemail and downed another bottle from the mini bar. He had listened to a few of the voice messages this morning as he wondered whether he needed another tiny bottle of alcohol to cure his lethargy or if he should try the thin, never-enough Nescafe coffee packets. So far he hadn't committed to either.

He looked out over his view. The sea in the early morning light was beautiful, but this particular stretch wasn't a vast millpond welcoming bathers to make their own splash. No, this sea had crushing waves, its white caps slamming onto the sand and shingle and making it sizzle. It was a sea in charge, one not to be messed with, yet still there were a couple of people in swimsuits poised at the edge, perhaps wondering which one of them would be brave enough to try to get in first.

Gianni breathed deep and admired the water. It reminded him of Riccardo. He could be the crashing, thrashing force the sea was right now. But he could also be calm and nurturing, caring for those who lived tucked beneath his waves. Gianni cursed under his breath and ripped off his sunglasses, dropping them to the table. What was he doing here? He had given this plan little considera-tion. He was looking for someone his mother had spent a few weeks with one summer. She only knew his first name. And since his mother had told him that, Gianni had discovered that 'Pan' or rather 'Panos' or even the much longer 'Panagiotis' was not uncommon in Greece. One of the employees on the reception desk even had that name.

He turned his attention away from the scenery and looked back at the sachets of coffee in his room. He wasn't going to waste the water. He was going to find some proper coffee in the hotel's restaurant.

* * *

The hotel was quiet. It was as if one of the rules was for all guests to remain in their rooms until the sun was up. Well, it was up now, and Gianni had places to go. Not that he knew where he was going to start. He had taken a peek at a vision board he had put together before his father's death and revisited the ideas he'd been having about their brand. Staying busy and grounded with the business was going to help him, he'd decided, while everything else in his life was spinning chaotically like fruits in a smoothie maker. Now maybe there was a diversionary idea...

Gianni pushed at the glass doors of the restaurant and entered. Tables were being laid and food was being put out under heat lamps. A collection of cats had their noses pressed to the windows, gazing at the buffet. He felt like one of those cats, sorely in need of food. But coffee was calling him first. You didn't get to be behind one of Italy's leading coffee companies without being a little bit addicted to the produce... Now where was the machine?

He saw a waitress putting butter packs into a white porcelain urn. 'Where are the coffee machines?'

The woman turned around to face him. 'Excuse me.'

'Where are the coffee machines?' he repeated.

'I heard what you said,' the woman answered. 'But you didn't say "excuse me". I know it's early but that was a bit rude.'

What? He was astounded. For a second he didn't know how to reply. Where was her name badge? Wait, she wasn't even wearing a uniform. In fact, what she had on wasn't appropriate attire for working at all. Short shorts showed off lean legs and her vest hugged an hour-glass figure which he took a beat to appreciate. And those eyes – the colour of almonds – they were unwavering in their evaluation of him.

'I am a customer,' Gianni informed her, his lack-of-coffee angriness biting at him.

She stuck out her hand. 'And I am a human. It's nice to meet you.'

He was caught between being appalled at this comeback and feeling a little in awe of her boldness. Because all the while she was *smiling* at him. How could you be mad at someone who was smiling at you? He wanted to bark a tight reply but his lips betrayed him and before he was able to stamp any control over what happened next, he was laughing. Hard.

'Oh my God,' Gianni said, his stomach aching as he was finally able to draw in some air and say something. 'I apologise. If I was rude.'

'You really were,' the woman replied, her tone brusque.

'And you are still not letting this go.'

He observed her some more. Auburn hair. No heavy make-up.

'Sorry,' the woman said, letting out a sigh and putting her tray of butter packets down on the side. 'I don't really work here and Gabby told me guests wouldn't be in until seven.'

'You don't work here?' he asked. 'So, you just, come in to fill the butter for fun?'

She smiled again, shaking her head. 'I'm helping a friend who has more jobs than any sane person should have.'

'Does this friend really work here?'

'So she says,' the woman whispered. 'But, you know, maybe she wears the uniform just for fun.'

This was... *something*. Something else. Something that wasn't his father being sick or his father dying or finding out he was not 100 per cent Italian.

He was just looking at the woman now and saying nothing, for some reason he had leaned in a little, his body language obviously on autopilot. He straightened up, felt the need to fold his arms across his chest.

'Why don't you choose a table and I will see if I can find you some coffee?' she suggested.

'Thank you,' he answered. 'Human.'

She smiled at his comment and headed towards the back of the restaurant. There was no doubt in his mind now that this was shaping up to be a triple espresso before nine kind of day.

13

Eve was all for helping Gabby, like she had done when she'd fed the donkeys before she'd even opened her cabin case yesterday, but here at this hotel it felt as if she'd been hurled into the deep end. And Gabby had literally disappeared, leaving Eve taking instructions from someone called Magda who was quite terrifying. Corfu was supposed to be a holiday. OK, it had also turned into a chance to get Ben on his own and find out what was going on with him, but essentially, when she and Gabby had talked about it on their FaceTimes and phone calls it had been sold as a girls' holiday. Time together. Sun, sea, rest and relaxation. Eve hadn't envisaged filling containers with tiny butter servings or dealing with grumpy tourists who definitely needed coffee more than they possibly knew. Although that particular hotel guest, despite the initial attitude, had been quite pleasing to the eye. Tall, lean, olive skin, dark hair not overdone with products and his laugh... That had been surprising. No one had ever laughed at her attempt at humour as much as this guy had.

And now she had his coffee, she was trying to find him in the restaurant area which was starting to fill. Looking out of the window, she saw him. He'd taken a table outside, under a large awning that was shading the majority of the terrace from the now fully risen sun. It had a view of a rather magnificent lagoon-style pool that was only a few steps away as well as the tumultuous sea beyond. She headed towards the bi-fold doors, carrying the jug of coffee.

'Your coffee, sir,' she greeted, arriving at his table.

He held an upright finger out into the air, thankfully not his middle one. She wondered what that meant. One cup? One moment? Stop? And then she saw he had his mobile phone pressed against his ear. He started speaking; it wasn't English and she didn't think it was Greek either. It definitely wasn't German. Well, she didn't need to know, she just had to pour his coffee and leave. She turned over the cup and started to tip in the coffee.

'Wait!'

OK, that was English. But was he talking to her or to whoever he was having the phone conversation with? Some of the coffee sloshed out of the cup and over onto the saucer. *Damn it.*

'*Paolo, ti richiamerò. Sì, ciao.*' He ended the call, put down his phone and shook his head at her.

'Your coffee, sir,' she said for the second time, smiling.

'Now I can really tell you do not work here,' he said, plucking up a paper napkin and mopping the spill in his saucer. 'And I am not drinking that.' He flapped the now slightly damp serviette towards the coffee pot on the table.

'But this is coffee, exactly like you asked for.' Eve looked at the jug and wondered what mistake she had made now. Even with Magda's heavy accent there had been no mistaking her telling Eve it was coffee.

'If you remember, while you were insulting me back there in

the restaurant, I was looking for the coffee *machine*. That is not coffee from any kind of machine I want to drink the product of.' He pointed at the pot again as if it might contain something akin to sewer rat excrement.

'Well,' Eve began. 'I don't know what other coffee they have here and... please don't make me go back in there. It's scary.'

He laughed good-naturedly at her, then motioned to the chair opposite his. 'Sit down.'

'I'm working,' she reminded.

'Not officially,' he countered. 'And although we are both humans, *I* am the customer and customers are always right. On that we can both agree, yes?'

'Well, I—'

'Please, sit down. Let us conduct an experiment,' he suggested, taking ownership of the coffee jug.

Eve pulled out the chair and sat down. She still didn't know where Gabby was and she could murder a coffee herself.

The man took off his sunglasses and laid them on the table next to his phone. Next, he turned over the cup that was opposite Eve and poured some of the coffee into it.

'Already,' he began. 'I know this is going to be bad coffee.'

'How?' Eve looked at the dark pool of liquid in her cup and got nothing but I-want-to-drink-this vibes.

'There is no smell,' the man told her, pouring some more into his cup. He lifted it to his aquiline nose and inhaled. 'Nothing. Pa!'

Eve lifted her cup to her nose too and took a breath in. There was something, a slight aroma, but it reminded her of something other than coffee.

'All I get,' the man continued, still smelling, 'is dirt. Like the coffee has been made somewhere else, far far away and this poor relation to it is the bit that should have been thrown into the garbage.'

Eve opened her mouth to make comment but stopped herself. She *was* getting dirt notes from this drink.

'Take a sip,' the man urged, lifting his own cup.

'I don't know if I want to now,' she answered. 'Perhaps I will go back and ask about the machines.'

'Come on,' he said. 'Take a sip. Just one.'

Eve put the rim of the cup to her lips and let the coffee pour into her mouth. It was barely hot, despite the thermal jug she had brought it in, and the taste, if you could call it that, was watery, powdery, weak.

'Ugh, God! This is worse than I thought,' the man declared. 'This is like coffee pretending to be tea.'

'It's not like tea,' Eve declared with certainty.

'It is.'

'It really isn't. I'm British. I know all about tea and this is nothing like even the very weakest cup.'

'But you agree it is bad,' the man asked, raising one of his eyebrows.

'I agree it's bad. But... I don't know what to do about it,' she admitted. 'Milk? Sugar?'

Eve watched him intently. He seemed to be pondering what action to take. The coffee might not be the best but did holiday-makers usually look into it in this much detail? Eventually he sat back, leaning against his seat, elongating that long frame.

'I do not think it can be fixed,' he stated.

'Oh,' she replied. 'Well, what can I do?'

'Want to find somewhere that does the good stuff?' he asked. It sounded as if he was describing the best place to get high-grade marihuana.

'I—'

'Don't work here,' he reminded.

'No, but I also don't go out for coffee with humans I don't even know the name of.'

'Gianni,' he said, offering out his hand.

It was a nice hand. Not that Eve went around sorting good-looking hands from not-so-good-looking hands, like some kind of body parts quality control. She took his hand in hers and shook. 'I'm Eve.'

His touch was warm and firm and apparently she wanted to hold on longer than was appropriate. And as her eyes found his again, something weird was happening within. She had only felt this feeling once before, the night she had met Mitchell.

And then memories of the previous night came running into her mind. The word Aleka had spoken: *Kafes*. Coffee. She snatched her hand away and got to her feet, feeling suddenly overwhelmed.

'I... should... find my friend,' she spluttered.

Why was she spluttering? Mitchell was in the past, that chapter wrapped in shrink-wrap and buried, and coffee, well, coffee was found in homes and hotels around the world. Aleka's words were not a premonition of any kind.

'Are you OK?' Gianni asked, sounding concerned.

'Find. *Fine*, I mean.' She nodded, gritting her teeth together and trying to implement the methods of control she taught to her students. Except she was *so* tired and how long was this shift at the hotel, that wasn't even hers, going to take? Ben was alone at Safe Animals which meant he'd either be sleeping in or getting up and needing to find a distraction. And despite him showing vague interest in the herd of goats that had blocked the road on the way yesterday, Eve was sure a vibrant holiday town would be more appealing than mucking out. Maybe she should find out if Acharavi had any betting shops...

'Eve,' Gianni said softly. 'Sit down. You look a little pale.'

She looked pale? Granted, she had only just got to this

sunshine island, but surely her skin had picked up a little colour. She did feel hot though. She took a step backwards away from the table.

'Stop!' Gianni called. 'The pool!'

Eve was falling before he'd even ended the sentence.

14

It was the deep end. Gianni knew that from the markers along the side. Two metres. And he didn't know if Eve could swim. Plus, it was early; no one was in the pool or lying around on the loungers. And this visual reconnaissance was taking too long. He just had to act. Without thinking more, he jumped into the pool.

A millisecond after he hit the water, he saw her resurface. Splashing, if not actually swimming. Her head was now out in the air and she was gasping. He trod water, moved closer to her. She looked a little angry.

'You are OK?' he asked.

'What are you doing?' she exclaimed.

Definitely angry.

'Making sure you do not drown,' he replied, kicking for the side now.

'I'm twenty-five years old. I can swim!'

What was he doing? He put a hand on the tiled surround of the pool and prepared to haul himself out.

'Argh! Argh!'

He shook his head, water droplets spraying. 'You can swim so I am getting out.' He put his other hand to the tile and pushed himself up and out.

'Help! I... have... cramp!'

Gianni stood up and turned around just in time to see a pained expression on Eve's face and then she disappeared under the water.

'*Merda*,' he cursed. He jumped back into the pool and swam over to the swirl of water she had sunk into, where he dived down and grabbed her, bringing her to the surface.

She gasped, starting to cough as he supported her, using his legs to power them further down the pool where hopefully it was shallow enough to be able to stand.

'You are OK?' he asked.

'I... had cramp in my leg,' Eve said, her face still pale. 'I couldn't move.'

'It is OK,' Gianni told her. 'You are OK.' His feet met the floor of the pool and he stood up, a little relieved to be out of the deep water.

'Sorry,' she breathed.

She looked exhausted and before he realised it, he had tightened his hold, supporting her more. He cleared his throat. 'How is your leg now? Can you stand?'

'I can try.'

Gianni gently let go of her body and she attempted to right herself. 'OK?'

'I think so... Ow! No, no, not good.' She gritted her teeth and grabbed hold of his hand.

'It is OK,' he told her again. 'There is no rush to get out.' And, if he was honest, her holding his hand was warming his insides in a far more pleasurable way than any coffee.

'Sorry,' Eve said, still looking as though she was in pain.

'Do you apologise all the time?' he asked as she looked up

at him.

'I did tell you I'm British.'

'You also told me you could swim.'

'I *can* swim! I can't help getting cramp.'

He smiled at her. 'I think perhaps you just wanted me to stay in the water. And this shirt, it is Louis Vuitton.'

'Sorry, Louis. Perhaps you should have just thrown me one of those orange life rings.'

'And miss out on this morning exercise?'

She laughed then and the sound made him smile. It was warm, light, sexy...

* * *

'Eve! What are you doing?'

It was Gabby's voice and Eve turned her attention away from her hot, dark-haired, coffee-loving saviour who looked even more attractive now his hair was wet and had a little curl to it.

'I—' Eve began.

'Magda's wondering why you didn't come back for the plates.'

What? Eve was doing her friend a favour here. She wasn't being paid for this early morning stint at the restaurant. And she had fallen in the swimming pool. She was drenched from head to toe and her leg went into spasm every time she tried to move it.

'Excuse me,' Gianni called to Gabby. 'We will need some towels. And some hot drinks that do not taste like dirt. Could you bring these to that table over there?' He pointed to where the coffee jug and his sunglasses lay abandoned.

Gabby seemed to take a moment and then she replied, 'You were at Petra yesterday. I served you ouzo.'

'And now I stay here,' Gianni replied. 'And I would very much like you to serve me towels and hot drinks.'

Gabby still hadn't asked Eve if she was OK. She knew her friend was busy but...

'I'll be back in a minute,' Gabby snapped, turning on her heel and heading off again.

It was only then that Eve realised she and Gianni were still holding hands. Did he know? Was he merely holding on to support her in the water? Yes, of course that's what it was. What else could it be? But it was apparent that if she moved her fingers at all he would feel it and then he would realise, if he hadn't already, and then the connection would be broken. And his hand felt so good locked with hers. It had been an eternity since she had held hands with anyone but a random person at a yoga class she'd been forced to go to.

'Let us get you out of the water,' Gianni said. He squeezed her hand then and, taking her other hand too, he coaxed her forward.

Eve moved her feet and her weak leg seemed to comply.

'That was your friend? The one who was shouting at you?'

'Yes, that's Gabby,' she said. 'She seems a bit on edge today.'

'Stress,' Gianni stated. 'It can do that to a person.'

'Yes,' she agreed. 'It can. But, before I got here, Gabby was always telling me how relaxed she is here in Corfu.'

The two things weren't correlating so far: the Gabby who had painted a picture of this Greek island being the ultimate place for relaxation and the Gabby who was barking orders from the crack of dawn and sprinting around a hotel before she went back to the animal shelter to muck out tortoises.

'You can live somewhere you love but still have pressures.'

'Is that why you're here on holiday?'

'I... am... taking some time away from home.' He nodded at the end of the sentence, something Eve found people did when they felt they needed more validation for what they'd said. The statement people made wasn't usually a full-on lie but often it meant there was a lot more to the story.

'Where is home for you?' she asked as they reached the steps of the pool. 'Another part of Greece?'

He shook his head. 'I am not Greek. I am Italian. I live in the north. Verona.'

'Is it nice? Without the pressures?'

'It is beautiful even with the pressures,' he answered with a smile. 'That is why Shakespeare wrote about it.'

'*The Two Gentleman of Verona*,' Eve said. 'I read it at school.'

'I was thinking more of *Romeo and Juliet*.'

There was no water between them now, no reason for her to need his support, her leg doing what legs should do. But they were still holding hands.

'Oh, *scusa*,' Gianni said, dropping her hand as if he had only just realised they were still connected. 'You are OK?'

'Yes. Thank you. For getting in the pool and ruining your shirt. Do you want me to... have it cleaned or something?'

The 'something' died on her lips because with his now free-to-move hands he pulled off the Louis Vuitton and proceeded to wring the water from it. Except Eve wasn't focused on the drips from the fabric, she was totally admiring his torso. Abs for days told her he looked after himself and that whatever pressures he had back in Italy did not extend to missing gym time... Finally, her eyes found another focus: Gabby arriving with pristine white towels. She watched her friend drop them onto one of the sun loungers and then skip off again, waving a hand.

'Hot coffees are on the table over there!' Gabby called, bouncing hair and the rest of her disappearing back into the main hotel building. What Gabby had said was merely direct, a statement, but the body language was definitely telling Eve she was annoyed.

'That dirt coffee!' Gianni cursed, a wry smile on his face.

'Sorry,' Eve apologised.

He only had to raise an eyebrow and she checked herself.

'Not sorry. Not my coffee.'

And now he was towelling himself off with the fluffy white towel, including under the waistband of his trousers. She needed to leave, get herself dry and find out when this horror hotel shift would be over.

'I'd better go,' she said. 'But I will see if they have better coffee for you.'

'No. It is OK. I have things I need to do. Calls to make.' He ran the towel over his hair and then rubbed it over his strong jawline. 'I will find good coffee. I have a nose for it.'

He had a gorgeous nose. Strong, unapologetic, masculine – the exact kind of nose Eve would pick out as pleasing in a nasal line-up...

'It was good to meet you, Eve,' he told her.

And that was her cue to leave.

'You too, fellow human,' she replied with one last smile.

15

SEE YOU COFFEE AND JUICES, ACHARAVI

'Hey, Paolo,' Gianni greeted, answering his phone.

He was dry now, in clean clothes, sitting outside a coffee shop on the high street in Acharavi, watching the world go by. Tourists coaches, quad bikes, vans bursting with fruit were all zipping past on their way to hotels, paths off-the-beaten-track and beaches. And this coffee he was drinking now – a double espresso – was far superior to what had been served up at his hotel. It was different to the Riccardo flavour but the richness definitely hit the spot. He took another sip.

'Hello, Gianni,' a female voice answered.

The cup nearly fell from his hands and he had to balance his phone on his shoulder to maintain equilibrium. It was his mother.

'Do not hang up. That would be very childish,' she continued.

'You're calling *me* childish?' he blasted. He altered his posture in the seat, edging forward, feeling tension through his torso. He lowered the volume of his voice but laced it with bitterness. 'You are the one who had a one-night stand with somebody on holiday and did not use protection.'

'And if I had, you would not be here! Plus, it was not one night and I do not have to explain my actions to you.'

'Oh, I think I'm the *only* one you need to explain your actions to. Because I have spent my whole life growing up with a man who was not my biological father!'

'Gianni, I did not call you to fight.'

'Then why did you? On Paolo's phone too.'

'Because you are not answering my calls or messages and I... have information.'

Now he was listening. What information?

'I remember a little of the place where Pan told me he was from. It either began with the letter "e" or ended in it and—'

'Mamma, you only remember one letter?' He closed his eyes. There were probably tens of villages and towns beginning with 'e' here. This was no help at all.

'I will know the name if I hear it, I am sure of it. And it cannot be far from Spartilas. He had a motorbike that was very old. It would not have been able to manage long distances.'

It might not be much, but it was something. He put his mother on speakerphone and then drew up the Corfu map on the screen.

'Are you still there?' she asked.

'Yes, I am looking at the map now.' Whirls of the mountain he was going to have to drive up later, lots of crosses depicting churches. But this couldn't be possible. There was only one village that began or ended with the letter 'e' near to Spartilas. Episkepsi. How did he pronounce that?

'Was it... Episkepsi?'

'Yes!' she exclaimed. 'Yes, that was it!'

'You are certain? It was over twenty-five years ago.'

'The "e" is pronounced "eh" I think.'

'Eh-piss-kep-see.' Gianni sounded it out. 'Is that right?'

'Oh!' his mother said, sounding taken aback.

'What is it?'

'You sound Greek.'

He sighed. He didn't want to sound Greek. He didn't want to *be* Greek. He just wanted to know who his father was. See him one time. Maybe even only because his father had asked him to.

'I am going now,' he said, ready to end the call. He took the phone back off speaker.

'Gianni, wait.'

'What is it?'

'I know you are still angry with me. I also know that you are very proud, like Riccardo, and it will take you some time to start to forgive but I want you to know that... I will help you, any way I can.'

'By remembering one letter of the name of the village where this man you slept with is from?'

'Do not cheapen it, Gianni,' she bit back.

Her tone had changed. Gianni took another sip of his coffee, cradling the phone between ear and shoulder again.

'As I said, Pan and I were not a one-night affair,' she stated. 'I told you, we had weeks together and I came back to Corfu after the other islands and—'

'It does not matter to me,' Gianni interrupted. 'One night. A holiday romance. It is all the same.'

'It's not all the same. I know you are angry but I do not want you to think that your being here was not... without love.'

He closed his eyes and inhaled. Love now. What next? They were soulmates who met at the wrong time in the wrong place?

'I thought you loved my father, Riccardo,' he said through tight lips.

'I did, Gianni. So very much. I still do but—'

'But what? He's gone so let's move on?' He sat forward in his seat. 'Where the business is concerned, I couldn't agree more.

And… I have been thinking… I do not want you to sign that new deal with Barista Irresistible.'

'What?'

'It is not right.'

'Gianni, we have worked those numbers ten times over. Riccardo even looked at them before he was confined to his room. Paolo is practically number-blind.'

'It is not the numbers,' Gianni said, his gaze going across the road to the supermarket, where shoppers were wheeling trolleys full of packs of water bottles to their cars. 'It is the concept.'

'What?'

'It is old-fashioned. That is not what our brand is about. We are missing a chance to show that our company can be about traditional quality but also innovation. I feel if we do not show them a different side to our business in conjunction with our long-standing taste excellence, they will get this from somewhere else. They should not need to.'

'Gianni,' his mother began. 'I am not sure this is the right time for you to be thinking about messing with a deal that is virtually signed and sealed.'

'*Messing* with a deal? I think you are forgetting who the new CEO of the company is.' Now he was angry. He knew the coffee business inside and out, had worked from the ground up. He still remembered his father making him work as a barista at events. He had been to where they sourced the beans, he had worked at one of the manufacturing plants, he had tasted more cups of the signature Riccardocino than anyone on the Earth.

'I think you are forgetting that I have a life interest in Riccardo's estate. Riccardo wanted me still to guide you. Protect you.'

'What?' Gianni said, the coffee he'd just drunk pooling at the back of his throat.

'Take this time to be away from the business, Gianni. Paolo and I, we will look after things here.'

'You cannot sign anything without my approval,' he reminded her.

'Not new contracts, no,' she replied. 'And this deal with Barista Irresistible, it is a good one.'

'Do not do that deal, Mamma,' he warned.

'I have to go. There is another call coming in.'

'Mamma! Do not end this call!'

It wasn't until he heard the dial tone that he realised he was out of his chair and standing, being observed by other coffee drinkers. He needed to regain control. And perhaps that started with a trip up the mountain.

16

SAFE ANIMALS SANCTUARY, EPISKEPSI

It was almost ten o'clock before Gabby was pulling the moped back in through the gates of the sanctuary. Despite what she'd said earlier, she hadn't suggested Eve take a turn on the front of the vehicle and had ridden driven all the more aggressively up the mountain than she had down it. Tight cornering, revving hard at any and every opportunity, ignoring Eve's pleas for her to slow down when her still-wet canvas shoes had started to slip off the exhaust pipe. Now Gabby brought the moped to a skidding stop, flicking up stones from the rough ground and wrenching off her helmet before she'd even cut the engine.

'Gabby! What's the matter?' Eve asked as her friend started to rush away across the forecourt, heading past their wiry-haired airport driver who was leading two horses across the ground.

'Nothing! I've got to check in with the vet and I'm late!' Gabby answered without even looking back.

'The vet is OK,' the man said. 'I made him mountain tea. He is in your office.'

'Thanks,' Gabby answered, finally seeming to breathe before she headed onwards to the outbuildings.

Eve sighed, still astride the moped, helmet in place. She didn't feel relaxed, she felt agitated. You weren't meant to feel agitated when you were on a beautiful Greek island. There was something up with Gabby, something she was hiding. You didn't live with someone after the worst time of your life and not know them inside out. They'd dyed hair together. They'd waxed each other's bikini lines. You didn't get closer than that.

'Are you staying on the motorbike?' the man called out.

Eve looked over to him. Even the horses seemed to be appraising her, looking all superior and judgemental. They were cute though. One was a mahogany colour with a white blaze down its face and the other grey.

'No,' she answered, getting down with a squelch. She fanned out her clothes, which were still damp, and began to unstrap her helmet.

'Did it rain in Almyros?' the man asked, his eyes going to the clear blue sky, an expression of disbelief covering the rest of his face.

'Oh, no,' she answered, putting the helmet down on the seat of the bike. 'I went for an impromptu dip in the pool.'

'A what?'

'A swim,' Eve said more simply. 'With my clothes on.'

The man laughed then, hysterically so, his whole body rolling back as the emotion took hold, his hands tightening on the horses' halters bridles, making their heads snatch back. 'You fell in!'

'Yes, well, it wasn't quite so hilarious at the time and I got cramp and that wasn't funny at all.' Her leg hadn't liked being tensed into position on the moped either, but she hadn't dared complain to Gabby when she seemed to be under a lot of stress already.

'You need tea,' the man said. '*Ela*. Come. We will put the horses into the field and then I will make you a drink.'

'Oh, that's very kind but I really need to put on some dry clothes and find my brother.' She was hoping Ben was still in bed. He had been the epitome of a teenager before she had left the family home, lolling in bed until midday, then getting up only to put one of their dad's old vinyls on his record player...

'Ben is in the field,' the man said, beginning to lead the horses off.

Her heart jumped. That wording! It wasn't the first time Eve had been told that exact thing. But surely here there wouldn't be a tent of drunken lads and a gas stove none of them had realised was still turned on.

'Do not look so surprised. He is good with the animals. He was up to help a little after you left with Gabby.' The man smiled, encouraging the horses forward again. 'Now he is exercising Phantom.'

Phantom. Savage. These animal names were very dark – potential names when they brought *Gladiators* back to TV.

'Phantom is a tortoise,' the man told her.

'What? How do you exercise a tortoise?'

'I joke with you!' the man said, all laughter again. 'Phantom is a horse. Now, you take Pnèvma here and we will find them. Come.'

And, just like that, a thick wadge of rope was pressed into her hands and she was suddenly in control of the brown horse.

* * *

Ben was riding. And not the hanging-on-for-dear-life kind of riding Eve had done on the back of Gabby's moped; her brother was gently moving in rhythm with the horse – Phantom – as it trotted around the paddock area that also seemed to be housing Vincent Van Hoff, more cats than Eve could quickly count and... was that a deer?

'He is very good,' the man said as he released the grey horse. It walked no more than three or four steps and stuck its head in a water trough. 'He has ridden before.'

'No,' Eve said. 'He hasn't ridden before. Well, a donkey once at the vehicle show.' And there had been a mechanical bull at a stag party in Weymouth she'd seen photos of on Facebook. But horses? Not that she knew of. The only thing Ben had ever had to do with horses was gambling away every penny he had on them. But then again, she hadn't known he had lost his job and his flat. Perhaps he could also ride greyhounds...

'Some people, they have more of a good connection with animals rather than with people, no?'

Eve swallowed. Did Ben currently have a better connection with this horse he was newly acquainted with than he had with her? How was that even possible when her job, her whole life so far, had been about connecting with people and unravelling their psyche?

'You want to ride Milo or Pnèvma?' the man asked.

'Oh no,' Eve said immediately, passing him Pnèvma's rope. 'You saw me on the moped and I wasn't even in charge.'

Somehow, effortlessly, the silver-haired man got aboard the horse – saddle-less and reins-less. He smiled down at her. 'It is the same with mopeds as it is horses. The ones with the engines are always in charge. You only have to know how to hold on.'

Eve smiled, the truth of that hitting her. 'What's your name?' she asked him. 'I don't know it.'

He smiled back at her as he gently stroked Pnèvma's mane. 'My name is Pan. *Xero poli*. It is nice to meet you.'

17

Eve was sitting on the grass in her now bone-dry clothes thanks to the intense Corfiot sun, watching Ben make light work of one of the giant packs of crisps he'd bought. This field was about the only flattish space at the sanctuary; the rest of it was bordered by olive and cypress and was as undulating as the rest of the mountain. However, the 'grass' was more like straw because of the heat and Pan had said the horses were only allowed out for a while to exercise until they had to be brought back into shaded areas.

'Have you had anything but crisps today?' Eve asked.

'Leave it out. I've already had three texts from Mum asking what I'm eating,' Ben snapped.

This grumpiness seemed to be catching. Eve snatched the crisps and stuck her hand in, grabbing a handful and pushing them all into her mouth at once. She hadn't had anything to eat today either but, after the feast at Nikos's grill room last night, it was a wonder she even wanted crisps now.

'Oi!' Ben shouted, taking the packet back.

'Do you know what's wrong with Gabby?' Eve asked when

she'd finished her mouthful. 'I went to help her at the hotel she works at and she was a bit off with me.'

'She's stressed at the minute, isn't she?'

Ben had said it like it should have been obvious to someone who was supposed to be her best friend.

'Is she?'

'She's got those people coming to scrutinise the sanctuary some-time. Could be today. Could be next week. They aren't going to say when it is. Like some weird secret hotel inspector shit. Anyone who books in for a visit – like tourist groups and stuff – she has to treat as potential trustees. She thinks they're trying to close the place down.'

And Ben knew all this how? Eve was certain nothing had been said at dinner last night and she hadn't been away having her fortune told for *that* long.

'Did she tell you that?'

'Who else would have told me? Are you sure *you're* all right?'

She nodded. 'Yes. Of course.' Apart from her ears feeling full of pool water.

'You seem a bit uptight. More uptight than you usually are,' Ben said, opening a bottle of water. 'And that's saying something.'

So her best friend was agitated and deeply worried about something and couldn't talk to her about it. And now her brother was calling her uptight. Perhaps all this softly softly and pussy-footing around was doing no one any good. Maybe least of all Eve.

'So, are you going to tell me why you've lost your job and don't seem to be looking for something else?' Eve blurted out. 'Or should I carry on pretending that I don't know and that it doesn't matter?'

'Fuck's sake, Mum told you,' Ben said, dropping the crisps bag to the ground.

'Yes, and I hate the fact that *she* told me, and you didn't. What's going on, Ben?'

'Nothing,' he said, breaking eye contact. It was one word that spoke volumes.

'Ben, are you in some kind of trouble?'

'Oh yeah, jacked in the tiling and thought I'd join a biker gang,' he scoffed.

'I'm being serious. I'm worried about you.'

'Is that why you brought me here? To keep an eye on me? Because I was hoping we could have some actual fun.'

'Well, I'm sure living a jobless existence having Glenda cook ready meals for you seems fun right now but, believe me, when you have no money to go out on a Friday night, or no credit to buy the new Arsenal shirt, the fun will evaporate quicker than Harry Styles concert tickets.'

'Is this how you talk to your students?' Ben got to his feet. 'Telling them to get their act together and pull their socks up? Do what society tells them they should do?'

'Oh, so this is about reclaiming your freedom of expression, is it? Exercising your human right to live life your way? It's not about wanting to arse around, wasting your life away until someone else has to pick up the pieces again.'

'Careful, Eve, that liberal mask you have on with your counsellor hat is slipping.'

'Dad would hate how you're being right now!'

The moment the words were out of her mouth Eve wanted to claw them back in. Who even was she in this moment?

'I'm sorry, I didn't mean that.' It was much better to apologise quickly. Anger could make you say and do things, but it could also fester if it wasn't addressed promptly.

'No one ever compares to Dad for you, do they?' Ben retorted, gathering up the crisps and his water bottle.

'I don't know what you're talking about.'

'You idolise him. Even now. He's like some fucking god to you. It's a bit pathetic really.'

Eve tried to breathe. This was just Ben swiping back at her. She didn't respond. A non-response would usually force the other party to fill the silence. She waited.

'He wasn't all that. What did he actually do when you think about it? Stuck tiles on people's roofs, drank beer, played darts. Hardly worthy of that bench at the rec really.'

As much as Ben's words were gnawing at her heart and her lips were itching to roar a defence, she held still, trying to ignore the heat from the sun mixing with her internal rise in temperature. Perhaps Ben needed this. And then, once he had rid himself of this pent-up rage or unreleased grief, he would be ready to accept change and her help to make it happen.

'He never made a difference to anyone, did he? He never put others first. He did exactly what he wanted, when he wanted and no one pulled *him* up on that. Not even Mum. He was a shit husband and a shit father.'

Eve couldn't let that go. 'Ben, that's not at all true! He was a loyal husband and a wonderful father.'

'Loyal? Huh, yeah.' He shook his head.

Eve gritted her teeth and stood up too. 'He *was* loyal. Unlike Glenda with Gene Reynolds! The man Glenda was rolling around in bed with while our father was strapped to a morphine drip!'

Ben shook his head. 'I can't listen to this.' He made to leave.

'Oh, that's right!' she yelled, completely not in control of her emotions now. 'Leave when you don't like what you're hearing! Run away! Avoid all your issues!'

And then she realised the only ones listening to her unhinged screams were three horses, the three-legged sheep and approximately twelve cats.

18

EPISKEPSI, CORFU

Gianni had driven through this higgledy-piggledy village once already. And then, finding there was nowhere to park his car, he had driven back through it again, finally squeezing the vehicle into a gap beside a wire fence enclosing chickens which had glared at him as if they knew he was an outsider. The village seemed to have one main road but off it were small streets, winding upwards to what looked like tiers of homes. There were tiny terraces set with mis-matched furniture, strings of washing hanging from eaves, dogs sleeping on steps. Some people sat on chairs right outside their front doors. Bright bougainvillea trickled down over lattice fencing, ivy licked up electrical poles and vines intertwined with whatever they could find to cling to. It was as unsophisticated as it got but something inside him relaxed at that. The second he acknowledged that feeling though, he straightened up. He wasn't here to relax. He was here to seek the truth. He wanted to look his biological father in the eye and find out what kind of man he was.

'*Yassas! Ela! Edho!*'

A man wearing a white shirt and trousers, with a fedora on his head, was beckoning him to a small patio area where a few chairs and tables stood outside a whitewashed building with a yellow painted door. Just beyond that was an old bell tower, its white stone faded and aged with damp.

Gianni waved a hand. '*Bon pomeriggio.*'

The man looked confused before speaking again.

'Very good for you. Very good for me.'

So he spoke English and he was well into his sixties, maybe older. This was exactly the kind of person who might know the man he was looking for.

'Hello, sir,' Gianni began, stepping across the street to get closer. 'I wonder if you could help me. I am looking for someone. His name is Pan. Maybe Panos or Panagiotis? I am told he is from this village and—'

'Very good for you. Very good for me. *Ela. Páme.*'

The man put a hand on Gianni's shoulder and drew him towards a table where there were two women already seated. A dark-haired woman about this mother's age, the other could have been older than God, with silvery white hair in two thick rope-like braids lying past her shoulders. She could definitely have been here her whole life...

'Eeee!'

'Not "e" again, Aleka. Everything cannot be "e".'

'Eeee!'

This felt very awkward but at least one of them was speaking a language he could understand

'Hello,' Gianni greeted.

The two women conversed in Greek and then both of them looked back to him. He noticed a white glazed sheen on the older woman's eyes. Was she blind?

'Aleka asks why you do not speak Greek,' the dark-haired woman said.

'I... do not know Greek.' Were they angry about that?

'How can you not know Greek when you *are* Greek?' the woman scoffed.

Gianni swallowed as the older woman turned her head slowly until she was facing him as if she could see him. 'I am from Italy.'

'Aleka says you must sit down. I am Vasiliki. And Spiros here will bring you some ouzo.'

The man in the fedora grinned. 'Very good for you. Very good for me.' He headed off into the building where other people were sitting inside.

This didn't seem to be a matter for discussion, although he wasn't sure he wanted any more ouzo given that he was in charge of a car. Gianni pulled out a chair and sat down. Immediately, two cats settled by his feet under the table.

Aleka whispered something to Vasiliki and Vasiliki seemed to appraise him from top to bottom. Then she whispered back to Aleka whose fingers were now on a tray that looked as if it contained seashells. Gianni felt out of his depth. Perhaps he needed to lead the conversation, ask his questions and leave them no time to talk amongst themselves.

'Aleka says you are Greek,' Vasiliki said, getting in there first. 'She also says that this morning you went swimming.'

'What?' Gianni exclaimed, immediately shocked. And then he smiled, lightly pointing a finger at his companions. This old lady was excellent at what she did. However, she might fool many a tourist, but she was not going to be fooling him. 'Very good.' He nodded. 'Very good. But she cannot see, right? That means all her other senses, they work much better. I did not have time to shower so she can obviously smell the chlorine.'

Vasiliki snorted. 'You do not know Aleka. In 1974, in a freak accident, an olive was somehow catapulted from a hammermill machine and became lodged in Aleka's nose. High up. Unable to reach by external means. One nostril she cannot smell anything at all. The only sense that works well is her hearing.'

Gianni didn't know how to respond.

More whispering.

'She says you look for someone,' Vasiliki stated.

'Yes,' Gianni said. It didn't take someone with fortune-telling insight to conclude that a stranger to this village not carrying a large bag packed with things for the beach might have another purpose, but at least it gave him an opportunity to ask questions and hopefully find some answers. 'Someone that used to live here, I think. A friend... of my mother. She visited here. Well, not this village, she spent time in Spartilas. It was a long time ago. Twenty-six years.'

Aleka's fingers began to move around the seashells in the tray, scraping them one way and then another, picking some up and toying with them in her hands.

'What is the name? Of the person you look for,' Vasiliki asked.

'Pan? Or Panos? Or—'

'And the other name?'

Gianni sighed. 'This I do not know.'

Vasiliki laughed then. 'You do not know?'

He bit his lip. Was this whole idea stupid, a fruitless ploy?

'How about the names of this Panos's mother or father, sisters or brothers?'

Gianni shook his head. He had literally nothing.

'Cousins?' Vasiliki suggested with a hopeful raise of her eyebrow.

He was about to shake his head again when he realised he *did* have something. His mother had spent time in Spartilas and Pan had worked at a restaurant near there. He didn't know the name of it but...

'He worked as a waiter at a restaurant.'

'In Spartilas?'

'Not *in* Spartilas. She said it was a... mountain café?'

Saying the words 'mountain café' felt alien. Were there such things as mountain cafés here? They sounded much more like places that could be found in Switzerland, not Greece.

'Ah!' Vasiliki said, as if a lightbulb had gone on in her mind. 'You mean Harilaos's Countryside Taverna.'

Gianni was suddenly flooded with adrenaline. 'Is it far from here?'

'It is only a few miles.' Vasiliki waved a hand and indicated the backdrop of tall cypress and olive groves clinging to the rugged mountain.

Aleka said something and Vasiliki leaned in close to her. Then she looked at Gianni again.

'Aleka says if you find this bird you will find who you look for.'

For a second Gianni had no idea what Vasiliki was talking about. He looked over his shoulder to the bushes and trees, expecting to see something flapping its wings, maybe with a helpful compass around its neck.

'The picture,' Vasiliki said, grabbing his shoulder and turning him back to the table.

Gianni dropped his gaze to the tray of seashells and his mouth fell open. Somehow, while he had been distracted talking to Vasiliki, Aleka had been moving the shells in her tray to form a quite detailed picture of a bird.

'I do not understand,' he said, addressing Aleka.

Vasiliki spoke Greek, presumably repeating what he'd said. Aleka replied and as she spoke, her hand reached out across the table, finding Gianni's. She had a tight grip.

'She says this bird lives near to the person you are looking for. That is all she can tell you,' Vasiliki said. Then she whispered,

'Sometimes her pictures do not make sense at first. But there is always an answer in the end.'

Gianni nodded and Aleka finally relinquished her hold on him.

Spiros arrived shortly after with a tray carrying short glasses, a bottle of ouzo and water. Gianni decided he would have one drink and then he would make his way up the mountain to this countryside taverna.

'Harilaos's may not be open now,' Vasiliki said, as if she were a mind-reader. 'In Greece we have siesta time. You should go this evening. After six.'

Spiros slapped him on the shoulder. 'Very nice. Very nice.'

19

BOSTONIA VILLAGE, ALMYROS

'Please, Gabby, please tell me you don't work here too.'

Gabby's visitors to Safe Animals had cancelled at the very last minute, after she had toiled and sweated and made sure every single inch of the sanctuary was running more like clockwork than Big Ben and was cleaner than Eve's beer taps at the pub. Gabby had screamed until she'd scared Bruno the pig and then Pan had suggested making mountain tea. But Gabby had decided that now she had a few hours free, she wasn't going to spend them at the sanctuary. Taking the Fiat Doblò and Eve, they had headed down the mountain to Almyros. But not to the hotel; instead, to a smaller accommodation complex that had the most beautiful pool and bar area and padded sun loungers set on grass that was somehow lush and green.

'I don't work here,' Gabby said, exhaling loudly, her hair splayed out behind her as she stretched out in a white bikini that only emphasised her wonderful tan.

'Thank God for that,' Eve said. 'Because I was starting to think that there weren't many establishments that didn't have you on their roster.'

'Or did have at one time,' Gabby said.

'You never mentioned you were working quite so flat-out in our FaceTime chats,' Eve said, adjusting her sunglasses and then shifting into a better position on her lounger.

'Didn't I?'

'You know you didn't,' Eve said. 'I'm just trying to work out why. Yes, you said you worked at a bar as well as the sanctuary, but you didn't tell me about the hotel and I'm guessing there are other places I still don't know about.'

Gabby sighed. 'Listen, Eve, I'm sorry I was a bit off this morning. I was just bricking it about this visit and then it turned out to be nothing... probably... I don't know.' She sighed. 'I'm sure it's a test of my nerve more than anything else. They want to catch me unawares. Find a reason to find fault and then get rid of me and maybe even close the whole sanctuary.' She suddenly sat bolt upright. 'What if that booking was the trustees? They could have falsely cancelled. They could still turn up now! While I'm here!'

'Gabby,' Eve said. 'Take a breath and have a sip of your grapefruit soda. If they turn up then your colleagues will be there, they can show them around the perfectly clean and organised shelter and they can phone you and let you know.'

Gabby picked up the bottle containing the fizzy pink liquid and sipped from the straw, nodding.

'You know, I would have liked to hear about this trustee visit from you rather than Ben,' she admitted.

'I wanted to tell you. I wanted to mention it before you came here but I thought if I told you about it and how I'm kind of on edge about it then... you wouldn't come.'

Eve sighed. 'Oh, Gabby, Corfu is really lovely and everything, but I would have come to visit you if you'd been heading up a shelter anywhere. Or not heading up anything at all. It's you I've come to see.'

'And you're seeing me in between feeding strays and folding towels and—'

'That awful woman, Magda,' Eve added. 'She is scary.'

Gabby laughed. 'She's OK once you get to know her. But I have to admit, the coffee there isn't the best.'

Coffee. Eve nodded in response, but her mind couldn't help doing a little detour back to her dip in the pool at the hotel and her interaction with the rather gorgeous Gianni.

'So,' Gabby said, swinging her legs around the side of her lounger and facing Eve. 'Who *was* that guy you were in the pool with? I saw him at Petra yesterday. He'd never tried ouzo before, can you believe it?' Gabby had said that statement as if it were a crime not to have tasted the Greek aperitif.

Eve wasn't sure how she was going to answer her question. Because she didn't have very much to share.

'He didn't like the coffee,' Eve said. 'I told him I would get him something else and... I fell in the pool.'

'He was holding your hand,' Gabby said, her gaze very direct.

'Yes, well, that was because I had cramp.'

'In your hand?'

'No, in my leg.'

Gabby began to laugh and it was good to see the tension release for a moment. Except then, Eve realised her face had heated up as if it could solve the UK energy crisis all by itself.

'You like him!' Gabby exclaimed.

'Don't be ridiculous. I don't know him. At all.'

'He looked good though,' Gabby said. 'Much better looking than Mitchell in my opinion.'

Hearing that name stopped the warmth gathering in Eve's cheeks. She picked up her own soda from the little table underneath the parasol made of reeds and drank. She absolutely hated the fact that just the mention of Mitchell made her react at all. She wished she could delete him like an unwanted Sky programme you had a vague memory of setting to record but definitely did not Series Link and absolutely would not want to watch a second season of. He had been her greatest mistake. He had wrapped her in affection, he had drawn her in when she had still been fragile and she had paid a heavy price for opening up, for showing him her heart, for falling for a totally calculated manipulation.

'But you've had dates since Mitchell, haven't you?'

'I actually... haven't had a lot of time to think about dating lately because I've been too worried about Ben.'

'So, what exactly is happening with him? Because he seems good to me. And he loves the animals.'

'I don't really know,' Eve admitted. 'The only things I know for certain is he's lost his job and his flat and he's living with Glenda.'

'Wow,' Gabby said. 'That's a lot.'

'Yeah, and he won't seem to acknowledge any of it. It's like it's happening to someone else and it's not his story to tell. And no matter what approach I take, nothing's working and it ends up with him shouting or me shouting and him storming off.'

Gabby pulled the hairband off her wrist and began to tie up her curls. 'Maybe you're too close.'

Eve sighed. 'I thought we were close but now I'm not so sure. He was saying some odd things about Dad too.' Or perhaps that had just been Ben's way of deflecting the conversation away from his own shortcomings.

'Do you want me to have a go?' Gabby asked.

'Have a go?'

'At talking to Ben. Sometimes it's easier hearing things from an outsider.'

'You're not an outsider, Gabby.'

'No, I know, but I haven't been there for a while and I'm not his sister so, I don't know, maybe I'll have a different approach?'

Perhaps Gabby was right. Maybe Eve was too near to it all, suffocating Ben instead of supporting.

'Do you remember when you opened up to my mum a bit about Mitchell?' Gabby asked.

She remembered Maureen finding her sitting on the floor of their kitchen in floods of tears and Gabby's dad, Richard, scooping her up and putting her on the sofa. Maureen had wrapped her in fluffy blankets, made hot milk and eventually eked out the beginnings of the story. When Gabby got back Eve had been ready to divulge the rest. Mitchell hadn't just broken her heart, he had sabotaged her career path too. What she had thought were conversations with her boyfriend had been Mitchell stealing her ideas, line by line, feathering his own future that had never really included her.

'Sometimes it takes someone slightly removed to get the ball rolling. Then, once the door is opened, it might all come flooding out.'

Eve should know this. She was used to being the grown-up, the one to nudge the answers out of her students.

'Come here,' Gabby said, opening her arms. 'No matter how stressy I am, I've always got time for you!' She put one hand to her curls and shook them. 'Want to smell my hair?'

Eve shifted on her sun lounger so she could cuddle her best friend and inhale that scent of warming coconut.

'I've got you, OK?' Gabby said, holding tight. 'Just like you've got me.'

'Always,' Eve answered, closing her eyes.

'So... is now a good time to tell you I'm working at another taverna tonight?'

'Oh, Gabby! Really?' Eve exclaimed.

'This is going to be fun,' Gabby reassured her with a grin. 'It's a big, fat Greek wedding.'

20

HARILAOS'S COUNTRYSIDE TAVERNA

It was almost eight o'clock in the evening and as Gianni drove up the mountain, he was still, for some reason, scouring the rocks and scrub for a bird that looked like the old blind woman's picture made from shells. He mustn't get too enthused about someone who thought she could predict the future, nor his conversation with Vasiliki and Spiros. After the ouzo had arrived and he had turned down a second glass, he'd left Episkepsi thinking every second person must be called Panos. And it was slightly disheartening that these villagers, people from the village his father had told his mother he was from, seemed to know every Panos on the island except the one he was looking for. Or perhaps they just did not know their secrets. Because Panos Dimitrias who was in construction might have four daughters and land pockets all over the north of the island, but he might also have a son he knew nothing about. The same with Panos the plumber and the four Panos's who ran eateries from Acharavi to Arillas. Twenty-six years was a long time...

Gianni slowed as he passed a long stretch of parked cars on the side of the road. Was he not nearly at the countryside taverna? He didn't remember seeing some tourist hotspot before it on the map. He needed to make a decision.

Reversing backwards, he parked behind the last car, then got out and locked up.

* * *

'This place is fantastic, isn't it?'

Her brother wasn't wrong; this place was as quirky and unique as it got, in all the very best ways. Their earlier argument hadn't been addressed but Ben seemed to have put it to one side when he heard Gabby was working at the wedding and everyone was invited.

Its first aesthetic had hit Eve as a tumbledown home made up of several different sections – brick, timber, glass, metal – combining together as if no one had really thought about the final outcome. Outside, the barrels, watering cans and hosepipes had been made into urns of bright flowers and fairy lights spiralled around everything from table settings to the trees on the edge of the road.

Inside was even more eccentric. The downstairs was exactly like walking into someone's living room if that living room was cool and a little cave-like. Tables seemed to appear out of nowhere, hidden in the smallest of nooks, with thick stone steps leading upwards to a larger space where everything was wooden – floors, walls and tables and chairs – except for the large front windows gifting the most incredible views. More stairs then led up to a third tier with more tables and more fantastic vistas. It was rustic yet homely and completely enigmatic. And it was up on this third tier that Eve and Ben were sitting at a table crammed with guests, carafes of wine running down the centre next to jugs of water, trays filled with succulent spit-roasted lamb, pots of thick *tzatziki*, hunks of fresh bread and oven-roasted courgette, aubergine and pepper. A band of musicians was playing in the corner and every so often the *bouzouki* player would walk around, heading downstairs right to the ground floor and back again so everyone was involved.

'It really is fantastic,' Eve agreed, squeezing her body forward as a wedding guest shimmied past her. 'Not at all like the last wedding reception we went to together.'

Ben laughed, taking a swig of his beer before making a reply. 'You mean Mum and Dad's friend, Wurzel. I'd say that was just as rustic, seeing as it was in a barn and he arrived on a combine harvester.'

'And he had a pig as a page boy,' Eve added.

'Shit, yeah,' Ben said, laughing again. He took another swig of his drink. 'Anyway, marriage is an outdated concept if you ask me. What's the point of it?'

'Sshh,' Eve said. 'You can't say things like that about marriage at a wedding. That has to be bad luck.'

'For who? Me or the "happy" couple?'

'Ben, you at least have to be happy for people who've decided they want to support the so-called outdated concept and become husband and wife. Especially this couple – Andreas and Mairi – when they're feeding us such delicious food.'

'Ha,' Ben said as if he'd discovered a secret. 'You've given yourself away, Eve. You *don't* think marriage is outdated.'

'I don't really have an opinion on marriage as a whole.'

'Wow, that was so quick it sounded like a stock answer.'

'Well,' Eve said, watching as the bride and groom arrived on their level and began to lead the guests in a circular dance, their smiles wide and faces flushed. 'I think two people should be able to commit to each other for life if they care deeply enough about each other.' She sighed. 'But, finding that person is rarer than most people think and that's why a lot of marriages don't last.'

'Because people pick the wrong person?' Ben queried.

'And for the wrong reasons.'

Her mind was back on Mitchell now. He had appeared to be the right person, made all the right moves, but what she'd seen hadn't been what she'd got. It had been false advertising from the outset.

Eve looked out of the window under the floral awning to the valley, where it dropped away from the mountain in pillows of greenery until it reached the blue of the sea in the distance. This place really felt like it was on another plane to anywhere she'd been before. And then, looking to the road, she saw a figure approaching. Tall, dark-haired, with olive skin, like most of the party here tonight. Except there was something familiar about him...

'Eve,' Ben called above the music. 'They're going to make everyone dance.'

She turned her attention back to her brother. He looked a little pale and he was off his chair and standing.

'I'm going downstairs to help Gabby,' he said.

Before Eve could make any response, he was across the floor of the taverna and heading for the stairs.

21

This place was even more eclectic than Episkepsi. There were tables dressed in white linen on scrub land outside what appeared to be a multi-layer family home. The chatter of people was louder than the band of musicians which Gianni could just see playing from inside. There were dogs chasing each other's tails, cats trying to avoid being chased by dogs and even more cars parked in every available gap. But as much as it was buzzy and loud it also somehow felt warm and welcoming.

He paused at the entrance, letting his eyes wander around the setting, the cicadas chirping from the trees. Was this what it had been like when his mother was here? It was hard to imagine his mother and her girlfriends, aged twenty, nothing but backpacks between them, sitting here drinking wine and eating food from a grill. Gianni had never seen his mother eat anything on a stick except an ice lolly and even with that she would complain about it making a mess. Had she really been carefree? Tried new things? Not been tied to her routines in Verona?

His eyes followed a waiter carrying a tray filled with drinks –

green beer bottles, coffees, jugs of wine. He had dark hair, a swarthy look, aged approximately in his forties. Could he be...

Suddenly Gianni was almost lifted off his feet. Then, he was spun around until someone's arm came down around his shoulders and he was somehow part of a circle of dancers all moving right, then left, then right again. It was like dance kidnapping. And it was testing. He seemed to be stepping left when he was supposed to be going right and vice versa – not that anyone seemed to mind. But the more it continued the more he realised this was as much cardio as a session on the treadmill in his home gym. Just as he was considering a ducking of his head and an arm retraction, he noticed a conga line coming out of the taverna – more notably, his eyes landed on one person. Was it really the girl who had fallen in the pool?

Eve.

Somehow his feet were now managing to move in time, and he found he didn't want to disengage, he wanted to stay dancing so he could look at her a little longer. He knew Corfu was a small island, that she had been at his hotel only a few miles away this morning, but, still, for her to be here at this restaurant where his mother had met his father. It was an eerie coincidence. But a coincidence nonetheless, right?

'*Opa!*' the circle of dancers all said at once.

Opa? Did that mean he was supposed to do something different with his feet? But then just like that, the music ended and everyone broke their hold and applauded. Gianni clapped too, his focus still on Eve. She was stood by a long table of drinks, selecting a glass of wine. He walked towards her.

* * *

Eve had no idea where Ben had gone. He had fled from the upper level as if something had significantly unsettled him and now he was nowhere to be seen. She'd found Gabby elbow deep in dough in the tiny little kitchen and asked her friend if she had seen him, but she hadn't. Now Eve was seeking something to settle her and she'd decided that something was cool white wine. She picked up a glass and took a sip. Piney, a little dry but still pleasant. And she had to remember that Ben was an adult who had to be allowed to make his own mistakes. No, not mistakes – that was already putting a negative spin on it – allowed to make his own *decisions*.

Taking another sip of the wine, Eve closed her eyes.

'Hello.'

Her eyes snapped open and there was Gianni standing right in front of her. So, she'd been right. It *had* been him walking along the road.

'We meet again,' he said, smiling.

'We do,' she replied, returning his smile. 'Do you know the bride or the groom? Or neither, like me?'

'This is a wedding?' Gianni exclaimed. 'Should I not be here?'

Eve shook her head. 'No, everyone is invited. I am finding that's how Greeks like it with most things.' But what *was* he doing here? This place was out in the middle of nowhere; maybe it was somewhere you stumbled upon in the daytime, but the evening?

And now neither of them was saying anything. Eve picked up a glass of wine and offered it to him. 'So, what brings you up here? It's quite a way from tourist civilisation.'

He took the wine. 'I was... recommended this place.'

'Really?' Eve asked. 'Like in a travel guide? Or someone at the hotel?'

'Actually, my mother,' he responded. 'She came here, years ago, when she was just out of college, and she said this was one of the places that she spent time. Back then she was into walking and they all wanted to walk the Corfu Trail.'

'That sounds very energetic.'

'I looked it up,' Gianni said. 'It is 220 kilometres. You are meant to start in the south of the island and end in the north. I am not sure how much of the trail she completed.'

'Feeling a little lacking just thinking about it,' Eve said, smiling.

'If I am honest, she has told me very little else about the trip.' An expression crossed his face which Eve read as his mind being elsewhere. But very quickly he recovered, as if he had realised it wasn't something he should be saying.

'Are you here with someone? Your angry friend? Gabby?'

'Yes. She's working again. But my brother is here too... somewhere.'

One of the tables closest to them became vacant as a couple bade their farewells and left the space.

'Shall we—'

'There's a table—'

They'd both spoken at the same time and Eve laughed. 'Quick, before someone else takes it.'

'Or they get us involved in dancing again,' Gianni added.

He stepped up to the table first and pulled one of the white plastic chairs out for her. *A gentleman from Verona.* Eve sat down, putting her glass on the table as Gianni sat down opposite her.

'So, you are here on holiday with your brother,' he stated, sipping his wine.

'Yes,' she said. 'It wasn't meant to be that way. I mean, I was supposed to come here on my own but, you know.' She shrugged as if that had given him any kind of answer at all.

'I do not know,' he said.

He hadn't changed the subject, meaning she would have to say something a little more substantial.

'Well, Ben's going through a bit of a tough time at the moment and Glenda isn't exactly Kofi Annan when it comes to keeping the peace so—'

'And Glenda is… your sister?'

His blue crystal eyes were studying her now, waiting for more. Why was she finding this so difficult? The answer was because she didn't share much with anyone but Gabby. And Gabby knew every scrap of her history and needed no explanations.

'Glenda is my mother,' Eve admitted. 'Ben's back living at home for a while.'

'And you call your mother by her first name?'

She nodded. 'I do.'

'Did she do something wrong?'

'Some *things* actually. Many things. Possibly a lot more than I even know about.'

She'd tried to keep her voice level but as she thought about Glenda, several images came into view in her mind's eye. Her dad in the hospice, that vacant look in his eyes that said there was barely anything left of him and then another, unproven, of Glenda and Gene Reynolds snuggled up in front of the wood burner watching *S.W.A.T.*

'Mothers,' Gianni said, cradling his glass in his left hand. 'I think they can be as complex as the very structure of our DNA.'

'Do you have a good relationship with yours?' Eve asked.

'Well,' Gianni started. 'If we were having this conversation a few weeks ago I would have said yes, we have a very good relationship.'

'And what's happened to change that?'

Christ, Eve, this was small talk at a Greek wedding, yet her question had rather come out as if she were addressing Gianni in her harmony hub. But it was too late to retract it and go for something lighter now.

'What has happened to change that is... my father died.'

Eve couldn't stop her intake of breath. 'Oh, I'm so sorry. This happened in the last few weeks? How... how awful for you all.'

'Thank you,' Gianni said, controlled, measured, exactly as Eve had been when people didn't really know what else to say to you when you were grieving.

'Was it a shock?' Eve asked. 'Sorry, I don't know why I asked that. Any death is a shock, isn't it? I mean, even though the Queen was ninety-six, my first thought was still that it was a hoax.'

Gianni shook his head. 'It is OK. He was sick for quite some time. We had to carry on around his illness, as hard as it was.'

Eve knew all about that. She had been doing A-levels when her dad first got diagnosed and her focus had not been on the exams. But what else could you do but try to carry on?

'But some of us found it easier to carry on every day than others.' He tipped back his wine as if it were a shot. 'So, I am here to perhaps find out more about who my mother was and maybe that will help me to work out who she is now.'

'That doesn't sound much like a holiday.'

'Ha! No, you are right. But my business calls are done for the day and we are in the middle of a wedding so perhaps the holiday can begin now. For tonight at least,' he suggested. 'Would you like another drink?'

Eve nodded. 'Yes please.'

22

'What is he doing here?'

It was Gabby asking the question, two trays full of *spanakopita* in her hands, ready to deliver to all the tables who hadn't yet had any. Gabby had just joined Eve outside the taverna and they began trying to navigate their way through more rings of dancers. Gabby's gaze was fixed on Gianni.

'Well, he said that this taverna is somewhere his mother visited once years ago and he wanted to come and see it.'

'Do you think he's stalking you? I mean, it's a bit weird, he turns up at Petra, he's staying at the hotel I work at, he's here now.'

'Wouldn't that mean he was stalking *you*?' Eve suggested. 'And this joke might be wearing thin but remember you work almost everywhere.'

'Not stalking then, just ever so interested,' Gabby said, making an expression that suggested innuendo.

'He didn't know I was going to be here. And unless he really is stalking you hard and he learned his craft from watching *The Capture* he can't have known you would be working here either. You said this event was a one-off.'

'It is a one-off,' Gabby assured, shimmying into some space and putting one tray down on a table. 'Pan asked me to help out. He works here most nights. I get the feeling he's worked here since before Athens had the Parthenon, but he won't do weddings.'

'What d'you mean he won't do weddings?'

'He hates them. No idea why. But you mention anything wedding-related to him and he either changes the subject really deliberately or he runs away. Anyway, I said I'd do it and he's going to clean out Bruno for a week for me. Usually I do Bruno because he keeps calm if I sing to him but, you know, Pan will have to learn how to sing like Katherine Jenkins, won't he?'

'Do *you* sing like Katherine Jenkins?'

'No,' Gabby said, laughing. 'But Pan doesn't know that.'

'Hey, I've brought more olive oil.'

It was Ben appearing at Eve's shoulder, a wooden trug containing glass bottles in each hand.

'Aww, thanks, Ben,' Gabby replied. 'Bring them over here.'

Before Ben could follow, Eve caught his arm.

'Ben, is everything OK?'

'Yeah, course.'

He was avoiding eye contact and nodding. There was that classic saying-what-you-absolutely-did-not-mean vibe again.

'You used to like dancing,' she reminded him.

'Give over,' he said, waving her away as if she were an annoying mosquito.

'You did!' Eve insisted. 'You even had a white glove like Michael Jackson and you used to—'

'Yeah, you can stop now,' Ben interrupted. 'I'm going to take these over to Gabby. Why don't you go and sit back down with that guy you've hooked up with?'

'I'm not. I haven't.'

'Careful, Eve, your body language is giving away all I need to know.'

And then he winked before embarking upon an ironically almost-dance-like shimmy through the animated groups of guests.

Eve's attention went back to Gianni, still at the table, his foot keeping a beat to the melody of the musicians who were now in the centre of the road seemingly not caring whether they were in the way of any vehicles. She enjoyed his company, this man she had bumped into. Enjoyed it already more than she had enjoyed the company of anyone of the opposite sex since those first weeks with Mitchell. Mind you, there had only been Mason, the PE tutor, trying to force her into after-hours burpees and Derek, who ran the canteen and had slightly too deep an interest in model villages. She sighed. One thing was certain, she really needed to stop thinking about Mitchell as a benchmark of any kind. And maybe what she also needed was someone else. An Italian for the holidays? There was only one way to find out...

23

'I brought you some food. I didn't know if you had eaten so...' Eve put a plate and cutlery down in front of Gianni. 'There's spit-roasted lamb, and then this – this is an absolutely delicious cheese and spinach pie with a difficult-to-pronounce name.' She pointed to the plate. 'Then there's the creamiest most garlicky *tzatziki*, oh, and this medley of vegetables – well, the way they're cooked just turns them into things you want to savour instead of things you want eat quickly because they're supposed to be good for you.'

Gianni smiled. He liked the way she made every sentence a lot longer than it could be. It was a bit like poetry. It was telling information, a story, in the most elongated yet beautiful way.

'Sorry, I sounded like an M&S Food ad then, didn't I?' she said, sitting down on the chair alongside him.

'It sounded like you think this is the best food you have ever had,' he answered, picking up his knife and fork.

'Well, I have to say, I'm already finding the tastes and flavours of Greece don't have to be about complex cooking. It seems to be all about the seasoning and letting things take their own time.'

Suddenly, Gianni was shot with a memory, something that had

never come to mind before. *His mother baking.* He leaned into the recollection, mentally searching and asking his brain for more. It was a cake. With walnuts and raisins. She had called it something. What was it? And then part of it came to him – it had something to do with a saint. That is what she had said. Then he realised he hadn't responded to Eve.

'You like Italian food?' he asked her.

'Doesn't everyone?'

He smiled but he was shaking his head. 'You make fresh pasta?'

'Literally every day.'

'Ha! You lie to me!' He dug his fork into the vegetables and put some in his mouth.

'No one normal makes fresh pasta at home,' Eve told him.

'No one normal? What is normal, human?'

She smiled and it warmed him as much as these vegetables were. She was right, the taste really was exceptional.

'These are very good,' he said, scooping up some more and closing his eyes as the sweet peppers burst all over his tongue.

'So, what is Italian food if it isn't pizza on a Friday night?' Eve asked.

'You insult me now!' he joked. 'You have never visited Italy?'

She shook her head. 'No. And I'd never visited Greece either before now.' She took a breath. 'I haven't really visited anywhere. My parents liked to holiday in the UK and then, after my dad died—'

He stopped eating. 'Your father, he has died like mine?'

Eve nodded. 'But it wasn't recent, it was... six years ago.'

But he could tell this still had the deepest effect on her. And why wouldn't it? To lose someone so close was as life changing as it got no matter how old you were or how long it had been.

'Was it a shock?' he asked, mirroring her question from earlier.

'Like your father,' Eve began. 'My dad was sick, but he refused to acknowledge it at the beginning.' She sighed. 'He was one of those people who got on with things, even when deep in the back of their minds they know something's wrong, but they think ignoring it will make it not true.'

'The very worst kind,' Gianni said with a shake of his head. And then he apologised. 'I am sorry. I did not mean that your father was the worst kind. I am certain he was an honourable man. I just meant he sounds as stubborn and stupid as my father when it comes to health matters.'

'Oh, agreed,' Eve said, smiling. 'So, have you travelled a lot? Sailed the seven seas?'

'I have only been around Europe and I have been to the UK once, to London. I liked it. Where are you from?'

'Nowhere like London,' Eve told him. 'I'm from a small town, nothing more than a village really, in Hampshire. It's about an hour and a half away from the capital.'

'Do you work in your village?' Gianni asked, picking his cutlery up again and forking into the lamb.

'Some of the time. I work in the local pub.'

'Pub,' Gianni said, smiling. 'I love that word. What does it say really?'

'Well,' Eve replied. 'It's a shortening of "public house".'

'A public house.'

'In ancient times they were also called "taverns" which is like "taverna", isn't it?'

* * *

And now Eve was giving him some kind of history lesson in the origins of pubs! She needed to tell him what else she did. Or tell him the reason behind her working in the village pub. But maybe he would then realise exactly how marooned on her own self-made island she was.

'I... also work at a college.'

'You are a teacher?' Gianni asked, turning towards her in his seat.

She shook her head. 'No, no, I'm a counsellor. I'm there to support the students' well-being. If they are... not turning in their assignments and the tutor thinks there is something more to it they get referred to me, or if they are having problems with a friendship at college or they don't have any friends at college or they've... lost a family member.'

She swallowed, stopping abruptly at the last statement. There hadn't been any harmony hub when she was grieving her dad, had been nothing for Ben at his school – not that he would have used it. Everyone back then either had to bury their feelings or break down, or sometimes it was a bit of both.

'It is important,' Gianni said, his eyes on her. 'For young people to talk about their feelings. If they do not let these things out, that sadness or that anger or that fear will shape how they are as adults.'

'It's that exactly!' Eve replied. 'When I was at college, only a few years before, there was nothing like what I hope I've created. I understand establishments have a budget but back then it was putting supplies over children's mental health. I think there's still a lot of work to do but it is getting better.'

He smiled at her. 'You are passionate... about this.'

His pause didn't go unnoticed and she nodded, realising that she was blushing. The way she had just spoken reminded her exactly how passionate she could be when it came to something she cared about.

'Almost as passionate as you about good coffee,' she teased.

'Well,' he began. 'Coffee... that is *my* job.' He leaned forward in his chair, reached into the back pocket of his trousers and took out his wallet. He produced a card, which he handed to her.

'Gianni Riccardo. Riccardocino.' She couldn't read the rest. 'Oh, can you translate?'

He smiled. 'It says master coffee producers then our slogan "Take time to taste". It is English on the other side.'

Eve flipped the card over. There was also his mobile phone number...

'I have been working for the business since I was able to drink coffee. Which in Italy is very young. And we might not be like Lavazza and Illy yet but I have hopes of exploring a different side to our market. I just need to narrow down my ideas.'

It all sounded very high-powered and not at all like The Hunter's Moon in Brookly Heath. Their coffee was Kenco and it came in slimline packets that usually went in the bin more often than they got used.

And then it came to her.

Coffee. *Kafes*. These were two coffee-related things now from the old kind-of fortune-teller...

'All my students drink boba these days,' Eve said. 'You know, bubble tea.'

'I am aware of it,' Gianni replied, his face falling a little. 'I do not understand it.'

'Have you tried it?'

He shook his head. 'I do not believe it is a drink. For me it is a dessert.'

'I admit I'm not a big fan of the tapioca pearls but some of the fruit-based teas and the other flavoured popping bubbles are really nice. And you can have them hot or cold.'

'Do they have this in Greece?'

'I don't know,' Eve said. 'I always thought it could be more though. Like, I don't know, some kind of adult version with popping alcohol... or, maybe a healthy version with key vitamins in the balls...'

'You have thought about this a lot.'

'I think you underestimate exactly how many of these drinks my students devour. It's big business.'

Gianni took a sip of his wine and sat back in his chair. 'I tell you what they devour here in Greece. Ouzo. I have had it twice already and I am not even sure I like it. And while I was being served ouzo I did not want there was a crazy woman who thinks she can tell people's fortune by making pictures with shells in a tray.' He scoffed. 'And she is blind.'

Eve's heart juddered. He had had his fortune told by Aleka too? Instantly she was wondering what his picture had been. She shook her head. This was ridiculous. There was no merit to it. Coffee could relate to literally anyone who drank it, around half the population of the world.

'One guy called Spiros got us the ouzo and this woman, Vasiliki, translated for the old lady.'

'I know them,' Eve told him. 'I mean, I don't know them very well, but I'm staying very close to Episkepsi. I've met them.'

'Really? Ha! Well, if you happen to know where I can find a strange-looking bird with spikes on its head let me know.'

A bird with spikes on its head. Could it be... Savage?

'Believe it or not,' Eve stated. 'I might be able to help you.'

24

SAFE ANIMALS SANCTUARY, EPISKEPSI

Eve didn't know why she was doing this, but it seemed she was doing it anyway. If she was saying she believed Aleka's shell picture made for Gianni, then she was also saying she believed in the picture made for her out of red wool.

Or maybe the retsina – the local wine – was driving things a little.

When she had suggested the bird could be Savage, Gianni had seemed almost excited about the prospect. So, without telling anyone where they were going, they had left the wedding, had got into Gianni's car and were now driving down the mountain to find the bird.

'You really think this could be the bird in the picture?' Gianni asked for about the third time.

'I don't know for sure, and it would have been good if you'd taken a picture of the shells but—'

'I never thought to do that,' Gianni admitted.

'It's a hoopoe bird,' Eve explained. 'Apparently, they found it on the road one day, it's wing damaged. It was repaired and it healed up and then the bird just never left.'

'So now it is a pet?'

'I'm not sure it's a pet. Just a long-term resident who doesn't want to leave. Some of the animals here stay, others get rehomed, like some of the cats and dogs. Wild animals they try to introduce back to their natural environment but it depends on what their ailment is and whether going back to the wild would be best for them.'

'You sound like you are running this place,' Gianni remarked, slowing a little for the next bend.

'That's another one of Gabby's jobs. Her favourite one. It's just round this corner and then a sharp left,' Eve directed. 'There, up this track.'

'You are serious?'

Eve laughed. She had thought that when she'd first been taken up here. But in the darkness now it seemed all the more intimidating. The branches of the olive trees stretched into the night like skinny, buckled arms, spooky and foreboding, the headlights of the car casting shadows. The track was like dry clay and rose at an angle of close to ninety degrees. It was not for the faint-hearted.

'I'm serious,' Eve told him.

'I took out the extra insurance to cover every aspect of this car but I did expect to bring it back in one piece.'

'You need to hit the gas quite hard to get up there.'

'I might close my eyes and pray,' Gianni said as he stepped on the accelerator.

Eve braced herself and held on as they climbed up the severe hill, Gianni skidding the car a little, until eventually the terrain flattened out, widened and then there was the entrance to the sanctuary.

'We're here,' she announced as Gianni pulled into the yard and found somewhere to park.

'I am surprised any of the rescued animals survive that hill,' he said, shaking his head.

'Apparently Vincent Van Hoff, the three-legged sheep, escaped once and they found him at the top of the drop just looking in disgust at the route out.'

'That sounds like a sensible sheep.'

Eve opened the car door and got out, taking a breath of the night air. It was a little cooler now, the temperature a few degrees lower, a hint of freshness to it. Gianni got out too and locked the car.

'Now, I don't know where Savage will be but he's been hanging out near Gabby's house on the balcony of my room.'

* * *

This is a crazy idea. You have come here to a wildlife shelter because a very old, very blind woman told you a mad-looking bird was the key to finding your father.

Gianni shook his head. But what other choice did he have? There had been no potential fathers working at the mountain café and he had tried to see if there were any wedding guests of the right age who resembled him with no success. Riccardo had talked about a similarity in looks but was that because he knew Gianni did not get those features from his mother? Or did his mother... have a photograph?

'Gianni,' Eve called. 'Are you OK?'

He had paused by the car as these thoughts tumbled into his brain. Where was he going to go next if today's search was fruitless?

'Yes, I am good,' he responded, stepping towards her.

'These are the stables for the horses. They live here all the time and sometimes children with special needs visit to groom them and those that want to can ride them around the paddock.'

There were three horses, all with their heads poking over the gates of their stables, interested in them, either looking for attention or perhaps getting ready to raise a warning.

'I've discovered my brother can ride and has probably told the horses more about how he's feeling than he has me,' Eve said, continuing with the tour.

'If only you could speak horse language,' Gianni said.

'I thought that. But unfortunately, I can't translate a whinny from a neigh.' She stepped on. 'Over here is where the dogs are kept – we won't go there because they'll start barking if we get too close or the light goes on. There is the cat shelter,' she said, pointing. 'And there is... wait!' She put a hand on his arm and drew him to a stop. 'Sshh. Keep still and quiet.'

'What is it?' he asked. All he could see was darkness and a fenced area up ahead.

'It's Savage,' she whispered. 'On the handle of that wheelbarrow.'

Wheelbarrow? It took Gianni a second to pick it out in the dim light, but when he did and his eyes had adjusted, he saw the bird. The plumage on its head was very like what Aleka had made out of shards of shells.

'I think this bird is what she meant,' Gianni said.

'But does it mean anything to you?'

'Nothing,' he answered, stepping closer as if a message might pop out of the bird's rear end.

'Don't get too close!' Eve exclaimed.

'Because I will scare it?'

'No, because it might attack you.'

'Attack me?'

'I haven't had the full back story yet but even Gabby won't get too close to it.'

Gianni laughed as he proceeded. 'It is not a bird of prey. What is the worst that can happen?'

'Losing an eye? Puncture wounds like on *The Staircase*?'

As he got within a few paces of the bird it started to make a rattling noise in its throat like it might be part of the snake family.

'Keep still! Do not move!'

It wasn't Eve shouting. It was someone else. A man. Tall, lithe, with a cloud of grey hair, he was carrying a bundle of rags.

'I said keep still!' the man repeated. 'Everything still. Do not look at me.'

Gianni held his breath and weighted his stance. And then there was another noise, a whistling, high and then low and back again. But it wasn't coming from the bird, it was coming from the man.

The bird's attention was away from Gianni now and as if the whistling was some kind of charming trick, Savage hopped from the handle of the barrow onto the fence and then took flight to land further away.

'You OK?' the man asked, flashing on a torch. 'You look white. Have you lost all your colour.'

'Thankfully I have not lost my eye,' Gianni answered.

The man laughed. 'Ha! This is true! Very true!'

'Thank you so much for coming to the rescue,' Eve said, joining Gianni. 'I did tell him not to get close, but he wouldn't listen.'

Next there was another noise that suddenly filled the night and it was coming from the bundle of rags.

'Oh my God!' Eve exclaimed. 'Pan, is that... a baby?'

Pan! Gianni froze. Had Eve just called this man Pan?

His whole body started to react then: his throat began to dry up, goosebumps broke out on his skin and a thousand thoughts fluttered around his brain like confetti. Gianni was more rooted to the spot now than he had been when first warned about the bird. He began looking at this man from top to bottom, seeking clarification, needing there to be visual clues to help provide some answers. Was there anything about him that seemed familiar? Something echoed in his body language? His jawline? His nose? Gianni couldn't be sure. But also, he couldn't *not* be sure. As Eve fussed over the wriggling child that was screaming its lungs out, Gianni had to wonder, was he now looking at his real father and was his real father somehow symbolically carrying a new-born baby?

25

Gianni was shivering, his body moving from muscle memory alone as he followed Eve who was tracking Pan who was apparently making decisions about a naked infant he'd discovered in a box by the office. As crazy as that situation was, Gianni's mind was whirring about other things, another child – him – the fact that his search might be over, that this man might be the man his mother had created him with.

They were entering a small, terraced cottage now, a combination of natural stone and flaking plaster, but it was tidy. A coffee table was right by the entrance, easy to fall into, and on it were books in a neat stack, a clean ashtray and an olive-wood candle holder. Behind the table was a two-seat sofa and an arm chair set to one side. There was a tiny kitchen area, washing-up done and draining, a bread packet tied up, a small teapot at the centre of the work surface...

'We need to call a doctor,' Eve said as Pan began to open cupboards and drawers, the baby lying in the crook of his arm.

'There is no need,' Pan answered. 'I have called the vet.'

'The vet!' Eve exclaimed. 'Pan, this isn't a puppy. It's a person.

And he... or she... is very, very small. He, she, needs medical attention.'

'It is a he,' Pan declared with a smile. 'The winkie has already pee-peed all over the cloths.'

'Well, what about the mother? If she's just given birth, she will need medical attention for any physical trauma and then some help with her mental state. She must have been scared and desperate to leave a baby at an animal sanctuary.'

'Eve,' Pan said, halting his search and looking directly at her. 'This baby has not just been born.'

'Well, how do you know?'

'Because he is clean. Because he has the button in his belly all tied and it is healed. I think baby is maybe four weeks old.'

'How do you know about babies?' Gianni asked. 'Do you have children?'

He hadn't meant to say that out loud but there it was all the same. His heart pumped hard as he waited for Pan to answer.

'I have delivered many kids,' Pan told him, straight-faced. 'Of goats.'

And then he burst out laughing as if anything about this situation was amusing.

Anger gripped Gianni. What was funny about someone abandoning their child? This little boy didn't know his mother or his father and was being swaddled by a man in his fifties who had called an animal practitioner to see to its needs. And Pan hadn't answered the question as to whether he had a family of his own. But judging by this house, if this *was* Pan's house, it was only set up for a single man whose hobbies seemed to be smoking and reading by candlelight.

'Pan,' Eve said. 'Let me hold the baby while you look for whatever you need to find. What *are* you looking for?' She offered out her arms.

'I have a tin of milk somewhere. In date.' He gave the baby over to Eve and began a more rigorous search.

'You can't give a baby tinned milk!' she exclaimed, beginning to rock the child.

'He is hungry and I do not have breasts full of mother's milk,' Pan answered. 'What else do you suggest?'

'I don't know,' Eve said. 'I don't know much about babies! But I do know you don't give them tinned milk. And what are you going to feed him with? Because he's too little to have a shot glass by the way.'

'We have bottles for the lambs. Or I can use a syringe. But I will take the advice of the vet when he gets here,' Pan said. 'Ah, here it is.' He got a tin from the cupboard and turned it upside down. 'As I said, it is still in date.'

'You need to call a doctor,' Eve continued, switching the baby's position. 'Is it super hard to find one on this island or something?'

'We cannot call the doctor yet,' Pan said as he brought out a tin opener and began to open the milk.

'Why not?'

'Because the doctor will have to call the authorities and they will come to take the baby away.'

'To make sure it's looked after by someone who cares for humans and not stray or injured animals. You are making that sound like a bad thing,' Eve said, settling the baby on her chest, one hand on his head.

'But if they take the baby away there will not be a chance for it to reconnect with its mother,' Pan said, 'when she realises that she has made a mistake.' He took the lid off the can of milk.

'And how are you going to find the mother? Surely the police can do a better job. They must have more resources than we have.'

'The police will either not look for the mother and the baby will go into care, or they will look for the mother to prosecute her for this crime.'

'What about a private doctor?' Gianni asked them both.

'Ha! You have money for this?'

'Yes,' Gianni answered confidently. 'I have money for this.'

'You also have money to pay this doctor to keep quiet?' Pan asked.

'If you think that is the right thing to do.'

Pan sighed, putting his fingers to his temples. 'I do not know what is the right thing.'

Gianni wet his lips before speaking again. 'Listen, I know there is a doctor on call at my hotel. I could... drive down there, arrange for them to come here, check the baby and I could... buy milk for babies from the supermarket.'

All he could think about were two things. One, getting out of here and trying to come to terms with the fact that he might have just met his father. And two, making sure he had a reason to come back.

'Oh, Gianni,' Eve said. 'I think that's a very good idea. A compromise. The baby's health is looked at, he gets some proper milk and tomorrow we can re-evaluate.'

'Gianni,' Pan said, pronouncing the name with a 'y'. 'That is your name?'

'No. Gianni.'

'You are not Greek?' Pan stated.

'No,' Gianni replied, unable to meet Pan's eyes. 'I am not Greek.'

26

Eve wasn't quite sure when her life had gone from relatively mediocre to off-the-charts crazy but here she was, sitting on the balcony of her room, a baby finally asleep in her arms, its fist wrapped around the hair scrunchie on her wrist. Gianni had been true to his word and come back to the sanctuary along with a doctor and a bag of baby essentials – formula, nappies, wipes. Once the baby had been declared fit and well, if a little hungry, and Pan had fashioned him something to wear out of a black polo neck circa 1985, Eve had taken first shift on care. She wouldn't ever have called herself a natural baby person who got melty eyed at the very idea of getting her hands on an infant, but she also wasn't one of those people who erupted in rage as soon as a child bleated on public transport. They needed to help this child. He had, for whatever reason, been left in the care of the sanctuary. And if Pan couldn't find the mother in the next day or so they would have no choice but to make a difficult decision.

Suddenly, the door that led from the loft room to the balcony burst open, slamming back against the wall.

'Jesus Christ, Eve! I mean, seriously, what the fuck? Do you have any idea what I've gone through these last few hours? I mean, don't you answer your phone? I've left you message after message on voicemail and I've texted about fifty times. And Gabby's texted too! You can't do that! You can't just fucking do that!'

Ben looked haunted. He was pale and clammy and was doing a good impression of the first symptoms of a heart attack.

In Eve's arms, the baby began to stir, tightening its grip on her hair band.

'What's the matter, Ben?' she asked, getting to her feet as gently as she could and keeping a rhythmic movement to her motion.

'What's the matter? Are you kidding me?'

He was pacing around the balcony area now as though he was doing sponsored laps for charity and they had to be done in a certain amount of time.

'You left the wedding! You left the wedding and that guy you were with was nowhere to be seen either and I know *nothing* about him and Gabby says she knows *nothing* about him either and you disappear and you don't answer your phone and I am thinking my sister would not just leave somewhere in a *foreign* country with a guy no one knows and not tell her brother or her best friend where she's going!'

Ben's voice was becoming louder still and the baby wasn't just *stirring* in his sleep now, his eyes were opening.

'Ben—'

'Anything could have happened to you. *Anything.* And what then, huh? Where would we even start to look for you on this island? With some guy? Walking around a mountain *in the dark!*'

Ben had said 'in the dark' as if it were an invitation to tea from Villanelle. Eve rocked the baby who was making an uncomfortable grunting noise but, right now, she was more concerned about Ben's reaction and his pallor.

'Take a long, slow deep breath,' she told him in as calm a voice as she could manage while rocking the half-sleepy, half-angry baby.

'I don't want to take any kind of breath,' Ben rattled out at speed. And then, almost involuntarily, he did, but it wasn't long and slow or deep; it was short, quick and shallow. 'I can't breathe,' he stated, eyes widening, panic written there. 'I can't breathe.'

Suddenly he was clawing at the neck of his shirt as if it was suffocating him, his skin fading with every second that ticked by. Eve looked at the baby, its face turning puce. And then she made her decision.

'Ben, I need you to hold this baby.'

She didn't let him challenge her statement, she just balanced the infant in one arm, drew Ben's arms up from his sides and then gave the baby to him.

'What? I... can't... I—'

Eve stayed close. 'You need to hold him, Ben. Focus on keeping him happy because otherwise he's going to scream and he has quite the set of lungs.'

She kept a watch on her brother, making sure the baby was safe, ready should this decision go horribly wrong. Ben was confused. Or rather his brain was being tricked. It had to quickly work out what was more important in this scenario: its need to panic or its need to not endanger a baby by panicking.

'I can't breathe, Eve,' he said, holding the baby a little closer.

'Yes, you can,' she told him. 'And you are. Just concentrate on the baby. He's only small. He needs you to hold him.'

'I don't know if I can.'

That was better. One step up from 'I can't'.

'*I* know you can,' she encouraged. 'Just come over here and sit down with him.' Straight suggestions, no 'why don't you' or 'perhaps you should'. Eve pulled up the second chair and ensured that he was able to lower himself safely into it. His breathing still wasn't controlled but it was getting there. Now she stayed quiet, let Ben continue to realise that he had been left holding the baby.

It was Eve's time to breathe for a second and take stock of what had happened tonight. The rustic taverna, the beautiful wedding, the Greek dancing, the talking to Gianni. There was no denying, on her part anyway, there was a draw to the Italian. And, when they were together, conversation just flowed so effortlessly. Except maybe after he had got back to Safe Animals with the baby supplies. Then he had seemed a little distracted but hadn't all three of them been? She looked out into the night, those knots of olive trees spiralling into the black, the hum of cicadas now a strange absence.

'Eve,' Ben said suddenly. 'What is this baby doing here? Who does it belong to?'

'Not me,' she replied. 'I mean, that would be quick work for leaving the taverna with the only man I've been closer than two metres to in years.' She hadn't answered her brother's question. 'Pan found him. He'd been left here.'

'What?'

'Yeah,' she said, sighing. 'So, if you got a little bit worried about being left by your twenty-five-year-old sister, imagine how he feels.' She stopped talking. She hadn't meant to belittle how Ben had felt. 'Sorry, I didn't mean—'

'I'm fine,' he said quickly, barriers restored. 'No drama. Just, you know, I worried. For a bit.'

Eve knew he was trying to make light of it but the way he had been, angry, clammy, panicked. Was this a sign of addiction? Could you get that kind of cold turkey when it came to gambling? Or was this something else?

'So, the Greek dude you went off with… what's that all about?'

'Oh, well, he's not actually Greek,' Eve said. 'He's Italian.'

'Yeah? Well, I wasn't actually asking for his nationality.' Ben's tone was hard as well as sarcastic.

'Well, he's Italian,' she said for the second time.

'Noted. Again.'

'I met him this morning at the hotel in Almyros. And, Ben, I am sorry. For not telling you I was leaving the wedding or where I was going. I shouldn't have done that.'

He shrugged. 'S'all right.' Then a smile crossed his face. 'Look, he's gone to sleep.'

The baby's eyes were tightly shut again and he seemed as content as he had ever been since Eve had been introduced to him.

'So, what do we do with him now?' Ben asked.

'We sit here until your arm goes numb and then we pop him in his vegetable box.' She nodded to the crate Gianni had fashioned for him to sleep in.

'And what happens to him after that?'

Eve sighed. 'I don't think anyone knows yet.'

27

ALMYROS

Gianni was on his third cup of coffee and it was only 8 a.m. Unable to face dirt coffee for the rest of his stay, he had bought a jar from the supermarket. Instant was not good. But it was a step up from soil. He drank some now and let it coat the back of his throat. He had found this quiet area of the grounds in the shade of a thick-trunked olive tree, had dragged a small table and a chair into the space, and claimed it as his own. The sun was up, the cicadas were awake, yet he was exhausted. He hadn't slept. He hadn't even got into the bed. It was suddenly all too much. All these questions he had no answers for. Not knowing if the man called Pan he had met last night was his father or just one of a lot of men on this island who had a variation of the name. The only real link that made this seem more possible was the blind woman and the shell picture of the bird that had almost attacked him. It was hardly any connection at all unless you believed in something spiritual.

Right now, he didn't know what he believed. He was used to dealing in facts and figures, truths you could not argue with on a spreadsheet if you had done your research properly. But this was something he had not known existed. How could you research when you had no idea where to start?

Gianni checked his phone again. He had texted his mother, several times, and still there was no notification that she had read the messages. He had started off light, asking her about the upcoming meeting, making sure she knew he had been serious when he'd told her not to do the deal. Then he had tiptoed into the arena of what he really wanted to ask about.

Did Pan like to read?

Did Pan smoke?

Did Pan like animals?

The texts looked a little pathetic now. All the more pathetic as they languished there unanswered. What next? He had to do something while he waited. *The baby*.

If he was honest, he hadn't thought about the child since he'd left the animal sanctuary last night. He'd made his excuses as soon as he could after dropping off the supplies, left Eve, left maybe his father, left a baby too... Perhaps abandonment was written across his DNA.

Gianni jumped in his seat as his phone started to ring. The cicadas briefly mute as if they were in shock too. *Mamma*.

'Hello.'

'Hello, Gianni.'

There was a silence. Exactly like all the silences there had been between them since his father had passed. It was like a game of who was going to break first.

He cleared his throat.

'It is early,' his mother began before he could speak.

'Here in Greece it is eight o'clock.'

'Is that cicadas I can hear? Where are you?' Gianni noted the fatigue in his mother's tone but also the pinch of remembrance. Perhaps this was how things worked when you got a little older; long-ago memories were pieced together slowly, bit by bit.

'I am in a place called Almyros.' He hadn't told her exactly where he was staying. Had she been here too?

'I remember the cicadas being so loud. They are not so loud in Italy.'

'Greece is not the same as Italy in many ways.'

'This is true.'

Another silence. He needed to cut to the chase or perhaps they would never get there.

'I think,' Gianni began, 'that I have found Pan.'

He heard his mother's sharp intake of breath perhaps before she had even realised she'd let it go.

A tabby cat appeared from the undergrowth, a small brown lizard in its mouth.

'Is he well?'

Asking after this man's health was not the first thing Gianni had expected his mother to say. But, then again, what *had* he expected her to say? He was finding out that his mother was more multi-layered than he had realised, a mix of contradictions.

'Did you not read my messages?' he asked, his tone a little bitter. 'He smokes.'

'Most Greeks smoke, just like Italians.'

'So, you *did* get my messages?'

'I asked you if he is well,' she said firmly.

'That is the first thing you think of? To ask if he is well? Not to ask how I might feel about meeting him?' If it *was* him. He still had nothing cast in iron.

He'd shown his exasperation and realised a little too late he had sounded like a child.

'I ask if he is well because you have lost one father already to ill health. I do not want you to lose another one.'

Gianni stayed quiet, contrite. He watched the cat devour the lizard in one savage gulp then lick its lips.

'Gianni, why have you messaged me with questions about this? Really?'

'You do not want me to tell you about my progress with the search?'

'You made the decision to go to Corfu. You did not want my input. Why do you need it now?'

Why *did* he need this conversation with his mother? Was it simply because he wanted some kind of validation for what he was doing? Because, as she had just said, he hadn't needed this from her before.

No, it was not that.

'I want to be certain it is him before I say anything about who I am. I want to have that knowledge before *he* has any knowledge.'

'Gianni, you talk like Riccardo. You want power like this is a business transaction to rise above a competitor.'

He shook his head even though she could not see him. The cat saw him and then turned its attention to biting its own tail.

'It is not about power,' he replied with conviction. 'It is about wanting to get to know this man, if he is the right man, before he knows I am his son. What if he is not a good man? What if... we have nothing in common? What if he... does not want to know me?'

He bit back the emotion that had leaked into his words. This only-just-better-than-dirt coffee was obviously affecting his emotions.

'The Pan I knew is a good man,' she said straight away. 'And you will only find out what you have in common with each other if you get to know each other.' She sighed. 'Things in common do not always come from how you are made, Gianni. They take time. Like when you try something new for the first time and realise that you enjoy it. It might be that you have your first taste of Greek mountain tea and you find you like it as much as coffee.'

Gianni bristled a little. He was not going to like any kind of tea better than coffee. Coffee was an integral part of who he was. Or was that true? *Was* it part of him? Or had it been percolated into him by the man who had raised him?

'I know what you are thinking,' his mother said. 'You are thinking that you do not want to find common ground with someone you do not know. That if you find that you get along with Pan it is somehow disrespecting Riccardo.'

Did he think that? It had been hard to get his head around the situation but it was more difficult now he thought he had located his father. This was *real*. There was no more pretending it wasn't.

'When Riccardo knew he was at the end he wanted you to know the truth and he wanted you to find your father.'

'And you did not,' Gianni reminded her.

'I know,' she replied. 'Because... I did not want to hurt you. In every way that matters, Riccardo was your only father and there was never one occasion in your growing up that I thought I should tell you anything different. Not one, Gianni. Because your father was the best of fathers.'

He could picture the scene back in Verona now. His mother in the open-plan kitchen, dressed ready for work in a designer trouser suit, her hair tied into a tight bun, the red lipstick providing a warning to whoever might think of getting in her way that day, a steaming macchiato sat on the granite countertop.

'But I see now that what I thought was for the best came from a place of fear.' He heard her take a deep breath. 'I have always wanted to protect you from anything that might hurt you, Gianni, ever since you came into the world, through getting your lip stuck inside one of your toy cars, to losing out on a deal I knew you wanted so badly. But, to truly experience the joy of life, you must also experience the difficult times and the pain. Without the highs and the lows, there is only ever "OK" and who wants only "OK"?'

He didn't say anything, he simply absorbed what he was being told, discovering this other different, compassionate side to his mother.

'I have something for you,' his mother told him. 'Claudia sent it to me last night.'

Claudia was his mother's longest standing friend. They were opposites in both looks and nature. Claudia's hair was very long, her manner was mild and calm and she lived with her mother who still looked after a large lemon grove with zero assistance. Claudia was also someone who had gone on his mother's Greek back-packing trip of her youth.

'It is old and faded a little. A Polaroid she carried all over Greece and back again to Italy and, well, you know Claudia, she is one of those people who spills things over everything – her clothes, her friends – so there are spatters of something over one corner.'

He wasn't entirely listening to what she was telling him. His interest had been piqued by the word 'Polaroid'. She had a photograph. An old photograph. But was it...

'It is a photo of a photo. The quality is not very good. But it is something that might help you. It is a photo of Pan and me.'

Gianni swallowed. *A photo of Pan.* Was it possible he could get definite confirmation this man at Safe Animals was or wasn't his father as easily as that? And how did that make him feel? What if this Pan wasn't the right Pan? Where did he start to look after that?

The idea that he might have to go back to a blind woman in Episkepsi for more hocus pocus seemed ridiculous.

'Gianni,' his mother said when he didn't immediately respond.

'Yes.'

'Did you hear what I said?'

'Send me the photo,' he told her. 'I will let you know.'

28

EPISKEPSI

'You know this is insane, right?' Gabby said as she held the wriggling baby in the air. They had just got out of the Fiat Doblò on the outskirts of the village and Eve wrapped her sarong around her body to turn it into a baby carrier.

'To be really truthful, I thought strapping a few-weeks-old baby into a makeshift car seat was the real insanity. I'm so glad your neighbour had a proper one in the end so we didn't have to use that builder's bucket.'

She wasn't tying this right at all. Pan had made it look so easy when they'd practiced.

'That *was* lucky, wasn't it?' Gabby said, smiling at the baby as his face creased up into the expression it wore as a prelude to screaming. 'If Lola wasn't more than seventy-five years old, I would be holding her under suspicion of being the mother.'

'I'm not doing this right,' Eve said in frustration.

It was very hot already and Gabby and Eve had been tasked by Pan to 'walk the village with the baby looking adorable' while he and Ben and the two other volunteers managed the sanctuary. It was sizzling in temperature, the road dusty and hot under their sandals, not a hint of breeze, cats taking a nap in any nook of shade they could find.

Finally she tied a tight knot and gave the fabric a tug.

'We can't take ownership of this situation for long,' Gabby said. 'I mean, how long can you keep a baby that isn't yours until it turns from "fostering" to "kidnapping"?'

'I did say we should call the authorities but Pan made it sound as if we would be sentencing the baby to a life where he was destined to be the Artful Dodger.'

Gabby laughed. 'Pan wants to look after everyone and everything. And if we lose an animal he cries harder than the baby.'

Eve put her hands around the straps of faux baby-carrier like it might be a parachute harness she was clipped into. 'OK, pop him in but, you know, don't let go until I say. Or be ready to catch. We don't want him dropping straight out of the bottom.'

A frantic minute passed with the baby's arms and legs being adjusted into the relevant holes, much to his chagrin, but finally he was in position, facing forward in the long black polo neck Pan had cut down to not-really-the-right-size until they got a baby-gro.

'He looks like a miniature Greek *yiayia*,' Gabby remarked as they started to walk down the hill where they had left the van. 'Baby Yiayia!'

'Baby Grandmother isn't a very cute name. And you are cute, aren't you?' Eve said, stroking the fine dark hair on the baby's head. She gently nudged Gabby's arm. 'So, how are you feeling today?'

'Wiped out from the wedding and no sleep. Wondering why I'm minding a baby in the few hours I have before I need to be somewhere else.'

'Any news on these trustees and the visit?'

'No and the whole cloak and dagger thing is getting on my nerves now. I get that they have to be confident in whoever is in charge but I've been here almost a year now and we're busier than ever with strays.' Gabby sighed. 'Not that that's a good thing but it shows there's a need for the work we do.'

Gabby sounded so impassioned. Something she had never sounded looking after Felix and Titania and handling Felix and Titania's carbon-neutral diet. Eve hoped that this visit was nothing but a tick-box exercise and not a deep dive into Gabby's management prowess. However, if it *was* the latter, she had no doubt Gabby was going to pass their tests with flying colours. Anyone who could teach geese to do 'The Electric Slide' had to be doing something right!

'And now that work includes looking after stray babies,' Eve answered.

'That has never happened before, that I know of,' Gabby admitted.

'Something else that hasn't happened before is Ben having some kind of almost panic attack,' Eve said, stepping carefully as a pale-yellow butterfly landed in her path.

'He was really worried about you when you took off last night. He made me text you even though I tried to tell him you'd be OK.'

'He tried to make light of it but—'

'Yabby! *Ela!* Yabby!'

'Oh, God, it's Vasiliki,' Gabby whispered, turning her face away. 'Don't let her see me, we'll never get away.'

'But aren't we supposed to be showing the baby to the village in the hope that the mother is here and she will see how cute he is and have second thoughts about having left him, or at least look to seek help?'

'Yes, but she doesn't like me,' Gabby said.

'Why not?'

'Because... I sat in the wrong seat once at the post office.'

Eve wasn't even going to pretend she understood but she was going to do what she had promised Pan. And if it all came to nothing, they would call the authorities and someone other than people with zero experience of the needs of babies would be put in charge.

'Come on,' she urged. 'We'll ask Vasiliki for help. She knows everyone, doesn't she?'

'She *bosses* everybody is what she does.'

'Smile,' Eve said. 'And be nice.'

29

SAFE ANIMALS SANCTUARY, EPISKEPSI

Gianni sat inside his car in the car park of the animal shelter and silently debated with himself. Should he go in? Should he stay away and take more time? Should he confront Pan? Should he not? He picked his phone up from the console and looked again at the photograph his mother had sent him. Yes, it was poor quality, as you would expect from something that was old and made with a camera lacking current technologies but there was no doubt. The man in the picture with his mother was tall, lithe, olive-skinned and had a mountainous amount of thick, dark hair. The hair may now be silver but there was no mistaking Pan's eyes or his smile. Gianni shivered. This Pan, here at the animal shelter, *was* his father.

Suddenly the car door was pulled open and there was the man from the photograph staring in at him. Gianni dropped the phone and tried to collect himself.

'Eve is not here,' Pan said. 'She has taken the baby to the village with Gabby to see if they can find the mother.'

Gianni got out of the car, desperately trying to act natural. Except how did you act natural when your father was stood right in front of you? He was already tuning in to every nuance, watching the man's expressions, taking in his stance…

'You want to wait? Have mountain tea?'

'Do you have coffee?' Gianni asked.

'Ha!' Pan exclaimed, slapping a hand to his shoulder. 'Coffee will kill you.'

'I think there is more of a chance that smoking will kill *you*.'

Pan smiled. 'We are both risks takers, yes? *Ela*. Come try the tea.'

Gianni hesitated. But the decision seemed to have been taken out of his hands. Fate? Or coincidence? Whatever it was it was an opportunity being handed to him.

'I will try the tea,' Gianni said as he locked the car and followed Pan across the dusty gravel and tarmac.

* * *

This was the house he had been in last night. Where he had cast an eye over the stack of books and tried to work out from that what kind of man Pan was. But then the idea that he might be his father was underpinned by a shell picture made by an octogenarian at the very least. Now Gianni had proof. It was real. Now every detail mattered even more. The olive wood ornaments, the skimmed milk, the bananas and orange fruits Gianni didn't recognise. He wanted to know. He wanted to feel some kind of connection.

'We will drink this outside in the shade. The house gets hot if I do not close all the shutters and then we cannot see without light. Light is not good for the planet and it is expensive,' Pan explained.

His father was not rich. His father had to worry about turning on lights. Riccardo had hated the dark. Been a little fearful of it. When they used to go out and were coming back late, Riccardo would leave on every single light in the house. It hadn't mattered about the cost to him or the cost to the environment. He needed it to be light, so it was. It was in complete contrast to how Riccardo had demanded his final days to be. Perhaps his shutting out of the light had been his acknowledgement that the end was nearing.

Gianni followed Pan out of the little house to a tiny terrace area that comprised of a few roughly cut stones, a table made out of pallets and two chairs that seemed only held together with rust.

Pan put the cups of this sweet-smelling herb tea on the table and presented it with a flourish. Gianni sensed an opening.

'Like the best waiter. Thank you,' he said, picking up his cup and cradling it in his hands.

'I was a waiter since I was very young,' Pan told him.

'Really?' He needed to go slower, take his time.

Pan nodded, sipping his tea. 'For most people on Corfu there are only so many opportunities. Hospitality. Olives. Building. Fixing cars.'

'You could not build or fix cars?' Gianni asked.

'I can do all those things. But they are not things I love.'

'You loved being a waiter?'

'I still am a waiter. I have shifts some evenings at the mountain café near Spartilas,' Pan answered. 'The very best bit of the work is getting to know the customers.' He slurped at his tea. 'In the summer, so many people from so many different countries all over the world, coming to visit this little island in Greece.' Pan shook his head as if in awe. 'It is powerful to make connections with people you will most likely not ever see again.'

So, Pan was a man of many connections. Had he sold his mother a love story like he may have done to countless women from all over the globe? Maybe there were other women who had had his children too. Perhaps Gianni had siblings in every corner of Europe, and beyond.

'You make a connection with Eve,' Pan stated, a smile on his lips as he leaned back into the pallet chair.

Gianni felt his stomach tighten. *Did* he have a connection with Eve? It was true he very much enjoyed spending time with her but he wasn't here to find anything like that. And, even back at home it was not something he ever dwelt too long on. His days were full and his nights could be full if he wanted them to be. He was never short of offers but, so far, none of those nights had been anything to get attached to. He also wasn't careless enough to have doubts about there being little Gianni's trotting around Verona...

'She is nice,' Gianni admitted.

'She is very nice,' Pan said. 'But the very first time I met her I felt this weight around her. It is like she is carrying bricks on her back all of the time. I think she needs someone to help take the bricks away.'

'Her brother is not helping... with the bricks?' Gianni asked.

'Ben is a good boy. Deep in his heart there is nothing but good things. But he struggles too. He has bricks of his own – some of them he has made himself – and he worries that his bricks are also making the pile of Eve's bricks bigger and he does not want that.'

'You sound like you know these people better than your own family.'

Gianni held his breath, wondering what answer Pan was going to give. Did he have a family? A wife? Children? This house was definitely the place of a single man but that didn't mean Pan hadn't ever married, did it?

'It is a gift,' Pan admitted, smiling. 'To sense things about people without them having to say too much.'

Once again he hadn't remarked on the comment about family. Gianni couldn't be any more direct. But perhaps there was another way. Just then a cat jumped up onto Gianni's lap and began rubbing its face on his hand.

'Ah!' Pan exclaimed. 'I know just by Thalassa jumping on to you that you are a good person.'

'How do you tell that?' Gianni asked, petting the ginger cat as it started to settle on his lap.

'She is called Thalassa for a reason. *Thalassa*, it is the Greek word for "sea". She and five other kittens were found in a bag washed up on the beach. She was the only survivor. It was a miracle. But she does not trust. She will not go near to Ben. She will not be near Gabby or the other volunteers. I am the one she comes to. Until now.'

What was wrong with this island? Why did everyone seem to have a sixth sense about things? Did this cat somehow know that Pan and Gianni were connected? He shook his head. No, that was craziness. He needed to get this conversation back on track, talk about Pan's early days as a waiter again...

'Pan! Can you come?'

Gianni turned his head to see Eve's brother running up the track towards the house looking terrified. Pan was up out of his seat in a second.

'What has happened?' he called back.

'One of the goats is down! No one can get him to move!'

'I am coming,' Pan said, rushing off.

'Is there anything I can do?' Gianni asked.

'Relax,' Pan told him. 'It is something I think you rarely do.'

And with that last sentence imparted, Pan disappeared up the path.

30

EPISKEPSI

'Baby Yiayia needs honey,' Vasiliki announced to the group who sat on the thick stone steps that led down to an open space in front of the church, an old two-bell tower grey against the azure blue sky. Vasiliki had taken ownership of the baby since she had whipped it out of Eve's carry pouch but claimed she had no idea who it could belong to. *Maria has got fat but that is down to* louka-mades *and* baklava, *not a baby. Amalia would be a prime candidate for the way she behaved all summer, but she has gone back to university. Limoni is only twelve.*

'I don't think babies are allowed honey until they're about six months old. I don't know why I know that but there was something on *GMB* about it last year,' Eve said.

'Soft *English* babies,' Vasiliki said. 'This baby, he is Greek.'

The woman had said it with such conviction Eve wasn't going to argue with the logic.

'I don't know what I'm going to do,' Gabby said, sighing. 'I can't have a baby at Safe Animals. I've got the trustees threatening to visit sometime and the last thing I need is them to find problems.'

'There are other problems to find?' Vasiliki asked. 'You cannot fix everything, huh?'

'There are no problems. I just don't have time to manage a baby as well as work my other jobs.'

'Why you work other jobs?' Vasiliki asked, lifting the baby up and down and pulling faces. 'You like to fold towels at the hotel? To serve plates of *souvlakia* at Petra?'

'No. I'd love to just work with the animals but bills are expensive. My moped has its KTEO coming up and I really don't know if it's going to pass.'

'What's a KT and whatever other letters you said?' Eve asked.

'It's an MOT,' Gabby said.

Aleka, who had been very quiet since they helped her down the steps to sit with them, her trusty *tavli* board/fortune-telling tray on her lap, suddenly said something.

'Yes,' Vasiliki said. 'Aleka says, why you not ask for pay rise?'

'Well,' Gabby began. 'Because I also get my accommodation paid for. That was the deal I signed up for.'

'But if bills are more expensive then the deal must change,' Vasiliki stated with a shrug.

'You make it sound so easy,' Gabby said. 'But, you know, sometimes I feel I'll never be as good as the last manager because I'm not Greek. And I try so hard with the language but it's not easy.'

'I do not know why you make things difficult! Send email! Ask for more pay! If they say no, then you leave,' Vasiliki said.

Aleka spoke again and Eve looked over to see that the woman had made another picture, this time out of olive stones.

'What is it?' she asked. 'Is this something to help us find the baby's mother?'

'Please, God,' Gabby remarked.

'Aleka says this is for you, Eve. She says it is drink. But this time, it is with bits.'

Eve shook her head. 'It's the awful coffee from the hotel you work in, Gabby. Gianni calls it "dirt coffee".'

'*Ochi. Ochi,*' Aleka said, shaking her head, silver plaits gently moving.

Eve knew that Greek word was 'no'.

'It's not?' she asked the old lady.

Aleka spoke again in Greek.

'Aleka says that this drink, in her olive stone picture, it is new and different,' Vasiliki said, translating. 'I do not understand exactly what she means but she said "pop".'

'Pop?' Eve queried, furrowing her brow.

'Maybe it's not a drink. Maybe it's my head exploding after all this stress,' Gabby suggested. Then she sniffed, before leaning a little towards Baby Yiayia. 'Cancel that. It's the baby who's exploded.'

Vasiliki gasped and held Baby Yiayia up off her lap like he was Simba from *The Lion King*.

31

SAFE ANIMALS SANCTUARY, EPISKEPSI

'Can you feel anything?' Ben asked Pan.

'I can only feel one hoof. This is bad.'

'What do you want me to do?' Gianni questioned. He was sweating, his designer shirt drenched, the sun relentless in the field where this goat had decided it was going to give birth. Pan still hadn't seemed convinced of the pregnancy until the goat got up off the sparse grass and began to dig with its hooves – allegedly a classic sign.

'Nothing yet,' Pan said, his hand inside the goat. 'We need to give her a little more time. To see if she can do this by herself. That is the best way. If I could just find the problem.'

To see if she can do this by herself. The irony that those words had come from Gianni's father. His mother, young and pregnant with Gianni, finding support from someone else.

'Do goats have one kid at a time? Or more?' Ben asked.

'More,' Pan said. 'Ah, I think this is the bent leg. If I can very slowly, move this...'

'Well, how many is she going to have?' he asked, sweeping his hair back from his face.

'I have no idea,' Pan replied. 'There is not much space in here. Would you like to add your hand?'

The goat seemed to answer for everyone by making a desperate bleating noise.

'Is she OK?'

'She does not like me moving her kid's leg but... ah! There we go, two hooves together, I think this one is coming. *Ela, mitera, páme.*'

* * *

There were four goats in total, each one different. Black and white, brown and white, pure white with one leg dotted in biscuit-coloured spots and the last one, a good deal smaller than the rest, was mainly grey. Gianni had helped to get that one out while Pan encouraged the mother to lick her babies. Licking them at the earliest opportunity meant the mother would get the scent of her new-borns and bond with them more quickly, identifying them as her own. It had been an experience Gianni never thought in a million years he would be part of. Yes, his clothes were covered in amniotic fluid and unless the hotel laundry was better than its coffee, they would never be the same again, but he had helped a goat bring kids into the world! It was the wonder of life and nature right there. It had seemed a little too much for Ben. He had left after the first birth.

'Gianni,' Pan said. 'Bring your goat closer to the mother. We need to make her lick it.'

Gianni rubbed the still sticky fur of the little goat by his feet, but it didn't move. His heart stalled until he heard the tiniest of breaths coming from it.

'There is something wrong,' Gianni said. 'It is not breathing as it should.'

Pan was across the short distance at lightning speed, picking the goat up and putting his ear to its chest, its skinny legs dangling floppy and loose.

'Get the water,' he said urgently.

Gianni stooped and picked up the bottle of Zagori, wondering what to do with it. He unscrewed the cap.

'You need to shoot the water up his nose,' Pan directed, turning the goat's face towards him. 'Squeeze the bottle hard and fast.'

'What?'

'There is no time for whats. Do it!'

Gianni squeezed the bottle into the goat's nostrils as Pan held on tight to the animal. Nothing was happening. Except the kid's eyes seemed glazed, terrified.

'Is it going to be OK?' Gianni asked, suddenly realising that he was shaking. It had to be OK, didn't it?

Pan wiped across the goat's nose with the sleeve of his white shirt and then the kid bleated sharply, taking long breaths, beginning to wriggle in his hands. Gianni felt as if the weight of the universe had been removed from his shoulders.

'Take him,' Pan said, holding the squirming baby. 'Take him before he falls. Put him in front of the mother.'

Gianni took the still slimy kid and put him on the ground and then he stepped back to give the new mother some space. Pan was at his shoulder, both of them watching the scene. Gianni was still holding his breath. And then, finally, the nanny goat dipped her head, paying attention to her tiniest offspring, nose twitching, a long pink tongue unfurling to clean.

'Oh my God!' Pan exclaimed. 'My heart cannot stand any more of this. Where are my cigarettes?' He patted down his jeans unsuccessfully. And then he put a hand on Gianni's shoulder. 'You did very well for your first-time delivery.'

'How did you know it was my first time?'

Pan laughed hard then. 'Ha! Because I thought you were going to cry when you got goat fluid on your fancy clothes.'

His fancy clothes. The smart look Riccardo had always adopted and Gianni had mimicked. *Appearance is important. If you look good, you feel good.*

Gianni looked at Pan. From his work boots with the fraying laces to the paint and now blood-spattered jeans to the off-white shirt also sullied. The differences were clear, but both 'uniforms' spoke of hard work, be it through physical graft or the art of conversational deal-making.

'*Ela*. Come, we will finish the mountain tea,' Pan said. 'But this time we will add some *tsipouro*. We have both earned this.'

'What is sip-o-ro?'

'It is very strong. Alcohol. For our shock of the new goats. I can make it with coffee if you do not like the tea.'

Alcohol in coffee was not new. But Eve had also mentioned alcohol in boba tea, vitamins and new flavours. Already Gianni's mind was whirring with the possibilities. Was this the something he had been searching for to take to Barista Irresistible? The reason he wanted his mother to not complete the paperwork just yet?

'Ah, you have somewhere else to be,' Pan said. He had moved over to the gate now and was unlatching it. 'I was young once. Places to go that are more exciting than nature.'

'No,' Gianni said, shaking his head. 'I have nowhere else to be. Let us drink sup-is-ro.'

'Ha!' Pan replied, laughing. '*Tsipouro*.' He shook his head. 'You can tell you are Italian.'

Gianni swallowed and then smiled. '*Sì. É vero.* Yes, it is true.'

32

Eve was so tired her eyes were sore and itching. It had taken Vasiliki only a few hours through the Episkepsi grapevine to find Baby Yiayia's mother. And now the baby was in Vasiliki's care while she and other 'elders' in the village put in place a strategy to help the young mum cope with the unexpected arrival and create a plan to move forward. She and Gabby had then headed down to Acharavi to pick up some supplies for the new goats. Eve had thought Gabby was going to faint when Pan's phone call had come through. First a human baby and then four surprise kids. What was next? Vincent Van Hoff wanting to get married?

All Eve could think about now was getting out of her sticky and slightly sicky clothes thanks to a bit of spit-up from Baby Yiayia and luxuriating even for five solid minutes in a cooling shower. She mounted the staircase in Gabby's little cottage, her fingertips brushing the cool of the stone wall and could almost feel the water grazing her shoulders. In fact, was that the shower she could hear? She tuned in to the sound obviously in her head – ribbons of cooling refreshment calming her sun-kissed skin, soothing her slightly frazzled mind – and the scents – the minty top notes of the shower gel Gabby had, the citrus seeping through the window from the lemons growing down below. She was already feeling fresher.

Suddenly the door of the bathroom flew open and there was Gianni. Soaking wet. Completely naked.

Eve's brain seemed to be taking a long time to decide what she should do. So long in fact that somehow her eyes were leading a trail that was sending lots of other messages, none of which were 'stop'. Glistening olive skin, the light definition of that six-pack she remembered from the pool, the strong shoulders that matched his jawline and his dark hair, both kinds, a little curly now they were wet. Everything else she shouldn't be looking at was also as pleasing as the rest. And the seconds were ticking on...

'Sorry,' she said finally, her eyes deciding now was the time to find the wooden floorboards of great interest.

'No,' Gianni answered. 'It is my fault. Ben... he said it was OK to use the shower. I should have gone back to the hotel.'

'No, I should have called out or something...'

Was he covered up now? Should she ask? Or did she carry on staring at a particularly striking knot of wood that resembled the face of an Ewok? She turned her head a little. The athletic legs were still bare.

'Eve,' Gianni said.

'Not looking.' She was starting to feel even hotter than she had been strapped up to Baby Yiayia.

'Eve,' Gianni said again, his voice sounding even closer.

Did he *want* her to look? That was a bit disconcerting, wasn't it? Or perhaps a tiny bit *sexy*. The only bare parts she usually got to see on a regular basis were when the screens went up on *Naked Attraction*.

'Eve,' Gianni repeated a third time. 'You're standing in front of my towel.'

Of course she was. As her libido plummeted down from a planet not even Professor Brian Cox knew about, she stepped aside. 'Oh, sorry.'

She waited for a waft of white towel to whip past, gave it a few more seconds and then felt safe enough to raise her head to meet his... eyes. Definitely his eyes.

'You do not have the baby?' Gianni asked, moderately clothed now he had tied the towel around his waist.

Was that her ovaries calling? Asking for a same day appointment? She internally shook herself. 'No, the baby is in the village being taken care of by literally everyone. The butcher, the baker and the kumquat candle maker. Not even kidding.'

'You found the father?' He paused. 'I mean... the mother?'

'We did,' Eve said. 'It's a story that involves an explosion and Aleka saying the Greek word for "pop". Which is *krótos* by the way.'

* * *

Pop. Papa. Pan. Gianni swallowed. So much had happened today it felt like days since he had spoken to his mother that morning. And he had a dilemma there. She had sent him that old photo of Pan and he had yet to tell her that it was certain that he had spent time with him. As of this moment, he was the only one who knew Pan was his father and the anonymity of that gave him greater opportunities and flexibility. The pressure wasn't there. Pan couldn't reject him. Gianni was just an Italian holidaymaker who happened to be staying nearby...

'Gianni? Are you OK?'

Had she said something he hadn't heard or responded to while his mind was wandering? He shook his head. 'It is the goats. When I arrived on this island, I did not expect to be delivering anything but my opinion on the hotel coffee.'

Eve smiled. 'And you do do that in such a passionate way.'

'I do?' he asked, a little playfully.

'You know you do,' she answered.

This was a moment. He sensed it inside before he began to sense it underneath his towel... Perhaps this was another opportunity he shouldn't ignore. After all, this trip was as much about finding out who *he* was as it was about finding his Greek father.

'Eve,' he said, the nervousness in his tone catching him by surprise.

'Am I standing in front of another towel?'

He smiled. 'No. I was just thinking... if you would like to come to dinner tonight?' A second ticked by and he wondered whether he'd been clear enough. 'For dinner... with me.'

He swallowed, his throat suddenly dry, his heart ticking a bit faster. This was new. Her answer mattered to him. He really wanted it to be a 'yes'.

'I'd like that,' she answered.

Was that an affirmative? Or was there more to come? *I'd like that but... I'd like that however...*

'But...' she continued.

Here it was. He felt himself tense, brace for impact even.

'But I'll need a shower first,' she finished, grinning.

He bowed towards her. He had no idea why and quickly straightened up. 'I will leave you in peace. And... take my clothes.' He picked up the pile he had left outside the bathroom door. 'Seven thirty? Eight?'

'Eight is perfect.'

'OK,' he said. 'Eight.'

And now he was leaving... in a towel... wondering where he

should get dressed again. But he felt *happy*. He moved his shoulders as if that idea of happiness could roll over him like a wave. A date *he* had suggested, and judging by the way his heart was reacting, it might just have leapfrogged any other evening he had been on in the importance stakes.

33

Gianni killed the engine of his car and took a deep breath. It was hot tonight and despite having had a second shower and putting the air con on, he was still feeling the humidity. Or perhaps it was something else that was getting him hot under the collar?

As he looked out over the olive groves, a tabby cat emerging from the undergrowth, he realised this was the first time he had instigated a date – ever. Most of the dates he had been on took the shape of business negotiations with the added bonus of sex. He much preferred to do business in the boardroom, but sometimes blending work with pleasure was the only way to have any kind of social life. So, sometimes he said yes and usually he woke up later that night, or very rarely, the next morning, feeling perhaps physically satisfied but emotionally empty.

He switched off his thinking when Pan came into view. His father, pushing something in a wheelbarrow. In a different shirt to earlier, but still covered in some kind of muck, hair like silver candyfloss, lips moving in speech Gianni couldn't hear.

He opened the car door and got out.

'Pan,' he called and watched as the man stopped with his barrow and turned his head towards him.

'You are here again, Mr Italy. Are you looking to take a job?'

Gianni smiled as he caught up to him. 'I do not think I have enough experience.'

'Ha! Nobody *starts off* with experience. It is something you have to earn. Look at this.' He indicated the inside of the wheelbarrow where tiny baby birds were sitting in a nest, their little mouths open looking for food. 'I do not know what it is with babies this summer. They are everywhere.'

Gianni swallowed. 'What are you going to do with them?'

'The nest was on the ground. I put it back into the tree and I hid to watch to make sure the mother came back.' Pan sighed. 'She did not. And if they do not have food they will die.'

'What do you feed them?'

'*Gyros*. Is it not obvious?'

'I—'

'Ha! I am joking with you! We will start with insects and then we will add a little moist dog biscuits. But they also will eat boiled eggs and liver.'

'And how do you know what to feed them?' Gianni asked, watching the birds bobbing their heads about, orange beaks opening and closing, begging.

'You learn,' Pan said. 'Trials and errors. The first baby birds I rescued – I was eight – they did not care for ION chocolate.'

'You've been looking after animals all that time?'

'Before then,' Pan told him, 'the animals and I, we looked after each other.'

What did that mean? Gianni opened his mouth, rather like the baby birds, and went to ask but Pan beat him to it.

'So, you are not dressed for exercising Phantom or fighting off Savage. Do you go somewhere nice?'

'I am taking Eve for dinner,' Gianni said, unable to stop the excited anticipation from flooding his senses.

'Let me give you advice,' Pan jumped in, taking what looked like a bug from the top pocket of his shirt and breaking it up with his fingers to feed to the birds. 'You do not have to take it but... it is me talking from *experience*.'

'OK.'

'Do not waste time. Do not hesitate in life.'

That was all Pan said and when he stopped speaking, all Gianni could hear was the chirping of the crickets and a distant bray of the donkeys.

'Is that it?' he asked.

'Weighing things up, wondering, worrying, looking at every tiny detail... that is a waste of moments. Think quickly and act always on your initial feelings. You like Eve, tell her. You want to kiss Eve, kiss her. You want to—'

'Whoa, I think I am getting the advice. Loud and in a little too much detail.'

'And make sure that when you say something to her... if you really mean it... make sure that she knows you are talking from the heart,' Pan finished off.

Now he looked as though he was reminiscing. Perhaps this was the perfect chance to ask a leading question...

'Here is Eve now,' Pan said before Gianni could take the opportunity. 'She looks very beautiful, no?'

Eve did look beautiful. Her hair was loose, pushed back behind her ears, fringe light on her forehead and she was wearing an all-in-one that cascaded over her curves, emphasising each one to perfection.

'I am leaving with the baby birds,' Pan told him, a hand on his shoulder. 'Tell her she looks beautiful. Before you say anything else.' He pushed the wheelbarrow forward.

Now Gianni's throat was dry and suddenly he was feeling pressurised. The heat on his skin began to rise again. His father giving him advice on dating. It was sending all his thoughts off-kilter.

'Hi,' Eve said, crossing the outside space at the front of the sanctuary, a chicken now following her. 'Honestly, the chicken isn't coming with us. I just sprayed myself with insect repellent and it's like she's been bewitched by the scent.'

Gianni smiled.

'And here I am spending a fortune on Dior when obviously Deet will do,' Eve said.

Why was he hesitating? She did look beautiful. Overthinking. Wasting moments.

He took a step towards her, visually drinking her in. 'You look beautiful.'

Without letting his mind grab hold of the reins he softly kissed her on both cheeks and then stepped back again.

'Shall we go?' he asked, offering her his arm.

'Yes,' she said, accepting it. 'Before this chicken tries to mate with me.'

34

MEDUSA SEASIDE, ACHARAVI

The restaurant was lovely. From the stone floor and the flowing water under little wooden bridges lit up by coloured lights, to the decked area right on the white stone beach where the turquoise water capped in white was caressing the shoreline. They had a table right by the sea, a view of the beautiful orange and pink sunset as it finally turned in for the night. Soft background music perfected the relaxed mood.

The delicious sweet white wine was relaxing Eve too and as the temperature dipped just a bit, she found herself becoming less nervy. They had ordered a mixed meze of starters but in the meantime they were ripping up large hunks of bread, smothering them in garlic butter and olive tapenade.

'Have you been to this restaurant before?' she asked.

'No,' he replied, taking a sip of his beer. 'I walked along the beachfront earlier and saw it. It looked like a beautiful place to have beautiful conversation with a beautiful woman.'

'Smooth. Very smooth,' she said, smiling and shaking her head.

'What?' he asked. 'You think I do not tell the truth?'

'I think there is a lot I could pick out of that sentence if I had my psychologist hat on.'

'Like what?'

'Like you used "beautiful" three times.'

'It is a beautiful word.'

She couldn't help but laugh then.

'I could replace it. I have other words in English,' Gianni said. He cleared his throat. 'So, I was on the beachfront and this restaurant looked like a *charming* place to have... *intelligent* conversation with... an *alluring* woman.'

Eve laughed again. 'I don't know what's funnier. You saying "charming" like that. Or that you've called me "alluring".'

'What is wrong with "alluring"? It means you are beautiful, no?'

'It means beautiful with an air of mystery,' Eve said, her knife moving over the dark purple olive paste. 'I don't think I have an air of mystery.'

He leaned a little into the table and Eve got a closer look at those gorgeous and unusual blue eyes. 'I think there is much more for me to know about you. That is mystery, right?' He smiled, picked a whole olive from the small pot they had been given and continued the conversation they had been having on the way over. 'And also, I am intrigued to know what ice cream van will be at the summer show at your village. Will this Ted or Stanley tell you?'

Eve laughed. 'If you really want to know I could find out.'

'The way you speak of it I can tell it is important to you.'

'Well, we have to make the best of it in Brookly Heath. It doesn't do ice cream like Italy. I mean, your country is the ice cream capital of the world, isn't it? I want to know about the best one you've had. Or your favourite flavour.'

'Gelato talk,' Gianni said. 'We have not yet had *antipasti*.'

'Are you a pistachio man?'

'Pistachio?' He hissed as if she might have offended him.

'Not a nut fan?'

'It is almost as bad as dirt coffee in my opinion.'

'Chocolate?'

'I like it. But it is not alluring.'

'You're going to have to tell me.'

'It is a flavour called *zabaglione*,' he said. 'It is made with cream and a Sicilian wine. It is based on an Italian dessert from years ago and then someone decided it would make a good gelato.'

'See, innovation! A dessert with alcohol made into an ice cream. Like my idea for bubble tea with boozy popping bubbles.'

'Do you really think this drink is a phenomenon? Tell me.'

'Well, my students say that a good boba can change their day. Feeling depressed, have a boba. Celebrating something, have a boba. To me an alcoholic version just makes sense. I mean, all those fruity flavours and then the kick of alcohol. Imagine.'

'I am imagining,' he answered.

'But, you know, I'm a college counsellor and a part-time bar person not... Touker Suleyman.'

'I have no idea who that is,' he said as his eyes met hers, deep and intense.

Suddenly the air seemed to charge. There was definitely something between them, nothing forced, just something organically, simply *there*. And Eve liked it. It was both unexpected here, now, on this Greek island and something not quite like anything she'd had before in the UK. It was almost a feeling of recollection. As if they'd always somehow known each other on some level.

And then their food arrived. Steaming platters of *keftedes* (meatballs), *saganaki* (fried cheese) and grilled vegetables – peppers, courgettes and aubergines – slick and slightly blackened at the edges. Peppers in Greece, Eve had discovered, were not bulbous slightly misshapen affairs like in the UK; these were slender and flat, like European supermodels in comparison.

'You really like Greek food, don't you?' Gianni asked, picking up the platter of meatballs and passing it to her.

'I am getting to *love* Greek food,' she admitted. 'It's all so *alive* somehow. Like at the wedding, it's... I don't know, you can taste the passion that created the original recipes all those years ago.'

'Wow,' Gianni said, smiling as he put some meatballs on his plate next. 'You are *really* getting to love it.'

'Don't you love it?'

'I like it very much,' he admitted. 'And I find it interesting that this is something my mother has experienced and has not really spoken about.' He smiled as he cut up the square of fried cheese. 'Greek food should definitely be talked about.'

'How is your mum doing? Coping with your father's loss?' she asked. 'Sorry, if that's too much. You don't have to answer.'

'No,' he replied. 'It is OK.' He took a breath and sat back in his chair. 'She has always filled her life with work and lunches with friends and shopping... and more lunches with friends. When I left to come to Corfu, she was surrounded by over a hundred people and standing next to a chocolate fountain. I think she is doing OK.'

'Well, people process things at different times. Loss can be felt immediately, but also it can be boxed away or hidden, either by choice because the person thinks it is better to internalise their feelings, or by impulse: the brain knows the person can't cope with what's happened, so it blocks it out, shuts off the hurt for as long as possible.' She sighed. 'But it never works long term. The grief always has to be addressed.'

Eve swallowed. She had meant to be talking about Josh and Kit-Kat but now her own words were resonating with her. She had boxed her grief up. She hadn't talked about it. Not with Gabby. Not with Ben. Not Glenda. And she carried that around with her every-where, a weighty, overflowing suitcase full of unaddressed hurt that desperately needed unpacking before it burst its zip.

'Your Glenda,' Gianni began. 'She has kept her grief inside?'

'No,' Eve said, putting down her knife and fork. 'I mean, I don't know.'

'She does not talk to you or Ben?'

She shook her head, those gritty, uncomfortable feelings edging inside her. Perhaps it was time to vocalise them, or at least unzip a front pocket on the case. 'Glenda... she... cheated on my father as he was dying.'

After the words had tumbled from her lips, she gave a sharp inhale, realising the pain that fact still caused her.

'Eve,' Gianni said, reaching for her hand. 'I am so sorry.'

He was squeezing her fingers, so gently, yet also firm, reassuring. Tears were at the corners of her eyes, but she didn't want to let her anger at Glenda ruin this night, this first date in so long.

'I can't speak to her. About anything. I can't forgive her for doing that. Ever. I mean, what sort of person does that to someone you've been married to for so long? When they're dying? There was her out. He was dying, couldn't she wait five minutes?'

'Eve,' Gianni said, still holding her hand. 'Look at me.'

'Sorry, I really *really* don't want to talk about Glenda tonight.'

'It is OK... to feel this way about someone, someone you are meant to only feel good things about.'

* * *

It was Gianni's turn to feel confronted by this conversation. The way he felt about his own mother had changed significantly, not only because he'd found out about her actions, but because of the fact she had kept it all a secret. How could you trust someone again when they had lied to you over and over for your entire life?

'Sometimes it is hard to believe that the people who have raised us were young once. That they were learning just like us.'

He swallowed. He had not been planned for as he had assumed, not a longed-for product of his mother and Riccardo's love for one another.

'What mistake did your mother make?' Eve asked.

And that's where his deep thinking had got him. Slipping up. A miniscule comment and Eve, insightful as she was, had picked straight up on it. Was he ready to let anyone in? Was he ready to let Eve in?

'She... chose a man who was addicted to good coffee, absolutely committed to making his initial small business one of Italy's finest. That kind of commitment comes with a cost. You either realise that you have to warm up many meals when he is late home from work, or you get as involved in the business. Echo his passion.'

'And what did she do?'

Now he had changed the way of the conversation, she had stopped crying, tears drying on her cheeks. He was taking that as a plus on both counts.

'A little of both. She ringfenced some family time, she got on with the rest. But now she has no meals to warm up she is paying more interest in the business than I would like.' He sighed. 'We have opposing ideas on how to move forward and that is difficult.'

'What are you going to do?' Eve speared a meatball with her fork.

'I am... going to treat her exactly the same way I would treat a business partner who is not my mother. I am going to pitch her my ideas and make her realise that the company can keep its traditional values and the products our customers know us for, and love, but it can embrace new avenues too.'

'Good luck with that,' Eve said, putting down her fork and picking up her glass of wine. 'In my experience, mothers are never keen on being "made to realise" anything.'

'Then I will have to be at my most persuasive,' he said, smiling.

'And how does that usually go?'

She was looking directly at him now, a flicker of amusement on her mouth but there was something more sensual pooling in her eyes. He liked it. He liked it a lot.

'My way,' he answered. 'It usually goes my way.'

She widened her mouth into a smile, holding his gaze. 'Confidence is attractive, Mr Riccardo. But don't let it spill over into arrogance. Arrogance gets you nowhere.'

'With mothers?' he asked, raising an eyebrow.

'With anyone who might be open to persuasion.'

Gianni liked the way this conversation was going. There was a hot coal in the pit of his stomach sizzling and spitting, alive.

He forked something on the platter between them and held it up. '*Melanzana?*' he asked in Italian.

'What does that mean?'

'It is Italian... for the aubergine?'

'Of course it is,' she replied, shaking her head but grinning as she did so. Eve reached out her fork. 'Well, it is my favourite. But I'm choosey about the variety and I'll only partake if it's very *very* well-prepared.'

And now that hot coal was jumping up into his chest, sparks fizzing as she connected her fork with his and took the segment from the prongs.

'Preparation and no arrogance,' Gianni said, nodding as confidently as he could while his libido shot up in hot flames. 'Noted, human. Noted.'

35

POET'S CORNER, ACHARAVI

After their delicious meal – the starters, followed by *kleftiko* (lamb shank slow cooked in the oven) for Gianni and *moussaka* for Eve – they'd decided to walk off their full stomachs, starting with a slow crunch over the white stone beach and then onto the main street of Acharavi. It was bustling with families, couples, all with slightly reddened faces from the day's sun, perusing menus outside the restaurants or admiring cute keyrings and calendars of cats and Greek scenes. Mopeds were zipping by and the light sound of Greek music was in the air along with the gentle aroma of spiced grilled meats.

Wanting a little quiet, they'd decided to take a detour off the main street and found themselves walking along what was denoted as the 'old village'. Here they had literally stumbled upon this tiny bar in which only around ten patrons could fit at one time. It was all traditional stone on the walls and thick wood and bottles of spirits on shelves, quirky objects adorning the walls – beer mats, toy cars, pictures of The Beatles and Demis Roussos.

Eve had ordered another glass of white wine but the barman had given her that *and* a shot of ouzo. Gianni had ordered coffee and although he hadn't had high hopes for the quality, he'd made no complaints so far. Now they were sitting on little green iron chairs outside the bar enjoying the cooling night if not the presence of more mosquitos.

'Still enjoying the coffee now we have the scent of some burning to get rid of the bugs?' Eve asked him. The smoke was rising from the small black pot the barman had set light to as, apparently, the mosquitos didn't like it. Eve wasn't sure *she* liked it either but it was better than getting bitten.

'I would much rather be drinking ouzo, but I am driving.'

'I could get a taxi,' she offered. 'Or...'

What was she doing ending the sentence there? She'd been more forward in her aubergine banter than she'd ever been before but was she openly suggesting that she didn't go back to Safe Animals?

'Or...?' he repeated, his eyes locked on hers.

He had undone a couple of his shirt buttons sometime during the evening and that hint of collarbone was enough to be giving Eve flashbacks to his entire naked body outside the bathroom. Eve was starting to ask herself exactly why her default position was always to hold back. Except she knew the answer really. Because when she had given her trust it hadn't been treasured, it had been abused...

'I... am not very good at this,' she blurted out. There it was. Flirty, alluring Eve had all but vanished.

'Good at what?'

'Oh God, please understand. Your English is so good, including your grasp of subtleties. Don't fail me now.' She felt one sentence away from putting her head in her hands. Not attractive.

'We have talked about aubergine,' Gianni said, his lips shaped into a wry smile now. 'And, for me personally, it was not a conversation about food.'

Eve had sensed *something* right at least. 'And I don't usually do that. Haven't done anything like that for... a long time.' She sighed. 'Do you have... someone in Verona? A girlfriend?'

'What?' he answered quickly. 'No.' He shook his head.

Eve let a long breath leave her and felt her shoulders relax a little. Perhaps that should have been a question to ask before she'd accepted his offer tonight. But it was good to know she wasn't treading on anyone's toes.

'I have a wife,' Gianni responded. 'And three children. Two boys and a girl who has my eyes.'

'What?'

And then Gianni laughed out loud. 'Eve, I am joking with you.'

'It's not funny.' A chill suddenly crept over her. She was feeling vulnerable now, stupid, naïve, the way she had felt after Mitchell.

'Eve,' Gianni said, his voice softer. 'I am sorry. I did not mean to... You are upset.' He reached across the table and took one of her hands in his.

She tried to swallow down her reaction but once it had bubbled up to the surface it was hard to battle it back down.

'Tell me,' he urged, his fingers lightly tracing her knuckles. 'Whatever it is that makes you feel this way.'

Eve shook her head. 'I don't talk about it any more. Every good counsellor knows there is a time for talking and then there is a time for moving on, that bringing it back up only reignites the feelings and gives them power.'

'OK,' he responded. 'So, like with the grief we talked about. You have not put this into a box and stuck down the top?'

'You're not allowed to use my techniques against me. That's a hard and fast rule.'

She was going to talk her way out of this; that's what people who were good with words did.

'Then I will have to guess,' Gianni said, seemingly unperturbed. 'Someone has hurt you. In the past.'

'I think we should go back to talking about... what did you call it in Italian? *Melanzana*?'

'Eve,' Gianni said.

'Shall I go and get us some more drinks?' She got to her feet. God, she was really going to run away from this.

'No,' Gianni said, standing up as well.

He was facing her now, his hand entwined with hers. The hold was firm, determined, a solid grip that said he didn't want to let her go but that he would if she so wished or countered hard enough. This was a turning point.

'Eve, there is nothing you can tell me that is going to take anything away from the evening we have enjoyed tonight. Nothing.' He squeezed her hand and she blinked away the tears, breathing fast.

'OK, *I* will begin.' He took a deep breath. 'Eve, I do not have anyone in Verona. And I only *ever* do casual. I do not ask people to dinner. I do not tell people about my family or how I feel.'

His eyes met hers then. What Eve was seeing was the very opposite of casual. There was intent, a swirling mix of passion and something she couldn't immediately identify.

'I do not know what is happening here, with us. It is not the same. And I cannot explain it. Maybe it is this Greek island. Perhaps it is because I have time. But definitely it is you, Eve. And me. There is something strong between us, no?'

She was feeling it right now, holding his hand, standing only a few centimetres away from him, their only company the dark night and the light sound of music from another bar. It *was* strong. It was thrumming through her veins, it was pounding in her head like the intensity of a thunderstorm building up, ready to release that first powerful lightning strike.

And then it all began to tumble out like hard rain.

'My ex-boyfriend. Mitchell. He used me,' she said, her voice shaking a little. 'He made me fall in love with him... and then he used my work, my ideas, my dissertations I had worked so hard on, to get a job he knew *I* wanted. I thought that when we bounced ideas off each other it was simply that, a brainstorm between two people who loved each other. But he took my thoughts and he made them his.' She let the tears fall, slowly, with a sense of resignation. 'And the very worst thing of all was he didn't see what he had done, never admitted the truth. He got the job, he made light of the fact he'd even *applied* for it – nothing ventured, nothing gained, great money no matter which one of us gets it – and then he asked me to marry him.'

She shook her head, remembering that Mitchell proposing had been the moment she'd really known something was off. She may have fallen for his slick charade from the outset but as the weeks had gone on, she had started to be able to read his tell, that need to touch his top lip very slightly with the tip of his tongue when he was telling a lie.

'He never wanted to marry me. I went through his emails. I saw all the attachments to the college principal. My words. My work. All my ideas. I'd served my purpose and he was moving to London.'

'*Bastardo*,' Gianni spat.

'For a long time afterwards, I hated myself, not him. How could I have been so stupid as to let someone manipulate me like that? Why didn't I read him sooner? How could someone feel they had achieved something by using someone else's ideas?'

'I do not know,' Gianni said, squeezing her hand again. 'But I do know that I want to one day see this man and give him something much harsher than my ideas.'

'I don't trust easily, Gianni. And I trusted him. And he broke that so, so badly.'

'I understand,' he whispered, drawing her closer, the words warm and soft in her inner ear.

'I haven't... been with anyone since then,' she continued, closing her eyes and resting her head against his. 'Not even casual. I still dwell on it, still hate him, still have this bitter disappointment in myself.' She took a breath. 'I like you, Gianni. And realising I like you is as terrifying as it is... exciting.

* * *

'Listen to me,' Gianni said, edging her away from him slightly. 'This man who hurt you, well, he is not a man. He is not even human. And there is nothing wrong with the way you read a situation.' He took a breath. 'All night long I have been thinking what it would be like to touch your face, to hold you in my arms, to taste you. I do not know if I am interpreting things in the right way but there is something moving between us, like an energy.'

It was as if he could hear the humid air, as if it was breathing, crackling, pushing against his skin.

'I have not had this feeling before,' he whispered. 'And I am thinking that to be casual would be an insult... to us both.'

'What are you saying?'

What *was* he saying? This was not how his romantic encounters usually went. The path was always written. Dinner. Sex. *Arrivederci*. But tonight, he was lost, perhaps on the precipice of something so unlike anything he'd previously experienced.

'I am saying, I think you are special,' he told her. 'And I do not want to—'

Gianni's words got lost because Eve had brushed his lips with hers and it was the most sensual sensation, pulling him in slowly, divinely with each tiny intention. There was no holding back now, no denying his body's reaction to her. He kissed her back, full-mouthed, passionate and then he took some of the control, backing them up against the old stone wall of the building, a private corner only for them. It was torture for his mouth to leave hers but finally he dragged it away, his eyes burning with desire as he gazed at her, two fingers resting on her cheek, just in front of her ear.

'You are making it hard...'

'I know,' she breathed out.

'...for me to drive you home tonight,' he finished.

'Oh.'

'Eve,' he groaned, leaning into her a little.

'You could stay,' she offered.

'In a room with your brother?' He shook his head.

'A stable? I'm sure Phantom wouldn't mind sharing.'

He smiled. He had a hotel room. Even closer to here than Episkepsi. A beautiful hotel room with a luxurious shower he would later imagine them both in. But treating this as a casual encounter just like all the rest felt like disrespect.

'Savage would find me and perhaps take my whole nose.'

'Is bird conversation the new cold shower?' Eve asked, putting a hand on his shoulder.

'I did not say we should make a cold shower yet,' he replied, thumbing her cheek then brushing her lips with another light kiss. 'But I am going to be a man of honour and take you home.' He took a strand of her hair between his fingers, teasing it apart. 'Because I want to do this again. I want to... continue to get to know you. If that is what you want too.'

He watched her, trying to read her expression, his heart jumping around inside him, not quite sure how to beat next.

'I would like that,' she answered with a smile, putting both arms around his neck. 'Besides, I already told you I like my aubergine very *very* well-prepared.'

That comment and the way she had elongated all the 'very's, hit him straight in the groin.

He leaned into her again, looking deep into her eyes. 'I get it,' he told her. 'But just know that some things, they can be marinated for too long.'

'Oh, I hear you,' Eve whispered, pressing her mouth to his.

36

SAFE ANIMALS SANCTUARY, EPISKEPSI

'Mountain tea. For your hangover.'

Eve opened her eyes and the scent of herbs and olives and whatever this concoction was scurried up her nose. She wriggled into a sitting position in the bed. She took the cup from Ben and then straight away had to pop it down on the bedside table before it scalded her fingers. The window was open, delivering a blast of warm air for the rusty fan to rotate around the room and the scent was one of P20 sun cream which meant Ben had been awake at least long enough to have covered himself.

'I don't have a hangover,' she replied. 'I had a few glasses of wine and a couple of ouzos and that was it.'

'Any Italian liqueur?' Ben asked with a raised eyebrow.

'Ben!'

'What? Not even limoncello?' he said, laughing as he plopped down on the bottom of the bed like he used to when he was six and wanted her to read him a story. Dinosaurs had been his obsession and Eve had to pronounce all the names correctly or he got stroppy.

'I was back here before midnight,' she reminded him.

'Like nothing dirty ever happens before then.'

'Ben!' She was not having a conversation like this with her little brother, even if he was very much an adult now.

'What's the deal with you and Gianni then?'

'We went out for dinner and drinks,' she said. 'In Acharavi. We didn't get on a flight to Vegas.'

'Yeah, well, I know it's the first dinner and drinks you've been on since that douchebag Mitchell screwed you over.'

How did he know that? How could he possibly know that? Eve set her face to neutral and then picked up the cup to hide the expression in case she slipped.

'I don't know what you mean, Ben. You're going to need to expand.' Her words were echoing around the mug and she was already regretting going down this path. She wasn't sure she was strong enough to pull off the bravado.

'Really? OK, so fact one, you're at college from eight in the morning until at least five. You supervise crochet club and LGBTQ+ club there, or at least that's what you told me. And you work at the pub at least five nights a week, meaning by the time you've caught up on *Money Heist* there's no space for dates.'

Eve kept her exterior measured while inside, her stomach turned into a home for energetic eels. She didn't like the fact her little brother was picking her routines apart. It felt unnatural for her boot to be on his foot.

'So, is that enough expansion?' he asked. 'Want to tell me what the deal is with you and Gianni now?'

Eve sighed. 'OK, it was the first date I've been on since Mitchell. There, I said it.'

'Gabby thinks you date at home,' Ben stated.

'I never told her that.'

'Let her think you did though. Why?'

'Because I knew she'd worry if I had to admit that... my life hasn't moved on since Dad died.'

This was not something she had thought she would be admitting to her brother this early in the morning, in Greece, or in fact, anywhere.

'Wow,' Ben said. 'Maybe I need to shake Gianni's hand next time I see him. Didn't think you'd ever own up to that.'

She shrugged as if it was nothing. As if her admission wasn't rocketing through her like a firework, the realisation and the whole saying-it-out-loud part of it bouncing off each other. 'Owning up to things is hard. No matter what the circumstances are. Right, Ben?'

Ouch. Turning the tables. Was that an act of deflection? Or, by her giving something to Ben, was he now going to return the favour?

'Gabby hasn't dated either, you know. Not since that crew member on the rich family's boat.' Ben managed to avoid the virtual spotlight she'd thrown on him.

'The one who wanted her to become part of a throuple?'

'Guy was just trying his luck big time if you ask me.'

'Totally.'

'I'm just saying maybe you both need to be more honest with each other. Isn't that what best friends do?'

He bounced on the bed, up and down, up and down, until Eve had to put her mug down for fear the mountain tea was going to spill all over the duvet. 'So, again, what's the deal with Gianni?'

'Stop bouncing!' she ordered.

'Had too much of it last night?'

'Ben!'

'What? I have grown up since *Harry and His Bucket Full of Dinosaurs* you know.'

'I know,' she said as Ben stopped his jumping. 'I know you

have. And I know I sometimes still treat you like you're going to ask me to reach up for your Minecraft mug.'

'Sometimes?'

She smiled. 'OK, a truth for a truth? I'll tell you about Gianni and you tell me something I don't know about you.'

'Not even going to shroud the counsellor bent now?'

'I'm game if you are, Aristotle.'

'Hit me.' He folded his arms across his chest.

'OK. So... I do really like Gianni. We gelled almost instantly and... I don't know what to say apart from that.'

'Yeah, well, you don't need to say anything else,' Ben said. 'Your face just lit up like the Brookly Heath bonfire when they finally have all the Guys on top.'

Eve put her hands to her cheeks and found a furious heat there. She smiled at Ben. 'OK, your turn.'

She watched him take a long, deep breath and then he spoke:

'I think I fancy Gabby.'

37

SUNROSE BEACH APARTHOTEL, ACHARAVI

Gianni sipped at the coffee he'd ordered – another great one – as he sat at a table on the decked area of this small apartment complex he'd walked to.

He had been true to his word. After the heat of his and Eve's kisses at the little bar in the old part of town, they had held hands and walked back to his car – it had felt as alien to him as drinking bad coffee when he'd first arrived here. Gianni Riccardo shook hands, he didn't hold them. But as their fingers were laced tight, the thumping need to keep that skin-on-skin connection had been so strong. He'd never wanted to sleep with anyone more. And when he'd kissed Eve goodnight it had been very apparent, to him and to her, that letting her go, opening that car door, getting inside and driving away was a challenge of epic proportions.

But as well as all that physical distraction, there was another very different driver, a need to spend more time with her, clothed if they had to be, talk with her, listen to her. Perhaps share with her the reason why he was here on Corfu...

He shook his head. He still didn't know what to do about that. Was it weird to want to be around Pan like this? Almost under a subterfuge? How long could that go on for before people started to wonder why an Italian businessman was spending so much time at an animal sanctuary?

His phone started to vibrate on the table. *Paolo*.

But was it really? Or was it his mother again?

'*Sì*,' he greeted, picking it up and putting it to his ear.

'Gianni.'

It *was* Paolo. And he was whispering.

'Why does it sound like you are in a dungeon?' he asked, getting up from his chair and facing the sea view.

'Because I am... locked in the wine cellar... at your house.'

What was going on? Was there an intruder? His father had installed a panic room for that purpose, with so many supplies that, in there, you could live life to the full for months. Or had his mother *put* Paolo there?

'Paolo, has my mother gone crazy?'

'Possibly she will if she finds out I have called you.' He was still talking in hushed tones. 'I have locked myself in here. To buy myself some time.'

'What has happened?'

'She is signing the deal with Barista Irresistible tomorrow afternoon. 5 p.m.'

Gianni gritted his teeth. This was not what he wanted to hear. His idea so far was nothing but jotted notes and a couple of pages on Word. He hadn't had time to do full research. He didn't even really know if the mechanics of it could work in reality.

'*Merda*,' he hissed.

Perhaps it was time to bring Paolo into his thinking. Before this phone call he had been wondering if he had a split camp. Paolo had been so close to his mother while his father had been unwell and Gianni wasn't sure whether Paolo's loyalties lay with her or with him. He hated that there was division.

'What do you want me to do?' Paolo asked.

That question and the fact Paolo was holed up in the dark, temperature-controlled basement, hiding from his mother surrounded by bottles of Sangiovese – some of which were worth more than his yearly salary – spoke loudly.

'Can you delay it?'

'I have delayed it,' Paolo replied. 'It was supposed to be today. I had to invent a hospital appointment. I am sure she was suspicious.'

God, what had his business come to? Lies and deceit, so completely the opposite to the way his father had run things. What could Gianni do? Nothing. From here...

'OK,' he said, taking a deep breath of the sea air, watching the waves crash onto the stones. 'OK.'

'OK?' Paolo shout-whispered again. 'What is OK?'

'Paolo, tell me, what is your true opinion on this deal?'

Gianni heard Paolo inhale before he started talking again.

'Your mother likes to pretend she is strong, but your father's death... it has rocked her more than she is prepared to admit. I feel it is blighting her decision-making. The deal makes financial sense, yes. But there is more we could be doing as a company. I know, from conversations I have had with others in the industry, that Barista Irresistible are looking for something ground-breaking and are in first negotiations with some of our competitors. They want to target the younger generation. And I am not talking about the usual demographic of twenty-somethings, I mean consumers as young as twelve. Coffee is not lost to them, it is still appealing but they want something more, something no one else has experienced yet.'

'Like the way they are with bubble tea,' Gianni said.

'What?'

'Never mind. I'm just brainstorming out loud. Listen, if I send you some things over email could you spend your "hospital appointment" making some sense of them, then email me back and hopefully tell me I'm not crazy?'

'I wish to do anything but freeze underground right now.'

'OK,' Gianni replied.

'And what about the meeting tomorrow?'

'I will be there,' Gianni answered. 'I'm coming back to Italy.'

38

QUALITY GRILL, EPISKEPSI

'You are bouncing Baby Yiayia too hard!'

Eve, Pan and Aleka looked on – or in Aleka's case, had to work out what was going on just from the vocals – as Vasiliki admonished Spiros.

Eve and Pan had come to the village to pick up some paperwork for Gabby that had been delivered to the post office. To be honest, Eve was ready to jump on any excuse to leave the shelter for a bit after Ben's earlier admission about 'liking' her best friend. They'd been playing the truth game, but that hadn't been something she'd expected at all. And what she was going to do about it she still didn't know. It just felt a bit *weird*, her younger brother feeling like that about Gabby. Not that she had been given the opportunity to quiz him about it. Ben had changed the conversation pretty rapidly before making an excuse to leave.

'You're still calling him Baby Yiayia,' Eve remarked. 'We only called him that because when Pan dressed him in his jumper he looked like…' She stopped talking, realising that she was just about to criticise the very fashion of Vasiliki and Aleka and almost every older woman she had passed by in the village.

194 MANDY BAGGOT

'You think we do not get the joke? It is funny! We laugh! It is true he looks like a *yiayia*. He also has these deep creases in his forehead like he is always disapproving. It is the way I look at my grandson. And he is twenty-four.'

'It should be the parents who choose the name,' Pan remarked. 'Not us.'

'Gorgios is right,' Vasiliki said. 'And there is plenty of time for that. The village is offering help while the mother is reintroduced to the baby slowly, so a bond can be reformed.'

It all sounded practical but why was Pan being addressed as *Gorgios*?

'Ouzo?' Spiros said, placing Baby Yiayia in the crook of his arm and picking the bottle up from the table.

'There's not ouzo in there is there?' Eve asked, suddenly alarmed.

'*Ochi*,' Vasiliki said straight away. 'And no one is having ouzo right now, Spiros.' She sighed. 'Where is Yabby? Why she not come? I ask *her* to pick this up.'

'She is back at Safe Animals,' Pan replied. 'She does not leave until her shift at the hotel or Petra is due to begin, in case we get the visit from the trustees.'

Vasiliki tutted. 'You make these people sound like an invading army. I am certain they are not going to come in and start rounding up animals like they are prisoners of war. What is she afraid of?'

'Most of all she worries that if the trustees cut down the funding or stop it altogether then the whole shelter will have to close and what will happen to the animals? And if she loses the job, the one job she enjoys and the home that goes with it, well, she might have to think about going back to England,' Eve said.

Vasiliki tutted again. 'But the trustees, they are animal lovers. That is the reason of the shelter.'

'But people struggle for money now,' Pan said. 'All over the world there are having to be cutbacks. The first things to go are causes for charity.'

Vasiliki shook her head. 'Why does everybody think that the trustees visit for bad reasons, huh? Maybe they come, and they see things that are wrong, and they give even more money to put this right? To make things better?'

'Because this is real life,' Pan said, pushing up the sleeves of his shirt. 'Not a fairy tale.'

'What is wrong with you people? It is like you are walking around with black clouds over your heads waiting for the thunderstorm to begin! We are in Greece! There is always sunshine!'

'Gorgios,' Aleka growled, her fingers resting in her tray that today was filled with sand.

Pan responded in Greek. Eve attempted to pick any words she recognised from the ensuing conversation but as she only really knew 'yes', 'no', 'hello' and 'goodbye' – which were the same word – she wasn't having much luck.

And if Pan had looked downhearted before about the potential for the shelter to be closed, whatever Aleka had just said – and shown him in the sand – was far worse. Any trace of colour on his face had been rinsed away and his hand, holding the coffee cup, was shaking.

'What did she say?' Eve asked.

Pan shook his head and got to his feet suddenly, leaving the table and the outside area of Nikos's grillroom, and walking up the street towards the belltower.

Eve leaned over the tray and tried to work out what picture Aleka had made. It was a circle with a fine spoon shape and round fruits. It made zero sense to her.

'It is a cake,' Vasiliki stated.

'And a picture of a cake made Pan leave his coffee and run away?'

'Pan?' Vasiliki queried.

'Gorgios?' Eve offered, pointing to Pan's retreating form disappearing around the corner.

'It is a special cake. It is *Fanouropita*. Named after Saint Fanourios. Greeks make this cake on 27 August to honour him, but also we make this cake at other times to help us find lost things.'

Eve's brow furrowed. 'So you make a certain cake and it helps you find things?'

'Yes,' Vasiliki said, as if there was no truer statement in the whole world.

Aleka said something else, low and slow.

'Aleka says Gorgios was once like Baby Yiayia. But this cake, it is not about *him* being lost. It is something else. Some*one* else. She does not "see" any more than that.'

Eve didn't understand at all, but she was definitely curious. She took a sip of her coffee and smiled at Baby Yiayia who seemed to be staring right at her with those large eyes he had. And then her own eyes went to the screen of her phone. But there was nothing except her lock screen wallpaper. She swallowed. What had she been expecting? A message from Gianni as soon as he woke up? She hadn't sent him one yet. Though she had thought about it. She had thought quite a lot about him already, in between Ben dropping bombshells.

She'd never been kissed the way he'd kissed her. She'd never kissed anyone the way she'd kissed him, or fantasised so much about the places she wanted to kiss him. But it was more than just the physical attraction; from the instant they'd met there was an unprecedented affinity.

'Eve,' Vasiliki said, pulling her out of her daydream. 'Aleka has made *you* something with the sand now.'

Oh no. She thought she'd avoided being the focus of the picture drawing. She looked into the box and saw that the picture for Pan had been destroyed and now there was a rectangle divided into three pieces.

'Is this another cake? A different one? Do I make this if I want to win the lottery?'

Aleka spoke in Greek and then Vasiliki translated. 'It is not a cake. It is a flag. Three colours.' She pointed to each segment in turn. 'Green, white, red.'

Already Eve's stomach was churning up this description. She knew what was coming before Vasiliki finished.

'The flag of Italy.'

39

SAFE ANIMALS SANCTUARY, EPISKEPSI

The timing could not have been worse, Gianni knew that. But what could he do? Put this very new introduction to his father and this very new interaction with Eve above his business? Put it above the company Riccardo had started and built up into a coffee empire, everything Gianni had known and lived by for the whole of his twenty-five years? You didn't turn your back on something like that, something that was the backbone of who you had always been.

The problem was, if he left Corfu now, if he got embroiled in this new idea he had, creating a new contract, delivering a different concept, starting something from absolute scratch... would he ever return? Was he going to end this? Could he know that his father seemed to be a good man, was doing great things with animal welfare, but never go any further than that?

It was late afternoon now and Gianni was still musing as he stood in the car park of the shelter, taking it all in. The stone outbuildings, some of their roofs made from sheets of corrugated iron bound together with wire to keep them intact; the edge of the paddock, bordered with olive trees, silvery green leaves bright in the light; Phantom, Milo and Pnévma grazing; the roofs of the two cottages beyond.

'We will have to begin to charge you for the parking space.'

It was Pan, appearing from one of the sheds, the mother goat on a rope, her babies trotting along behind.

'How are they doing?' Gianni asked.

'See for yourself.'

He walked nearer, the mother bleating loudly, the babies hot on her heels.

'Can I touch them?' The kids were paying him a little interest now, stepping gingerly forward on their super-long legs.

'Of course!' Pan answered. 'Pick them up, rock them like human babies, they love to be touched. And Mama will not mind. She is close.'

Gianni didn't have to make the decision. With one ginormous leap, the brown and white goat leapt up into the air, and he caught it, staggering back and trying to hold it less awkwardly. All Pan seemed capable of doing was laughing.

'It is going to lick my face!' Gianni exclaimed, jerking his head back.

'He likes you,' Pan said. 'Here.' He put his own hands on the goat. 'Move your hands underneath his body, support him there, let his legs be free, like that.'

It felt strange. Him holding the goat. His father moving his hands around, advising, guiding.

'He is so relaxed now,' Pan continued. 'He could fall asleep at any moment.'

'Do not say that,' Gianni said. 'I have things I must do.' He paused for a second before carrying on. 'I... have to leave here. Early tomorrow.'

'Leave?' Pan queried, tightening his grip on the rope. 'You stay somewhere else on Corfu?'

Gianni shook his head. 'No. I must return to Italy.'

Pan frowned. 'It has been a short holiday for you. You have only started to get to know Eve.'

'Yes,' Gianni said, sighing. 'I know. It is not ideal for me to go now, but I have a problem with my business, and I need to return to try to fix it.'

'I thought all business can be done through the internet these days.'

Gianni smiled. 'Not looking after goats. Or convincing business partners they are wrong. Unfortunately.' The goat in his arms began to wriggle as if it were uncomfortable so he placed it down on the ground where it wandered a few wonky steps back to its mother.

'You are coming back? When you have made your business partner see things your way?'

Gianni looked directly at him, noticing not for the first time the similarities between them – the curls in the hair that Gianni desperately tried to tame, the cut of his jaw, the length of his nose – if not the tip which Gianni had got from his mother and his *nonna*. Pan was wearing his trademark shirt, sleeves pushed up to his elbows, smart, though still covered in the tell-tale signs of his work here. Jeans a little too loose at the waist, staying up only because of the well-worn belt. He lacked every refinement when compared to Riccardo and there was nothing in his mother's taste in men that tallied here except perhaps a strong will and a good heart. Maybe that was the only correlation needed...

'I do not know,' he finally said. He took a deep breath, the sunshine prickling his neck as well as the anxiety that was now crawling over him like a troupe of grasshoppers.

'You do not know,' Pan echoed in response.

Neither of them said anything further and then one of the baby goats shattered the tension as it broke wind.

'There is something crazy about him,' Pan said, coddling the kid and rubbing its ears. 'Goats, they are free spirits but this one pushes all limits. One day I will come into the shed and find him swinging from ropes like it is a trapeze.'

'Life would not be how it is if we were all the same,' Gianni said.

'That is true,' Pan agreed, matching his gaze.

Should he tell him? Now? They were alone here apart from the goats. Gianni was leaving anyway. It would be a shock but Pan could run from it or not run from it.

'Well,' Pan began before Gianni could say anything else. 'Eve is not here right now. She has gone with Gabby to try to catch two lizards.'

Gianni didn't understand. 'Lizards? But there are lizards here, wild ones; I have seen them, on the walls, on plants at my hotel.'

'Yes,' Pan agreed. 'But these two are originally from Germany. They are pets. They have escaped from the owners who took them sightseeing.' He rolled his eyes. 'If they are not found it could cause chaos in the ecosystem. They will eat lizards that are meant to be here, they will breed and make babies with three heads that are *not* meant to be here. Big problem.'

'OK,' Gianni replied.

'OK?'

'Well, it is not OK for the island... or the lizards but—'

'What time do you leave tomorrow?' Pan interrupted. 'You change at Athens?'

Gianni shook his head. 'There is a direct flight to Verona at 6 a.m.'

'A direct flight,' Pan said, surprised. 'When I was your age, there was very little direct from Corfu to anywhere.'

The mother goat seemed to be getting restless, thumping her hooves into the earth.

'She is struggling,' Pan said. 'Not wanting to exercise. Some-times when mothers have a baby they think that their job is done, that the kids do not need them. But this is far from the truth.'

'Yeah,' Gianni replied, swallowing a lump in his throat.

'Exactly like with Baby Yiayia.' He shook his head. 'Perhaps it would have been best to hand him over to the authorities.'

'What makes you say that?'

'Because deep down he will always know that his parents did not want him, even if a solution can be reached.'

Gianni inhaled deeply before responding. 'We do not know he was not wanted. We only know that his mother is finding things hard. What if he does not ever know what happened to him? What if he goes on to be brought up in a stable home with this whole village around him, supporting him?'

'Well,' Pan said. 'You cannot change history. It is fact. His mother let her cousin put him in a box. His father... he is nowhere to be seen.'

Gianni's heart was racing now. This was his in. 'What if... his father does not even know he exists?'

He could hear his heart in his ears; it was thumping, whoosh-ing, overpowering everything else, even the impatience of the mother goat clattering her hooves.

Then Pan made his reply. 'Maybe he has not been told in words by the mother. But, if he put himself in that position, if he loved deeply enough to create a chance of this happening then some-where in his heart there is a part of him that must realise there was potential for this.'

Gianni was holding his breath now, so many thoughts and feel-ings in combat with each other. What was he supposed to make of that? How was he meant to stand here knowing that Pan *had* put himself in that position, with his mother, and Gianni wasn't just potential, he was a fully formed reality.

'I should go,' he said, retreating a step with his feet, a thousand miles with his heart.

'You want me to tell Eve you came by?' Pan asked.

'No,' he answered. 'I will... call her.'

Unable to manage anything else, Gianni got back into his car and slammed the door shut. He closed his eyes and tried to stop the white noise invading his brain – the crashing of the sea from earlier, the cicadas, the hooves of the goat.

He leapt in his seat when knuckles rapped the window. Pan was there, looking in at him. Gianni had no choice but to lower the window.

'The lizards are in Old Perithia,' Pan said, the goat still in his charge, the kids bleating by her side.

'What?' he asked, his mind scrambled like well-beaten eggs.

'The lizards that have escaped! And Eve and Gabby. They are at Old Perithia.' He pointed away from where they were, his finger directed more to the sky than the earth.

'OK,' Gianni said, nodding, still not fully computing. He went to put the window back up.

'Gianni,' Pan said.

He'd pronounced it with a 'y' again. 'It's Gianni,' he corrected.

'*Signomi*,' Pan said. He took a breath. 'Sorry.'

The silence seemed to somehow intensify between them. Was that it? Had Pan been going to say something more? Or was 'sorry' what he'd wanted to say? Sorry for what?

The mother goat let out a guttural groan and launched a hoof at Gianni's car door.

'I must go,' Pan said, steering her away, the goats scattering briefly before regrouping around their mother. '*Yassas*.' He turned from the car.

'*Ciao*,' Gianni finished.

40

OLD PERITHIA

'Who takes two lizards on a minibus?' Eve asked, putting another container of strawberries and sliced peeled cucumber under a bush.

'Eve, you've been saying that for the past two hours,' Gabby said, hands grappling the undergrowth, bamboo cane stabbing the ground to ward off any snakes caught unawares. 'And you know their names are Tony and Brenda. The owners, not the chameleons. I don't actually know what the chameleons are called. Perhaps we should have asked.'

Two hours they had been looking for what were actually chameleons and although Tony and Brenda had said they'd started out as green-coloured, chances were they could be brown now to match the dry, split ground or golden yellow to blend in with the jars of local honey on sale here at this used-to-be-abandoned village. From what she could see from trekking over cobbled paths, the village was now overflowing with tourists, if not quite back to being populated as it had been years before. There were five tavernas in all, each having tempting dishes on menus hanging from the stone walls or written in chalk on the blackboards, covered wooden tables under vines, cushions on stone seating areas and plates of meats, pastas and vegetables arriving from the kitchens. Eve's stomach gave a lurch then; hunting reptiles was hungry work.

'Have you ever successfully found escaped chameleons before?' Eve asked as Gabby pushed her way through hay-like grass that was almost up to their waists.

'What do you think?' Gabby replied, curls swinging. 'It's a fruitless exercise really.'

'I wouldn't say that,' Eve said, her eyes going to the container of watermelon slices and grapes she was cradling for the next drop off point.

'I mean this is like looking for one particular grain of sand on a beach.'

Eve frowned. 'I thought you said the chameleons were big. Like sixteen inches.'

'They are but, look at this village, and the mountainside and the people. They're reptiles. They aren't going to be just sitting outside Taverna Evdokia ordering a Mythos, are they? They're going to run and hide and wait for everyone to stop interfering. Make a break for it while they can.'

Gabby stabbed her bamboo cane at the ground with the grunt of a desperate Wimbledon player. Was this conversation still about chameleons?

'Gabby, are you OK?' Eve asked, coming up alongside her.

'Yes,' she replied but her expression alone was challenging that answer. 'No.'

And there it was.

'You're not still worried about this trustee visit, are you?' she asked. 'Because Vasiliki really seemed like she was worried about you worrying. And I said you would call her.'

'That woman doesn't like me. She's always telling me I don't speak enough Greek. And she interferes as if everything that happens in or even *near* Episkepsi is her business!'

'I think she could help you with these trustees if you let her.'

'That would be showing the trustees that I can't cope.' She prodded her cane into some tall grass. 'And that's the last thing I want. Because I want them to accept me and I want to keep my job.'

'There's nothing wrong in asking for help, Gabby. I keep reminding Ben of that.'

'But Ben's doing OK now,' Gabby stated. 'Isn't he?'

'I hope so,' Eve said. 'But you can never really know with Ben. He always keeps things in, holds back, diverts his true emotions. He masks.' She took a deep breath. 'I know there's something he isn't telling me. I'm only hoping it doesn't involve steeplechases at Newton Abbot.'

Ben's gambling had been so very destructive to the whole family. It had crippled him, financially, emotionally and mentally. It had taken everything he had, everything he had worked for, and set it on fire. And just recalling those very worst of times when her brother had been at his lowest ebb, then going through it all over again when he relapsed, was all still so tender.

'I don't think it's that,' Gabby said with a shake of her head.

'No?' Eve asked. 'Has he said something to you?'

'Not anything specific, but gambling, it wasn't the vibe I was catching.'

'What vibe were you catching?'

'I don't know,' Gabby answered. 'But I got the feeling something might have happened at work. With his friend, Charlie.'

'What did he say?'

'He didn't say anything direct, but he just sounded a bit off when I mentioned Charlie.'

A bit off. It was barely anything to work with. But even before they'd lost their dad Ben was a sensitive soul who had never seemed truly prepared for life's harsh realities. He always wanted to believe the best in people and usually, when people found out his softness, it was never equally reciprocated and, at worst, it was taken advantage of. Was it any wonder he now retreated inside his shell when it came to admitting mistakes or needing help? Perhaps they were more alike than Eve had ever realised.

'Ooh, I see something!' Gabby exclaimed, shielding her eyes from the sun, and looking past the empty, roofless but beautiful stone building nearest to them.

'Is it one of the chameleons?'

'Not unless it's become six foot tall and is channelling shades of blue. I'd say it was Gianni.'

It was Eve's turn to change colour, predominantly red.

41

FOROS TAVERNA, OLD PERITHIA

'*Yamas*,' Eve said, raising her glass and clinking it with Gianni's as they sat at a table outside Foros Taverna. There were green vines dangling from above them as well as a fan, its blades set to warp speed, delivering what breeze it could manage. It was still light, but the sky was morphing into that pinky purple stage it got to before the sun was completely extinguished. The lights from the tavernas were casting the old village in a warming haze you could see the moths leaping into.

'*Yamas*,' Gianni replied, taking a sip of his drink.

He didn't feel in a very celebratory mood. He was here to deliver the news that he was leaving for Italy in the morning, just when they had spent the most wonderful evening together. Whatever it was they shared, a deep mutual attraction, a thread of similar values, he was about to cast a big cloud of doubt over it. Because when he got back to Italy, he knew the business would take over again – as it always had. Corfu would be far away, he would have enough distraction to push Pan's existence to the very back of his mind, his life would be stable again. If he could forget...

'I can't tell you how relieved I am we caught one of the chameleons,' Eve said.

He smiled. She had been flushed when he'd arrived, carrying a container of fruit pieces as if they were precious jewels and then Gabby had got a call from someone saying a chameleon was hiding out in the lavender at a guesthouse around the other side of the village. By the time they had sprinted around there, Brenda and Tony had caught their pet and it was back into its carry container.

'But, you know, we can't really celebrate until we get the other one back. If this was a hostage situation you wouldn't just give up on the second twin, would you?'

'I guess not,' he replied.

'You *guess* not?'

'I am sorry,' he said quickly. 'My mind. It is not here.'

'Oh,' Eve said. 'Well, that was honest at least. Do I need to order something stronger than ginger beer for this conversation?'

'What?'

'Is this the talk we're going to have that starts with "I had a great time last night but"?'

'But what?' Gianni asked.

'I don't know. You've realised that the peak of last night was the grilled peppers and not anything else we shared?'

He smiled. 'The peppers *were* exquisite.'

Eve sighed, not smiling at what was supposed to be a joke. Maybe he just needed to get this over with.

'There is no easy way to say this and I wish it had not happened this way but... I have to leave tomorrow. To go back to Italy.'

'Oh.' There was heavy disappointment in her expression and her posture, until she seemed to catch herself and she straightened up, resetting her mouth to a neutral expression. That was a position her mouth had definitely not been in last night.

'I thought I would be staying longer but something is happening with my business and I need to get back for an important meeting.'

'Is everything OK? You sound a bit on edge.'

'You are good at your job of listening,' he said, a finger grazing the rim of his glass. 'The meeting will be challenging. Like finding chameleons.' He smiled. 'But, I hope, at the end of it, to have reached a new decision about the future of Riccardocino.'

'Focus on how exciting that sounds,' Eve said. 'Not on how scared you are.'

'I am not scared,' he answered quickly.

'Tell that to your hand that's scrunching up the serviette.'

Gianni hadn't even realised he was doing it. He unfurled his fingers and then flattened out the tissue paper. 'I do not always do this.'

'What, assault napkins?'

'Why is it not easy for me to leave this place? Why is it not easy for me to leave you?' He gave an uncomfortable shrug.

'Are you asking me and expecting an answer?'

'Eve.'

'I'm still listening,' she half-whispered, leaning closer into the table.

He met her eyes, and that charged tension was right there again, spinning between them, challenging, thrilling. And then it occurred to him. Perhaps the solution.

* * *

'You... could come with me,' he breathed, taking hold of her hand.

'What?'

'I leave early in the morning, 4 a.m. But you could come too. I will have the meeting and some business, but I could show you where I am from. Verona, it is a special place and—'

Right away, Eve's mind was back in Episkepsi, and that sand drawing made by Aleka. *The flag of Italy*. This was insane! It could not be happening and it *wasn't* going to happen. She had got on a plane to Greece to see Gabby, to make time for Ben and so far all she seemed to have done was work at various hospitality establishments, eat her body weight in oven-roasted deliciousness and learn that mosquitos were not her friends. And then there was Gianni. Someone she had bumped into by chance and now, now he was one of the few people she'd told the entire truth about Mitchell to.

'That would be weird, wouldn't it?' she interrupted. 'I mean, we haven't known each other very long.'

'It would be weird?' He looked unconvinced by her suggestion, with a hint of dented pride maybe.

'Please don't feel you have to invite me to Italy just because we had dinner and after-dinner... refreshment.'

'After-dinner refreshment?'

Why was she saying all this? Did it matter why he'd invited her to Italy? He'd invited her to Italy! And whatever god Aleka was worshipping at the altar of, someone had deigned it worthy of a blind woman's fortune-telling sand image. It was akin to holy scriptures unearthed by Indiana Jones.

'I'm just saying I don't want you to think I'm going to collapse into a heap of desperate break-up-esque emotion just because you have to go and we felt something for each other. Briefly.'

'Maybe we should just have had sex,' Gianni suggested.

He'd said it so directly, those glorious eyes hitting hers with all the intended sultriness, that for a second Eve was caught not knowing what to do. But then her brain, or rather, her usually parked and wheel-clamped libido, caught up.

'There's still time. Four in the morning you said?'

He smiled then, perhaps thinking exactly like her, about how that scenario might play out. How sizzling that could be...

He squeezed her hand. It wasn't a touch that said he wanted to bed her, it was more than that, maybe *better* than that. Although those flashforwards of her undressing him before slipping naked into a swim-up pool were intensely distracting.

'Come with me,' he practically purred.

'I've been told that takes practice,' Eve said, faltering over the words slightly.

'That depends on how well-prepared the aubergine is.'

'Stop,' she said, stuck between getting hot in the knickers and laughing at the corniness of their eggplant banter.

'I am serious, Eve. Come to Italy with me,' he said again.

She couldn't, could she? There were things to consider. There was the fact she had known Gianni only days. Did she know enough about him to get on a plane to another country? Did she *like* him enough to get on a plane to another country? There was... Ben. She'd ignored a text from Glenda this morning. It had been a sarcastic question mark, presumably because she was annoyed Eve hadn't answered her previous text.

'I can see you are thinking deeply about it,' Gianni said as the light faded further and solar-powered fairy lights sparkled to life in the trees.

'I am,' she admitted. 'I really am.'

'It does not have to mean anything, if you do not want it to,' he said, still holding onto her hand.

'Does it not mean anything to you?' she asked. 'Do you invite a lot of women to jet off somewhere with you?'

She watched him hard, ready to draw on all her experience in identifying body language. Would he tighten up? Shoot a look to the left with his eyes or cover his mouth with that serviette he'd been scrunching up?

'No,' Gianni said with a fair degree of determination. 'It *would* mean something to me.'

His admission lifted her heart rate a touch and it made the decision harder. If she was only thinking for herself, because she had been brave enough to let him know a part of her she usually kept tied tight, it would be a yes. But she wasn't thinking only about herself. There was Ben. And she had brought him here.

'It is OK,' Gianni pre-empted. 'I get it. You are here on holiday with your brother, to see Gabby—'

'It isn't just that it's a holiday,' Eve interrupted, squeezing his hand. 'It's trying to be a good sister.' She drew in a breath. 'I know that I have to trust Ben; he's a grown man and he isn't stupid, despite some of the things he's done. Some might think it's safer for him being here, away from the temptations of things at home, that bad set of friends, but without me here he might go looking for those distractions in Corfu. And, if he starts looking, he *will* find them.'

Gianni raised her hand to his lips and placed a kiss on the skin. 'You do not have to explain anything else. You are a good human. I have seen that from the moment we met.'

She smiled then. 'I don't think I'm really cut out for hospitality though.'

'Serving dirt coffee and falling into pools,' Gianni said.

'I was actually talking about my inability to fold towels into the shape of swans.'

'Definitely you cannot ever work in a hotel,' he agreed. 'I pay extra for my towels to be made into different things every day.'

'Flowers... fans... phallic vegetables.'

'Now *you* must stop,' Gianni told her, his tone thick.

'Or...'

'Or seasoning will... start to crumble.'

'Sexy and hilarious. The perfect combination.'

He held both of her hands now and Eve realised that she hadn't ever felt this calm before. He absolutely excited her but sitting here, holding his hands, she felt so much stillness, like she was at peace with herself for the first time in so long.

'Bring Ben,' Gianni said suddenly.

'What?'

'Bring Ben with you, to Italy. While I am at my meetings, you can see the sights together. The arena, Juliet's house; there is a tourist train that goes around the city and—'

Eve interrupted. 'If I don't come to Italy, will I ever see you again?'

She saw his expression as he fought with the options. She knew the answer really. He lived in Verona. She lived in Brookly Heath. Perhaps if they'd had longer together it would be different.

'You have my business card,' he said, 'and my number in your phone.'

'Thank you, Gianni,' Eve said, reaching up to rest her hand against his strong jawline.

'For what?'

'For making me realise that there are good guys out there.'

He shook his head, shifting her hand, holding it tight. 'No,' he said, sounding a little cross. 'I am not going to let other "good" guys realise what a special person you are when we have not had long enough to get to know each other.'

He put her hands down then, reaching for his phone and tapping at the screen.

'What are you doing?' she asked.

'I am booking two more seats on the plane to Verona tomorrow morning.'

'Gianni!'

'Give the idea more thought, Eve. Give thought to the idea of us being more than the very little we have explored so far. Ask Ben. Tell him the tourist train is a bit bumpy and cheesy but our ice cream is the best in the world.'

Eve shook her head. 'You're crazy.'

'And sexy,' he reminded her. 'And hilarious. Like you said.'

She lost those gorgeous eyes to the screen as he carried on tapping.

'But what if you're wasting your money?'

He raised his head then, one eyebrow moving before his lips did. 'Ah, but what if I am not?'

42

ALMYROS

It was three minutes to four the next morning and Gianni hadn't really slept at all. It was freezing in his room, the air-conditioning unable to make it anything but Arctic for some reason but there was nothing he could do about it now. He was leaving... in three minutes.

He sipped his coffee – still adequate at best – and looked at his phone again. What was he expecting? Yes, Eve might have kissed him hard last night and held him tight but there had been sadness tainting her tone. It had still been a goodbye. He was competing with Ben and Eve's relationship and her need to protect him. It was hard to understand fully, not having a close sibling like that himself. But Eve was a conscientious person, loyal, dedicated. He would have expected nothing less.

Two minutes to four.

He also couldn't deny that he was looking at his phone as much for the time as he was for a message from Eve. A text to say she was coming. That she and Ben were on their way. Despite the fact he was going into battle with his mother and hoping to charm Barista

Irresistible with mere sketches of an idea, he wanted to spend more time with her, to see what it could be.

Still two minutes to four.

Suddenly there was a knock on his room door and any notion that he was being cool about his invitation went right up into the freezing climate-controlled air as he dashed to answer it.

Disappointment hit the second he saw the receptionist.

'Mr Riccardo?'

'Yes,' he answered.

'There is someone in reception to see you.'

The giddiness was back, flooding into his brain and floating it. He pulled the room card from the slot by the door and followed the employee down the corridor.

His good mood started to deplete when, stepping into the vast foyer space, he found it empty. Low lighting had been deployed given the hour and a slow hum from the fridges behind the bar was the only sound. Gianni turned to the receptionist.

'You said there was someone to see me?'

'Yes,' she answered. 'He is outside.'

Not wanting to give any credence to the 'he', assuming that it could be Ben and that Eve was not far away, he looked to the glass entrance doors and took in the scene. Definitely not Eve and not Ben either. Tall, silver-haired, a plume of smoke meeting the early morning air.

Pan.

The doors opened automatically as Gianni got close and Pan turned around to greet him.

'*Kalimera*,' the older man said, nodding.

'You have brought Eve? And Ben?' he asked hopefully.

Pan shook his head, frowning. 'No? Are they supposed to be here?'

'I guess not,' he answered with a sigh. And then he caught sight of something by Pan's feet.

'You are coming to stay here? At this hotel?' He indicated the rather ancient-looking duffle bag.

'No,' Pan replied, taking a drag of his cigarette.

Gianni waited for him to elaborate but nothing was forthcoming. A hornet buzzed around the outside lights, dazzled and disorientated.

He checked his watch. Two minutes past four. He needed to get going for the airport. It was a forty-five-minute drive and his plane left just after six. 'OK, well, I have to get to the airport so—'

'I am coming to Italy with you,' Pan announced. 'We need to take your car because Gabby will need the van while I am away.'

'What?' Gianni was caught between deep confusion and even deeper panic. *Why* was Pan going to Italy... *with* him?

'I have not been out of Greece in over twenty years. But I have an updated passport. I was meant to travel to Albania to collect a feral dog everyone say is a wolf. No one could catch him. Someone wanted to shoot him. They called the sanctuary.' Pan shrugged. 'The day I was due to leave on the boat, a fisherman saw the wolf-dog just walk into the sea. Imagine that? A dog just walks into the sea, no swimming, no thrashing and fighting to breathe when the water goes over its head. It walks into the tide and never comes back. It is like it knows that it is different. That it is not wanted.'

Gianni swallowed, not knowing how to respond. Still he had no answers.

'I do not tell you this story because of the passport,' Pan continued, dropping his cigarette to the ground and stamping it out with his boot.

'No?'

'The people, they did not know what the wolf-dog was. Was it this? Was it that? Where had it come from? Where did it belong? It was like until they had made the decision of what it was, it was crazy, it was weird, it was scary,' Pan carried on, gesticulating hard. 'But, you know, the truth was, it did not matter if it was a dog or a wolf, or a mix-up of the two things... it only mattered that it existed. It owed nothing to anyone else to be this way or that way. It was who it was. It was the opinions of others that drove it mad. It should do this. It cannot do that. Those behaviours, of the people, made it think "this is enough".'

'Listen, Pan, I do not know what this is about but my flight leaves soon and it is a long drive to—'

'I am saying... that dogs or wolves or dog-wolves, there are reasons they are here. We might not know them, or understand them, but the universe has made it so and we should respect that.' He inhaled hard, fixing his eyes on Gianni. 'Things that are some-times regarded as mistakes, it does not mean they happened without thought... without love.'

And just like that, Gianni got a head rush so strong it almost knocked him sideways. It was as if he could hear everything inside him and none of it was stable. His blood was on fire, boiling hard, the whooshing and pounding echoing in his ears. His mother had said something very similar on the phone to him.

'I know... who you are, Gianni,' Pan said simply.

Gianni felt as though he was going to be sick. Pan couldn't know, could he? This was Gianni's situation to control. Gianni was the one who decided when or even if Pan became aware of the facts.

'I did not know the very first time we met. But the second time... when I did more than glance at you.' Pan shook his head. 'I saw... pieces of her looking back at me.'

'I do not know what you are talking about,' Gianni rushed out. He put a hand to the wall, needed to hold onto something solid, keep himself from spinning.

'And then I saw pieces of me too,' Pan concluded.

Then Gianni *was* sick. Unable to stop himself from vomiting into the beautifully manicured hedges surrounding the outside area. This was too much. He wasn't prepared. It wasn't meant to be this way.

'You *know*,' Gianni said, his voice barely more than a whisper, his hand wiping at his mouth.

'Yes,' Pan replied.

Gianni was shaking his head so much it was beginning to hurt.

'You know,' Gianni started, 'that you... are my father.'

'Yes,' Pan answered.

How could he be replying so calmly? Like he was saying yes to someone commenting on the weather, that it was hot for the time of year. Like he was detached. Perhaps that was the answer; Pan *had* been detached. For all these years. And it was Gianni coming here that had opened things up, changed everything.

'You are OK,' Pan stated.

He was far from OK. He felt even more lost and in freefall than he had the moment Riccardo had passed away. How was that possible? And how was it possible that Pan now had the advantage, that Gianni was on the back foot? A hand landed on his back between his shoulder blades. He didn't want it there, couldn't stand to be touched.

'Stop,' he pleaded, straightening up, moving away and wiping his mouth with the back of his hand for a second time.

'I do not know why you are acting like you are shocked,' Pan said, coolly. 'You are the one who knew what the situation was when you arrived on this island.'

Gianni shook his head. 'And I am the one going back to Italy.'

'Without wanting to ask any questions?' Pan asked him. 'Without asking me for answers—'

'For answers?' Gianni scoffed. 'What answers can you give me?'

He stopped abruptly then. 'Unless...' Now, as well as shock, there was bitterness. 'Did you know? About me? Did you know you had a child, before I came here?'

'No,' Pan said, his tone finally showing some signs of instability, of emotion. 'No, Gianni, I did not know.'

'It is *Gianni*,' he said through taut lips. 'With a "g". Because I am Italian.'

He didn't know what else to say. His biological father was right here, springing this on him now, before he was about to leave, when there was no time to discuss anything. *Time*. Gianni checked his watch. It was four fifteen. He needed to get his luggage, grab his phone from the charging lead, return the key card to reception...

'We can talk about this later,' Pan said, picking up the duffle bag. 'In Italy. When we see your mother.'

'I do not think that is a good idea,' Gianni stated.

'Well, I am going to Verona even if you think it is a bad idea. If you like I can drive your car. I know a shortcut. It will get us there more fast.'

'And if I say no?' Gianni challenged.

Pan shrugged then. 'I will call a taxi. You can drive your car. I will get to the airport first.'

There seemed to be no other option.

43

IOANNIS KAPODISTRIAS AIRPORT, CORFU

'Maybe this is a mistake. Maybe he didn't mean it,' Eve said, the skin on her arms coming out in goosebumps as she stood with Ben outside the airport. It was five o'clock in the morning and they'd been here since four forty-five, expecting to arrive at a similar time to Gianni. The airport wasn't so large that they would miss him and at this time in the morning, even though it was summer, there were fewer flights coming in and going out.

'The dude bought you a ticket,' Ben reminded her. 'He bought *me* a ticket too. I think that means he meant it.'

'But he's not here,' Eve said, checking her watch again.

'Goat traffic?' Ben suggested.

She gave him a look that said she wasn't buying that. She was nervous. Concerned that being here, deciding to take a chance on this, was putting herself out there too much. It was the most transparent she had been in a long time.

'Maybe we should go back,' she suggested, shivering now despite the humid air.

'I am not taking you over that mountain on the back of this moped again. I could hear you screaming through the helmet.'

'Your cornering wouldn't pass muster in the UK.'

Ben laughed. 'Pass muster? Please don't say that to Gianni when you're in Italy. It makes you sound like Stanley from the pub.'

'Why don't you come?' Eve asked, toying with the tag on her cabin bag. 'You know, it will be fun.'

'You just said "fun" like you said "pass muster".'

'Ben, I'm being serious!'

'I know, you always are.'

Eve flicked him on the arm.

'Ow! That hurt!' Ben rubbed the sore spot. 'I thought you'd stop doing that when you hit, I don't know, twenty-six.'

'I'm twenty-five!'

'Just testing.'

'Yes, you are!'

Ben grinned then and jostled into her, wrapping an arm around her neck and pulling her into a loose supposed-to-be-affectionate headlock that was definitely going to mess up the hair she'd styled to look casual.

'OK, Ben, you win. Stop with the wrestling.'

'Listen to me, OK?' he said, giving her little choice in the matter.

'Listening. Also trying to breathe.'

'Go and have proper fun with Gianni in Italy. Take a break from being hybrid-sister-mum, OK?'

'Ew! I don't like that title. It makes me sound at least twenty-six.'

'I'm OK,' Ben said, his tone less playful and much more serious. 'I mean it, Eve. I'm OK.'

'OK?'

'Yeah, I mean, I'm not 100 per cent. But I'm getting there, you know?'

She didn't know how to respond to that. He was gently easing the door ajar. She held her body still, Ben's arm slightly laxer now.

'And... I'm not gambling again,' he said in a rush, as if it took real effort to commit that to the Corfiot air.

'No?' Her heart was battering heavily but slowly. She wanted to believe it was the truth, wanted Ben to give her slightly more.

'No,' he said more definitely this time. 'You don't have to worry about me while you're away, OK?'

He gave her another squeeze and then released her to right herself. She could already feel her hair was much more messy than casual. But right now, she didn't care. She reached out quickly and squeezed his face.

'Ow!' Ben complained, shifting away and almost knocking into the moped he'd parked just behind them on the road.

'Look after Gabby for me,' she said.

'She doesn't need looking after. She's literally the definition of "life management". From a three-legged sheep and a display team of geese and a whole shelter of other misfits... to that crazy woman in the village... to a freaking baby that looks like a grandma. Not to mention a hotel, a taverna and whatever else she makes time for.'

'Just, look after her. She's really worried about the shelter. I don't know, take her for dinner, keep her off Facebook. I'll be back in a few days.' She checked her watch again and did another appraisal of the road outside. Another minibus with 'Auto Union' and 'Simpson Travel' written on the side pulled up alongside them.

'You didn't tell Gabby what I said, did you?' Ben asked, now looking a bit sheepish himself. 'That, you know, I kind of, like her?'

Eve shook her head. 'Sibling loyalty trumps best friend needing to know everything.' She paused. 'Why? Have you... changed your mind?'

'Oh no,' he said with conviction. 'She looked really hot in those dungaree shorts yesterday.'

Eve slapped her hands over her ears. 'Can't hear! Cannot hear!'

Ben pulled her hands away from her ears and put on a soft version of his serious expression as exhaust fumes from a nearby coach puffed into the atmosphere between them.

It was then she gave him the biggest hug, one that almost lifted him off the floor.

'Whoa! Save that kind of energy for whatever hotel room you're in with Gianni.'

She let him go. 'Actually, he was talking about us staying at his home, which sounds like a palace. But I think he saw me getting excited about the word "en suite", so he played it down after that.' She shook her head. 'Plus, I told him I wasn't going so—'

'Well, now you can tell him you *are* going,' he said, putting his hands on her shoulders. 'Turn around.'

He moved her a bit and then she did the rest on her own. Pulling a small case out of one of the minibuses from the hire car companies, was Gianni.

'Go on, go!' Ben ushered her forward. 'Text me when you land safe and... send me pictures of all the tourist stuff... or his bathroom, I don't care.'

'OK,' Eve said. 'But you text me back, OK? No ignoring me or I'll call. And enjoy the horses but don't get too close to Savage and—'

'Clear off now! Leave!'

With one final wave over her shoulder, Eve trotted along the pavement, heart palpitating as much from the half-jog as it was from the feeling that this was a leap outside her comfort zone.

But before she had reached Gianni who, as she got closer, was looking decidedly sombre, someone else popped out of the mini-van. *Pan.* What was Pan doing here? He had a big grubby-looking holdall with him. Was he travelling somewhere? And then she had an awful thought. What if Gianni had given Pan her ticket? Or Ben's? She had told him she wasn't coming. He'd made other plans and now it was just going to feel awkward.

She turned around, looking for her brother, wanting to be able to sprint back to him without anyone else seeing. But Ben was already on the moped, helmet on, preparing to depart.

'Eve!'

It was Gianni's voice and he sounded pleased to see her. Swallowing away her doubts, she turned back around, smiling as he approached, pulling his case behind him.

'I... didn't think you were coming,' he said when he had reached her. 'Is Ben here too?'

'He was,' she said. 'He brought me. On Gabby's moped. But he didn't want to come to Italy. I think he wants a bit of independence away from his nagging sister and—'

What she was going to continue with got swallowed up – literally. Gianni pressed his lips to hers, putting an arm behind her back and drawing her close as he deepened the kiss.

'I am so glad you decided to come,' he said after he had broken away, still holding her to him.

'So, you haven't given mine or Ben's ticket to Pan? He's not coming with us? He's just getting rid of some old stuff in that bag? Are there animals in there? A litter of piglets?'

Gianni shook his head. 'No piglets. That I am aware of.' He sighed. 'But... he is coming to Italy.'

She waited for a further explanation. Because it was very odd if this wasn't an I-have-a-free-flight-to-Italy situation. And Gabby needed all the workforce she had with this visit still looming.

'Can I explain to you later?' he said. 'It is not a normal situation.'

'O-K,' she replied, her eyes leaving him and going to Pan who was hauling the large bag up over his shoulder.

'Let us go, yes? Before we are too late to board.'

Eve watched Pan struggling with the bag a little as he walked towards the sliding glass doors into the terminal.

'I'm not sure Pan's bag is going to fit under the seat in front of him,' she murmured under her breath.

44

VALERIO CATULLO AIRPORT, VERONA, ITALY

The flight had been short. A tail wind apparently and Eve was grateful. It was an almost full plane. Her seat had been on the aisle, whilst Gianni had been by the window of the opposite three seats. Pan was somewhere in the middle. She'd heard him charming a stewardess and getting her to help him squeeze that massive bag into the overhead locker. Quite the feat it had sounded like, even from at least fifteen rows away.

There had been no chance to talk, only a brief conversation when passing in the aisle but they couldn't really get into anything. It was more an it-won't-be-long-until-we-land, the-coffee-had-an-innovative-filter kind of chat. In a way, Eve was glad to keep it casual. It *was* casual. It wasn't entering into a joint mortgage or even purchasing a Two Together railcard, but it was the most commitment Eve had shown to a guy since Mitchell had destroyed her faith in men. She was acknowledging that, noting it was there and then, like the best meditation podcast, she was going to try to respond rather than react. This was an opportunity to see another country, a chance to be taken.

As they'd come to land, Eve had looked out at the landscape. It was different to what she'd been treated to on arrival in Corfu. Here it was flatter, wider, patchwork fields of varying degrees of green and brown not that dissimilar to England. There were clusters of houses, stone barns and trees, the vibe very much rural, not the city she'd been expecting. And now here they were, walking through a rather small and deserted terminal where it seemed theirs was the only flight arriving or departing.

'We can walk?' Pan asked, bag on his back as if he was a mule carting provisions to a far-off village.

'No,' Gianni answered. 'My house, it is a drive away. There will be a car waiting for us.'

'I will drive,' Pan said. 'We will get there faster.'

'No,' Gianni said firmly. 'No one is driving. My driver is collecting us.'

'You have someone to drive so you do not have to?' Pan asked, incredulous. 'Do you not like to drive?'

'Yes, I like to drive,' Gianni snapped. 'But my cars are at the house.'

You didn't need to be an expert in body language or be able to distinguish the 'fingerprint' of someone's vocal tone to realise that there was tension between them. And Pan was staying at the house too? This was getting more and more odd. Eve took her phone from the front pocket of her bag and checked to see if she had signal yet. Two bars. She would send Ben a quick text to say they had landed safely.

* * *

'Your *cars*,' Pan said. 'How many do you have?'

'There are sixteen at the house. They are not all mine. Some of them are my father's.'

Gianni's lips clamped together as soon as the last word was out into the air. This was so difficult and his brain was finding it hard to choose which task to give focus to. He was back in Italy – his home – but he was with two strangers to the country. One he wanted to show all the places he had grown up with, the cafés, the culture, the spots that held childhood memories. The other he wanted to hide away until he was ready to face that reality here with his mother. And then there was the initial reason for this visit. His mother's insistence that *her* plans were what was going to take the coffee business forward...

'Sixteen cars,' Pan said, seemingly caught between disgust and awe. 'And does your driver use all of them for you?'

Gianni saw that Eve was a few paces ahead, her eyes down on the screen of her phone. He took hold of Pan's arm and drew him to a halt.

'This has to stop, or it is not going to work,' he said sternly.

'What has to stop? And what is not going to work?' Pan asked, looking oblivious.

'I have money,' Gianni stated. 'I am not going to apologise for that. I have a driver for convenience. He has driven for my father for over thirty years. Yes, I could drive myself, or get a taxi, but then I would be putting a virtual member of my family out of a job. Davide has a wife, five children and two grandchildren. In Italy family comes in many shapes and it is very important.'

Pan snorted. 'Family is just as important in Greece. And I know, sometimes, the family you are given are not the people you end up choosing to be close to.'

Was that a dig? At Riccardo? Or perhaps his mother? Was Pan angry? He certainly sounded that way and Gianni was well aware that this situation could be incendiary.

'Why did you come here?' he asked, wanting to know. 'What is it that you are hoping to achieve?'

Pan straightened up, the bag on his back still across his shoulders. 'I want to see Valentina. And I want to know why she did not tell me that I have a son.'

'Not so loud,' Gianni hissed. 'Eve does not know about this.'

Pan shook his head. 'Still so many secrets.'

'And this stays a secret until I can... find a way through it,' he stated, glancing over at Eve, who was still on her phone.

'Find a way through it?' Pan asked. 'You speak like it is a path in the woods.'

'A forest,' Gianni said. 'A dark, old, thick, scary forest that time has forgotten about.'

Pan raised an eyebrow. 'You should not speak of your mother that way.'

'Is this a joke to you?' He brought his voice down a notch.

'No, Gianni,' Pan said, the 'g' distinctly pronounced. 'It is not a joke to me that I find out after all these years that I have a child. That he comes to me and I see the woman I love reflected back at me. I can think of nothing that is less amusing. But what do I do? I cannot change it. And so, I am here. To work out why Valentina would make such a decision. And to see the man she *did* decide to marry.'

A knot formed in his throat then. Of course, Pan had no idea about Riccardo. Why would he? The way Pan was pushing back his shirt sleeves now made it seem like he was preparing to arm-wrestle for his mother's affections. As though he still cared for her. Frankly, Gianni was surprised that Pan remembered her name. Surely she must have been one in a long line of tourists he had wooed. Regardless, there was no point in delaying the truth here.

'My father,' Gianni began. 'The man my mother married. The one who raised me.' He took a deep breath. 'He is dead.'

The words still kicked his heart, still made him feel like his foundations were rocky, that there was less substance and support in his life now.

'Gianni,' Pan said, his hand moving as if he might be about to reach for his shoulder.

Gianni stepped away, pulling his case with him. 'I do not need pity. I need you to keep quiet until I say it is the right time. I have a very important meeting later today and nothing is going to stand in the way of that.'

He looked to Eve, now finished with her phone, eyes on him. She was the brightest, purest light in the midst of all this. The way he was starting to feel about her showed that he was not closed off to matters of the heart. The business was so important to him, it had been the structure he'd clung to and he knew, going forward without Riccardo, that he could lead. But could he also love

'Is everything OK?' Eve asked as he caught up alongside her.

'*Si*,' he answered. 'Let us go to my house.'

45

GIANNI'S HOME, VERONA, ITALY

Eve had never seen such a spectacular house in the flesh before. This home was the kind that got its own special section on *A Place in the Sun* – the piece where they went to villas that could only be afforded by lottery winners or oil barons. In fact, it didn't look like a singular house at all. There were parts of it in one place, another section that looked as if it continued around the corner, huge lines of garages and a perfectly manicured garden comprising of topiary hedges, patios that looked like chess boards and fountains dancing in different spray styles that changed every couple of minutes.

'It is like Disneyland,' Pan commented, picking his bag out of the car and throwing it onto the driveway before Davide the driver could get there.

'It is nothing like Disneyland,' Gianni replied, closing Eve's car door for her.

'It is almost as large as the hotel in Almyros,' Pan continued. 'How many people stay here? Do you stay here...' He addressed this to Davide. 'With your wife, five children and two grandchildren?'

Davide did not reply, for Gianni was speaking to him in Italian.

He got back into the sleek black car – an Alfa Romeo – and drove it around the central hedge display which was a bit like an elaborate roundabout.

'Do you have horses?' Pan continued.

'No.'

'But those buildings over there... they are like stables.'

'It is a home gym and spa.'

'Much better than stables in my opinion,' Eve commented. 'No one ever says "let's lie back and relax in the saddle".'

'Exactly,' Gianni agreed. 'So, let me show you to your rooms and I will organise some drinks.'

Pan moved towards the marble-style steps that led up to the main body of the impressive house with its imposing pillars and large windows. Eve followed.

'Wait,' Gianni said. 'Not you!'

'Me?' she asked, turning around.

'Not you,' Gianni repeated.

'*Not* me?' Eve asked again.

Gianni took her hands in his. 'Forgive me, please. Eve, go into the house, look around, make yourself at home. I will be only a minute.'

'Oh, OK,' Eve said.

She stayed where she was, her shoe caressing only the very bottom step while she watched Gianni take Pan by the arm and lead him away from the house, past the flowering borders and around the corner.

It *was* beautiful, this house. Large, stately, yet there was also a lightness to it. It was cool and pale, the stone reflecting the sunshine streaming onto the front porch where expensive-looking furniture was set facing towards the focal point of the fountains. She pushed at the door and it swung open, revealing a central atrium, light flooding the tiled space from a glass dome set into the high ceiling. It was like all of someone's décor dreams made into reality and in a very classy way. Eve left her bag by the door and walked further into the house, noting the paintings of landscapes in gilt frames showing the green and brown flat land she'd seen from the plane; the azure and turquoise sea; lemons and olives, plump, bright, good enough to eat...

'May I help you?'

Eve jumped, rebounding into a hostess trolley and making all the probably expensive glassware rattle and chink. She hadn't expected there to be anyone in the house. Was this woman a maid or something? If she was honest, she would kill for a bottle of ice-cold water. Italy was just as hot as Corfu.

'Gianni said to come in and look around,' Eve said as the woman walked purposefully towards her. Definitely not a maid unless maids in Italy wore designer heels. This had to be Gianni's mother.

'Oh, he did, did he?'

It was an unusual reply. Nothing of meaning. Not moving the conversation on. Not encouraging more interaction. Eve only had one response. Introduction. It usually calmed conversational storms and brought about a less confrontational atmosphere.

'I'm Eve,' she said, extending a hand.

'I believe you,' the woman responded, stopping two metres clear and maintaining that commanding smile that did not say foe but definitely did not say friend either. She was showing expertise in not giving away any clear signals from what she was saying. Or doing.

Eve's hand was hanging; if any more time went by, she was going to have to edge it further still in a challenge or retract.

The door flew open, making an audible whoosh and Gianni swept into the space, his cabin case with him.

'Mamma,' he greeted.

So, this *was* his mother. Well, she was certainly nothing like Glenda. Although Eve shouldn't be surprised. Any woman with enough money to have a glass dome in her ceiling and designer shoes obviously had enough cash to look after the rest of her wardrobe and anti-crease her forehead.

'Gianni,' the woman answered. 'Were you not expecting me?'

'I—'

'Did you think I would be staying at the apartment in town?'

'I did not think that you would know that I was coming back today.'

'Did you not?'

Eve watched the exchange with interest. There was definitely more being said by what they weren't saying than what they were. It wasn't a traditional mother/son dynamic but, again, who was she to judge when her relationship with Glenda was about as far from traditional as you got? And right now, she was trying desperately to blend in with the gilt wallpaper...

'Is Paolo here?' Gianni asked.

'Why would Paolo be here? It is not yet 9 a.m.'

'I just did not know what you had planned for business today.'

'Oh, Gianni, I have many plans today. It is unfortunate that you did not tell me you were coming. I could have involved you somehow. Alas.'

Such was Eve's effort to press herself against the wall and pretend to be invisible amid this awkwardness that her head nudged one of the framed paintings. It fell to the floor with a crash.

'Oh my God! I am so, so sorry,' she said, dropping to a half-crouch position and picking the picture up.

'It is OK,' Gianni said, rushing to her side and taking the painting from her. 'Unfortunately, it is not broken. I really hate this one.' He stared at the picture – an open window looking out over another house with an open window. 'I have never understood it.'

Gianni's mother snatched the painting from her son's grasp and swung it into her arms as if it were her most cherished possession.

'Your father had that commissioned for me.'

'I can guarantee he didn't.'

Eve put her hand out again. Perhaps a mistake when the person she was now offering it to had a hand full of open windows.

'I'm Eve,' she said again. 'What should I call you?'

'Eve, I apologise, I was not expecting anyone to be home,' Gianni said. 'This is my mother, Valentina. Mamma, this is Eve. Eve will be staying in my wing of the house.'

Just as Eve processed the phrase 'my wing of the house' Valentina pressed the painting back into Eve's hands.

'Do you know what this represents, Evie?' she asked, standing next to her now, a bit too close.

'It's Eve,' she corrected.

'Gianni's father always thought a window looking onto another window was like a maze for the eyes. There is no escape. It is a window, then another and then, you see, just there in the distance, another window. Incredible.'

'But others might say that the windows are open,' Eve joined in. 'How can there be no escape with *open* windows?'

'Exactly,' Valentina agreed. 'It is all about an individual's perception.'

'I agree.' Eve held the painting tight. 'But it would be interesting to know what the artist was thinking when he chose to paint this piece.' She sighed, bringing the picture closer to her face. 'I suspect some people, when they look at it, cannot see the bars painted in front of the windows.'

'What?' Valentina asked. She snatched the picture back and started to examine it.

'Perhaps that's what Gianni's father could see,' Eve offered.

46

This 'wing' of the house comprised of four bedrooms, each with its own bathroom, a light-filled lounge, a study and even a kitchen. It was self-contained, bigger than most people's homes all on its own and the style was much more contemporary than any of the rest of the property Eve had seen already. She could see how Gianni fitted here, the businessman, the man who looked after himself. The bathroom adjoining this final room (his bedroom) was made for someone who spent a considerable amount of time there; the study with its twin screens told a story of spreadsheets, profit and loss, a lamp for long dark nights. It was minimalist, not much out of place, not much here at all that didn't serve a purpose.

Eve was snapping a photo of the bathroom to send to Ben when Gianni spoke.

'I must apologise,' he began. 'For my mother being here unexpectedly.'

Eve faced him. 'Is she not supposed to be living here?'

He smiled. 'No, she does live here, I just didn't think she would be here today, this morning.'

'I'm not sure she thought very highly of me. I'm sorry if my talking about bars on the windows didn't go down so well.'

He laughed then. 'Ha! That was perfection! My mother, she has never understood art. She buys pictures because she thinks she ought to. Amongst her friends there is deep rivalry over such things. Everybody wants to find that breakout artist. They have pieces they do not even like gracing their homes, hoping one day they will be worth a fortune only so they can show off about it to their other rich friends.'

'Glenda does that, but the opposite way. She used to brag to her friends about how *little* she spent on things.'

'This is something you like about her?' he asked.

'Let's not go too far.' She smiled.

'*Dio!* I am so sorry, Eve. I have offered you nothing to drink. I am a terrible host. Come, let us sit on the balcony and I will make coffee. Riccardocino coffee.'

* * *

Eve drank down the glass of water first and it was heavenly. Here, sitting on this balcony that jutted out and off from Gianni's lounge, there was a magnificent view of the grounds, every manicured inch tended to by a team of gardeners, or so Gianni told her. She couldn't imagine growing up here. As much as it was beautiful, it was also perfectly presented. Placed. Like an exceptional table setting. Where did a younger Gianni ride his bike? Where were the trees he could climb without fear of disturbing the had-to-be-tamed branches? She couldn't imagine Valentina rolling out the Tupperware in a heatwave, shaking out a blanket and declaring it an evening meal of picky bits.

Eve was struck by a memory then. Sausage rolls dipped in mustard. Homemade quiche – bacon, egg and pickles – her dad's favourite. Ben desperate to swing across the river on a tyre he couldn't even climb up on. Glenda and Dad barefoot, laughing together, dancing to something by Fleetwood Mac. Where had that love gone? Did it happen to all partnerships in the end? She shook the thought away.

'OK,' Gianni said, a small white porcelain cup in his hands. 'Are you ready?'

'You're making it sound like it might be a challenge,' she replied.

'Not one without pleasure,' he said with confidence. 'It is about learning to taste coffee the Riccardocino way.'

'Hmm.' Eve was simply enjoying looking at him. 'I suppose that means not slugging it back in seconds and longing for another one.'

'You could do that with an espresso. But in five minutes you would feel a head rush like you would not believe.'

Whenever she was near him, Eve usually had a head rush she couldn't believe so who knew what the coffee might do. She took the cup from him. 'What is this one?'

'This is our signature cappuccino. The drink that my father designed and created long before I was born and it has been pleasuring Italians for years.'

There was that head rush from his comment and Eve hadn't even sampled the coffee yet.

'So how do I drink it?' she asked, looking at the liquid. It was dark around the outside, a layer of white froth on top and Gianni had somehow drawn a perfect leaf in the centre, the kind you only got with an experienced barista. She had a sudden thought. 'Or do I? Is this really a work of art? A test to see if I would ravage it? Should I pop it on the wall next to the open window painting?'

He smiled. 'If you did that, I think my mother might burst into flames. But no, I want you to drink it. However, like with wine, it begins with the aroma. So, take it a little closer to your nose.'

'Is the foam going to burst out and spatter me?'

'It depends how close you hold it.'

Oh God! Why did every conversation turn sexy? Coffee. They were talking about coffee!

She held the cup nearer and inhaled. All at once she was hit with the kind of scent you usually got from entering a coffee shop that grew in strength the closer you got to the machines. But here and now, on this balcony, there was no richer, deeper aroma than the powerful coffee magic coming from this cup.

'How long do I have to hold back from putting it in my mouth?'

Gianni smiled. 'The intensity needs to build. Well-prepared, remember. Like the eggplant.'

'Stop! *I* might be the one who bursts into flames,' she said, laughing. 'It smells so good.'

'You get everything? The dark, wild underbelly? The light sweeter notes?'

'It's good, Gianni! Please let me taste it!'

'I like it when you beg.'

She wasn't going to wait for his say so any more. She put the cup to her lips and let the first hot, wet morsel singe her mouth.

Wow! Just in that tiny droplet there was flavour beyond any coffee she had experienced before. This was the king of coffees; this was coffee *par excellence*. And Eve already knew one was not going to be enough.

'What do you think?' Gianni asked, his expression telling her that her answer was going to mean a lot to him.

'I think it's velvety... but also raw and fresh.' She shook her head, taking another drink and doubting what she'd just said. Because it didn't make sense to have those combinations in equal measure bursting with each mouthful.

'It is a combination of the very best beans, harvested quickly, then roasted slowly, in a secret process my father developed. As far as I am aware, nobody does it quite like Riccardocino.'

'No one does it like you?' Eve said, her eyebrow raising of its own accord.

'I am as certain as I can be about that,' he replied, confidence oozing.

Eve waited a beat and then asked her next question. 'What is your meeting here about? It must be important for you to have to leave Corfu so suddenly.' She took another sip of the drink. It really was good.

Gianni didn't answer right off. She watched his expression cloud a touch, perhaps a guard come up, before he made his response.

'The business has a new deal to be made. It was something my father had some hand in despite him being unwell. But it was not fully finalised. He got sick and I focused on that. My mother, on the other hand, thought she would take care of things.' He shrugged but Eve sensed that there was much more behind it. She could see it in the depths of those eyes.

'So, you are fighting with your mother over this?'

'Not fighting,' he said. 'We have a difference of opinion.'

'And when is this battle?' Eve asked. 'Sorry, I mean meeting.' She took another drink of the coffee, stretching her legs out towards the sun.

'It is today,' he said. 'This afternoon. I am sorry, Eve. To be here and not to be with you. But once it is over, I promise there will be time for me to show you Verona.'

'And what about Pan?' she asked, finishing the coffee and putting the cup on the table.

Another change of expression, a few seconds of deliberation written on his brow.

'Pan,' he said. A ploy to buy more time.

'Tall man. Bush of silver-coloured hair. Had the biggest cabin luggage Ryanair have ever seen.'

'Yes,' Gianni said, nodding.

Still no answer. How long would she keep trying before it got weird?

'Did you know his name is Gorgios?'

'What?'

'Pan. In Episkepsi, Vasiliki kept calling him Gorgios. I asked him if that was his name and he got a bit like you're getting now.'

'How I am getting?'

'Gianni, I don't even know why Pan is here with us. But as he *is* here, why isn't he staying in one of the en-suite bedrooms? Where even *is* he right now? Is there another guest wing he has all to himself? Or... the garage?'

Gianni moved his wrist then. Was he looking at his watch? Something was not right with this whole situation. It was as if Pan had been squirrelled away somewhere. Like he was a secret.

'Gianni,' Eve said seriously. She took hold of his hand, forcing him to look at her. 'Tell me, what's going on?'

'God, Eve,' he said, sighing hard, a troubled look on his face now. 'I do not know even where to begin.'

'You can start anywhere,' she said. 'People who say it's best to start at the beginning don't really know what they're talking about.'

'I will tell you. Everything. I swear it. I just need... today. Can you do that? Just give me today to work things out. I know how that sounds but I have this meeting this afternoon and I really need to make it count.'

She squeezed his hand. 'I want you to know you can trust me with whatever it is, OK? Whatever trouble, whatever difficulty, there isn't much I haven't heard and I don't judge.'

'No?' he asked, looking up at her as she held his hand and he held on. He looked younger all of a sudden.

'Never,' she replied, seriously.

He exhaled then. Like he had been holding and storing tension his whole life. 'Why do we meet now, Eve? Why do we meet when I am in the middle of a crisis, with my business, with life, with everything?'

'Would you have come to Corfu if you weren't in a middle of a crisis?' she asked him.

She was working her way around the limited knowledge she had here. She didn't know if she was on the right track, but she did know that whatever was happening, she was on his side.

'No,' he answered. 'I would not have come to Corfu.'

'Then whatever has happened, it has given us the chance to get to know one another,' Eve said. 'And whatever happens next, whatever it is you have to tell me, I am grateful for that.'

He let go of her hand and softly palmed her face, his fingers tracing the edge of her fringe. 'I am grateful for that too. So grateful.'

'Then go to your meeting. Do whatever you have to do. I'll be here waiting to listen when you're ready.'

'Thank you,' he whispered. 'But I can do a little better than that. Come into Verona with me. Then, when my meeting is over, we can see the sights, have dinner, and we will talk.'

'I'd like that. But can you promise me one thing?'

'Anything.'

'Promise me Pan isn't locked up in the villa dungeon or something.'

She'd said the comment in jest but something flashed over Gianni's face for a split second.

'Gianni!' she exclaimed.

'I promise he is not locked in any dungeon.'

And that appeared to be all she was getting.

47

'Help! Help me! Somebody!'

Gianni shook his head as he approached the door, keys in one hand and a tray in the other. He slipped the key into the door and turned to open it. But before he could go any further the door shot forward, slamming into him and knocking the tray clean out of his hands. A cup, a plate and a jug of water all toppled to the floor, smashing to the ground as Pan burst through the door looking like a frantic trapped animal, eyes bulbous with terror.

'Look what you have done! My mother is going to kill me!' Gianni shouted as he attempted to pick up the broken porcelain together with the panini and San Pellegrino that were now also scattered on the tiles.

'Your father has been planning all the ways to kill you since you locked him in this place!' Pan yelled.

'You are behaving like this a jail! You have a widescreen television and a Coco-Mat mattress on the bed!'

'It has small windows and a locked door. That was all I see!'

Gianni picked up everything he could and then abandoned the tray, putting it on the bench outside the door to the guest suite. It was then he looked at Pan more closely. He really *did* look terrified. He was pale, clammy, shaking. Was he unwell?

'You are OK?'

'No, Gianni. I am not OK. I come here with you and you lock me in a cupboard!'

He was about to protest that the guest suite was about as far from a cupboard as you could get, with surround sound and great coffee, but it appeared all its merits were lost on Pan.

'I had brought you something to eat but...' He indicated the spoiled food and drink along with the broken plates.

'What are you afraid of, Gianni?' Pan asked him then.

'I should ask you the same question. You are shaking.'

Pan put out a hand as if he needed visual confirmation of it. He clamped one with the other and took a breath. 'I will be OK if this door stays not locked.'

Gianni looked over his shoulder. He thought he had heard his mother go out earlier, but her usual car of choice was still parked in the garage. Soon he would have to phone Paolo and set up a pre-meeting meeting to go through his plans for later.

'You do not want your mother to see me,' Pan said, realisation dawning. 'Well, I am here and I will not stay hidden the whole time.'

Gianni walked away from the guest suite, striding into the garden and looking out over the lawns. He heard Pan follow.

'These are good gardens,' Pan stated, inhaling deeply.

'My father had them designed. Every part.'

'He had good taste.'

'You do not need to say that,' Gianni replied. 'He was nothing to you.'

'No,' Pan agreed. 'But I did see him. Once.'

It was Gianni's turn to look shocked. What did that mean? How could Pan have ever seen Riccardo?

They walked on to the next section of the garden, following a gravelled path that spiralled around manicured hedges.

'I am thinking that your mother did not tell you anything about me,' Pan said. 'Did not even mention her time in Greece or me, someone she once knew that she cared about.'

Gianni shook his head. 'No.'

'Perhaps I am not the one to say anything. Perhaps if I do, that fierce side of her will come out.'

'Perhaps if you do not say anything I will never know,' Gianni said with a sigh. 'And I think there has been far too much of that already.'

Pan paused in his walking and took another long slow breath, the sunlight on his face, which had recovered some colour now. 'I was very much in love with your mother, Gianni. And I thought she was in love with me. We made plans together, in our heads, the kind of plans that begin with so much excitement and hope, more like they are dreams than plans. Perhaps that was what they were for her. A fiction, never to be reality.'

'She was young. She was on holiday. I understand how things work. A lot of things can be said under the influence of alcohol.'

'You do not know how it was for us,' Pan said. Then, he sighed. 'For me at least. It was like when I first saw her there was no sunshine in the sky that was brighter than her smile. And then, when we talked with each other, every small conversation became something important, something necessary.'

Gianni swallowed. It was hard to think of his mother with Pan. It was as though, if he did try to conjure up how that might have looked, it was a betrayal of the life they had all shared with Riccardo. But there was also a piece of him that could relate. It was like that the moment he had met Eve.

'I loved her,' Pan said. 'There was no doubt in my mind. But...'

He left the sentence hanging. They'd reached the corner of one section of garden.

'But?' Gianni asked.

'But you do not clip the wings of a bird,' Pan said. 'How do I explain?'

He mused for a second before beginning to walk again and Gianni followed in step.

'Like with Savage at the sanctuary. If we had clipped his wings when he was better and tried to make him stay, it would not have worked. Instead, we let him go and guess what, he decides to stay anyway.'

'Comparing my mother to a wild, violent bird,' Gianni remarked. 'You really did know her every side.'

'I asked her to marry me,' Pan admitted, stopping again. 'She was leaving to go back to Italy. I did not want her to go. So, instead of clipping her wings like, I do not know, destroying her passport or locking her in a room... I gave her a choice. A question. A promise to devote myself to her.'

'And she said no,' Gianni guessed.

'No,' Pan answered stiffly. 'She said yes.'

'What?'

Gianni hadn't meant it to come out but he couldn't keep his shock inside. How had his mother said yes to a proposal? Because, before she had given birth to him, she was already married to another man. It made no sense.

They had arrived at one of the ornate benches along the path, somewhere Riccardo had liked to sit and take coffee, away from the house. Gianni gripped the metal now.

'I had never felt so happy in my life before. This beautiful exotic woman from another country, from Italy, had come to my island and wanted to stay, with me, to love me, to live with me, to make it forever,' Pan continued. 'Someone wanted me for me. Just as I am. And that someone was vibrant and warm and passionate and everything anyone could wish from a partner. She would see something, something she had never seen before, maybe the simplest of things and it would excite her. She would list all of its attributes, ask questions. Like, Greek bread. Why is it so very fresh? What do they do to it?'

Gianni dropped down onto the bench now, putting his head into his hands. He didn't know how to cope with this.

'I do not know what happened. Maybe, she thought her only option was to say yes. Perhaps she said yes to make me happy but, deep down, she was never going to stay. I thought that giving her a choice was not clipping her wings but perhaps that is exactly what she thought it was.'

Pan dropped down onto the seat next to him and neither of them said anything for a while. It wasn't an easy silence by any means; there was tension in the air above the fragrance from the rosemary and lavender. Then suddenly Gianni remembered what Pan had said.

'You said you saw my father. Riccardo.'

He watched Pan make a small sombre nod. 'It was two months after your mother left Corfu. I tried to forget her. I came up with a new dish for the taverna menu every day, rearranged all the tables, took on the feeding of ducks and chickens, tried to fill my mind with anything I could, but it was pointless. She was never going to leave my thoughts until I had tried one more time. If she could not leave Italy, perhaps I could leave Greece.'

This sounded like a huge commitment to make for someone you had only spent weeks with. Gianni's mind went to Eve then. Where was their beginning of a relationship going? How could he contemplate starting something when there was nothing in his life that was stable right now? But then again, how she made him feel, how he loved talking to her, that was real, that was something that was his and hers alone, not mixed up in all this drama.

'I took a very old, very long ferry that took over a day to arrive and then I hitchhiked the rest of the way. Valentina had told me about this place, Piazza Bra, and the benches around the amphitheatre under the trees, her favourite restaurant with the bright red awning, which served green olives almost the size of plums...'

Gianni closed his eyes. They had visited that restaurant so many times as a family, his mother always *always* asking for more of those olives, her smile stretched wide every time she popped one into her mouth. It was her place of choice for date nights, meetings, birthdays... and that had been something she had told Pan about.

'I sat on benches, moving with the sun, I shared my lunch with pigeons and I watched these beautiful people striding so confidently across the cobbles, the background this striking old colosseum like from a movie.' Pan paused, drawing in a breath as a butterfly suddenly appeared in front of them, touching down on a plant. 'And then I saw her. For a moment I almost did not recognise her. She was wearing these special clothes like she was dressed up for a party and her hair, it was not loose with salt from the sea making it curl, it was straight and tied into a bun.' Pan sighed. 'But the thing I notice the most was her holding hands with a man. A tall, broad, large colossus of a man who looked like a movie star. He had the smart suit, the black shiny straight hair, this way of moving that was like a ship gliding through the sea.'

Pan's recollection of Riccardo resonated deeply with Gianni. That was exactly how his father was. Supremely confident, effortlessly chic, oozing supremacy, not in an ill-mannered way, but in a way that spoke of his inner belief in success. And Riccardo had

had success, in his business, in life, in love... Cancer was the only thing that he hadn't been able to conquer.

'I watched them,' Pan said. 'He was a gentleman. He pulled a chair out for her, he offered her the menu first, all the things that I had done. And he looked at her like I had looked at her. Like he loved her.' He sighed again. 'That was when I realised that he loved her too. And what match was I for a man like that?'

'Well,' Gianni said, adjusting his position on the bench and turning his body towards him. 'What did you do?'

'What did I do?' Pan repeated. 'The only thing I could do. I picked up my bag and I hitchhiked back the way I had come.'

'What? You did not speak to her? You travelled all that way, on a ferry, in the cars of strangers and you did not say anything?'

Pan got to his feet, incredulous. 'What was there to say? She was not the same person in her fine clothes, in this expensive restaurant. On Corfu she would wear shorts made from old jeans and pick pomegranates to eat from the bush.'

'But if she loved you like you thought she did, if she said yes to your proposal of marriage, then surely you had to give her a chance to explain?'

'So, you think I should have gone into that fancy place, in my jeans and my sandals, with my hair like it is, and stood in front of your mother and your Hollywood-looking father and said, "Valentina, I know you left in the middle of the night without saying anything but here I am! Come to tell you I love you all over again! Let us get married! I will live in Italy! I do not know how we will make money or ever eat in a restaurant like this but we will have each other!"'

'Well, why not?'

'Because of everything, Gianni. The way your father would look at me, like tumbleweed blown over from Greece. How Valentina would look at me.' Pan's voice began to get choked up.

'The last time I saw her on Corfu, she was happy, she was smiling. And that was how she was here now with this man. That was how I wanted her to be, always. And if she saw me in that restaurant, that smile would have disappeared. Because I was intruding, I was uninvited in her life here.'

Gianni let Pan gather himself for a moment before he made his reply.

'She might have told you she was pregnant.'

Pan turned to face him, tears in his eyes. 'And that is my only regret. And that is why I am here now.'

Gianni sighed. 'It is all such a mess.'

'No,' Pan said. 'Not a mess.' He sighed again. 'I believe that things are what they need to be for a reason. Yes, I would like to have known about you but what could I really have done? If your mother had told me and then we had got married, it would have been *because* of you. You remember what I say about clipping the bird's wings.' He pointed to a small sparrow that was chirping its song from the branches of a tree. 'I had nothing to offer you back then, I have nothing to offer you now. But the time is right for me to be here and ask questions. Because not telling me at the beginning, starting a new life with your father looking after you both is one thing, but *never* reaching out in all this time...'

'Yes,' Gianni said. 'I know.'

'So,' Pan said. 'No more locking me in rooms. I want to see Valentina.'

48

VERONA, ITALY

Eve gasped as she stepped out of the car, her eyes on the imposing amphitheatre just up ahead. It was like something out of a film. The ancient crumbling stones towering up to a magnificent blue sky, all beautiful arches, bird song in the air, the buzz of people crossing the cobbled piazza, mopeds zipping along the road, green trees providing shade from the heat of the day.

'This is what I imagine Rome to be like,' Eve said as Gianni joined her, standing close.

'Ha! Do not say that to a gentleman from Verona. Verona is better than Rome. That is why it is not the capital.' He waved a hand as if he was dismissing the notion. 'Who wants the title of being the busiest, most over touristic city?'

Eve laughed and then she quietened, catching the sleeve of his shirt. 'Are you sure your meeting is cancelled?'

'I am sure,' he replied.

'But that was the reason you were coming back here and leaving Corfu, wasn't it?'

He nodded. 'It was.'

'Then what happened?'

He took a deep breath. 'Just about everything. There *is* a meeting, just one that I will not be involved in for now.'

'And you're not going to tell me,' Eve said, resigned to the fact now.

'I *am* going to tell you,' Gianni assured her, taking her hands in his as a small cream-coloured train pulled up beside them. 'But before that, we are going to join the ride.' He put a hand on one of the tiny doors of the train as if it was connected to what he had just said.

Eve paid more attention to the train on wheels. It was exactly like the kind you got at Bournemouth and other British seaside resorts: a Dotto train. Was a man with an almost limousine-like car going to take them on a tour in this?

'Eve, are you scared of the train?' Gianni asked, grinning.

'If I was scared of the train, you smiling like that would be very, very triggering.'

She watched him straighten his face as if he really was concerned she had a train phobia. And then she laughed.

'I'm not scared of the train, Gianni. I'm just discovering many things about you without you having to tell me too much at all.'

'You are reading me,' he said. 'With the hocus pocus of a counsellor.'

Eve laughed again then. 'I can't believe your excellent English-speaking skills extend to the words "hocus pocus".'

'I have a good teacher.'

'And I don't deal in witchcraft.'

'I note it,' he said. And then he bowed, moving his hand as if he was beckoning her to join him for a dance at a regal party.

The train was rapidly filling up, so Eve scooted in and Gianni sat down next to her, his knees touching the inside of the carriage. And as soon as the train was full, off they went, juddering across the cobbles as an automated and rather childish-sounding tour guide voice came over the tannoy.

'We do not have to listen,' Gianni said. 'I can tell you what we are seeing.' He slipped his hand into hers then pointed with his other. 'The arena. It has been here for a million years.'

'Gianni, the right dates please or I will listen to this child over the speakers.'

'OK,' Gianni said. 'I may not get everything completely correct but this is not my first Dotto train ride.'

'And I don't want to know about all the other girls you have taken on here.'

'Oh no, Eve.' His expression was serious then. 'I have never ridden this train with any other girl before.'

There was that wriggling in her stomach that she so enjoyed and had thought she might not experience again. She was getting to like it. Maybe getting too used to it.

'Facts and figures and add in any romantic stories,' she said, settling back into the seat of the train.

'Romantic stories,' Gianni said with half a smile. 'Like all the tourists who visit Verona, you only want Romeo and Juliet!'

'Well, theirs is one of the greatest love stories. If a little tragic at the end.'

'One of the greatest love stories so far,' Gianni said, squeezing her hand.

There was the fluttering inside her again, happy tiny birds beating their wings and reaching for the sky.

'OK, here we are leaving Piazza Bra. It is the largest piazza in Verona and surrounding it are wonderful restaurants and cafés and then there are benches, cedar and pine trees above for shade. There is a bronze statue; he is the very first King of Italy on his horse. Of course, the jewel in our crown is the arena. It was built around two thousand years ago and is now an entertainment venue. Many different types of music can be heard here. Rock, pop, operatic—'

'Opera,' Eve breathed, her face to the sun, taking in this lovely city.

'Yes. You like opera?'

'I've never been. But the idea of it...' She had to stop talking as shivers were running up and down her spine. She imagined the voices as if they were echoing around the ancient walls.

'I have been once,' he said. 'I was very young, perhaps eight or nine. My parents had tickets right at the front, close to the stage. But I would not sit still. I left our expensive seats and I climbed right to the top level, the very highest point of the arena and I sat there to listen.' He smiled. 'My parents, they looked like tiny ants, the performers too, but I liked the way the sound carried.'

'It sounds amazing.'

'OK, here,' Gianni said, pointing. 'That is Aldi. A very nice supermarket.'

'Gianni!'

'Take in the tree-lined streets and the mopeds in rows. Here is a large clock and another amazing archway.'

'You're spoiling it now,' Eve said, taking her hand out of his. 'I know you've seen all this before, but I haven't.'

'I am sorry,' he said, re-threading their hands. 'I will be better.'

She liked him reaching for her hand, so she leaned into him a little and relaxed into the up and down of the land train.

There was another park coming up, with areas of green grass, more trees and fountains, a kiosk and playground, children on swings, parents watching.

'I thought it would be different to this,' she admitted.

'How different?'

'I don't know. I suppose I imagined it less open, not parks and lawns, the buildings nowhere near as beautiful, dry and not so green.'

'It is a city for everyone,' Gianni said. 'Charm, peace, the old buildings, the river flowing through it.'

Eve curled her body into him. 'I love it already.'

49

PIAZZA DEI SIGNORI, VERONA

Seeing Verona through Eve's eyes had been the best thing. She had absorbed so much more of the city than Gianni did on a daily basis, because it was brand new to her, fresh and exciting. Standing in the courtyard, looking up at Juliet's balcony, ivy cascading down the bricks, she had had tears in her eyes. He had been about to remind her that these two lovers were fictional, made up by Shakespeare, but he had stopped himself. It would be unromantic to make comment. Why would you want to spoil the idea of two lovers whose tragic demise reunited their families, whether it was real or not? Somewhere, somewhen, this most probably *had* happened in reality. And Eve wanted to revel in it, breathe life into the idea that two people could love each other so much that the thought of life without the other was not possible.

Gianni's thoughts had strayed to Pan. Loving Valentina so much that he had left everything he knew to travel to another country with no money, nothing but a bag and his heart on his sleeve.

He had ignored all the messages from his mother, which had begun to come in about half an hour ago when she'd realised he had postponed the meeting with Barista Irresistible. Perhaps that was what he should have done from the outset, back in Corfu when Paolo had called him. But then he had not known that Pan had guessed his identity. And now Pan was in Italy. There were bigger things to think about right at this moment. He was deciding to put family before business. That was what Riccardo had always done, no matter how big the deal. It wasn't about buying himself time to perfect his pitch for his new idea, it was about respecting Pan and his need to ask his questions. And from what he had heard, his mother owed Pan that chance.

It was evening now, the coffees turning to beers and wines, and there was an end-of-the-working day atmosphere under canopies in the squares and narrow side streets. They had walked to this piazza, one of his favourite spots, tucked behind the main thoroughfare, a courtyard flanked by imposing yet outstanding architecture, the buildings connected to each other by arches and loggias. In the centre was a statue of Dante, the poet and philosopher, and above them was one of the most famous towers in Verona, *Torre dei Lamberti*, eighty-four metres of stone and marble.

'This tower,' Gianni said to Eve, gesturing. 'It was starting to be built in the eleven hundreds, I think. They added the very top section later and then that was struck by lightning.'

'So, it's a cursed tower?' Eve asked. 'You've taken me to dinner by a cursed tower. What kind of hocus pocus is that?'

He smiled. 'I like it here. At this time in the evening, it is cooler, and it is not as busy as the restaurants in the Bra.'

'Tell that to the pigeons,' Eve said, indicating the gang of feathered friends meandering around looking for scraps, others perched on the overhangs of buildings ready to poop on tables or patrons. He had never minded, even when one of them had deposited right into his glass of Coke.

'Pigeons, they are a part of any large city,' he said in defence.

'But Verona has the best. Look at the ones with feathered legs. Kings of pigeons.'

Eve laughed but Gianni was distracted as his phone screen lit up again. Mamma. He turned it over in one quick flip.

'Gianni, it's OK if you want to answer that,' she said. 'I don't mind.'

'*I* mind,' he told her. 'I want to have dinner with you. I want to hear you talk about the romantic arches of Verona again or make more squeaking noises about the designer shops.'

'I did not squeak,' Eve countered. 'I never squeak!'

'That will remain to be seen,' he said, deliberately connecting with her gaze.

'Careful there, Mr Coffee, you're swirling up that ripening marinade.'

'Always,' he said as their food arrived.

The second the waiter had left their dishes – a traditional Veronese risotto for Eve and gnocchi for him – his phone rumbled again.

'Is it business? About the meeting you cancelled?' Eve asked, topping her dish with some parmesan cheese.

'Yes.' He sighed. 'It is my mother.'

'Has she decided I can't stay? Do I need to find a hotel? I didn't mean to annoy her about the painting, really.'

He shook his head. 'She is angry because I postponed the meeting. At the moment, in our family, it is like a game of chess. Each person trying to out move the other. I do not like it but...'

'But?' Eve asked.

'Sometimes it is necessary.' He picked up his fork and then put it down again. 'I am sorry, you need more wine.' He took the bottle from the silver cooler at the side of their table and topped up her glass. 'You are not saying anything.'

He looked across at Eve, so beautiful, her hair a mix of gold and bronze in the evening sunlight. She was looking back at him, quiet. Then he understood.

'You are doing the counsellor thing. When you say nothing and hope that the person will keep talking.'

'You got me. But to keep talking is always a choice.'

'OK,' Gianni breathed. 'I will speak.' He nodded, his mind made up. He began, 'Pan... he is...'

Why could he not just say the words? He took a deep breath.

'Pan... he is my biological father.'

There, it was out. Simple, the truth.

'Well,' Eve began, pressing her napkin to her lips. 'I was not expecting that.'

He watched her put the napkin down again, then take a sip of her wine. There was no loud exclamation, no shock, just calming words.

'I was also not expecting it,' he admitted.

'To tell me?'

'No, no,' he said quickly. 'I was always going to tell you. Sometime.' He took a breath. 'It just, is new to me. It is... a revelation.'

'You found out recently?'

'My father told me. That is, my father who is not my father told me. As he lay dying.'

'Oh, Gianni,' Eve said. 'I am so, so sorry. That must have been very, very tough.'

He shrugged but it was not a shrug to make light of the situation, it was a shrug that said there had been nothing he could do about any of it. The ball had never been in his court. His father had made the decision to tell him. His mother had held it back his whole life and might *never* have told him. But now he had all the cards, it was, in some way, his choice what happened next

'I was not on holiday on Corfu. Or on business. I was there to find my biological father. I wanted to see what kind of man he is, to see if I felt any connection.' He forked his gnocchi but didn't eat.

'And did you? Feel a connection?'

'I do not know,' he said. 'And I was going to leave Greece without saying anything. Without telling Pan who I was. I could see he was a good man. A simple man, perhaps, but a kind, generous person with a big heart. Perhaps that was all I needed to know. But I did not think about *him*. What *he* might want to know.' He sighed. 'He turned up at my hotel before I was leaving for the airport and he told me he knew who I was. Had guessed for a while since I had arrived. He booked the flight. He wants to talk to my mother.'

'Wow,' Eve said. 'That is a lot. Is that why she's calling you?'

'No, she is calling about the business. She does not know Pan is here yet. That is why I locked him in the guest suite.'

'Gianni! You told me he was not locked in anywhere.'

'I believe I said he was not locked in any dungeon.'

'And where is he now?'

'He is at the house. Not locked anywhere, I promise.' He sighed, picked up his wine glass and took a sip. 'I left him with some old photo albums, pictures of me when I was younger, photos of my mother and Riccardo, until my mother goes home and...'

He didn't need to finish the sentence.

'Will they be OK on their own? I mean, it's going to be a shock for your mother, isn't it?'

Gianni hadn't considered his mother much in his thoughts. He was still angry at her for keeping this from him, for seemingly never wanting him to know. And now he had met Pan and now he knew Pan had been as oblivious to the situation as Gianni had been, he felt for the man. But what about his mother? How was she going to react? Were there things he didn't know yet? Different circumstances of which no one but she was aware?

'I do not know how she will react,' Gianni said. 'But I guess we will be finding out.'

Eve reached out across the table and put her hand on top of his. 'You have a lot going on.'

'I know.'

'It's a lot more than me chasing missing chameleons around Old Perithia.'

He tilted his head, musing on her comment. 'I do not know. My mother could rival a chameleon in changing her appearance. She has many, many clothes.'

'Gianni,' Eve said softly. 'If you want to go back to the house and be there with them to, I don't know, referee or something, I would understand. Don't feel you have to be my tour guide. I'm quite capable of drinking more of this beautiful Italian wine alone and getting a taxi back to the house, or somewhere else for the night to give you some space.'

'No,' he said at once. 'No, Eve. That is not what I want.' He squeezed her hand tightly. 'It is not what I want at all.'

'Honestly, spending the day with you has been something I've enjoyed more than anything else in a very long time and—'

'And I don't want that to end prematurely,' Gianni interrupted. 'I would much rather be here with you than in the crossfire with... my parents.'

He baulked a bit on those last two words. They were his parents. They were about to be in the same place together for the first time since before he was born. It wasn't a small thing. But there was nothing he could really do about it now. It would go how it would go. Perhaps he would return home to find smashed glasses, if his mother had flown into a temper, or perhaps there would be laughter and Pan making tea. Maybe it would be a mixture of both.

'It must feel strange, having a different dad to the one you thought,' Eve said, still holding his hand.

Gianni nodded. 'It hurts. I still do not know if it has sunk in. I did not understand how it could be possible that I had no idea. I also still do not understand what made Riccardo tell me when he did.' He closed his eyes briefly, thinking back to that warm, sticky afternoon, Riccardo's breathing getting slower and slower...

'Sometimes there's never a right time to tell someone something so hard,' Eve said. 'Remember what I said about not having to start a conversation with the beginning of the story?'

He smiled at her. The evening light had diminished further now, the flame of their candle on the table more apparent, the footfall of visitors lessening, soft music playing from one of the trattorias. Despite all this heaviness in his life, there was this beautiful, light, enchanting melody they were creating together. Somehow it was like a score of notes leading them through the changes in tempo.

'I am not answering my phone tonight,' Gianni said, his fingers grazing the skin of her hand as his gaze held hers. 'For anyone. For anything.'

Again, Eve made no reply, but he watched as her pupils dilated, the reflection of the candlelight dancing there.

'I invited you here to show you Verona, my city, and to spend more time with you,' he said as sincerely as he had ever said anything. 'To see... if we can like each other in Italy as well as Greece.'

'Ah, so that was your plan,' Eve teased, her hair swishing to the side as she picked up her wine glass, her other hand still with him. 'Impress me with Italy. Well, I've had a Dotto train and Romeo and Juliet and I have definite plans for gelato.'

'I have no plan,' Gianni said. 'I ask for, just... time.' He pressed the pad of his thumb to the base of hers. 'Can we take tonight for us? Leave everything else for tomorrow?'

She captured his thumb, ran hers over his and internally he quivered.

'*Sì*,' she said. 'I liked you in Greece. I think I might like you even more in Italy.'

'*Grazie Dio*,' Gianni said, bringing her hand to his lips and kissing it.

50

PIAZZA BRA, VERONA

This city was simply so beautiful and its charm extended into the night where low lights came on in bars and restaurants and bicycles still whizzed across cobbles and took their chances amid taxis and mopeds on roundabouts. Eve took another mouthful of the ice cream she was trying to savour as much as the humidity would let her. It was pistachio – the cone part-covered in chocolate and multi-coloured sprinkles with a round wafer stuck into the top. Gianni had let out an audible groan when she'd ordered it. His favourite made with Sicilian wine wasn't even on offer, so he'd opted for *menta* – mint. And now they were strolling back across this piazza, the chatter and buzz from the restaurants rising into the night, the hiss of the water from the fountain duelling with loud conversations from the queue of smartly dressed people waiting to enter the arena.

The arena looked even more beautiful at night. Its presence dominated the square like a circular layered cake, arches etched into the icing, parts of it crumbling, struggling to be held in place, but still perfection, like time might have eroded some of the brickwork but had destroyed none of the majesty. Now, against the dark, the arches glowed, warm and atmospheric. It felt special to just be here to see it, be part of it, under a perfect sky, with the best ice cream and someone she was connecting with by her side.

'How is Italy's world-famous ice cream?' Gianni asked, nudging her elbow.

'Heavenly,' she answered. 'How do I say that in Italian?'

'*Celeste*.'

'*Celeste*,' Eve attempted to copy. 'Ugh, it sounded a lot sexier when you said it.'

'Did it?' he said, those gorgeous eyes flashing a little.

'Maybe,' she admitted.

'I like the way you say it more,' he told her and little sparkles of intensity danced up her back. 'So,' he said, stepping ahead of her and then turning to face her, walking backwards across the cobbles, ice cream dribbling. 'Where would you like to sit to listen to the opera?'

'What?' She gasped, excitement hitting her. Surely he wasn't serious? Judging by the number of people waiting to get through the gates to find their seat, it was going to be a full audience.

'I am sorry, I could not get tickets,' Gianni said. 'But we can still listen.'

'How?' Eve asked.

He moved alongside her and draped an arm around her shoulders. 'Look at the shape of the arena. It is made this way for a reason. An amphitheatre. It amplifies the sound.'

'I am aware of the concept,' Eve said, smiling.

'So really,' Gianni said. 'We do not have to be inside to appreciate it.'

'Please tell me we aren't going to climb up any of the scaffolding,' Eve said, her eyes now roaming over the old building and trying to work out what Gianni meant.

'No,' he answered. 'Come, let me show you.'

He took her free hand then and pulled her across the piazza.

* * *

Gianni had never been to the Terrazza Arena Sky Lounge Bar on top of the Milano Hotel – but he remembered Paolo telling him about it last year. Paolo had taken his boyfriend there for a date night and the next day they were engaged to be married. Not that Gianni was about to propose but he wanted tonight to be as special as he could make it. Because that was what Eve deserved.

Now they were here he could see why it was the perfect setting. There was a phenomenal view of the only original remaining 'wing' of the arena as well as down below to the piazza.

'Oh, Gianni, this place is incredible,' Eve exclaimed when they had taken their seats, huge white modern shapes each side of a table next to some glass that supposedly was to stop you from falling. 'It's a total contrast. These contemporary tables and chairs and the age of the arena, it's so beautiful.'

And so was she, her smile lighting up the night more than the stars in the sky above them. He swallowed the unrecognisable emotion caught in his throat. It was more than wanting to sleep with someone. It was more than liking someone. But it was too soon for anything truly deeper, wasn't it?

As the first notes of the orchestra hit the air, Gianni felt goosebumps break out on his skin. The music was so clear, echoing around the amphitheatre and then spiralling out, gifting those outside with almost the same experience. As the very beginnings of the vocals drifted into the evening, his eyes went to Eve, and he could see how much the sweet melody was affecting her too.

* * *

Eve couldn't understand the language, but she was completely captivated by the operatic voices. She found she was looking across at the arena and creating a vision in her mind of the stage she couldn't see. How many voices were there? What was the story? What colours were the costumes?

'It is *Carmen*,' Gianni whispered.

Eve nodded, too scared to speak in case she burst into floods of tears. Being here in Italy was somehow even more affecting than having been in Greece. Corfu was a safe space where she had Gabby. Verona was a step into the unknown. So far away from that cushioning she had built around her life in the UK since her dad had died. This was not the Brookly Heath vehicle show or changing barrels at the pub or consoling one of her students. It wasn't Glenda or Gene Reynolds or worrying Ben had a secret account on Bet365. It was a full moon, a sky full of stars, gelato and Gianni, sitting opposite her. Gorgeous, smart, funny Gianni. He meant something to her already and that worried her a little. Their relationship had snuck up on her, woven itself into her time in Greece like those first red strings in Aleka's picture of the coffee cup. *Coffee.* Perhaps fate was leading the way because if she'd thought too long and too hard she would have pushed Gianni away like everyone else. Tonight she was glad for the helping hand, for not having turned her back on the chance.

As the tenor's vibrato launched into the night, Eve reached across the table and took Gianni's hand in hers. Both of them had got to this point together despite the most difficult and unusual circumstances. Perhaps because none of it had been straightforward, it made the realisation that she *really* liked him that much more poignant.

She slipped her fingers in between his and held on tight.

51

GIANNI'S HOME, VERONA

'I can't hear any arguing,' Gianni whispered as they left the car and approached the house. The night was completely black but the air was still humid, moths dancing around the lights that showed the pathway around the rose bushes and ornate hedges.

'If I'm honest,' Eve whispered, 'I can still only hear the opera.'

'Me also,' Gianni said, taking her hand in his.

What was unusual was that the house was in total darkness. Not one light was visible from the front, not on the porch or through the downstairs rooms, nor any upstairs. This wasn't what Gianni had been expecting. Though he still wasn't 100 per cent sure what he *had* been expecting. Or what he wanted the outcome to be. Pan and Valentina both unscathed perhaps. Externally if not internally.

'Do you think anyone's home?' Eve asked as they approached the marble steps.

'This is most likely my mother's way of showing me she does not want to talk to me tonight. It would not be the first time,' Gianni said. 'When I was younger, if we got into a fight, she would bolt the front door so I could not get in with my key.'

'She won't have done that tonight, will she?' Eve asked, looking a little concerned.

Gianni smiled. 'I have been careful ever since that night. I have another key for my wing of the house.'

'Maybe you should check your phone,' Eve told him. 'In case anything's wrong.'

'No,' Gianni said defiantly. 'I said I was not doing that and I meant it.'

'OK, but I'd really like you to,' Eve told him, pausing at the bottom of the steps.

'Eve...'

'Please, Gianni, just check there's no messages from the emergency services or the local hospital and then I will relax a bit. Not too much, because your mother slightly terrifies me, but enough to...' She ended the sentence there.

'Enough to?' Gianni said, feeling that delicious prickling in his gut again.

'Enough to... I don't know... take all my clothes off and... get in your fountain.'

The visualisation was suddenly front and centre and his eyes did a reconnaissance of her body, the dress she was wearing that traced every curve. His hand was already reaching into the pocket of his trousers for his mobile phone.

'A quick check,' he told her. 'For you.'

Seconds seemed to lengthen as he powered on his phone and waited for any notifications to appear. There were many. A stream of missed calls from his mother, two from Paolo, emails from some of their suppliers, one from Barista Irresistible, a slew of offers for things he never remembered signing up for. An iMessage from his cousin, Luna, asking him to be a plus one... He didn't read further. There were no messages from his mother. No voicemails.

'There is nothing we need to concern ourselves with,' Gianni said, pocketing his phone again.

'You're completely sure?' Eve asked.

He silenced her with a firm kiss and then quickly another and then one more as he caught her up in his arms and half-walked, half-carried her around the side of the house.

'Gianni!' Eve shrieked, laughing as he kissed her cheek and missed slightly, getting a mouthful of her hair. 'You must really want me in your fountain.'

'I do,' he answered. 'I very much do.'

'Well,' she said, running a hand down the front of his shirt. 'You'll have to catch me first.'

Before he had time to feel that rush of passion escaping like pressurised steam from a coffee machine, she had pushed him backwards with her palm and sprinted off across the grass. He laughed to himself as she screamed, all their whispering and trying to be quiet forgotten about, as the sprinkler system activated every time she ran past a sensor, each new arc of water soaking her dress and her sun-kissed skin. He followed, watching her. It would be easy to catch up to her quickly but the sound of her shrieks and laughter was infectious and he only wanted to elongate this moment, savour it.

The grass gave way to a gravel path. And then there the fountain was. The ridiculously large, big-enough-for-the-middle-of-Piazza-Bra marble structure, the centrepiece of this particular ornamental garden. Gianni had never much cared for it. It was the part of his father he never really understood. He got the luxury cars and the large house, he definitely got the donations to charities, but these expensive decorations just because he could? However, now, seeing Eve backed up against the stone, her dress dripping, her hair dripping more, the water trickling then spurting as it danced to a rhythm, well, the ostentatious feature was growing on him.

He took a step forward, his shoe crunching on the stones.

'You... didn't tell me you had sprinklers,' Eve said as he drew closer.

'I did not think you would be running through the garden,' Gianni answered.

'That is a fair point,' she said, her voice shaking a little.

'Are you cold?' He was now so close to her he could reach out and touch her. He held off.

'Wet,' Eve said. 'Not cold.'

And that statement made his libido zing into a different stratosphere. He did reach out then, slowly, his hand shaking as he used a finger to part her saturated fringe, then trace a line down over her cheekbone to her jaw. She shivered, the whole of her body reacting to his one fingertip. He began to imagine how she might react to something more, but before he could dwell on it, she had got hold of his shirt and ripped it open, some of the buttons hitting the ground.

'I... was not expecting that,' he said as her lips met his collarbone, delivering tiny kisses along its length.

She lifted her head and met his eyes. 'No?'

'No.'

'What were you expecting?'

'I do not know,' he admitted, suddenly feeling a little stupid that he had made such a comment.

'There's more to me than the dutiful sister,' Eve told him seriously.

'I know that. And I like that you surprise me.'

'So now you can take the rest of your clothes off and get in the fountain.'

'This is really what you want?' Gianni whispered, his lips finding the space just below the lobe of her ear.

She lowered her mouth to *his* ear. 'I think if we don't get naked together now, we'll both go from well-prepared to in danger of being overdone.'

'Then what are we waiting for?'

He pressed his mouth to hers, hot and hard, relishing her response in more than equal measure. Then, in one fluid motion, he scooped her up into his arms and as she laughed and kicked, he climbed into the fountain.

52

Eve had made coffee as quietly as the machine would allow in Gianni's almost en-suite kitchen and now she was sipping it slowly as she stood back in the master bedroom admiring the view. Not the view from the window, the almost maze-like privets and the cascading terraces of steps that led further into the acreage of the ground visible from the balcony, but Gianni. He was still completely naked, one buttock partially covered by the Egyptian cotton sheets. That was the view she'd been enjoying well into the early hours of the morning. It had started in the fountain – steamy kisses, hot foreplay and then a head-pounding, heart-thumping experience that had left her with tingling in places she didn't even know she had – and then it had moved into the bathroom and continued in the bedroom until neither of them could breathe. Suffocation by smooching sounded like a nice way to go but now she'd let Gianni in, *really* let him in, physically as well as emotionally, she didn't want to go anywhere just yet.

Suddenly her phone burred. She put her coffee cup on the chest of drawers and picked up her phone. She'd sent Ben and Gabby texts. Just to check in. Not because she was dutiful or at all worried about them. But the message wasn't from Ben or Gabby. It was from Glenda. Immediately there was that icy feeling running over her shoulders. She took another glance at Gianni, still stationary, still looking like Michelangelo's David... and then she clicked on the message.

I need to talk to you ✖

That was it. And the 'x' wasn't an 'x' like someone might add to represent a kiss; it was a cross, one of those big red scary x's that you found in the 'symbols' section of your emojis. Was that what it was meant to be? A warning symbol? Eve read the message again just to make sure she wasn't missing anything somewhere between the six words and fiery cross. Nothing. She checked the time of the message. It had been sent late last night in England. For some reason – signal, network, water from the fountain – it hadn't got to her phone until now. But there was no follow-up, no bubbles with more information pending, so Eve could only assume it wasn't a dire emergency.

'Buongiorno.'

She put her phone down and gave Gianni her full attention. He was sitting up in the bed now, the sheets covering him from the midriff down except for one leg he had bent up, teasingly it felt to her.

'Buongiorno,' she replied, picking up her coffee cup, and the one she had made for him, and stepping towards the bed.

'You have made me coffee?' he asked, running his hand through frankly delectable bed hair, all dark curls after the fountain and the rainfall shower.

'Well,' she said, passing him the cup. 'I can't guarantee it will taste as good as the one you made me, but I really tried.'

Gianni took the mug and put it to his lips, taking a sip. 'Ugh, made to the same recipe as my Greek hotel.'

'What?'

He laughed then, that wide, full-mouthed smile, his eyes creasing at the corners. 'I am joking with you. It is good. Although there is little you can do wrong with Riccardocino once you have the quality beans.'

'To be really frank,' Eve said, lowering down onto the edge of the bed. 'I wasn't sure I was going to be able to press the right buttons.'

He grinned then, dipping that curly-haired head into her space. 'Are we still speaking about coffee? Because, if we are not, then my buttons have no reason to complain.'

She rested her cup on her knee and smiled, palming his cheek. 'My buttons are also feeling nothing but complimentary this morning, if a little tired.'

He kissed her palm. 'We did not get much sleep, no?'

'It was so quiet,' Eve said. 'I mean, I thought Corfu was quiet but then you factor in the donkeys braying and the chickens and the geese and—'

She had been about to mention Savage's awful squawking that, according to Google, no hoopoe bird should ever do, when a high-pitched, might-crack-crystal scream stopped her saying any more.

'That is my mother.' Gianni gasped, throwing back the sheets and searching the floor with his hand. 'Have you seen my underwear?'

'Not since around midnight. Sorry, not funny.' Eve dragged her eyes away from the full-frontal display and hunted for his black Armani trunks. 'Here!'

She threw them to him and then regarded herself in the full-length mirror – Gianni's shirt and her cargo pants. The scream had sounded urgent. Whatever she had on would have to do. Gianni scrambled for the door.

53

Valentina was in the middle of the kitchen and she was holding a carving knife. Her whole body was shaking, her eyes directed toward the French doors that led from this room to the garden.

'Mamma, what is it?' Gianni asked, heading across the tiles towards her.

'Stay back!' she warned, whisking the knife to her left and almost catching him on the shoulder.

'Mamma! What is going on?' he said, stopping in his tracks.

'That is what I want to know from you! You are trying to discredit me! I see that now! Saying you are back for the meeting and then cancelling the meeting and now... this! Well, I will not let you try to prove I am mad. It will take more than hiring an actor with a passing resemblance.'

'What?'

'I cannot stand it! I cannot take it! I can't! I can't!'

Suddenly there was whistling. An upbeat tune, slightly off key. Gianni turned around to see Eve, her pursed lips making the sound. Her hands were performing jerky motions, to the left, then to the right, up high, down low. Was that 'Y.M.C.A'?

But before Gianni could say or do anything, Eve had swished around right in front of his mother, still whistling, still in some sort of dance break. His mother seemed as bemused as he was. And then quickly, without incident, as if with a magician's sleight of hand, Eve was suddenly holding the knife.

She put it down on the granite work surface, out of reach, The whistling stopped and, next, Eve was resting a hand on each of his mother's shoulders, looking deep into her eyes.

'There we are,' she said softly and calmly. 'There we are, Valentina. Everything is calm now. You are safe. Everything is fine.'

She was talking to his mother as if she were a small child who had stood too close to a fire and narrowly escaped injury. Any second now and his mother was going to erupt like a volatile volcano, the way she always did when someone tried to take control of her. Except the only thing Valentina was doing right now was keeping her eyes on Eve, and not in a way that said she was about to leap for another kitchen aid to bludgeon someone with, but instead in a way that suggested she was beginning to calm down. Already, Gianni noted, her body had stopped quaking quite so much.

'Gianni,' Eve said, still calm, obviously now somehow in control of this situation. 'Please make your mother some hot water with lemon and sugar.'

As he dived for the kettle, he watched Eve lead his mother to one of the white rattan chairs around the table.

* * *

'I am seeing things,' Valentina whispered as Eve made sure she sat down safely. 'Ghosts.'

'Ghosts?'

'You think I am crazy,' Valentina said. '*I* think I am crazy. Ghosts, they are not real. They are tricks of the mind.'

'I didn't say I don't think ghosts are real,' Eve said as she pulled out another chair and sat down opposite her.

'You believe in them?'

'I believe that our brains can bring us reminders of things and that those reminders can take the shape of anything.'

'You have lost someone and seen them again?'

Eve sighed. 'I lost my father. It was a few years ago now. But most days I can see something that makes me think of him.'

'I am sorry for your loss,' Valentina said. 'But it is not the same. I see Riccardocino many times a day. I drink Riccardocino more times a day than I should but I do not see the form of Riccardo walking around the garden.'

'Is that what you saw?' Eve asked. 'Gianni's father walking around the garden?'

'Yes,' Valentina said, voice trembling again. 'But not that one. It was a vision from my past. The same. But different.' She went quiet for a moment, as if she was catching her breath, then: 'It was mountain tea, not coffee.'

Now Eve began to slowly realise what might have happened and it seemed Gianni had too, because he was there, abandoning the drink-making and standing next to the table with them.

* * *

'Mamma, did you not come home last night?' Gianni asked.

She shook her head. 'I was so mad with you. I am *still* so mad with you.'

Gianni put his hands to his head and squeezed the curls there. This wasn't how this was supposed to go.

'I stayed at the apartment in town. I had awful takeout and too much wine.'

She hadn't come home. She didn't know anything other than that he had postponed the meeting with Barista Irresistible. There was no use avoiding the subject now. Gianni was going to have to come out with it.

'Mamma, did you see Pan in the garden?'

Wide, frightened, glazed eyes looked up at him then, lips back to trembling. Next came the anger.

'So, this *is* what you do! A lookalike to throw me into panic before our meeting!'

He lowered himself into a squat and took hold of his mother's hands. 'Mamma, you are not seeing things that are not there. And it is not a lookalike.' He squeezed tight, keeping his eyes on her. 'Pan... he is here.'

'No!' she gasped, eyes bulging.

'Breathe, Valentina,' Eve encouraged. 'Slowly in and slowly out.'

Gianni continued to hold her hands as she heeded Eve's advice and drew in a long, loud breath and then let go of an even longer but much quieter one.

'You... found him,' she said, her words sounding scratchy and packed with emotion. 'You never said.'

No. He hadn't said. Because he was somehow still trying to make her pay for the fact she had kept this from him all these years. Like a juvenile. But this situation was bigger than his hurt feelings. It really wasn't only about him.

He swallowed. 'No,' he began. 'I didn't tell you. But yes, I found him. And he is here.'

Valentina burst into tears then. Loud shrieks of crying and a waterfall of tears. She let go of Gianni's hands and covered her face. If it proved only one thing it was that his mother *was* still human. That the kind, warm, if strict, mamma who had raised him was still there under this tough, all-business exterior she had perfected in recent years.

The doors to the garden flew open then and a rush of humid wind attacked the air-conditioned sanctuary. And with it came Pan.

'I heard screaming. Is everyone OK?'

Gianni stood up and nodded. 'We are OK.'

'OK,' Pan said, nodding too. But Gianni saw that his eyes were very much set on the sobbing wreck of his mother, who was still sitting in the chair, looking back at him.

'Do not look at me!' she scolded.

'I was not,' Pan replied. 'I was... looking at your chair. It is a fine chair. Handmade I think.'

'Why are you talking about chairs?' Gianni's mother yelled, hands coming away from her face.

This was good. Despite everything, even though Gianni knew the emotional breakdown he had just witnessed was necessary and for her own good, his mother shouting now, reverting to type, was somehow better.

'Gianni and I will make some tea,' Eve said as if she was in the middle of the most normal scenario in the world. She took hold of his arm and edged him towards the kitchen worktop.

'You are right,' Pan said. 'I did not come here to talk about chairs.' He sighed, a deep inhalation that Gianni felt carried the weight of years and years of being kept in the dark. 'I came here to talk about our son.'

Eve switched on the kettle and it began to rumble into action. All the while, Gianni kept his eyes on his mother's expression. He could almost see her mind working overtime, her eyes glazing over, her brow a concertina of fine lines not knowing which way to form. And then everything crumbled again.

'I am sorry, Pan. I am so, so sorry!'

'*Ochi, agapi mou. Ochi. Ola endaksi.*'

'I still... do not speak... any Greek,' she sobbed as Pan rested a hand on her shoulder.

'I say, no, my love,' Pan told her. 'Everything, it is OK.'

54

I need to talk to you ✖

Eve was sitting on a swing seat on a terrace off the guest suite, away from the main house. After she and Gianni had got properly dressed, she had stayed in the house for a while, making everyone hot lemon water and then tea whilst no one said very much. Then she gave them the suggestion that the approach to conversation should begin from a place of calm, with mutual respect, plus the understanding that no matter what, the past could not be changed. She had finished by saying that if they decided they needed her help as a 'talk expert' once conversation got going, Gianni knew where she was.

I need to talk to you ✖

The text wasn't going away. She put the phone on the seat next to her, face down, and kicked her legs a little, making the seat roll up and out into the sunshine, her toes almost interfering with the flight of a beetle. And then the phone began to ring.

Eve sat forward, one foot prodding the ground in an attempt to get the seat to stop swinging, and then she picked up the phone. As if somehow Glenda knew the message was weighing on Eve's mind, it was *her* name on the screen. Maybe it was serious after all. Except Ben was fine, Eve had just been messaging him. What to do? Answer? Let it go to voicemail? Would Glenda even leave a voicemail? Eve thought about what she had only just said some twenty minutes or so ago to Gianni, Valentina and Pan about mutual respect and not being able to change the past. Should she practice what she preached? If only for five minutes? Before she thought more, she pressed to accept.

'Hello.'

'Oh, you're there,' Glenda said. 'You didn't answer my text.'

'I wasn't sure it was from you.'

'It was my number, wasn't it?' Glenda snapped.

'It said you wanted to talk. You never want to talk to me.'

'That's not true. *You* never want to talk to *me*.'

Eve sighed, eyes passing over the beautiful garden all around her. She tried to channel its tranquillity. 'What do you want to talk about?'

'I found something.'

God? Another widower on Facebook?

'In your brother's room,' Glenda continued.

Now Eve was alert. But the counsellor in her, the one who spoke to many parents as well as students, knew what she should be saying next was spiel on boundaries and privacy. Except the last time there had been 'something' in Ben's room, it wasn't a crusty sock or an inappropriate screensaver on his laptop, it had been paperwork for a bank loan.

'I'm listening,' Eve said, both feet back on the ground now.

Glenda inhaled for so long Eve began to wonder if she was

actually going to say anything. Until: 'It was a betting slip. Tucked inside his pillowcase.'

Eve's heart sank and all those terrifying feelings she'd had the last time Ben entered therapy came rushing back. It felt as if she was the lead actress in a horrendous, glass-shattering, metal-bending car crash scene. This couldn't be happening again. It just *couldn't.*

'Are you sure?' Eve asked quickly.

'What d'you mean, am I sure? I've got it right in front of me now. I know what a betting slip looks like.'

'Well, what does it say on it?'

'Does it matter what the horse is called?' Glenda shouted. 'It says Race Three, "FrogInMyThroat", 2.40 p.m. Fontwell. And this is the worst bit. It says £100 to win.'

Eve closed her eyes and inhaled, her heart beating hard in her chest and in her ears. This was not what she wanted to hear. But she had to keep some perspective. All might not be what it seemed.

'Is it a printed betting slip? Or handwritten?'

'What bloody difference does that make?'

Eve gritted her teeth. 'It makes a difference if it's in Ben's bloody writing!'

'Oh... I see what you mean,' Glenda said, sounding a smidge contrite. 'No, it's printed. Square, no... rectangular. It says Totepool on it. And there's one of those funny square bar code things.'

'It's from a racecourse,' Eve said. She didn't know much about horseracing but she did know all the different kinds of betting slips. For some reason, Ben hadn't ever destroyed the evidence of his gambling, he had kept them like souvenirs of his destruction. 'There must be a date on it.'

'Yes,' Glenda said. 'There is. It's only three months ago.'

It was the exact opposite of what Eve wanted to hear. The foundational bricks of trust she'd thought Ben had been building since his last stint in therapy were starting to erode before her eyes. Nothing had changed. He was still gambling. This was why he had lost his job and the flat and why Charlie wasn't speaking to him. He had been nicking off to racecourses and betting again. And he had lied to her about it. How could Ben have done that again?

'Are you still there?' Glenda asked.

She didn't want to be still here. She wanted to soak her head in Gianni's fountain and rewind to the memories of last night, back when this issue wasn't a thing, and she was thinking of herself for once. What a short time that had lasted. She pressed her fingers into the fabric of the cushions on the swing seat, making an indent, trying to realign her thinking. 'Yes, I'm still here.'

'Well, you need to ask Ben about it,' Glenda said. 'Now, while I'm on the phone. I think we went too soft last time. I listened to you and let you do whatever it is you do to hypnotise the college kids and what good came from it? It took twice as long for him to realise the gambling was destroying him and get to therapy than it would have done if I'd just marched him there.'

Eve was caught between commenting on the word 'hypnotise' and Glenda's accusation that her approach had delayed Ben getting help the previous time. She knew, unlike Glenda it seemed, that the person who needed help had to very much be *on board* with getting help if any intervention was going to work.

'No one "went soft" last time,' Eve responded. 'My approach just didn't involve putting Ben into some kind of strangle-hold like you wanted to.'

'Put Ben on the phone!' Glenda ordered.

'If you wanted to speak to Ben, why didn't you phone him?'

'Don't you think I tried? Before I messaged you?'

Of course she had.

'He's not responding to my texts and he's not answering my calls. Because he's probably betting on whatever they bet on in

Greece! Plate-smashing or something! And I need to stop him because you'll take too long and it will be too late! Now, put him on the phone!'

'I can't,' Eve said.

'Evelyn!'

'I can't put Ben on because he's not here.'

'What d'you mean he's not there? Where is he?'

'He's in Corfu.'

'I know that. You came and took him and apparently moaned about me packing sun cream. Stop messing around, Evelyn!'

'I'm not. He's not here. Because I'm... in Italy.'

Immediately there was a ghost of guilt, popping up like a spectre and declaring a big, fat, boo! She had been nervous about coming here and leaving Ben, but Ben had been fine. Except now apparently Ben was not fine, Ben was hiding the fact he was still gambling and she had left him unsupervised in another country while she had been eating delicious Italian dishes.

'Sorry, what did you just say?'

'I said I'm in Italy right now. Ben's still in Greece.'

There was a silence then that seemed to stretch longer than the ads on ITV. Eve braced herself for whatever was coming. It was far better to let someone get something off their chest than pre-empt the strike.

'You've left Ben in Greece! On his own!' Glenda raved. 'You said you were taking him with you so you could keep an eye on him. Get some sense out of him about his job and the flat and what happened with Charlie!'

Truthfully, she'd just wanted Ben under better guidance than a woman who thought a microwavable pie was a balanced meal. But then she'd got on a plane to another country...

'He'll have fallen in with the wrong crowd. He'll be drinking too much and going to sleep in bins on the beach!'

OK, this was getting too much now. Time to speak and get Glenda to calm down. Eve wasn't sure her whistling trick was going to work this time.

'He's not going to be in a bin on the beach,' she said with certainty.

'How do you know?' Glenda shot back. 'Can you see Corfu from Italy?'

'He texted me, just now. He said he was fine.'

'Well, he's not exactly going to say anything else, is he? Especially if you're roaming around in Rome without him!'

'I'm not in Rome. I'm in Verona. Listen, there's no point shouting at me about this. It's not going to solve anything.'

'I didn't want to shout at you! I wanted to shout at Ben, but, as I said, he's not answering his phone. Probably because he's sold it for euros to go gambling!'

The pull to just disconnect the call now was so strong. Make the noise and the accusations and all the usual Glenda-drama stop. But she was bigger than that. Better than that.

'I blame your father!'

Now Eve's skin bristled and her irritation started to morph into anger. She went to interrupt but Glenda carried on.

'He was a terrible role model really. No enthusiasm for anything but standing at the end of that bar after work. He should have been playing football with Ben, spending time with him, keeping him on the straight and narrow.'

'I'm not listening to this,' Eve said. Her dad *had* spent time with them. They'd *all* gone to the pub. There had been those bottles of Coke and scampi fries, cockles from the fish man, choosing tickets for the meat draw. Fun family times.

'No, of course you're not listening! Because you still think your dad was a saint!'

Glenda had said the last sentence with such brutality it

shocked Eve. 'What are you talking about? How is any of this Dad's fault?'

There was quiet from the other end of the phone then, just the occasional jagged inward breath coming from an obviously pent-up Glenda.

'Just talk to your brother. Stop him from pawning his good trainers and his iPad. Whenever you're back from wherever you've gone to. Goodbye, Evelyn.'

55

'Are you two going to say anything to one another? Or are we to sit here and stare at this lemon water until it goes cold?' Gianni asked.

He, his mother and Pan might be sat around the kitchen table but it was as much a boardroom type tension as he had ever felt. Maybe he should go and get Eve. Someone who was distanced from the situation might be able to suggest what to do. He knew he was supposed to be calm and respectful but, right now, no one was saying anything at all.

'I hate the idea of this drink,' his mother admitted, pushing the cup and saucer away. She got to her feet. 'I will make coffee.'

'Coffee will rot away your insides,' Pan said calmly. 'I told you this when we first met.'

'And I am still here, am I not?' she countered. 'All of my insides still inside.'

'Sit down, Mamma,' Gianni said. 'And, as you have been the first to try to escape by standing up, you can begin.'

'I do not know what to say,' she replied, folding her arms across her chest.

'Let me make a suggestion,' Gianni said. 'How about you tell

Pan why you told him you would marry him and then you left and married someone else.'

The colour drained from her face and she shot a harsh look at Pan. 'You tell him this?'

Pan shrugged. 'The boy is twenty-five years old. Does he not deserve the truth?'

'Yes! But not only *your* truth!'

'Is what I say not true?'

His mother thumped down into her chair again. 'There is a lot more to it than that.'

'And that is why we are here together,' Gianni said. 'So, Mamma, please begin.'

She shook her head, her discomfort plain to see.

'You were never short of words on Corfu,' Pan commented, reaching for his cup and taking a sip of his lemon water.

'You were much more handsome back then,' she snapped.

Pan smiled and looked at Gianni. 'I *was* very handsome back then.'

'And you flattered every woman you met,' she carried on, her fingers fiddling with the lace on the edge of the tablecloth.

'I complimented people, that is all,' Pan said. 'It is important in hospitality that your customers feel special. Is it not the same in the coffee industry?'

Gianni sighed. Perhaps he shouldn't be here. Maybe his presence wasn't helping. He stood up, as insignificantly as he could, moving into the kitchen, giving them some space.

'It is not the same,' his mother told him. 'Our brand is about luxury. Special coffee for customers who already know they are special.'

Pan laughed, hard, and for a considerable amount of time. 'Oh, Valentina, you really are not the girl I met in Greece.'

Gianni leaned against the worktop and waited for his mother

to respond. He wasn't sure he had heard anyone talk to her quite how Pan was talking to her. Not even Riccardo. But Pan did talk that way to everyone – he was open and honest.

'Is that why you are here?' his mother asked abruptly. 'To see if I am the same stupid person full of crazy dreams you met back then?'

'You were not stupid,' Pan said, softer now. 'And your dreams were not crazy.'

'They were the dreams of someone who thought only of herself,' she countered.

'That is why they are called dreams,' Pan said. 'But you did not only think of yourself. I was once a part of those dreams.'

She sniffed and Gianni looked at her, her face crumpling again as she began to cry.

'I could not stay in Greece. Not... after I got that phone call.'

'What phone call?' Pan asked.

She shook her head. 'My mother, she had her first stroke. She was in the hospital. That was why I had to leave.'

'Valentina,' Pan said, reaching for her hands and taking them in his.

Gianni watched, but no sooner had Pan made contact than his mother withdrew, sitting as far back in her seat as she could.

'I know what you are going to say,' she began. 'You are going to say that I should have told you. That you would have come to Italy with me. That whatever happened with my mother, we could have adapted our dreams.'

'I would have said all of that,' Pan said, assuring her. 'But the decision would have been yours to make. That was how our relationship was, was it not?'

'Oh, Pan, we made decisions about what cliff edges to jump from or... whether to order *tzatziki* or *tirokfateri* with our bread. We did not have to think about physio and rehabilitation or... babies.'

Gianni pressed his back into the worktop. *He* was the baby. He was *their* baby. Now he felt he needed coffee more than anyone else.

'But to not tell me. About your mother. And later, about the baby,' Pan said. 'You know how I feel about family. You know about... my childhood.'

'Is this something to do with why some people call you Gorgios?' Gianni asked.

Both Pan and his mother looked at him as if they had forgotten he was even in the room. Neither of them said anything in response.

'Is that your name?' Gianni asked.

Pan began to speak. 'Gorgios was the name given to me by my mother. When I was nine months old, she put me in a box outside the church of Saint Vasilios in Episkepsi and she left the island with her Albanian boyfriend.'

'What?' Gianni said, shocked.

'They tell me, when I was older, that I ate half of the cardboard before I was found. See, I have never known family in the traditional way, Gianni. I too have never known my father. I was left exactly like Baby Yiayia.' He sighed. 'I was looked after by the priest. He was a good man, but he was strict. He kept locked doors.'

Suddenly Gianni understood more than ever, and guilt invaded him about how he had treated Pan.

'At thirteen, I decided to make my own way.'

'Thirteen,' Gianni said. 'You lived alone when you were thirteen.'

'Not alone,' Pan said. 'With nature. Always with nature. That is why I change my name. Pan, it is the name of the god of shepherds, of fields. Historically he has the body of a man and the legs of a goat.' He stretched out his legs and wiggled them a little. 'I think they look more like a goat as I get older.'

'You are still stupid,' his mother remarked.

'And you are still beautiful,' Pan whispered.

'See!' she said, her tone accusatory. 'A charmer! Someone who flatters every chance they get.'

'Someone who makes people feel special,' Gianni interrupted. 'Like Riccardo.'

His father's name in the air got the hush the mention deserved and then Pan looked at his mother.

'I want to know about Riccardo. Tell me about the most wonderful man who helped you raise our son so well.'

56

Eve closed her eyes as the ringtone beeped slowly. On, then off, then on, then off again. *Please answer.* She was pacing Gianni's lounge room, her phone pressed to her ear, trying to enjoy a little air conditioning after getting a bit sun-blushed outside in the garden. The call timed out. Now it seemed Ben wasn't answering *her* calls either. Was there a reason for that or was he out on the horses? Perhaps Gabby had got him to help at the hotel in Almyros. He was definitely not in a bin on the beach.

What time was it in Corfu? She checked her watch. Mid-morning now. Glenda had got into her head. But this time there was evidence, hard evidence in the form of that betting slip. She had to speak to Ben about it. But maybe all those missed calls from Glenda had given him a heads-up that he was sprung.

There was only one other thing she could do from here and that was to call Gabby. She hoped at least one person she knew in Corfu would answer her.

'Hello. Eve?'

'Gabby, you're there. Great. Good. Where actually are you right now?' she asked, striding towards Gianni's desk.

'I'm at Petra. They called me in to do a shift and—'

'OK, so is Ben with you?' She closed her eyes again and tried to wish it true.

'Ben? No, no, why would Ben be with me? I'm working so Ben isn't here, at all.'

Eve opened her eyes, struck by the fact her friend had said her brother's name three times. 'Gabby, what's going on?'

'Argh! You know, don't you?' she said. 'I told Ben you would know. You *always* know, even when we're not in the same country. It's like a person-reading sixth sense.'

Eve swallowed. 'What has he told you? Because Glenda is freaking out.'

'What? How does your mum know? Has she got software on his phone? I mean, Ben said he was pretty sure she tracks his iPhone but—'

'Gabby,' Eve interrupted. 'What has Ben said to you?'

'Said to me?'

Why was this so difficult? She turned around, nudging the edge of Gianni's laptop with her hip. She could hear the sounds of Corfu down the phone, the Greek voices, the music from the radio, the burr of a moped passing by, the crush of the waves... It all felt so terribly far away. She put a hand to the computer and straightened it back up. No more beating around the bush.

'Ben's gambling again. Glenda found a betting slip in his bedclothes. It's... only three months old.' She hated how the words sounded coming from her mouth, being voiced to someone else, making the situation a whole lot more real.

'What? I mean... that wasn't what I thought you were going to say and... well, do you think it's really true?'

Eve frowned, her fingers grazing the corner of the laptop screen, unhappy it wasn't safe on the edge of the desk. 'Glenda has a betting slip that's only three months old. In her hands.'

'I heard what you said. I just... I mean... there could be other reasons for it, right? Or, he could have had one slip up, three months ago and now he's fine again.'

Eve shook her head. That was what she'd wanted to think. This wasn't serious. It was a habit that could be easily broken. Like eating fewer takeaways or not straying onto the Black Friday deals. But it was nothing like that. She needed to sort this the same way she had sorted it at home. By being prepared.

'So, Ben hasn't said anything to you about it? Nothing at all, even something over a couple of beers that could, in any way, have been about straying back to his old ways?'

'No,' Gabby said. 'But, there is something you should know. Ben said not to say anything yet but... we kissed,' Gabby said. 'Ben and me. Last night. Outside Nikos's.'

Eve closed her eyes again, her heart sinking. If she hadn't had that phone call with Glenda, would she be feeling differently? Her brother and her best friend, she loved them both so much but now, after the news of FrogInMyThroat and Fontwell, well, Ben was not in a place where he could make those kinds of decisions and there was no way she wanted Gabby to be a part of this upcoming horror show. She used her thumbnail to trace a line across the trackpad of Gianni's laptop and suddenly the screen came to life.

English words appeared...

Regeneration for the new generation

Global Boba – flavours from around the world infused with Riccardocino premium coffee beans

Vitamin-T – coffee boba including your daily vitamins and minerals

Not Sober Boba – the ultimate night out with alcoholic popping bubbles

A good boba can change your day. Feeling depressed, have a boba. Celebrating something, have a boba.

'Eve, did you hear what I said?'

Eve's hand started to shake as she scrolled down further. On the screen was a rough business plan, an outline for different drinks, their target markets and how Riccardocino was going to implement the expansion of its range. Was this what Gianni's meeting had been about?

'Eve.'

She wanted to throw up. Because now it was completely clear. This was what she had talked about with Gianni. Conversations between them she thought were just conversations. But they had been reconnaissance for a new business enterprise. These were her *exact* words she was reading. *Her* ideas. She had told Gianni what Mitchell had done to her and he had done *exactly* the same. All those memories of reading Mitchell's job application and *her* dissertation accompanying it were playing like scenes from a movie now. Mitchell's ease of trying to manoeuvre his way out of what he had done, making her feel like she was overreacting, that he had applied for this job for them as a couple. And then there was Glenda's voice in her head, telling her her brother was betting again, Ben drunk and out of control, stealing from his friends, taking from her... This was too much. This was an emotional Armageddon.

'Eve, are you still there?' Gabby shouted.

'Yes,' Eve answered, turning away from the laptop as the first tear escaped her eyes and her head began to pound. 'I'm here.' She took a deep breath. 'But... I'm coming back. I'm going to be on the first flight out to Corfu.'

57

Gianni was exhausted, his eyes stinging as he sat on the uncomfortable sofa. He had always hated this sofa. It seemed to have been made to make you sit upright with its straight back and stiff cushions. But he wasn't in the mood for the softer couch in one of the other sitting rooms just yet. He wanted upright for a minute longer. And then, when he had regrouped, he wanted to get Eve and get out of here, make some time for just them.

'Gianni.'

It was his mother, standing under the archway, her shoes off.

'Please tell me you have not killed Pan,' he breathed. 'Because I am too tired to be burying any bodies.'

'Don't be crazy! Why would you say such a thing?'

'Because you shout at each other like you are married. The way you used to shout at Papa... it is the same.' He rubbed at his eyes and tried to lean forward.

'Oh no, Gianni. We do not argue like your father and I used to argue,' she said, coming closer, stockinged feet slipping over the tiles. 'Riccardo, he had a way of arguing like no other. It was almost like a dance.' She smiled. 'He would start off very slowly, like a waltz, deliberate statements pounding and then when I would counter, he would up the speed – jab, jab, jab – until he turned purple. And usually then he would run out of energy and then I would say something that would make him laugh.' She smiled again. 'And you remember how much he used to laugh and how—'

'It would make the ornaments on the walls shake,' Gianni finished for her.

She moved in front of him. 'May I sit down?'

Gianni shrugged. 'It is not comfortable.'

'I know. Awful thing. Did I tell you, it was Riccardo's mother's. It is as straight-backed as she was. I had it re-covered but it always feels like she is standing behind me when I sit on it.' She sat down, her feet not meeting the floor. 'And it is too high.'

'Where is Pan?' Gianni asked. 'If he is not dead.'

'I made ciabattas. I told him to take one to Eve. I know you keep no food in that kitchen of yours, the poor girl must be starving.'

'I am going to take her to lunch,' Gianni said. 'I want to make this trip special for her no matter the family circumstances right now.'

His mother took his hand in hers and squeezed. 'I want to say sorry, Gianni.'

He drew in a breath. 'What for?'

'Everything. Just... everything. I do not even know where to begin. For not being there so much for Riccardo when he was near the end, for putting business first, for—'

'Not telling me I have a Greek father?'

She nodded. 'Especially for that. You know, I could always see him in you, Gianni. Pan.' She paused as if in thought. 'Do you remember that homeless dog in the city? The one you fed your gelato to? It followed you all day and you would have taken him home if I had let you. You were like Pan then, wanting to look after a stray, telling it it was the most handsome dog you had ever seen.' She laughed. 'It was so flea-bitten, with a torn ear and teeth that were too long.'

'And it smelled very bad,' Gianni said, recalling.

'You do remember!'

'Yes,' he said. 'We took him back to the office and he tried to eat Papa's tie.'

'That's right,' she said, laughing. 'He was so angry, but then you said that his tie and your ice cream might be the only thing that poor dog had in its stomach for the rest of the week.'

'And Papa bought him steak and took him to the rescue shelter.' He hadn't realised that he still had these small memories from his childhood.

'I thought about Pan that evening. I thought about what he might think of his son being kind, putting others first. But then I looked at you, sitting with Riccardo, copying everything he did like you were his shadow and... I made another cake.'

There was that memory again. His mother usually such a reluctant cook, forgetting she had turned on the oven, burning things when she did remember, yet he recalled her baking this cake – walnuts, raisins, orange juice. Always the same cake.

'I remember the cake,' Gianni said. 'It was called something to do with a saint.'

His mother gasped then. 'You remember this too!'

'It was the only thing you ever cooked that you took care with.'

She nodded, as if accepting that was true. 'Gianni, I loved Riccardo with all my heart. No, more than that. I loved him with every part of me. We were destined to be together. But love, it is complicated, and sometimes, only sometimes, I would make the cake and I would wonder what Pan was doing or who he might be married to, whether he had children, if he was happy.' She sighed. 'Greeks make the cake every 27 August in honour of Saint Fanourios. But, also, it is meant to help you find lost things. Pan made it with me in the kitchen of the little mountain taverna where he worked, and he said... if we always made the cake, we would never lose each other.' Tears were escaping her now. 'I feel that perhaps you and I should make it together so we can never lose each other.'

'Mamma,' Gianni said. 'That is not going to happen.'

'But the business and—'

'We may have different ideas, but what is a family business without conflicting opinions?'

'Gianni!'

Pan's voice was urgent. He rushed into the room, a filled ciabatta on a plate in his hands.

'What are you doing?' his mother asked, struggling to get up from the sofa. 'You are supposed to be giving that to Eve.'

Gianni could see something was wrong from Pan's expression.

'What is it?' he asked, standing too.

'It is Eve,' Pan said. 'She is gone.'

58

VERONA, ITALY

'Gianni, you will wear out the soles of your shoes if you carry on like this!'

'Calm, Valentina. Shouting at the boy is not doing any good.'

The truth was, *nothing* was doing any good. Because he had walked around the whole estate, his parents on his heels for the most part, searching at first, phoning when he was really convinced that Eve *had* left and still, he had no real answers. What had gone wrong? He knew he had left her by herself while he tried to sort out this twenty-six-year-old mess, but she'd said she understood, said she was going to chill in the garden. How did it go from that to everything of hers being gone from his room – the dress she'd been wearing last night that had still been damp on his bedroom floor, that hair tie she sometimes wore around her wrist, her rucksack.

He turned around sharply, hIs mother almost walking right into him. 'I don't know what to do! Where is she? Why has she left me?'

When he'd said the last sentence, Gianni realised exactly how much he cared about Eve and how scared he was that this was the end when it had only just begun. He swallowed down the emotion, the sunlight offering not warming consolation but blinding ferocity.

'You have called her and she has not answered,' his mother said. 'This means she needs space.' She put her hands on his arms and squeezed.

Pan snorted. 'So, he has to what? Do nothing?'

His mother glared at Pan. 'When a woman needs space, it is usually for good reason.'

'But that is the point. I do not know the reason. Everything was fine. More than fine. It was good. It was…'

He stopped talking, either because he didn't feel comfortable sharing something this personal aloud or because he didn't want to commit to the air that this connection with Eve had stepped over every self-imposed boundary and elevated itself to a whole different level. Perhaps it was a mix of both.

'You need to talk,' Pan told him. 'You need to find her and you need to get to the root of what has happened. Because something must have happened.'

Gianni nodded.

'And you really have no idea what?'

He shook his head.

'And you have called other people?' Pan asked, as if he was going through a mental checklist.

'I spoke to Ben. He said he did not know anything. That Eve had texted him this morning and that she had sounded really happy. Now he is worried too.'

'Do not worry, there is always a chance to put it right,' Pan said, placing a hand on his shoulder. 'Or at least a chance to have a conversation, find out how she is feeling. When you find her.'

Gianni's phone rumbled in his hand and his eyes darted to the screen. 'It's a text from Ben.' He scanned it quickly and then his shoulders sagged. She had left the country. 'Eve's on her way back to Corfu.'

'That is good,' Pan said, nodding in a satisfied manner.

'Good?' Gianni asked, looking away from the phone. 'How is it good?'

'Because you now know where she is. And you can take action.'

'Yes,' Gianni said. 'Yes, I can... get on the next flight back there and I can find out what's going on, talk to her and—'

'No, no, no,' his mother said. 'You cannot do that. I will not let you do that.'

'Mamma—' He wanted to do something, go, take action.

'No, Gianni. At least, not yet. Eve has chosen to go, without saying anything to anyone. This means whatever made her leave is serious, yes?'

'I guess so,' Gianni answered, feet still itching to run.

'You have to take a step back,' she said. 'You do not have to tell me how much you care for her, it is written right the way through you, and I see it in your eyes. But you have to think of Eve now. Not you. Not what you want. What *she* wants. And if she wanted to talk to you right now then she would have stayed.'

He turned to Pan. 'What would you do?'

'Oh, Gianni,' Pan said, shaking his head. 'Do not ask me what I would do. I believe you already know the answer to that.'

'OK, I am asking for your opinion,' Gianni said. 'What do you think *I* should do?'

Pan sighed. 'On this occasion, only temporarily, I think that your mother may be right.'

Gianni gasped, hands going to his head, feeling an acute internal pain as he realised he was going to have to accept the situation. For now, at least.

'Gianni,' Pan said. 'I am not saying that you do not follow Eve back to Corfu. I am saying only that you wait. Let her get back.

Give her time with her own thoughts and feelings, no matter what they may be. It will give her the space it seems like she needs and it will give you the opportunity to work on your plea.'

'Pan!' his mother exclaimed. 'What are you talking about?'

Pan splayed his hands out and shrugged at the same time. 'One thing I have learned over the years is that giving up on something is different to letting something go.'

Gianni already knew he wasn't going to give up. He was emotionally invested. He wanted to know how Eve was feeling and make it better. But he also didn't want to crowd her, to make her feel pushed into a situation. Maybe she'd had second thoughts this morning and come to the conclusion they had gone too fast last night...

'OK,' he said, a more controlled breath leaving him. 'OK.'

Except, what *did* he do now?

'I know what you are thinking, Gianni,' his mother said, looping her arm around his and beginning to walk with him slowly along the path.

'I am thinking that I am still thinking about Eve,' he admitted.

'Exactly. And you need a distraction for the rest of today. Something that does not involve watching two middle-aged people arguing about who is right or wrong in situations we cannot change. Like Eve herself said about the past, it cannot be altered.'

Gianni sighed. 'What do you suggest?'

'I suggest that you show me your new ideas for Barista Irresistible,' she said.

'How do you...' He stopped himself from talking because he knew the answer. 'Paolo.'

'He is a loyal friend to you, Gianni. But you underestimated my powers of persuasion.'

'What did you do to him?'

She laughed then. 'You talk like I might have skills as a government interrogator.'

'Mamma,' Gianni said, his tone demanding that she give him a straight answer.

'I let him have the use of Riccardo's boat for the weekend. Full crew. Everything he and Giovanni could need.' She squeezed his arm. 'Now, I will make coffee—'

'No coffee for me,' Pan interjected. 'I will have the hot water with lemon.'

'Mamma, could you just give me a minute?' Gianni said, unhitching himself from her.

'Of course.' She took hold of his hand for a moment and squeezed it tight. 'I will be in the kitchen.'

She moved off and, as soon as she had gone, Pan put a hand on Gianni's arm.

'You are OK,' Pan said.

'I think so,' Gianni replied.

'It was not a question, Gianni. I am telling you. You are OK.'

Gianni nodded. 'And you? Are you OK?'

Pan didn't immediately come back with anything.

'That *was* a question,' Gianni clarified.

'I am OK,' he said. 'I am desperate to have a cigarette but... I am glad to be here. I have some of the answers I was looking for. I may not like all of them, but we cannot change the past, yes? We can only look forwards, not back.'

But where was Gianni's forwards now? It was such a short time ago since Riccardo had died, since he'd found out he had another father, that he was Greek, and still the coffee empire was where his future had been set. Then meeting Eve had introduced him to something else, another side to him, one that was usually buried deep. He'd enjoyed who he was when that came to the fore. He didn't want to cover it over again.

'Strong foundations can never be completely destroyed, Gianni,' Pan said, intuitive as always. 'If you and Eve are meant to be together it will be so.'

'But you and my mother,' Gianni countered. 'It did not work that way for you.'

Pan laughed then. 'Ha! Is that what you think?' He slapped a hand hard on Gianni's back. 'You are the proof that, in some way, we will always be bound together.'

It was enough for Gianni to raise a small smile. 'When I said I would give Eve time I want you to know I do not intend for it to be twenty-five years before we have our next conversation.'

'I agree,' Pan said, walking alongside him, boots crunching on the gravel path. 'And do not make the same mistake I did. The next time you see her, talk. And more importantly, listen. Listening, *really* listening to a woman, is the greatest skill a man can possess.'

Gianni nodded. He only hoped Eve was going to give him that chance.

59

QUALITY GRILL, EPISKEPSI

The village was buzzy tonight. From residents gathering around a fish man's van to a group of men and women sitting on plastic chairs outside the tiny mini market. The cats were waiting in the shadows in the hope the fish man dropped something they could snatch and there were half a dozen people inside Nikos's grillroom, bottles of Alfa and Mamos beer between them. In normal circumstances it was a backdrop Eve would find endearing. Relaxing Greek life going on around her, the tourist in her wanting to take photos of the doors with peeling paint, broken shutters and the archaic tractor that would never start again. But tonight, all she felt was shattered and hollow.

'OK?' Ben asked, pouring some white wine into her glass.

He'd been asking that a lot since she'd turned up at Safe Animals, dusty, sweaty and longing for a shower and a bottle of water. Ben had called her when she'd been in Bari – a connection she hadn't anticipated making – asking if she was OK and telling her that Gianni had been phoning the sanctuary. She'd said very little on that call but she'd told Ben if Gianni called again he could pass on that she hadn't been kidnapped by the Mafia and to leave it at that. She had said nothing else to her brother yet. Because the truth was, she didn't really know where to start. But what was it she kept saying to everyone else? You didn't have to start from the beginning – not that she was even sure where the beginning was – you just had to start somewhere. One small sentence and then build.

'It's good to be back here,' she said.

'Yeah?' His tone was tentative. As if he didn't quite know what she was going to say next.

'It's good to see you.'

'Eve, you've been gone a day and a bit.'

And so, so much had changed.

'Glenda phoned me,' she said, tightening her fingers around the glass of wine.

'Is it because I haven't been answering her calls?' Ben asked with a sigh. 'The last time I spoke to her she was panicking about some earthquake she'd heard about here. I looked it up. It was like a million miles away from Corfu. She worries about me more than you do.'

Eve wasn't sure that was true. Not the way she was feeling now. But this conversation had to be had, didn't it? She absolutely did not feel strong enough for it, but burying her head in the sand wasn't going to solve anything.

'She found a betting slip in your room.'

Eve concentrated on her brother's expression, waiting for that tell-tale drawing in of breath, pupil dilation, a flick of his tongue over his lips as he prepared to lie to her.

'Right,' Ben said with none of his usual hallmark facials. 'So, was it Fontwell or was it Newbury?'

'What?' She shook her head, failing to comprehend what was going on here.

'Was she snooping around my pillowcase or my jumper drawer?'

'I—'

'So what did you say to her?' he asked, the beginnings of anger definitely starting to brew. 'When she told you this?'

'I... said I would speak to you about it.' Eve swallowed.

'So, you didn't, like, both jump to the conclusion that I was gambling again, right? She hasn't been on the phone to GA trying to get confidential information again, has she?'

'Ben—'

'That's what happened, isn't it? You both assumed I'd fallen off the horse and that that's why I've lost the flat and why I've lost my job and fallen out with Charlie!'

The people inside Nikos's had turned away from the television now and were looking towards their table. Even the birds in the cage above the door weren't chirping like usual.

'Well,' she started. 'To be fair you haven't told either of us what happened with any of that and when she said she'd found that slip I—'

'Eve,' Ben said, his expression serious. 'I told you, before you went to Italy, that I wasn't gambling again. And I was being honest.' He picked up his beer bottle and gestured with it. 'So, what, you didn't believe me?' He swigged back the drink.

'No... I did. I just—'

'Took the word and the "evidence" of someone you don't even like over *my* word? Thanks, Eve, that makes me feel really special.'

How had she got this so wrong? This was supposed to be a low-key, calm, no finger-pointing and accusations evening together and it was fast turning into an episode of *EastEnders*. Somehow, she had to rescue it.

'You can't blame us for thinking the worst,' she said.

'What? Are you kidding me right now?'

'Ben, things were bad the first time but the last time they were a hundred times worse. We don't want to see you like that again.'

'Well, funnily enough, I don't want to *be* like that again either!'

'Then talk to me!' she said, raising her voice. 'Tell me what's going on. All of it. Your job, the apartment, Charlie.'

Ben shook his head and now his expression did change. But it wasn't someone attempting to cover up something, a face Eve had seen many times before, it was like fear was taking over. The hand holding his bottle of Alfa began to tremble ever so slightly.

'I... don't want to,' he said, the words barely making it out of his mouth.

'Why not?' she asked. That was a stupid reply from someone who should know much better. She rephrased. 'OK, I can tell you're feeling really uncomfortable about whatever it is but, trust me, Ben, there's nothing you can't tell me.' She took a breath. 'Nothing, even if it *is* that you're gambling again, OK?'

'For fuck's sake, Eve. I'm not gambling again!'

He'd shouted the statement and very quickly afterwards someone turned the television volume up. The football match was now louder than the fan rotating close to them. She watched Ben, who was gripping his bottle now, his face a picture of conflict. Was he going to tell her?

Finally, he let out a sigh. 'I have three betting slips,' Ben admitted. 'Fontwell is in my pillowcase. Newbury is in my jumper drawer. And I brought Salisbury with me.' He sighed. 'On the back of each one is the phone number of my sponsor – Rick. They were never my betting slips. They're from a stack they have at therapy. Some people can't go near them, others like to challenge their power. Yeah, I could have written Rick's number on a piece of note paper but, for me, it's about feeling that slip in my hand and knowing that I'm in control now, but also knowing that if I ever feel like I'm out of control, Rick's number is right there, on the back of something that tried to destroy me.'

'Ben—' Eve had tears in her eyes. Half from embarrassment because she hadn't taken him at his word and half from sadness at not knowing that he had this catch-net.

'For the last time, I am *not* gambling again.'

He took a long, deep breath, his chest heaving. She sensed there was more coming.

'The truth is... I... have anxiety.' He put his hand to his chest. 'I have panic attacks and... that's why I lost my job and that's why Charlie won't talk to me any more... Because I'm scared that no matter what I do, I'm going to have another one and put someone else in danger.'

The second the tears started to fall from her brother's eyes all Eve's training went spiralling into the humid air. She leapt up from her seat, moving to the other side of the table and throwing her arms around him.

'I had a panic attack... on the scaffold... because I thought Charlie was going to fall off,' Ben carried on, crying hard. 'And, in the end, I almost... *caused* him to fall off. And they couldn't have me putting people at risk.'

'Shh, it's OK, Ben, just breathe.'

'It's not OK. It's lame and... it's scary and... I don't know why I have this after doing everything I've done to get on the right track.'

'I know,' she said. 'I know how hard you've worked, and I am so, so sorry that I doubted you.' She smoothed a hand over his hair the way she had done when he was younger, tucked up in his bed with the army camouflage duvet cover, his toy owl in the crook of his arm.

He wriggled a little, his hands in fists, trying to fight with his emotions as well as her affection. 'No one's looking, right? They're all watching the football.'

'No one's looking,' she reassured him, rubbing his shoulder. 'Well, except those cats over there. But I think it's because the fish man's gone and they know we have ribs coming.'

Ben tried to laugh at her comment, but it came out weak. 'Listen, Eve, I don't want you to full-on worry about it. I've seen the doctor and I'm on the waiting list for a counsellor, but you know how things are with the NHS.'

She talked to college students suffering from anxiety all the time. She should have known. She should have seen this coming and been able to head it off before it got out of control. She couldn't help her expression giving her away.

'Don't look like that,' Ben said.

'I wasn't.'

'You were. And I know you could do the sit-me-in-a-leather-chair-and-hypnotise-me stuff but... I really just need you to be my sister. Not my therapist.'

She nodded, doing her best to look like she understood his reasoning. She did understand. But she didn't have to like that she felt a bit helpless.

'Anyway,' he said, plucking a serviette from the container on the table and blowing his nose. 'In Corfu, when I'm not worrying about something happening to you, things have been... better. I mean the wedding reception was a bit full on and when you disappeared that night, I lost it a bit. But, in general, I'm doing better here. I feel calmer, working with the animals and not thinking about what's going on in the UK.'

'Really?'

He nodded. 'Yeah, really. Greece is good for me.'

Eve smiled. 'That's so good to hear.'

It was then that a huge platter full of ribs was put down in front of them, together with a mound of oregano-sprinkled fries.

'Wow,' Ben said. 'Good job I'm starving.' He went in for the fries first.

Eve took a slow sip of her wine, letting the alcohol soothe her. Ben was still battling hard. It might not be the war that she and Glenda had thought it was, but it was no less tough. And he had been trying to manage it on his own, with that consummate blokes-can't-have-issues-if-they-want-to-be-blokes attitude. Telling her had been huge for him and she was so glad he'd finally opened up.

'Eve,' Ben said, stopping himself pawing at the chips as two cats crossed the road to take up a position under their table. 'You didn't leave Italy because you thought I was gambling again?'

She shook her head quickly. Was it 100 per cent the truth? No. But it had been the culmination of concern for Ben and reading her ideas on another laptop screen in such similar circumstances to one of the most awful times of her life that had made her throw everything she'd packed back into her bag and leave the country.

'So, what happened with Gianni?'

'Can we not talk about it? Just for now. Just for tonight. I'm so tired and I really only want to eat this food and drink this wine and for you to catch me up on you and Gabby.'

Immediately, Ben's face lightened, and he broke into a smile. 'You're not mad, are you?'

'Why would I be mad?'

'I dunno. I thought maybe there was some best-friend-can't-date-my-brother code of conduct you'd get pissed about.'

'Ah, so you're dating now,' Eve teased. 'I thought it was only one kiss.'

'Leave off,' he said, blushing.

Eve smiled, her eyes drifting to the street where just down the road she saw Spiros and Vasiliki in conversation with someone on the terrace. As much as she was pleased to be back in what was becoming familiarity, it all felt a little different now, the shine diminished, the anticipation of being at the start of a romance extinguished. She sighed and looked to the sky. Even the stars didn't have the same sparkle.

'You OK?' Ben asked.

She nodded as convincingly as she could manage. 'I'm fine.'

60

SAFE ANIMALS SANCTUARY, EPISKEPSI

Hard work was absolutely the answer when you were working through things. And Eve was repeating that statement as she pitchforked horse dung and damp straw into a wheelbarrow. Milo and Phantom were out in the field; only Pnévma remained nearby, her head hanging over the door of the stable, watching Eve's every move.

It had been two days since she'd got back from Italy and despite making the most of the endless sunshine, helping Gabby with a shift at the mountain café as she covered for Pan, and spending time with the animals and Ben, she'd be lying if she said her mind hadn't often wandered to Gianni. And she loathed herself for that. He was not who he had made himself out to be. He had listened to her heartache then used the same *modus operandi* as Mitchell and put it into a business plan. Did she need to know why? Why did it matter? She'd been there before, seeing her ideas passed off as someone else's. This time it was being used to make money, for Gianni to buy himself more fountains, to have sex with the next gullible woman.

She grunted in frustration, lifting another smelly load on the pitchfork into the barrow and blowing her fringe up and off her face. She was thinking about him now, again! His dark hair that got curlier when it was wet, the beautiful opera they had got caught up in together, the warmth of his embrace, the heat of his skin next to hers...

Maybe the fact that he had used her ideas like that was out of character, but perhaps what he had shown her had no truth attached to it in the first place. And coming to Corfu hadn't ever been about finding a romantic connection anyway, it had been about seeing Gabby and spending time with her brother. This tiny little meaningless frisson of something wasn't worth worrying about, was it?

'Help me out, Spirit,' she said, addressing the horse. Her ears pricked up as if she knew she was being spoken to. 'Tell me that I did the right thing, cutting loose before I got any deeper.'

But, in truth, she had been deeper than she had been with anyone since Mitchell, any deeper and she'd have been needing a lifejacket. She still hadn't opened up to Gabby or Ben about what had happened. All she had said was a rather dramatic yet aloof and non-descriptive, 'Italy wasn't quite what I thought it would be'. It told them precisely nothing and she knew she wasn't going to be able to keep holding off for long.

'Yabby!'

The horse whinnied and Eve came out of the stable to see who was approaching. Shielding her eyes from the sun, she saw Vasiliki, Aleka and Spiros making their way across the courtyard towards the stable block. She wasn't sure she had ever seen Aleka walk, so to find out that the old woman could was heartening, even with a stick to aid her. Then Eve noticed Spiros had Baby Yiayia in a shawl across his front.

'Ah, Eve, we are here,' Vasiliki shouted. 'Where is Yabby?'

'*Kalimera*,' Eve greeted, brushing her hands together, straw falling from her fingers as she approached. 'Yabby – Gabby – is with Bambi the rabbit, painting his mange medication on him and then she has to go to the other side of the island to collect a turkey who has his head stuck in a bucket, if they can't get the bucket off before she gets there. It's fine for the minute, it's just noisy and frustrated apparently.' She turned to the baby, taking one of his little fists in her hand and waving it up and down.

'Aww, Baby Yiayia, it's so good to see you.'

'Yes, speak English to him,' Vasiliki encouraged. 'We can make him speak both languages.'

'Very nice for you. Very nice for me,' Spiros said, smiling.

'What happened to your hat?' Eve asked him, noticing he was without his trademark hat today. She did the actions for putting something on her head and then tried to make the shape of it with her fingers. Spiros patted his head with his hands as if this was a game until Vasiliki translated into Greek.

Spiros instantly replied but Eve didn't understand so the man made actions of his own, arms outstretched, Baby Yiayia jiggling up and down as he did an impression of... was that a plane?

'He say that a bird with spikes on its head flew over him and plucked it from his head when he was hanging out his washing. That was three days ago. He has not seen it since.'

Gabby had said Savage hadn't been seen for a while...

Aleka took told of Eve's arm then, using her stick to get up close. She spoke in Greek, low and soft, her long grey plaits tickling Eve's skin.

'Aleka, Eve cannot speak or understand any Greek,' Vasiliki said rather brutally in that way she always did.

'I can say a few words now,' Eve defended.

'Let me guess. "Good morning", "hello", "wine"—'

'*Signomi*,' Eve interrupted with the word for "sorry".

'Very good,' Vasiliki said, clapping her hands together. 'You will use that one very much when you cannot speak Greek.'

Aleka banged her stick on the floor.

'*Endaksi,* Aleka,' Vasiliki said. 'Aleka says that she wants to draw you another picture.'

'Oh,' Eve said. 'Oh, no, that is very kind of you but—' She really didn't want any more fortune-telling. She'd followed the Italian flag and look where that had got her.

'I am sorry,' Vasiliki said. 'My words must have got lost in the translation. Aleka is *going* to draw you another picture.'

When Eve looked around for Aleka, she was already moving as though she could see where she was going, stopping by the wheelbarrow full of dung, her hands tracing the edge of the metal. Then, before she could say anything else, the old woman was digging her hands into it, scooping up straw and brown-coloured dollops and beginning to drop them into patterns on the ground.

'It is amazing, no?' Vasiliki said, watching. 'The way she cannot see but can make pictures out of anything.'

Eve went to speak, to say that making art out of horse droppings wasn't really her cup of tea but then she remembered some of the exhibitions at the last college trip she'd supervised – there had been everything from varnished bread rolls to a papier-mâché foetus hanging from the ceiling.

Aleka began to talk as she drizzled and everyone drew closer. Baby Yiayia began to blow raspberries and Spiros gave him a large leaf to hold which he immediately put into his mouth.

'Aleka says this is a woman. With long, blonde hair in curls,' Vasiliki translated. 'And there is a man. A tall man with dark hair.'

Eve watched the picture taking shape. It was bigger than Aleka's other offerings, no longer constrained to the board and it *was* quite something how she was able to turn random items into drawings without being able to see what she was doing.

Baby Yiayia let out a squeal, kicking his legs, teeth gnashing on the plant he had in his fist.

'There is a letter. G. Like Yabby,' Vasiliki carried on.

Now Eve was confused. Was it a 'g' or a 'y'? She watched Aleka making it and hoped it wasn't going to be a shape from the Greek alphabet. Could it be 'g' for 'Gianni'? She swallowed.

'And a letter "R" too. G and R,' Vasiliki said.

GR. GR. No, it couldn't be. *Gene Reynolds*. That bloody man! Was this some sort of sign to check his Facebook status? Was there a current connection to Glenda that had gone undetected?

'This mean something to you?' Vasiliki asked.

'I don't know. Maybe. I know a man with those initials.'

Aleka spoke again.

'Is not your Italian,' Vasiliki said. 'Aleka just said. And she say the GR, it is the woman, not the man.'

Now Eve had no idea what this was, but the outline of the man did have an edge of familiarity somehow... A woman with long blonde hair? There was no one who immediately came to mind.

'*Kalimera*, Vasiliki,' came a voice bearing greetings. '*Yassas*, Aleka, Spiro. Aww, Baby Yiayia!' It was Gabby. She had Bambi the rabbit in her hands and splashes of its mange paint on her top.

'Ah, you are here, good,' Vasiliki said. 'We will begin the tour.'

'Tour?' Gabby asked, a confused expression on her face.

'Oh, Yabby, do not tell me you have not worked it out,' Vasiliki said, shaking her head. 'And I thought you were smart.'

'I have no idea what you're talking about,' Gabby said. 'You're going to have to spell it out for me.'

'In Greek letters?' Vasiliki asked.

'Only if you can do it with just vowels,' Gabby replied, petting Bambi's head.

'Yabby, we are the trustees of Safe Animals,' Vasiliki announced, arms outstretched.

Eve watched Gabby's expression move from confused to even more confused to finally settling on some kind of awkward realisation.

'Is this a joke?' she asked, passing the rabbit to Eve and putting her hands to her hips, standing as if she might be ready for battle.

'No joke,' Vasiliki answered.

'But you told me the trustees didn't live here.'

'A small lie but we had to be sure.'

'Sure of what?'

'To be certain that you are the one to look after the shelter long term.'

'But... I've been here for over a year.'

'Call it a very long interview process,' Vasiliki said. 'And I realise that we have not made it easy for you.'

Gabby shook her head and Eve saw the utter exhaustion behind her eyes. She loved her work here; she loved this island but doing all those jobs to make ends just about meet had taken its toll.

'Plus, we had to wait for Aleka to get her injection for her arthritis or she would not be able to visit. That was why you did not have a set date for us to come.'

'You could have told me,' Gabby said. 'You *should* have told me. I've been worrying and not sleeping and... worrying some more.'

'For that I apologise. But everything is set to change,' Vasiliki continued. '*Ela*, come, we will look around and you will tell us what improvements need to be made and we will talk about a budget.' She put an arm around Gabby's shoulders. 'We will also talk about your rise in pay. Come on, Spiro, give Baby Yiayia to Eve and help Aleka.'

Before Eve could say anything else, Spiros was unfurling himself from the baby carrier and Eve was wondering what she was supposed to do with Bambi.

61

HARILAOS'S COUNTRYSIDE TAVERNA

It was very much the same atmosphere as the wedding reception, except this time the star of the show was a one-year-old girl named Marianna and it was her baptism party. There were fairy lights in the trees again and a pink piñata in the shape of a donkey hanging from a sturdy olive branch; the adults were starting to take turns with it now because none of the children had been able to burst it yet.

Eve had been helping Gabby, Ben and the other waiters deliver drinks and food to the guests and, on occasion, playing tag with the children.

Now the sun was about to go down and she was taking a moment to put on insect repellent before her bare arms took another attack.

'I'll have some of that,' Ben said, appearing at her shoulder, whipping the bottle from her grasp.

'Hey!' Eve said, trying to snatch it back.

After a quick spray to his arms, Ben handed it over.

'I think that christening cake is even bigger than the wedding cake was,' he commented, nodding toward the five-tier cream icing and rose-decorated stack in the centre of the long trestle table outside the taverna.

'It definitely is,' Eve agreed. She passed him the spray back. 'Make sure you do the back of your neck.'

'All right,' he said. 'Not a baby any more.'

'I know,' she answered with a sigh.

Though it hadn't been until this break in Greece that she had realised exactly how fast her brother was growing up. He was taller, broader, most definitely a man and having to deal with what life had thrown at him already.

'I called Mum,' Ben said then, rubbing the liquid on the back of his neck. 'I told her about the betting slips and... I told her about my anxiety.'

'Did you?' And then, realising that it might have come across that she didn't believe him, she continued. 'I mean... that was really, really brave, Ben. It must have taken a lot.'

He nodded. 'Gabby helped me. She asked me what I was frightened of. She told me to compare it to all the other times I've felt afraid and to rank this situation.'

That was sound advice and Eve knew *she* had given that nugget of knowledge to Gabby back when she had been petrified about telling her parents she was staying in Corfu and not returning to England.

'And where did it place?' Eve asked, folk music filling the air.

'Way down the list. Lower than when my stick insect lost a leg.'

'O-K. And what did Glenda say? When you told her.'

'She cried,' Ben said. 'You know that really noisy crying she does when there's a death in *Emmerdale*.'

Eve nodded but, in truth, she was finding it hard to imagine Glenda getting emotional like that. She had seen *some* tears with Ben's trips to therapy and his relapses, and she had seen equal amounts after their dad passed away, but to Eve it had never seemed enough for the severity of the situations. But perhaps even if Glenda could cry tears like the Hoover Dam had burst, it wouldn't be enough for Eve…

'Eve,' Ben said, his voice low and so serious it jolted her from her reverie.

'What is it?' She sensed this was going to be bad news. Lately, when wasn't it?

He reached for her hands and held them tightly in his. 'I want you to give Mum another chance.'

Her stomach was already turning over at the thought; it was like a muscle memory reaction. She tried to get her hands back but Ben held on hard.

'No, don't try to get away, this is important. I think you need to hear this now.'

She tried to tune into the musicians and the happy laughter coming from in and around the mountain café. Exactly what did she need to hear now?

'I don't know what went on between you and Gianni in Italy but from what I saw I do know that you were good together. I liked the guy. And, OK, I might have been a teenager when you were with Mitchell, but I *never* liked him. His vibe was off from the very beginning.'

Eve tried to edge her hands from his, hopefully so slowly he wouldn't notice. It wasn't working.

'It's just, I don't want you basing any decisions you make for your future to be because of what you *think* is the truth. Because I don't think that's fair. And I get Mum's side of it, I know she's trying to protect you, but I think I know you better than she does,' Ben carried on. 'I think, taking everything into account, that you would want the truth.'

Now Eve was a bit scared. What was her brother talking about? What truth? What was Glenda protecting her from?

'So, I'm going to tell you now and I am going to be here for you, because I know that this is going to hurt you.'

Eve shook her head. She didn't want hurt. She wanted to keep working, mucking out whatever needed to be mucked out at the sanctuary, passing out plates here at the baptism reception. That was what she wanted, *positivity* for the people she cared most about, definitely not hurt.

'Mum 100 per cent did *not* have an affair with Gene Reynolds,' Ben said.

Eve wrenched her hands from his then, anger bubbling. It was exactly like Glenda to do this. Whilst Ben had been telling her about his anxiety and what had happened with Charlie and the truth about the betting slips, she had wormed something into his head and was using him to do her bidding.

'Why do you let her do this to you, Ben? If you can be so brave and strong fighting all the other demons in your life, why can't you fight her? Ignore the rubbish and lies she feeds you?' Eve stepped out from under the olive tree.

Ben grabbed her arm. 'It's not a lie,' he said, keeping his voice calm. 'Mum... she didn't have an affair.' He took a breath. 'Dad did.'

The last two words seemed to bounce off the trunk of the gnarly old tree and echo down the valley. Eve went ice cold. This wasn't true. It *wasn't* true. How could it be? This was Glenda, using Ben like she had always used Ben.

'No,' she said. 'I saw the messages. The messages between Glenda and Gene Reynolds. They were not platonic-thumbs-up-emoji kind of conversations. They were explicit. They were—'

'Copies of messages from our dad to Gina Reynolds that Gene found on his wife's phone and sent to Mum.'

Eve's heart burst into a million tiny sharp fragments which were all tearing her insides apart. 'I can't—'

Ben held her arms tight. 'When you accused Mum of having an

affair, she didn't know what to do, so she let you believe it was the truth, so you always had that perfect image you have of Dad.'

Tears were spilling from her eyes now, those memories of her dad raining down on her brain like confetti. Paper thin. Weak. Dissolvable.

'She's taken all the no texting or phone calls, all the sharp comments when you've had to speak, the calling her by her first name all these years and the blaming her for something she never did. All because she loves you and because she knows how much you idolise Dad.'

Eve didn't want to hear this. It was like Ben was back in his graffiti days and was taking a spray can to a cardboard cut-out of their dad and defacing it. How could she believe this version of events? Her dad, her precious, wonderful, solid, *good* dad an adulterer? It just made no sense.

'If there's one thing I've learnt from my experiences with fighting addiction and facing up to things, it's that covering up the truth never works. It hurts everybody. The person hiding the secret, the people you're trying to protect. Nothing good comes out of it.'

Eve was shaking now and she wanted Ben to stop talking. She could hear the music and the sounds of the happy party vibe coming from the taverna, but it all felt out of reach, muted under this desperate, dark tornado funnel above her head. And then into her mind came Aleka's picture on the ground near the stables. The woman with long, blonde hair and the man, that tall, wide shape she kind of recognised. That shape had been her dad. And GR. Not Gene Reynolds but Gina, his wife.

'Eve, talk to me,' Ben said.

'I... have to go and find Gabby. She'll... need help in the kitchen.'

She wrestled her arms out of Ben's grasp. She needed distance from what she'd heard. She wasn't ready to even start to process it. Because how could you process something that had completely rocked the core of what you lived by? The memories of her dad shaped everything she did. She helped people at college because there hadn't been enough help for her when she'd lost him. She worked in The Hunter's Moon because it was like being in a living museum of those times with her dad when he'd been living his best life – laughing, joking, losing money at dominos. But now there were other times coming into her head. Times he'd got home late. Times he'd missed family dinners. Times he'd said he was one place and Eve had known it wasn't true. Had there been some tiny part of her that had sensed this all along? Had she simply buried it deep within her?

She turned away from Ben and began running down the road.

'Eve! Eve, wait!'

62

Eve was not in appropriate footwear for running and it was getting darker by the second. Every ten or so seconds she was being hit in the face by an insect and it was very hard to cry – or breathe – with a closed mouth because you were afraid of swallowing a hornet. But she couldn't stop. Because if she stopped then she had to address this and she really *really* didn't know what happened then. This changed everything. It altered how she felt about her dad. It made her question every conversation she had or hadn't had with Glenda these past years. She was already questioning decisions she'd made based on her almost hero-worship of her father. Not applying for another job at a different college after Mitchell had taken her dream. Working at the same pub. Playing it safe when it came to life and love. Imparting advice to keep people balanced, clinging to what she thought was a tightly tied and supportive cargo net when really it was nothing but fraying weak string.

The tears fell faster, her heart beating harder as she increased her speed and then, before she could do absolutely anything about it, she had collided with something as hard as rock and before she could stop herself, she was flying through the air.

* * *

'You are OK.'

'Was that a statement or a question?' Gianni asked as he drove the latest hire car up the mountain from Acharavi.

'I am asking,' Pan replied.

Gianni was tired. Their flight to Corfu had been delayed and then everything had seemed to slow from that moment. Collecting the car, the traffic in Corfu Town because of a parade, Pan needing to stop for tobacco. All he wanted to do was get to Safe Animals and do something. Whether that was being able to talk to Eve or talking to Ben or Gabby first. He couldn't wait any longer. Now he felt that letting time go by was not about giving Eve space, but about increasing the distance they were apart – actually and figuratively – and he didn't like it. He knew he had to be honest with her about how he felt, about how much she meant to him and that was what he was going to do. Then perhaps they could have another chance.

'I am OK,' he answered. 'But I will be better when I am doing something other than driving this car.'

'I need to not eat for a week,' Pan said, one hand on his still flat stomach. 'Your mother has cooked more food for me over these days than I would eat in a month.'

'She has cooked more food for us than she has cooked my entire life,' Gianni admitted. 'And it was not burnt.'

'I still do not know how I feel about Italian olives,' Pan admitted. 'They are not like Corfiot olives. The Italian ones, they are too big and bright green and like they are showing off with their slick outsides.'

'Do you insult my country?' Gianni asked.

'You have two countries now,' Pan reminded him.

Gianni still wasn't sure how he felt about that, the fact that half of him was Greek, whether he wanted to adopt it or not. It felt like a betrayal of Riccardo who had been proudly Italian in everything he did, his heritage flowing through him like the River Adige ran through Verona. Except Riccardo had wanted him to find Pan. To go through the rest of his life with the truth by his side. Maybe that included embracing a new culture, one which wasn't too dissimilar from the Italian way of life if he was honest.

'It is OK,' Pan said. 'You are you, Gianni. As independent as your mother. As strong as your father, Riccardo, has made you. You can be anything you want to be.'

The statement hit Gianni hard. Pan was perhaps the person most affected by all of this. To have loved a woman and lost her, to have never known she had had his child, to remember how it felt to be unwanted by his own parents, to change his name, to crave family...

As Gianni's eyes glazed over, he barely noticed the obstruction in the road until it was almost too late. He hit the brakes hard, turning the wheel away from the mountain edge and veering towards the other side, narrowly avoiding the blockage in the road.

The front of the car skimmed the brush and rocks at the side of the road and then finally came to a stop.

'Did you see that?' Gianni asked, already undoing his seatbelt.

Pan coughed, crushing the end of his lit cigarette with his fingers and putting the stub into the top pocket of his shirt. 'Goats. One injured and on the floor.' He undid his seatbelt too. 'You forget to tell me you are like F1 racing driver.'

Gianni got out of the car, made sure that the tail-end of his vehicle wasn't going to be an obstruction for anyone else and then he got his phone from the pocket of his jeans. He turned on the torch. Walking quickly, he shone the beam at half a dozen goats standing almost in a circle formation around a larger goat lying on the floor. But it wasn't the colour of the goat's coat that was drawing his eye, it was that not-quite-light-brown-not-quite-auburn colour he knew too well. And it was then he saw the goat wasn't the only thing lying on the ground.

'Eve!' he shouted.

Pan stopped in his tracks and turned back towards the car. 'I will get a blanket. Do hire cars have blankets?' He stumbled back up the road. 'I will get whatever they have or something from my bag.'

Gianni pushed the bleating goats out of his way, the bells around their necks ringing as he slid down onto his knees on the rough tarmac. Her eyes were open, she was breathing, but it was obvious she was hurt. Her palms were facing skywards, bleeding grazes and deeper divots plain to see.

'Don't move, OK? Tell me where does it hurt?'

He was almost too scared to touch her. Too afraid that even the gentlest of movements was going to disturb something crucial and set off a chain of bad events.

'Gi... anni?' Eve said, her voice faint.

'Yes,' he breathed. 'Please, Eve, keep still. I am going to phone for an ambulance.'

'Noooo,' she said. 'Don't... do that. I think... I think I'm just winded.' She tried to take a deep breath but it didn't quite hit any heights and it was clear she was in pain.

'Can you sit?' Gianni asked. 'If I help?'

'I don't know... ow... is the goat OK?'

Gianni had forgotten all about the goat on the ground. It had left his mind the second he saw there was a person. *His* person. The person he never wanted to hurt but somehow had.

He put a hand onto the goat's midriff, felt an in and out. 'He is alive.'

'Good,' Eve said. 'Because... I don't want the responsibility of... its death on my hands.'

He frowned. 'You have a car here? You hit the goat?' He gasped. 'Is the car over the side of the mountain?'

'No,' she rasped. 'I... hit the goat with my body. I was running and—' She stopped talking and tried to take another deep breath. This time it worked and Gianni saw the relief on her face. She put her hands to the ground in an attempt to sit herself up and then she winced.

'Let me help.'

'I don't want you to help. Ow!'

'Eve, your hands are cut. Please, let me help.'

'I left you in Italy.'

'And now I am in Greece.' He didn't wait for her to reject his assistance again; he moved behind her, supporting her shoulders as she worked her way into a sitting position until she was leaning against his chest, his legs stretched out in front of him.

'What are you doing here?' she asked as she tried to straighten herself.

'Currently I am wondering what Pan could be getting from the car. It is taking so long.'

'Pan is here too?'

'We just arrived. Our flight was late. We were heading to Safe Animals when I almost drove into the goats. And you.'

She nodded slowly, as if the action was painful and that was all the explanation she needed. He wanted more. He wanted her to tell him why she had left Verona without saying a thing. He wanted to know what he had done. But she was injured, and it was obvious, even though she had taken his help and was sitting with him on the road, that their dynamic had altered. She felt closed. A locked door, no sign of the key. He needed to go slow if he even had any chance at all.

'Why were you running?' he asked.

'What?'

'You said that you hit the goat because you were running.'

* * *

Eve *had* said that. But she didn't want to say any more. Her chest hurt, her hands felt as if she'd sanded them with glass and she was taking comfort from sitting in the arms of someone she had walked out on. He was an untrustworthy guy like every guy she had met before – including her own dad.

'Listen, you do not have to say anything but when you feel you are able, we should get you off this road.'

It was so dark now, the beautiful colours gone; the only disparity between the rocks and the brush were their edges – solid for the mountain granite, more fluid for the branches and leaves. The road was usually quiet but it would only take one vehicle not expecting to see a large prostrate goat and two people sat in the road and there could be another accident.

'I have a bright yellow sleeveless jacket, a fire extinguisher, a road map of Corfu, a T-shirt and three pairs of socks.'

It was Pan, some of those items he'd mentioned in his hands.

'Hello, Pan,' Eve greeted, shifting herself away from Gianni's firm torso and checking how things were with her legs. 'Can you please... look at the goat.' She used Gianni's shoulder to heave herself up from the ground and despite feeling like she had, well, hit a goat, she was able to stand without too much pain.

Pan put his fingers in his mouth and whistled. No sooner had the piercing sound met the air, the stoic goat jumped to its feet, letting out a loud and somewhat angry-sounding bleat.

'Sometimes they just forget what they are supposed to do,' Pan said. 'You fall down, you get up. You do not fall down and stay down and wait for something else to hit you, no?'

Those were wise words even if you weren't a goat. But after

hearing the truth of her parents' relationship, that it wasn't what she had believed at all, she wasn't sure whether she was able to get up. Hypothetically.

'I should go,' she said, readjusting her sandals and looking back up the mountain. She wasn't sure how far she had run, or how long it would take her now to walk back to the animal shelter.

'We should all go,' Pan said. 'I am having withdrawal symptoms from not having mountain tea for days.'

'Eve, you cannot walk,' Gianni said as she began to do just that.

Except she was doing it very badly, with a bit of a limp and a sharp pain fizzing down her side every time she took a step. She stopped.

'Let us take you in the car. We will be there in five minutes. You can rest or have a cool shower...'

The last word seemed to die on Gianni's tongue and all the memories of their lovemaking in the fountain and his en suite hit Eve like sharp, sexy darts. She swallowed. But what was the alternative? To take an hour, maybe more, stumbling around in the dark without even her phone to light the way? No, she needed to get back to her room and she needed to be on her own and probably spend what was left of the night crying.

'I can make us all some tea,' Pan offered.

'OK,' Eve agreed.

63

SAFE ANIMALS SANCTUARY, EPISKEPSI

Under the tepid water of the shower, Eve's back was hurting much more than she had first realised. There was definite bruising and scrapes and perhaps she was lucky to have only run into a goat rather than a vehicle. Except what was currently worrying her most was that she had run into Gianni. He was back here in Greece. Close. And, at some point, she knew he was going to want to know why she had left Verona.

But as she grabbed a towel and began to dry herself off, it was suddenly all too much. She couldn't remember the last time she hadn't felt on the edge of something. Ben's addiction. Losing her dad. Fighting with Glenda. Hating her naivety over Mitchell. Work was the only place that she could tune everything else out and what did she do there? She listened to other people's problems. Corfu had felt like a carefree choice, as had Italy at the time, except it hadn't taken long for a crisis to hit.

Tears were flowing again now as she wrapped her robe around her. Maybe these issues weren't the problem; she was the common denominator, maybe the problem was her. But what did she do with that?

She opened the bathroom door and then screamed, clutching at her chest. Gianni was there, a tiny white kitten in his hands.

'I am sorry,' he apologised. 'This little one escaped from the shed when I went in. She – I think it is a she – came in here and—'

'She's the last one,' Eve said. 'We've been calling her Áspro which is the Greek word for "white". She was the only one who wasn't tabby or ginger. The others have homes now,' Eve said, taking Áspro from him and holding her close.

'How are your injuries?' Gianni asked.

'Fine.'

'Eve—'

'Don't. Please, Gianni. Please don't.'

She knew he wanted to ask her. She could see it deep in those gorgeous blue eyes of his. But she wasn't ready to give him an explanation, not tonight, not when she was feeling lower than the belly of a Greek snake and had been catapulted into the air by a Greek goat.

'Eve, I came back to Corfu because I could not stand to have the distance between us. I did not come back before tonight because whatever happened, whatever you felt to make you leave, I wanted to let you, I do not know, have space to think about it?'

She tried to focus on Áspro wriggling in her arms and ignore the change in rhythm of her heart. She *had* thought about it. And all she had remembered was it happening once before.

'What changed?' Gianni asked, seemingly not having listened to the fact she'd said 'don't'. 'What did I do? Because, please, whatever it is... give me the opportunity to fix it.'

Perhaps it was better to tell him now. How much worse could tonight get? How many more rugs could be pulled out from underneath everything she thought was solid, fixed-down carpet?

'You can't fix it,' she said bluntly. And with that said she headed down the stone steps to the living area. The front door was still open and she needed the air.

She stepped out onto the courtyard, still coddling the kitten.

'I do not want to believe that,' Gianni said, at her heel. 'Talk to me. Like we've always talked from the moment we met.'

She wanted him to leave so she didn't have to face this. She pressed her nose into the kitten's fur.

'Eve, please,' Gianni said, putting a hand on her arm.

That touch. She had always loved his touch. But he had betrayed her.

'You really want to know what happened?' she asked, facing him.

'I really do.'

She took a deep breath, her chest uncomfortable about the motion but compliant nonetheless. 'I saw your business plan. On the laptop in your bedroom.'

'OK...' Gianni said.

'Nothing you want to say yet?'

She was scrutinising him now. From the expression on his face to the tension in his core to any subconscious movement of his hands. He wasn't even giving her the courtesy of his cheeks reddening now he knew the cat was out of the bag. The cat that wasn't in any bag seemed to sense the strain in the air and was still for once, eyes flitting from one person to the other.

'You saw the business ideas for the boba with alcoholic bubbles and vitamins and flavours from around the world?'

'Exactly! My words!' She took one hand from Áspro and pointed at him, accusing.

Gianni said nothing in reply for a moment as if he was waiting for her to carry on. Why wasn't he getting this? Did she have to spell it out?

'*I* gave you the idea about alcoholic popping bubbles and vitamins. I told you I'd often wondered about it when my students come into college with the drinks! I said bubble tea can change their day!' Eve yelled. 'It was *my* idea!'

* * *

Was this *it*? Was this *really* why she had left without saying a word, got on a plane and headed back to Corfu? Gianni couldn't believe it.

'Are you serious?' he asked.

'Yes, I'm serious! You talked to me about boba tea and I told you because I thought it was innocent conversation and yet without saying anything to me, you've put it in a business proposal!'

Gianni shook his head. 'I cannot believe this.' He took a step back.

'I opened up to you about what Mitchell did to me. He stole my words and my ideas, he stopped me from getting my dream job, lying to me, using me, and you... you've done exactly the same!'

'OK,' Gianni said, nodding now.

'OK?' Eve shrieked. 'What do you mean OK?' She couldn't read his expression. He looked passive yet aggressive. And somehow sad.

When he began to speak there was a tremor of emotion in his voice.

'I thought you understood me, Eve. I thought we connected with each other on so many levels. But... if you think I could do something like that to you, then... perhaps you never knew me at all.'

He took one long look at her and then he turned away, saying nothing else and starting to walk back towards the main building.

Eve didn't know what to do or what to say. This wasn't how things were supposed to go. She was meant to tell him how hurt she was by what he'd done and he was supposed to either accept he had been caught in the act and realise it was over and why, or alternatively tell her she was wrong, *why* she was wrong and put up a defence. Instead, he had done neither and she felt completely wrong-footed.

Had she got *this* wrong as well as so much else in her life?

64

'There is nothing like a Greek sofa-bed is there?'

Gianni came to with Pan shaking the wooden arm of the most uncomfortable piece of furniture he had ever had the misfortune to sleep on. The thick upholstered brown cushions with a swirling flower pattern were partially worn in places but should have provided adequate comfort, however the sofa-bed was short, the arms were wooden and there was no possible position to get settled for sleep. As his aching neck and shoulders were attesting to right now as he sat up.

'Do you ever sleep on this?' Gianni asked.

'No, are you crazy?' Pan answered. 'It is so uncomfortable.'

He checked his watch: 10 a.m. He stood up and began to tuck his shirt back into his trousers, sweep back his hair, remember what he was doing here. 'Why did you not wake me? It is late.'

'We did not get to sleep before two. You needed the rest,' Pan answered, pushing open the shutters on the one small window. 'I clean out the horses, check on the goats, feed the cats and the dogs – not to each other – and call the vet. Then I come back to see you.'

Last night. Getting here from Italy, tending to Eve on the roadside, having her tell him why she had left him, drinking ouzo with his Greek father... It was a lot.

'How you feel this morning?' Pan asked, pressing a steaming cup of mountain tea into his hands then putting a hand on his shoulder and urging him back down to sit.

Gianni had a headache but that was nothing compared to the ache in his heart. He had lost Eve. He had found out why she had left and he had lost her. Because obviously he had been wrong about how she felt about him. The Eve he had got to know through this intense period of his life would not have let something that could have been resolved from a conversation dictate her actions. 'Like... how do you say shit in Greek?'

'*Skatá*,' Pan said.

'I feel like that.' He slurped at the tea and it burned his tongue. 'Ow.'

'It will pass,' Pan assured. 'And, once your pride has dissolved you can make things good with Eve again.' He patted his shoulder and moved to sit down in his armchair.

'Once what? What do you mean when my pride has dissolved?'

Pan began to roll a cigarette, with just as many strands of tobacco going onto the floor as were making it into the paper. 'I listen to you last night when you tell me what happen with Eve. You sound like I did once. Your need to be strong in every situation way above any other feeling.'

'I do not know what you are talking about,' Gianni said stiffly. This wasn't about pride; it was about someone getting beneath his usual flat calm and stirring the deepest parts. It was about not wanting to believe that he had misinterpreted it all. Or that it hadn't meant anything near as much to Eve.

'Why are you angry, Gianni?'

'I told you last night. I am angry because... she thought I was the same as the guy who hurt her. She was positive that I could do something like that to her. How could she think that?'

'Put yourself into the boots of Eve,' Pan said, licking the paper of his cigarette. 'This man hurt her. She lost her father. Ben, he has problems. Eve, she does not speak very well with her mother. It is not this bubbly tea with ouzo inside balls that really make her leave. It is everything that scares her. The whole world she feels that hurts her. And let us not forget, you invite her to Italy and then a man you know only a little of comes along for the ride and there is shouting and lemons in hot water and the force that is Valentina.' He flicked his lighter until it produced a flame. 'It is very much.'

It was very much. It was very much to him. How could he imagine what it was like for someone else? To be thrown into the centre of this crazy situation, to expect someone to set it all aside and begin a romance when he was having a hard time accepting who he was. Who could be ready for that? Especially someone already carrying the weight of her own world.

'How do you know all that? That Ben has problems, that Eve does not communicate well with her mother?'

He watched as Pan lit the cigarette and blew a thick fast plume into the air. 'I tell you before. I listen.'

'You mean you overhear things when people are talking,' Gianni said. 'Things not meant for you.'

Pan shook his head. 'I did not say "hear". I said "listen".' He leaned forward in the chair. 'Sometimes it is not words that are being said. It is the words that are *not* being said.'

'I do not know what I am supposed to get from that.'

'You want to give up with Eve? Be angry forever that you think she has misjudged you? Move on?'

He didn't want that. The very thought of going back to Italy and never seeing her again made him feel nauseous. He shook his head.

'Then you have to approach things a different way,' Pan said. 'With less judgement. With more understanding. Because, if you care about her the way I think you care about her, her happiness should be the only thing you worry about.' He scoffed. 'I know how it is to wear pride like it is a bulletproof vest; I am Greek. But I have learned all these years that there are a great many things more important than that. Remember what I tell you, about seeing your father, Riccardo, and knowing how happy he was making your mother?'

'Do you have regrets about walking away from my mother and father in Verona?'

'Life is too short for regrets.'

It was an answer from a motivational calendar.

'Do you think things would have been different if you had approached them that day? If my mother had known you had come to Italy?'

Pan shook his head. 'Do you not listen? Eve's happiness must be *all* that matters. Valentina's happiness was all that mattered to me.' He sighed. 'She was happy, Gianni. She told me this week that Riccardo, he took on the care of her mother, paying for the best doctors and making her life as comfortable as possible. And he became the father to you, Gianni. Neither of you would be who you are today without him.'

'But if you had told my mother how you felt—'

'Gianni, the mistake I made was not in Italy, it was back in Corfu.' He sighed. 'Back then, when I did not know better, I heard the words she said rather than listening for the ones she did not.'

'I do not understand.'

'She said she would marry me but she said yes only to stop me from asking. I would never have been enough for her. I am a simple man. Valentina, she deserved much more. And your father, he gave that to her. What happened, it was meant to be. Just like you coming here at this time, knowing that I exist now, is the way it is meant to be.'

Could that be right? That instead of secrets being kept and things feeling 'wrong', that actually this was the way it was always meant to turn out? If that was the case, then how did that approach fit with him and Eve? Were they meant to be together for only such a short time? Was there nothing he could do to alter that?

Pan slammed the flat of his hand on the arm of his chair. 'But we do not talk of me. We talk about you.'

Gianni sighed, putting his head in his hands. 'I still feel like *skatá*.'

'Because you need to make a decision. A decision for you, Gianni.' Pan had said his name with a 'y' again. 'Sorry, G—'

'It is OK,' Gianni interrupted. 'Maybe, in Greece, I can be Yianni.'

Pan laughed. 'You do not have to do that. I am a stupid man in the middle-age, set in his ways.'

'No, I mean it.' He smiled at Pan. 'I would like you to.'

Pan smiled back and nodded. '*Endaksi*. OK.'

65

ALMYROS BEACH, ALMYROS

Despite the sky being painted the kind of ultramarine that speaks of the perfect peaceful holiday, today, the sea was a different story. Eve was standing in her bikini looking at the swirling white water.

'What are you waiting for?' Gabby asked. 'It's so hot today, the water will be lovely.'

'In temperature maybe,' Eve replied. 'But I don't possess any surfer-style skills that give me confidence I'm going to be able to keep standing up in that sea.'

Gabby laughed. 'That's the fun of this beach! The first time I came down here I rushed out there full of "embrace the moment" energy and I ran in. The waves pushed me right over and I lost my sunglasses.' She laughed. 'I've often wondered if there's a crab down there wearing them.'

Eve took her sunglasses off, throwing them on top of her clothes and bag. 'And that story is supposed to make me want to get in?'

'Well,' Gabby said, linking arms with her. 'I don't think the sea is as choppy as your life right now.'

Wow. Blunt. Typical Gabby, and that was one of the qualities

Eve loved about her. The swirling water didn't seem quite so bad when the alternative was conversation about the contents of her head... and her heart.

'Come on,' Gabby said, squeezing Eve's arm tight with hers. 'Let's get in. This is my first swim now I've only got one job.'

The way Gabby had said the sentence – with such relief and excitement – made Eve very happy. There was a lightness about her friend now that had definitely been missing when she had first arrived.

As they made tentative steps into the waves, the water sloshed over her feet. It was refreshing – not cold, not quite warm, but definitely enough to cool them from the heat of another sizzling Corfiot day. By the time Eve was up to her thighs though, she was being buffeted by the strength of the water, waves crashing against her back. Not great when she was bearing the grazes from her clash with the goat and the road.

She kicked up her legs and dived into the water, letting it wash over her whole body in the hope of some kind of restoration.

'So,' Gabby began once Eve had resurfaced. 'Ben told me what he talked to you about last night.'

Eve didn't know how to respond so she said nothing, swirling her hands in the sea, kicking her legs to stay afloat.

'That must have been so hard for you to hear,' she continued, unperturbed by Eve's silence.

It *had* been hard to hear, for so many reasons. Glenda was no longer the villain of the piece. Glenda hadn't done anything wrong, her dad had. And Eve still didn't want to believe it, even though something inside her was instinctively telling her this *was* the truth. Another thought hit her in that moment and this time she vocalised it.

'Did you know?' she asked.

'About your dad and this Gina woman?' Gabby clarified. 'No!

Of course not! If I had had any idea I would have told you, you know that.'

Eve sighed and focused a little more on keeping her arms going in a steady rhythm. 'Sorry, I don't know why I asked that. I just... feel so stupid that all this time I thought Glenda had cheated and it turns out that not only didn't she cheat but she didn't tell me the truth because she wanted to protect me and preserve the adored over-the-top memory of a man who absolutely didn't deserve it.'

Now the tears were there again, slipping out and mingling with the salt water of the sea, threatening to hinder Eve's ability to keep her head above water.

'Listen,' Gabby said, moving a little closer to her. 'One thing I've learned being here is that people move at their own pace.'

'Particularly the goats,' Eve said, sniffing up the emotion and trying to smile.

'No, I mean you can't make someone get over things at the same speed that you do. Some people move on fast. Others take longer. Some might not move on at all.'

'Are you trying to out-psych the psychology expert?'

'I'm just saying that maybe Glenda didn't want to tell you the truth because she was waiting until you were ready, until you'd moved on from losing your dad,' Gabby said, treading water. 'And, well, I don't think that's something you've really been able to do, is it?'

Gabby hadn't said it harshly, it was matter of fact and it was honest. Eve *knew* she hadn't moved on. She also knew that it had been because she hadn't wanted to. That was what living in Brookly Heath, working at the college she used to attend and evenings and weekends at The Hunter's Moon was *all* about. She had surrounded herself with the past and as well as that being an unhealthy way to exist, clinging to those memories as if they were the most important things she possessed had prevented her from creating any kind of new future.

'I tried to move on with Mitchell,' Eve said, putting her feet down and standing instead of swimming now. 'And when that ended, I think I used it as an excuse to move backwards again. Almost like saying to the world, "well, I took a trip outside my comfort zone, I tried to find something new and look what happened".'

'And no one could blame you for licking your wounds over that prick.'

'Yeah,' Eve agreed. 'Except I didn't just lick them, did I? I did the equivalent of putting myself on a longer than long NHS waiting list thinking they needed professional attention.'

She sighed. Had she known this really, deep down? Had she used what she'd thought had been her mother's infidelity to shape her every thought process, from never wanting to remember the times when Glenda had actually been a kind, caring, humorous mum and fixating on her dad being the perfect man that no other person in her life could match up to?

'So, that brings us on to Gianni,' Gabby said, leaning backwards and floating in a star shape.

Gianni. His response to her last night had been surprising. If it had been one of her students trying to flip the responsibility in that way, she might have thought it was an admission of guilt, but his words were still echoing in her mind. *Perhaps you never knew me at all.*

Tightening her core, Eve aimed her midriff at the sky and stretched herself out into the same shape as Gabby. They were currently the only people mad enough to be trying to keep still in this turbulent water.

'I liked Gianni,' Eve admitted, the water hitting the back of her neck. 'I liked him a lot.'

'Eve, you're *really* using the past tense?' Gabby asked, craning her neck, almost coming out of the star shape. She flapped her arms like a seal to keep herself straight.

'He's angry with me,' Eve said. 'And I don't even know if he has any right to be angry with me. Because he hasn't *actually* answered anything I said about incorporating my idea into his business plan.'

'Is that what he did?' Gabby asked, mouth wide open for a moment, then quickly shutting again when the salt water sloshed over her chin.

Eve quickly explained.

'So, you had some conversations about bubble tea.'

'Yes.'

'And he's started a business off the back of it?'

'Well, no, it was a page of ideas, like a pitch for a meeting. I didn't read it all, but things I said to him were on there.'

'OK,' Gabby said. 'And when you asked him about it, he said...'

'He said... something like... if I could believe that he could do something like that then perhaps I didn't know him at all.'

Gabby didn't immediately answer and, with her curls still soaking up the water, Eve didn't know if she had heard her. Until: 'Do you think that you almost kind of wanted Gianni to have done the same thing as Mitchell?'

'What?'

'Don't take it the wrong way but, you know, you admit that when you tried to move on with Mitchell after your dad died and then Mitchell hurt you, it sent you sailing back into that grief. You were holding onto the comfort of the past and those familiar situations and surroundings,' Gabby said. 'Maybe you left Italy because you were starting to really care for Gianni and that scared you and you were looking for reasons to, I don't know, regress again.' Gabby took a breath before carrying on. 'But now Ben's told you about your dad, that safe place you go to isn't quite like it was before and—'

'All right,' Eve said quickly, her heart picking up in pace. 'I get what you're trying to say.'

It was a deep conversation. Too deep to continue to float like a starfish. Eve dropped her feet back to the sand.

'I didn't mean to be blunt,' Gabby said, dropping out of the position too and touching Eve on the shoulder. 'I just... don't want what *anyone* did to you in the past make you assume everyone else is going to do the same.'

What was it Glenda used to say to her friends when Eve was little? *Don't tar everyone with the same brush*. Was that what she had been doing? Expecting the worst to happen each and every time she was presented with a new opportunity. And now with someone wanting to fall for her...

Gabby pulled her in for a hug and Eve took the opportunity to smell her friend's hair. Coconut. Sea salt. Possibly horse. A hint of goose...

'Please talk to Gianni. Tell him how you feel. Find out *exactly* what he has or hasn't done. And don't go into it with a Mitchell-shaped clouded judgement.'

'OK,' Eve said softly, relaxing into the cuddle.

'Promise?'

'I promise,' she said with a bit more conviction.

'OK,' Gabby said, letting her go and dipping back down into the water. 'So now you can tell me why Gianni is staying in Pan's tiny cottage and not at that expensive hotel in Almyros. It's like they're suddenly best buddies and, to be honest, that bromance chemistry is surprising.'

Eve put a hand on Gabby's shoulder and gave it a squeeze. 'OK, so brace yourself. Because I found out a lot in Italy. And I mean a lot.'

66

SAFE ANIMALS SANCTUARY, EPISKEPSI

It was blistering hot but the hard work at the sanctuary had to continue and Gianni needed the distraction. Carrying two large planks of wood, he headed from one of the large sheds towards the field, two cats at his heels as if he might be carrying food for them.

He had spoken to his mother that morning. She had wanted to know if he and Pan had arrived safely in Corfu, asking that before saying anything about Riccardocino. Gianni knew business had to go on, that he couldn't be on this break in Greece forever, but he wasn't quite ready to go back to Barista Irresistible and rearrange their meeting. Something was holding him back from pitching the new idea and, he wasn't stupid, he knew that it was Eve. It didn't feel right without her. *He* didn't feel right without her.

'Over here!'

Ben was waving at him from across the field. Gianni propped one wooden plank up against the fence as he opened the gate, the cats ignoring the opening and slinking through the bars.

'Pan says something has eaten the fence,' Gianni commented, putting his load down on the ground.

'Some things I reckon,' Ben answered. He ran a hand across the old wood. 'Here it looks like wood beetle has been attacking it. That's made the wood crack and either the horses have been eating it or... maybe Savage.'

'That bird is crazy,' Gianni remarked.

'Yeah, kind of like my sister,' Ben said with half a smile.

Gianni swallowed, stepping back and knocking into one of the lengths of fence he had propped up.

'Whoa,' Ben said, stopping it from hitting the grass and leaning it back again. 'You all right?'

'I think,' Gianni started, 'that your sister might be making me a little crazy.'

Ben put the pencil he'd been holding behind his ear, bent down and passed Gianni a two-litre bottle of water.

'If it's any help, Eve's pissed with me at the moment too.' He sighed. 'I had to tell her something quite hard last night and she left the taverna, running off into the night.'

'That is why she ran into a goat,' Gianni said, nodding.

'She ran into a goat?'

'She is OK.' Gianni began to unscrew the lid on the bottle and then took a swig. 'She is mainly angry with me, and I do not really know why.'

'Have you asked her?'

'She says I am like this guy who hurt her in the past. This Mitchell.'

Ben whistled through his teeth and then narrowed his eyes. 'She told you about Mitchell? Piece of work he was.'

'Yes.'

'So... are you? Like him?'

Gianni shook his head. 'I would never hurt her.'

Ben seemed to study him for a minute or so, as if he was trying to work out whether he was genuine or not. Gianni passed the bottle back to him.

'I believe you,' Ben said after a moment. 'And I probably know why Eve doesn't.'

'You do?' Gianni leant against the fence and wiped water away from his top lip.

'Yeah, and I'm pretty sure it's not as simple as the Mitchell factor. It's everything really. It's our dad dying and it's me screwing up with gambling and then telling her last night that it wasn't our mum who had an affair, it was our dad who was screwing Gene Reynold's wife and, well, it's shouldering everyone's shit because that's what she's always done. Her students at college, me... mainly me...'

Gianni ran the facts back in his mind. He thought he had it straight. And he knew exactly how Eve felt about each of her parents. She adored her late father. She had spent a long time despising her mother. This was going to have turned her world upside down.

'Eve never puts herself first. Like ever. Even when we were little kids she was, I dunno, like everyone's hype girl. The first to clap for a mate who won a sports day race or there to say it didn't matter if they fell over and lost. She was one of those kids who put their hand up for anything if it helped somebody else out, manning a stall at the church Christmas fair, helping me with my homework when I didn't have a clue how to do it... she even used to stack shelves with our mum when she worked at the local Co-op.' Ben sighed. 'Eve cares. Too much. And she listens. Too often. So, she's, I don't know, kind of surprised when someone wants to treat her right. She doesn't ever expect it. For someone who wants to make the world such a positive place, she always expects negativity to come her way.'

Gianni mused on what Ben was saying before replying. 'Perhaps she has fought so many battles it is now set into her nature that she must fight, even against herself and what she might really want.'

Ben nodded and wagged a finger. 'That is spot on. She's ready and expecting some kind of warfare before she's even gathered any intel.'

Gianni sighed. 'I should have not got on the high horse.'

'You what?'

'I tell Eve that I am angry. I say that if she believes I am like this Mitchell man then she does not know me.'

'Ouch, can't imagine that went down well. Did she give you one of her looks? That's basically worse than punching you if she did it right.'

'I should not have said what I said,' Gianni replied. 'I should have told her we should talk. That I would listen, fully.'

'You're talking like this battle is over,' Ben said, fingers grazing the damaged wood again.

'Because I do not know where to begin.' He put his hands into his hair and tugged with frustration.

'Anywhere,' Ben said. 'Eve taught me that. All this starting at the beginning bollocks is just that. Bollocks.' He picked up a nail from the few he had gathered on the fence post. 'Listen, my advice would be wait until Saturday. There's a whole big festival in Episkepsi. It's called a panny-something or other. Gabby said the whole village and all the neighbouring villages come, and there's dancing by the church and down the streets and stalls selling shit that lights up for the kids and doughnuts and stuff.'

Gianni frowned. 'I should wait until it is noisy and there are doughnuts?'

Ben placed a hand on his shoulder, a smile of solidarity on his face. 'Believe me, I don't like crowds and noise either, but I'm going to try really hard for Gabby. And Eve loves this stupid vehicle gathering show we have in Brookly Heath with crap ice cream and cold hotdogs and a beer tent. If there's anything that's going to put her in the right mood for you to talk honestly with her then it's that.'

'OK,' Gianni said, exhaling as if he'd been holding his breath for an eternity.

Ben smoothed his hand over the fence again, bending down to look closer as if there might have been something he'd missed. 'I don't know if it was wishful thinking Pan saying Savage might have bitten this. To me it looks more like one of the horses.'

'My father is missing that stupid very wild bird,' Gianni said, shaking his head.

Ben shot up into a standing position, a confused expression on his face. 'You what?'

'I said that Pan, he is worried where the bird has disappeared to.'

'You didn't say it like that,' Ben said. 'You said "my father".'

Had he? He paused. He could backtrack. Make out it was because his mind was elsewhere, that 'my father' could just as easily have come out of his mouth as 'the grumpy man'. But what would be the point of that? Riccardo would always be his father, but that father's wish was that Gianni found Pan. And acknowledging who he was had to be part of that journey.

'Yes,' Gianni said. 'I did.'

'Pan's your dad?' Ben said, looking shocked.

Gianni nodded. 'It is a very recent thing. The finding out, not the making of... well... you know.'

'Bloody hell,' Ben said, his mouth still agape.

'I am hoping my hair does not go silver too soon,' Gianni joked. 'Or stick out as much as his does.'

'You've got a lot on your plate,' Ben said, shaking his head. 'And I thought *I* had issues.'

'I would like my plate to have space for Eve,' Gianni told him. 'If her plate has the room for me.'

Ben patted Gianni's shoulder again. '*Kali orexi*.'

'What does this mean?' Gianni asked.

'It's like the Greek for *bon appetit*,' Ben said.

'*Buon appetito*,' Gianni said, nodding. 'I guess we will find out.'

67

'We can only take animals to the festival that are going to behave,' Gabby said as she wandered through the sanctuary, touching the screen of her iPad as if she was jabbing someone she didn't really like. 'No to Vincent Van Hoff. People are going to be drinking and dancing and he's obviously not steady on his legs even without that going on so—'

'But the children love Vincent,' Pan said, taking a strong hold on the rope the mother goat was attached to, her kids tottering behind, eager mouths searching for teats. 'And when we had the last fundraiser here you did not let him come out because it was when he was going through that time where he was shitting in the shoes of people.'

'God,' Gabby said, pausing in her walking. 'I'd forgotten all about that. That was awful. I had to buy a cheap pair of shoes from the China shop when he totally ruined my Vans.'

'Eve,' Pan said. 'You vote for Vincent to come to the festival, yes?'

Eve looked up from her phone. She had sort of heard the conversation, but more like it was background noise, that television show you had on to make you feel like you weren't on your own but also weren't really watching. Had she been walking across the yard? She didn't remember that either. 'Sorry, what?'

'Pan wants Vincent to come to the festival but I said he's unstable on his feet and it's going to be busy,' Gabby recounted.

'Spiros is unstable on his feet too and he will be there, won't he?'

Pan laughed hard at this comment, the motion making the piece of rope the mother goat was attached to shake. She let out a complaining bleat of displeasure. 'That is so true.'

'Who else do you have on the list?' Eve asked, paying proper attention now.

'Po, Dipsy and La-La,' Gabby began. 'Tinky Winky can't go near anyone with his eye like it still is. He's on more antibiotics now. Bambi the rabbit can't come with that toxic-smelling stuff we have to paint on her fur—'

'We could take Phantom,' Pan offered.

'He's too big.'

'The goats then?'

'The babies are still nursing and it will be noisy.'

'So, we have three tortoises? The village will wonder if we have any animals in the sanctuary!' Pan exclaimed.

'They are all welcome to come and look around any time they like as long as they make a nice healthy donation in the box.'

Eve stepped away from the good-natured bickering and looked back at her phone. The message from Glenda was super-short, but she was struggling to handle it. Should she text back? That was the slightly safer, less emotional option. Or should she put her heart on the line? The much harder way-out-of-her-comfort-zone option.

Can we talk?

'Eve, I've got to shoot off!' Gabby suddenly shouted. 'There's a dog that's been dumped at the recycling centre. I'm taking Ben!'

'OK,' Eve answered as her friend rushed across the yard towards the van.

'Lots to organise for the festival tonight,' Pan said, suddenly at her shoulder. 'The mayor will be collecting only the very best white plastic chairs to put out for everyone.'

Eve smiled but her heart wasn't in it. Bits and pieces of it were floating around somewhere but none of them knew what they were doing or where they should settle or if they were ever going to land.

'Gianni will be at the festival.'

'Will he?'

She was as surprised as she was excited and she knew she hadn't hidden either of those sentiments in her reply. She hadn't seen anything of Gianni over the last couple of days and Gabby and Ben didn't seem to know whether he was still staying with Pan or whether he had gone back to Italy again.

'He has been staying in Corfu Town. Working, how do they say, with a remote?'

'Remotely,' Eve said.

'He has been doing that,' Pan said. 'But tonight, he will be here in Episkepsi.'

And now her heart was thundering as if Phantom, Milo and Pnévma were all galloping to the finish line in a highly contested horse race. She wanted to see him. She wanted to know if she had judged too quickly, if maybe there was still a chance for them, despite everything they both had going on in their lives.

'We will make it a celebration. Gabby having only one job. Me getting the new job title of her deputy with pay! Ben staying to help here for the rest of the summer. It is good!' Pan declared, his arm waving in a way that was disgruntling the always hungry kids.

It *was* good. They hadn't set a fixed time to return to the UK. Eve still had the rest of the college summer holidays and Ben had told her he didn't want to put a date on his return at all. Maybe he would go back with her before the beginning of September, maybe he wouldn't. He did seem happy here, calmer and in control, and Eve was definitely noticing how his connection with Gabby was growing. He might still be living a bit of a see-saw existence, fighting to keep balanced, but right now he was owning that. For the first time since his last spell in therapy, Eve could see that Ben was acknowledging his issues and facing each day as it came with optimism.

'You want mountain tea?' Pan asked. 'I put the goats in the field and then I make some.'

'OK,' Eve replied. 'I'll be there in a second. I just have to do something first.'

She waited until Pan was gone and then she took in the magnificent surroundings – the abundance of olive groves bordering the sanctuary, the cats lying out on the low walls soaking up the sun, the slick sliver of sea sparkling in the distance. She was calling for nature to give her the courage to take this next step.

Drawing in a deep breath, she looked back at the message on her phone and made her decision.

It was six agonisingly long ring tones until the call was answered, but Eve knew exactly what to say.

'Hello, Mum.'

68

THE ROAD TO EPISKEPSI

Gianni had been able to hear the music coming from the village as soon as he was within half a mile of it. And now, as he drove up the mountain, there were guitars and a higher-pitched stringed instrument he couldn't place accompanying a soulful, warbling Greek voice.

'This is like going back in time,' his mother remarked, her head halfway out of the window.

'Mamma, do not lean so far out. If you do not get whipped by the passing grass, you will soon have a face full of mosquitos.'

'Nothing has changed here,' she continued, taking no notice of him. 'The trees, the little houses... it is like it was when I left.'

His mother had been immediately nostalgic when Gianni had picked her up from the airport that morning. Expecting her usual Louis Vuitton parade of luggage, he had been surprised when she had met him off the Ryanair flight with nothing but a Moschino backpack.

'Did you come to the festival before?' Gianni asked.

'I did. I drank beer out of a can. Can you believe that?'

'Actually, I can.'

Since meeting Pan and gaining a small insight into who his mother had been before Italy and her own mother's fragility had called her home, he could see her here now, younger, without any responsibilities, dancing underneath the stars...

'Does Pan know I'm coming?' she asked suddenly, pulling her head in from the window.

'You asked me not to tell him,' Gianni reminded her.

'Yes, I know but maybe I should not have done that. You have your own relationship with him now and I shouldn't be asking you to keep things from him. There has been enough keeping things secret for all our lifetimes, no?'

Gianni nodded, turning the final corner. He was confronted with a line of cars, vans and mopeds stacked up in every available space. He drew his vehicle to a stop. It looked like the festival was going to be busy. 'Well, in a very short time he will know that you are here and there will be no secret.' He pulled on the handbrake, turned off the engine and prepared to get out. His mother put a hand on his arm to stop him.

'Gianni, I am not in Corfu for Pan,' she said. 'I am here for you.'

'I know.'

'And if you decide that you would rather I went back to Italy and left you to get to know Pan more on your own then I—'

'Mamma, I know you still love my Italian father.'

That was what Riccardo had been named now. He was the Italian father and Pan was the Greek father. It was the only thing that felt right, to give each of them a rightful place in the family tree.

Gianni watched his mother's eyes tear up as she nodded.

'But I also know now that loving someone, it is complicated.'

He looked out of the car window, the pots of bright bougainvillea spilling forth on terraces crowded with chairs and surrounded by drying washing, cats lazing between balustrades.

'There is no clear-cut path,' he continued. 'No easy route, no set of directions that fits every scenario. But, I have discovered, there is one thing that everybody has in common when it comes to love.'

He took hold of his mother's hand and gave it a supportive squeeze. 'No one knows how much time they have to enjoy it... to savour it... to bathe in the beauty of it!'

His mother laughed. 'Who are you? And what have you done with my son?'

'I am still here. I am just a version that sees things differently.'

'Because of Eve,' she added. She hadn't even posed it as a question.

'Because of Eve,' he agreed. Then he sighed. He was certain there was no going back for him, no wanting to cool off and put his feelings down to grief from his father's death or shock about finding out about Pan. This was no brief holiday romance for him. This was something he wanted to elongate, work for, *fight* for. 'But she might not feel the same.'

'No,' his mother agreed. 'But no one ever really regrets putting their heart on the line, do they?'

He took a moment to process that thought and then she passed him the tightly wrapped foil bundle she had been nursing on her lap.

'It is hot in the car,' she said. 'Take the cake. Let us find some beer in cans!'

69

THE EPISKEPSI PANEGYRI, EPISKEPSI

'It's just like the vehicle gathering, isn't it?'

Ben nudged Eve with his arm, a stupid grin on his face as they sat at one of the white plastic tables in the thick of the bustling *panegyri* – translated as 'festival for everyone'. There were tables packed wherever there was space: on the grass, half on the road, in a pocket of land near the church; the concrete space next to the church had been reserved for the band and the dancing. There were stalls selling hot sizzling sticks of pork *souvlaki* served in foil trays, lambs rotating on spits – their meat cut up into hunks to be devoured by hungry customers – and *loukamades*, doughnut balls sprinkled with sugar and drizzled with honey or chocolate sauce or a combination of both. Cans of local beer were on offer as well as small bottles of Malamatina retsina, and Coca-Cola Light or water for the non-drinkers.

'It's really not like the vehicle gathering,' Eve replied, sipping some of her wine from the plastic glass she'd been given.

'Come on,' Ben said. 'There's plenty of vehicles gathered on the road to get here and some of them are older than the vintage ones on show at Brookly Heath.'

'It's better than the vehicle gathering,' Eve said. 'I'm going to have to eat some *souvlaki* in a second because the smell of it is making my stomach rumble.'

'I ate a whole tray earlier,' Ben admitted. 'Gabby wanted doughnut balls so I bought some meat to keep me occupied while I waited in the queue.'

'Where is Gabby?' Eve asked, sitting up in her chair and scanning the crowd. It had been a good twenty minutes since her best friend had leapt out of her seat and gone to try and fix something that needed attention.

'She's taking Vincent Van Hoff around to see the kids. Pan has Áspro on a lead and Dipsy, La-La and Po in a box. He's hoping someone will want to sign up to adopt the kitten.'

'Does she need any help?'

'She specifically told me not to let you do anything tonight.'

'Why?'

'I think she thinks that it hasn't been much of a holiday since you got here and she really wants you to chill out a bit and hopefully stay a few weeks longer.'

Eve exhaled as if his words had tapped into a pressure release valve she didn't even know existed. Chilling out sounded perfect to her.

She looked at Ben and then decided to press on. 'I spoke to Mum earlier.'

'Yeah?'

'Apart from moaning about the price of Lurpak whenever there was an awkward pause in conversation, it was... OK.'

'OK?'

'I just think it's going to take time. She told me everything. About finding out about Dad and Gina Reynolds, how she and Gene both had their suspicions and got in contact with each other.' She sighed. 'She protected us both when it happened and then, when I found those messages and jumped to the wrong conclusion she knew if she told me the truth, I wouldn't have believed it.'

'Yeah,' Ben said, holding onto his drink as a line of dancers meandered past their table.

'So, when did she tell *you* about it? And why didn't you tell me before?'

'I hacked her Facebook after that big showdown at the cemetery. I read *all* the messages, unlike you, so I found out it was Dad who had had the affair. I asked Mum about it and she made me promise not to tell you. I hated it, Eve. I hated having this secret between us and the more you clung on to the idea that Dad was infallible the worse it got.' He shook his head. 'I don't know, in therapy we talk about unpacking our trauma suitcase and the more progress I thought I was making, the more I realised that keeping that inside was holding me back.' He fixed his eyes on her. 'And I thought... it was holding you back too.'

Eve nodded. He was right. It had taken her a long time to realise it but she needed to work on how she was going to move forward. With her memories of her dad tarnished, it wasn't going to be straightforward but perhaps it began with making steps to repairing things with her mum. She had given Glenda the toughest ride over the past few years and none of it had been deserved.

'You don't hate me for keeping it from you, do you?' Ben asked, his forehead creasing the way it always did when he was worried about something.

'No, Ben, of course I don't. I'm sorry you were put in that position. Mum and I are both guilty over that.'

'No more guilt, Eve. For any of us, OK? I think we've spent so long swimming in it we're all as wrinkled as the old pickled onions at your pub.'

Eve hit him on the arm and Ben laughed, almost losing his balance.

Then suddenly a shiver ran down Eve's back as she spotted someone in the crowd, making their way into the thick of the village. *Gianni*. The humidity seemed to kick up a notch and Eve began to feel flushed and a little bit nauseous.

Be calm. Serene. Although it was hard to channel that mood when everyone around them was hyper, chatting loudly, dancing crazily, grilling furiously...

'Gianni's here,' Ben said. 'With an older woman.'

Eve's interest was piqued. She observed the scene a little more closely before replying, 'That's Valentina.'

'Who's Valentina?' Ben asked.

'Gianni's mum.'

Ben took that on board for a second. 'So, that's who... you know... with Pan... twenty-odd years ago.'

'Probably don't say that to any of them. So, Gabby told you? I told her not to tell anyone.'

'Gianni did.' Ben got to his feet. 'Right, I am going to see if Gabby needs me to take a turn with Vincent. If he falls over, it's on me and Pan to get him back up.' He paused. 'Unless you need me to play wingman or something.'

Eve shook her head, getting to her feet too. 'No, it's OK. And I'm not going to sit here and wait. I'm going to take a gamble.'

The moment she said it, her whole body flushed. 'Oh, God, Ben. I did not mean that. I shouldn't have said that. It was—'

'It's what the sheep do, right? Ben said. 'And probably the goats too. They gambol about in the field all day.' He put a hand on her shoulder. 'It's just a word. You can also say "horse", "jockey" and "evens favourite" without me breaking into a sweat, all right?'

'All right,' she said, nodding.

'Now, crack on and go and speak to Gianni,' he ordered.

70

Eve had made the decision, been all gung-ho about it with Ben, yet now she was hanging back, sandwiched between the makeshift bar and a stall selling a light-up helicopter-style toy that most of the villages' children were throwing into the air as if they really thought it might land on the moon.

She couldn't even see Gianni now. But she could see Pan and Valentina. Valentina seemed to be deciding whether she wanted to pet Vincent, her hand outstretched towards the sheep but not actually making contact. Pan was at her side, laughing, and Valentina was smiling more broadly than Eve had ever seen. *Second chances. Forgetting the past.* They seemed to be running themes here in Greece.

She looked towards the dance floor, down and across those stone amphitheatre-style steps. She could just make out Spiros and Vasiliki in the circle of dancers, swaying right then left, Spiros having to put a hand to his new hat to stop it falling off. Aleka was sitting outside the church doors, her infamous tray on her lap, clapping her hands together to the music.

Then Ben came into view, his hand clasping Gabby's, looking

as if he was about to join everyone in the dancing ring. But then she saw her brother hesitate and turn away from the crowd. Eve held her breath, watching on. Next, Ben smiled and joined both his hands with Gabby's, making their own personal ring and copying the steps of the other dancers. It warmed Eve's heart completely.

'Is this hiding space only for one?'

Now her heart reacted as if someone had just shocked it with a defib. Gianni wasn't in her line of sight because he was standing right behind her. She hit her hip against the wood of the bar, probably giving him the answer to his question about the space.

'I wasn't hiding,' she said. 'I was just...'

'Taking a minute because this festival is crazy?' Gianni suggested.

'Yes,' she said, nodding. 'Exactly that.'

And now neither of them were saying anything, though Gianni seemed to be saying quite a lot with his eyes. Those beautiful, clear blue eyes that gave off both sexy and intense vibes. Any second now, Eve's eyes were going to stray lower, across his stubble-peppered jawline, down the curve of his olive-skinned neck and across his chest past the two unfastened buttons of his shirt...

'Eve,' Gianni began. 'Can we talk?'

She nodded.

'Maybe not next to the bar and the toys for children?' he suggested.

'Oh, yes. That's a good point.' She stepped out of her nook into the lights and sounds of the *panegyri*, the aromas of smoky meat and sugary batter dominating the night air.

'Let us go for a walk,' Gianni suggested.

* * *

Gianni's hands were shaking but he had made the first step towards something, and they began a meander along the main road through the village. Episkepsi really was alive tonight, with scores of people who he assumed must occupy the houses that were dotted upwards, winding along narrow side alleys with paths outlined in white. Children fired bangers, chasing each other on bikes; parents deftly put sticks of meat between slices of bread and made kebab-style sandwiches; mopeds buzzed past, two or three children squeezed onto the backs. It wasn't until they were past Nikos's grillroom that things began to quieten, most people heading towards the music and dancing rather than away.

'How are you?' Gianni asked.

'Fine,' she answered hurriedly. 'Keeping busy, you know.'

'No,' Gianni said. 'I do not know.' He sighed. 'But I would like to.'

He waited a second for her to respond but quickly realised she wasn't going to. They kept walking, close but not touching, the streetlights dim against the darkening sky.

'Ben, he told me about your father,' Gianni began. 'About how he was the one to—'

'Don't,' Eve interrupted. 'You don't have to... say the words.' She took a breath. 'I'm still processing it and it's... difficult.'

'I can imagine,' Gianni answered. 'I have been imagining.'

'Have you?' Eve asked, her tone fragile.

'I did not say the right things when we last spoke. You told me what you had found on my business plan and I told you that you did not know me.'

'Gianni—'

'No, Eve, let me tell you what I should have said that night.'

They walked past a rusty old tractor which Gianni had noticed had been parked against the wall since he had come to the village, opposite a one-storey house almost hidden by the burgeoning blooms of hanging flowers.

'My ideas for a new arm of Riccardocino did begin from what you said about bubble tea,' he began. 'And then Pan, he mentioned alcohol in coffee too and it all began to make sense. And what you saw on my computer *was* something I was going to try to sell to Barista Irresistible. But, Eve, I was going to tell you. I was going to tell you everything about it and, more than that, I wish you had read further down that page of ideas.'

'Gianni, I know that running away was stupid,' Eve said. 'It was infantile, and it was not the action of someone who was thinking straight. And it wasn't just your business proposal. My mum phoned and I was worried about Ben, and everything started to implode and...'

She'd stopped talking, perhaps not knowing quite what else to say. All he wanted to do was put his arms around her. But he had to be patient. He didn't dare to hope that they were on the same page yet. He drew his phone from the pocket of his jeans.

'Eve, take a look at my proposal again. All of it.' He pressed his screen a few times before holding the phone out to her.

* * *

'You don't have to do that,' Eve said, ignoring the mobile between them. Despite the warmth of the night, she was shivering. 'I need to learn to not immediately think that everyone has ulterior motives and people are setting out to hurt me.'

'Please,' Gianni said, offering the device again. 'I want you to see.'

Eve took it from him and began to read, recognising the words she had first seen on his laptop in Verona.

This time she scrolled down, reading further.

Possible Riccardocino venues?

Our own café chain?

Names?

All Day for the café?

After Eve for the bar

Her name. Her name potentially on a bar sign. Her idea used, yes, but acknowledged in the sweetest of ways.

'You were going to name a bar after me?' she asked, looking up.

'I would name everything I own after you if you give me another chance.'

She passed him back his phone. 'Gianni, so much has happened since I landed on this island.' She sighed, beginning to walk again.

'For me too,' he replied, staying beside her. 'I found my father.'

'Yes,' she said. 'And I feel like I lost mine all over again.'

'You are angry with him. For not being the person you thought he was.'

'Yes. Exactly that.'

'But, Eve, although what he did was wrong it would also be wrong to let his one mistake change the way you feel about him, about all the other times you shared together,' Gianni said. 'Like when you tell me he carries you on his shoulders singing a song about apple pie and custard. Or... when he turned wooden vegetable boxes into a go-cart for you and Ben.'

Eve didn't know what to say, still sore from the situation.

Gianni put a hand on her shoulder as they reached the small walled area with a stone pillar monument inside. 'Remember how you introduced yourself to me that first moment we met?'

She nodded as tears pricked her eyes. 'I said I was a human.'

'Human,' Gianni repeated. 'We are all human. And as humans, we make mistakes. That is one of the things that makes us human, no?' He found one of her hands and held it in his. 'I am not perfect, Eve. I am as flawed as the next person and I do not always get things right. But the one thing I did get right in Corfu was opening myself up a little.' He squeezed her hand. 'Opening myself up to you.'

'Gianni—'

'I did not think that I would ever find someone who made me feel that being me was enough. Someone who did not want me for my business status or my homes and cars, someone who has been by my side almost all the time I have been lost here, trying to find my father, trying to find out how I feel about that and stepping into an uncertain future.'

Her tears slowly fell then, as she looked deep into his eyes. 'I have been so selfish.'

'No,' Gianni said at once. 'That is the very last thing you are. The very last thing.'

'I shouldn't have left you in Italy,' she admitted. 'I should have talked to you. I should have trusted you. Because I think I *do* know you, Gianni. And I should have believed that feeling.'

She was holding her breath now, the pace of her heart quickening.

'I have never felt for anyone what I feel for you, Eve,' Gianni said, his fingers tracing the outline of hers. 'And it makes no difference that I am in the middle of this situation with my family and the business, you are always there. You are in my thoughts, you are in my business plan, it is Eve, Eve, Eve and there is nothing I can do to stop it.'

'No?'

'No.'

They were standing closer together now, turned towards the view down the mountainside, spots of light from houses between the trees like fairy lights.

'I am going to stay in Corfu for the rest of the summer, at least,' Gianni said. 'I want to get to know Pan. I want to take a break from Riccardocino. I really do not know if I am even going to pitch these ideas to Barista Irresistible.'

'Really?'

'As much as my Italian father dedicated his life to the business, he never put business before family. I am going to make sure that I focus on what is most important to me. And right now, that is hoping that you will give me the chance to spend more time with you.'

She swallowed, seeing exactly how he felt about her written all over his expression. It might not be the right time or the right place, given that they lived in different countries, but she was certain Gianni was the right person to take this next step with.

'I missed you,' she whispered. 'It's only been days and I missed you so much.'

She fell into his arms and he held her tight, as if he never wanted them to be apart.

'I missed you too, human,' he answered, his hand cradling the back of her head. 'I missed you too.'

71

'What is this cake, Valentina? Can I call you Valentina, by the way? Or should I call you Mrs Riccardo?' Ben asked, crumbs on his face.

'You are a very polite boy,' Valentina answered, cutting another slice of the cake she had brought and popping it on a paper plate. 'You can call me Valentina, of course.'

Eve shared a smirk with Gianni as they all sat at one of the white tables with the best view of the dance floor below, the music still soaring into the night, the food still being sold in vast quantities, as too were the annoying helicopter toys that were still whizzing past people's heads.

'It is a cake called *Fanouropita*,' Pan informed him, passing slices around the table. 'In Greece we make this cake to help when we are looking for lost things.'

That story again. The last time it had been told she had seen Pan get upset about it. But now he was smiling as he shared a look with Valentina and it was obvious to Eve he definitely still had deep feelings for Gianni's mother.

'Should I make it every time one of the animals makes a break for freedom?' Gabby asked with a laugh.

'Animals make breaks for freedom, Yabby?' Vasiliki queried, raising her head from a container of *souvlaki* sticks and putting fingers to a paper plate of cake at the same time.

'Er, no, I didn't mean that,' Gabby said quickly. 'I mean with my new budget I will be able to repair the fences and buy new locks and—'

'I'm going to be there to help,' Ben piped up.

Eve saw her brother put his hand over Gabby's and link their little fingers together. It made her want to reach for Gianni. Under the table, she lightly traced her hand over his thigh.

'What are you doing?' he whispered. 'My mother is just over there cutting up a cake to find lost things.'

'I know,' she said. 'That doesn't mean I can't go on my own physical reconnaissance, does it?'

'Do I need to find the nearest fountain in Corfu?' he whispered, turning his body towards her.

'There's a whole waterfall not far from here in Nymfes.'

'Let's go,' he said, his lips grazing hers.

'Very good for you. Very good for me.'

The sound of Spiros's voice jarred the moment and Eve looked over her shoulder to see the man standing behind her, Aleka with him. The woman had her tray in her hands and she started to speak in Greek.

'Aleka says she has another picture to make but she does not yet know who the picture is for,' Vasiliki translated.

'What is happening?' Valentina asked, putting the cake knife down and paying more attention.

'Is nothing,' Pan said straightaway. 'Just a crazy *yiayia* who thinks that she can tell the future. Nothing to think about. We should cut more cake.'

'Gorgios! Aleka might not understand your English but I do,' Vasiliki admonished.

Spiros pulled an empty white plastic chair back and helped Aleka settle herself in it. Then he moved cans and plastic glasses and empty foil trays, so she had room to place her board on the table.

Eve couldn't help but position her chair closer, leaning in to see.

'You believe in this fortune telling?' Gianni asked.

'Not usually,' Eve admitted. 'But I have to say when I think about all the pictures Aleka made for me, she was actually pretty spot on.'

This time Aleka was using serviettes, pieces of them all scrunched up into tiny balls. Her fingers moved them around quickly, then slowly, and a shape began to form. Was that an apple?

'Aww! Look at Baby Yiayia!' Gabby said, her comment directing everybody's gaze towards the dance floor.

Eve looked and saw the baby in his young mother's arms, smiling, drooly mouth open as she rocked him gently to the sound of the band. She hoped that he stayed as happy as he was now and she knew this village would see to it that he was helped with any struggles he might have. That was what family did and Baby Yiayia's family was bigger now than his mother could ever have imagined.

'What is that you make?' Valentina asked, now standing at Eve's shoulder and surveying Aleka's tray. 'Is that a pair of bells like on the tower over there?'

Aleka said something and Pan scoffed.

'What did she say?' Eve asked.

'She does this for me,' Pan replied. 'She knows how I feel about weddings. It is a joke.'

'Weddings?'

'Aleka said that the picture is the bells. And that they will ring for a wedding,' Vasiliki translated.

Eve looked at Gianni and then immediately heat hit her cheeks. What was she thinking? She turned away, not wanting to gaze at him and give herself away. But then she saw Ben look at Gabby... and Valentina look at Pan, and then Spiros glance towards Vasiliki...

But before anyone could do or say anything else there was an almighty squawking that pierced the night. Eve screamed as something large and brown and green landed smack in the middle of the table.

'Oh my God!' Gabby shrieked. 'It's Tony and Brenda's missing chameleon!'

Another screech and flapping of wings and Savage settled on the back of Ben's chair. If it was possible for birds to pull expressions, the hoopoe looked mighty pleased with himself.

'Savage, you're back,' Ben said, turning in his seat and putting out a finger.

'Ben, don't do that!' Gabby ordered. 'He'll devour it like a ravenous *I'm a Celebrity* campmate.'

Pan shook his head. 'It is your cake,' he said to Valentina. 'Bringing us back lost things.'

Eve looked back to Gianni then and he slipped an arm around her shoulder, drawing her close.

'So, the picture says there is going to be a wedding,' he whispered in her ear.

'Well, I'm not sure anything made from scrunched up serviettes is akin to something written in formal legislation.'

'But you believed the pictures when they *weren't* about weddings?' Gianni teased.

'Aleka didn't know who the picture was for,' Eve reminded him.

'Or maybe it's simply that someone at this table is just going to, you know, be *invited* to a wedding.'

Gianni smiled. 'I liked the way you looked at me before you thought too hard about it.'

Eve blushed again. 'I didn't think you noticed.'

He kissed her. 'I noticed. But, you know, it is not a wedding that is on my mind this summer. It is something a little like another religious ceremony.'

'Oh?' Eve asked as he slipped his hand into hers.

'Mmm,' Gianni said. 'Like a baptism. Without our clothes. Where did you say that waterfall was?'

Eve laughed and as Gabby captured the chameleon before it tried to make a run for it and Ben very *very* slowly reached out to touch Savage on the beak, she realised that although her summer under a Greek sun had been challenging, it had also been the absolute best time of her life.

ACKNOWLEDGMENTS

Thank you to the best agent an author could wish for! Tanera, this book is dedicated to you and if 2022 proved one thing to me it was that you are the absolute best at what you do. If I told the world some of the things you had to fix/manage/sort out last year no one would believe it, but those stories will make it into a book one day... maybe!

A huge thanks to the rest of the team at Darley Anderson – Laura, Mary, Georgia, Sheila, Rosanna and everyone who has taken such care with my books and aimed to get the most out of them.

A huge thank you to Boldwood Books! I cannot wait to publish these next books with such a dynamic, always ambitious, driven and already so successful team. I am very happy to be a part of it and I'm delighted to be back working with Emily Yau as my editor. Hooray!

Thank you to the two friends who are always there for me no matter what time of day (or night!) it is – Sue Fortin and Rachel Lyndhurst. Another rollercoaster year of constantly ironing me out! Thank you for being the best bitch crew!

However, the biggest thanks of all goes to the members of The Mandy Baggot Book Club and every single reader who has chosen to read my books or listen to them on audio. Without your support I would not be able to keep writing full-time bringing you love stories you all adore so much! Every sale, every recommendation to a friend, every library borrow is really so appreciated. THANK YOU! Here's to many more Greek adventures to come!

MORE FROM MANDY BAGGOT

We hope you enjoyed reading *Under a Greek Sun*. If you did, please leave a review.

If you'd like to gift a copy, this book is also available as an ebook, hardback, large print, digital audio download and audiobook CD.

Sign up to Mandy Baggot's mailing list for news, competitions and updates on future books.

https://bit.ly/MandyBaggotNews

ABOUT THE AUTHOR

Mandy Baggot is a bestselling romance writer who loves giving readers that happy-ever-after. From sunshine romantic comedies set in Greece, to cosy curl-up winter reads, she's bringing gorgeous heroes and strong heroines readers can relate to. Mandy splits her time between Salisbury, Wiltshire and Corfu, Greece and has a passion for books, food, racehorses and all things Greek!

Visit Mandy's website: www.mandybaggot.com

Follow Mandy on social media here:

         facebook.com/mandybaggotauthor
         twitter.com/mandybaggot
         instagram.com/mandybaggot
         bookbub.com/profile/mandy-baggot

Boldwͻͻd

Boldwood Books is an award-winning fiction publishing company seeking out the best stories from around the world.

Find out more at www.boldwoodbooks.com

Join our reader community for brilliant books, competitions and offers!

Follow us
@BoldwoodBooks
@BookandTonic

Sign up to our weekly deals newsletter

https://bit.ly/BoldwoodBNewsletter

9 781805 493624